THE
TELLER
OF
SECRETS

THE TELLER OF SECRETS

a novel

BISI ADJAPON

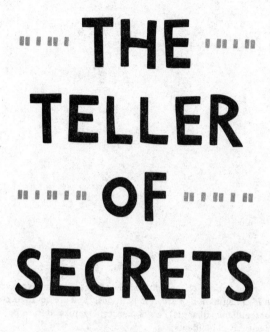

HarperVia

An Imprint of HarperCollinsPublishers

THE TELLER OF SECRETS. Copyright © 2018 by Bisi Adjapon. All rights reserved. Printed in the United States of America. No part of this book may be used or reproduced in any manner whatsoever without written permission except in the case of brief quotations embodied in critical articles and reviews. For information, address HarperCollins Publishers, 195 Broadway, New York, NY 10007.

HarperCollins books may be purchased for educational, business, or sales promotional use. For information, please email the Special Markets Department at SPsales@harpercollins.com.

Originally published as *Of Women and Frogs* by Kachifo Limited under the Farafina imprint in 2018.

FIRST HARPERCOLLINS PAPERBACK EDITION PUBLISHED IN 2022

Designed by Yvonne Chan

Library of Congress Cataloging-in-Publication Data is available upon request.

ISBN 978-0-06-308899-3

22 23 24 25 26 LSC 10 9 8 7 6 5 4 3 2 1

For my father, D.E.K. Adjepon-Yamoah, who gave me a passion for books, and my irrepressible mother, Adetayo Adetona.

In loving memory of my other mother, the gracious and incomparable Charlotte, and my siblings: Efuah, Aba, Ewurabena and Ato. Always in my heart.

CHAPTER ONE

*M*Y FRIEND ELISHA *says I should watch out for frogs after it rains. She says, if a frog jumps on you, you'll turn into a man. I don't want to be a man and have hair growing around my mouth—that's the worst thing that can happen to a girl. Elisha is eleven, so she knows more things and she's named after a prophet in the Bible. I am only nine, with an ordinary name, Esi, the name they give to every girl who is born on Sunday.*

Papa and I are spending the night in a hotel room in Accra because I have to see the ear doctor tomorrow. I'll never tickle my ears again with rolled-up paper or sticks of grass. I did that because my ears kept itching from the day I got sick and Papa drove me up the mountain to the medicine woman with half a lip who ground up wet leaves and squeezed them into my ears. Even though he says those who have gone to school should stay away from juju people with their potions. Now my ear is swollen and the pain feels as if someone is hammering a nail inside it.

The hotel has lovely little houses sitting around a circular lawn. We have a room with a bed that Papa calls king-size. We don't need a sitting room or kitchen because we can sit at tables on the marble floor around the lawn, and men and women in white uniforms bring us anything we want to eat or drink. The jollof rice with fried-fish stew was so delicious I nearly chewed my tongue.

I'm in bed alone now. I don't mind because I can hear Papa sitting on the veranda talking to a woman. I want to stay awake and wait for him, but the night is warm and he and the woman speak in low voices that hum me to sleep.

Papa is the person I love most. At home he opens his accordion and music pours out and he laughs when I dance. He makes me a cup of Milo every night before I sleep, and then we lie on his bed and read the Uncle Arthur's bedtime stories that come in big boxes from England.

The bed is making *shweequaw shweequaw shweequaw* sounds. I open my eyes. The moon is shining and Papa is a shadow on top of a woman who is also a shadow. The *shweequaw shweequaw* is because of the way they are moving. Something tells me I shouldn't be watching, but my eyes won't close. The bed rocks harder than before. Papa is groaning and twisting like something is poking him everywhere. Then he falls down beside me. I can see his white teeth and hear his lips smack. He is whispering *Thank you, thank you,* so I know he's happy. How can he be groaning when he's happy?

It's not so dark now. The woman's copper-colored skin is light against Papa's very black skin. When I sit up, she lifts her head and looks directly at me and I have to cover my mouth with both hands because it is the woman who served us our supper.

"She's awake," she whispers, shaking my father. I lie back down immediately and pretend to be asleep.

"She's asleep, she's asleep," Papa mutters.

"No, she's awake."

"She's asleep, I tell you." Papa sounds awake now. "I gave her the medicine. She can't be awake."

I remember the tablet he gave me to swallow when we were eating our supper by the fountain. The way he looked around him and blinked made me think of someone telling a lie. So, I brought the glass of water to my mouth, and when he looked away, I threw the tablet under the table. Now I understand. The medicine would have made me sleep and I wouldn't have heard any *shweequaw shweequaw*.

The woman props herself up on her elbow and clutches the sheet to her chest and says, "But I saw her sit up."

Papa laughs. "I'll prove to you that she's asleep. Her ear is very painful. If she's awake, she'll shout the moment I touch it."

I quickly make my body go hard so it won't hurt that much. He reaches over and tugs my ear. The pain is like a knife cutting me but I stay quiet.

He heaves away. "See? I told you she was asleep."

"But—"

"Shh. Come here."

"No." Giggles.

"Do you have a baby in your stomach?"

"No . . . please . . . aaah."

"If you have a baby in your stomach, tell me."

"My stomach is empty. Please . . . do it."

The bed is squeaking again so I open my eyes. Papa is climbing like a baby trying to get on his mother's back, which is weird because he is too big for that. I close my eyes. There are slapping sounds but I know they're not fighting. They bounce me up and down and groan and weep and then Papa's nose is like a car engine. I feel like running the way ants scatter when something interrupts their line.

Once, when I saw two dogs stuck together outside the house and pointed them out to Papa, he got angry and told me to get away from the window, as if I had seen something bad. So why is he doing it with a woman? I can't ask my stepmother, Auntie, because she'll wave me away and say that only a bad child asks so many questions. I can't ask my mother either, because she disappeared when I was four.

We used to live in Lagos, with my brother Kwabena. Just the four of us: Papa, Mother, me, and my brother. It was fun when Papa danced with Mother and they laughed, and when they let me sleep in their bed. There was no bouncing or groaning. But everything changed. The only thing I remember is being at the airport with my mother. She was standing between Kwabena and me, holding each of us by the hand. A man in a uniform asked for boarding passes. She was supposed to let us go but she didn't. She held my hand so tightly it almost hurt.

"I am not going to cry," she said. Her voice was firm. "I am not going to . . . Oh God. My daughter. My son. They're leaving, but I'm not going to cry." Her voice broke and she crushed us to her, sobbing, her powdery smell all over me. I didn't understand why she was upset. My chest hurt to see her cry, so I cried too. So did Kwabena. The man felt so sorry for her he let her climb into the plane with us. She whimpered like a wounded dog. But she wouldn't leave so the men took her by the elbows. I reached both hands for her, fighting against the belt, *iyá mi o*! Then the door slammed shut. It fries my stomach that I can't remember anything else.

Now we live in a town called Kumawu. It's not like Lagos where the streets were clogged with squeaking cars and hawkers yelling and music pouring from every store. Kumawu is a forest. Nothing but plantain trees and insect noises. Elisha says the town got its name from a fetish priest. He planted a kum tree in the town but the tree died. That's where Kumawu comes from. *Wu* means dying, which to me is the loneliest thing of all. Because that's the way I feel when I want my mother.

When I woke up in Ghana without my mother, I found myself with a new family, as if a witch made her disappear and replaced her with them: Auntie and four sisters with names that took me forever to get straight: Oldest Sister Adjoa, Sister Abena, Sister Yaa, and Sister Mansa. We call Sister Adjoa "Her Royal Highness" because she tells everyone what to do. I don't see her often because she doesn't live at home. I don't understand how come my sisters are so old when they are also Papa's children. When I ask him, he just smiles and his newspaper goes up to hide his face. What I know I glued together from pieces of grown-up conversations.

He had to run away from Ghana because people wanted to remove the prime minister, Kwame Nkrumah. Papa liked Nkrumah because he did good things for Ghana, but those people were his friends. Someone with a slippery mouth told on them, so Papa ran away to Nigeria, which is where he met Mother and I got to be born. Nothing bad happened to him when he slipped back to Ghana, and I never heard him mouth off about Nkrumah. Which is just as well, because Sister Mansa belonged to the Young Pioneers that Papa says was like the Red Guard of China, which is communist, whatever that means. If you told Young Pioneer leaders that your father said bad things about Nkrumah, soldiers could come cart your father off to that awful Nsawam Prison and he'd never come back home. But the CIA removed Nkrumah, together with the KGB people from Russia who lived at the presidential castle.

C I A. K G B. The alphabet people are like spirits. No one sees them or knows who they are, but they know how to find people who don't like presidents. My head hurts thinking about it. I'm happy Nkrumah is hiding somewhere in Guinea where he can't get at Papa. I never have to worry again about Papa disappearing and never coming back home. When I am lying next to him, I am happier and warmer than an egg under a hen. His loud snoring doesn't bother me, and I don't dream of the giant animal with wings spread wide, swooping down on me and screeching. But I can hear the frogs outside the window. I know they're hopping around, waiting to jump on me and turn me into a man, even now as Papa snores between the woman and me.

My ear is on fire. I feel a trickle of warmth running down where I wear my earring. I don't want to wake Papa up. But what if something bad is happening to my ear? I reach with my forefinger and poke his shoulder.

"Papa." He doesn't move. I poke harder. "Papa."

He jerks up, breathing as if he is carrying something heavy. "What is it?"

"My ear hurts. Something is coming out of it."

"Is that so?"

I nod.

"All right, let's go check it out in the bathroom." He covers the whole bed with a sheet so that the woman is hidden. In the bathroom, he flicks on the light and peers into my ear. I like how his breath warms my face. "Hmm," he says, "it's a little bloody. Looks like you had a boil in there that burst open. Let me clean it for you." He tears some toilet paper and dabs at my ear the way you touch an egg. He is smiling at me. Breathing soothing air on me. The opposite of what he did when he tugged my ear. "You'll feel better in the morning," he says.

By morning, the woman is gone.

CHAPTER TWO

I SQUAT BY THE gutter that runs along our back veranda, sticking my neck out to make sure there's no frog crouched inside, its sides blowing out and in with breathing. Only a millipede the size of a fountain pen crawls along the rough cement, its feet crowded like a toothbrush. We live in Kibi, a bigger town than Kumawu. Kibi too is all green and bushy with lots of creatures like this millipede.

"Esi!" my stepmother, Auntie, calls from the kitchen.

I won't answer. She wants me in there with her, I'm sure.

"Esi!"

Ha, she thinks I didn't hear her. I stand up, looking around to see if I can find a stick to poke at the millipede. I'm not going to hurt it. Just a touch to watch it roll into a spiral and play dead. Kwabena and I do that all the time. Where is the twerp, anyway? Just because I called him a fool for chewing his shirt collar is no reason for him to go off on his own.

"Esi Agyekum!"

Yie, Auntie sounds angry now.

"Yes, Auntie!"

"Where are you? What are you doing?"

"Nothing!" I don't want to tell her that though I'm now eleven, I still watch out for frogs. It would be terrifying to wake up with a deep voice and bushy armpit hair and new things hanging between my legs.

"Nothing? Come and help with the cooking!"

I wish Papa hadn't rolled off in his Mercedes. I could be reading with him instead of getting yelled at for playing. He's probably sitting at a bar sipping urine-colored beer and laughing loud enough to shake the walls. Which is fine by me.

He drove Hotel Woman and me all the way across the border into Togo where people spoke French. All I understood was *wee* and *non*. He took me to a bar with bamboo walls and sat me at a wooden table. He placed a sweating bottle of Fanta in front of me, and told me to enjoy myself. He and Hotel Woman would be back really soon. The afternoon air felt heavy, and I let the orangey liquid slide sweet and cool down my throat until two men at the counter lunged at each other with broken bottles.

By the time Papa and Hotel Woman returned, I'd backed my chair into a corner and pulled my knees to my chest. *She* was all teeth, clutching bags filled with new clothes he had bought for her. *Oh, we bought so many things, Esi. What a good girl you are for waiting.* I wanted to break the Fanta bottle on her head. Now I let him go to the bar without me. In fact, I will . . .

"Esi Agyekum! Are your ears clogged? Come this instant!"

"I'm coming, Auntie!"

I dart through the gate, cross the cobbled yard, and enter the kitchen. She is seated, hunched forward, fanning the coal pot. Steam rises from the aluminum pot above it, covering me with the smell of palm nuts.

"Look at you," she says with a bite to her voice. "You're a girl, stay in the kitchen. Learn how to cook. Hmm, one day, your husband will send us your bad soup and it will be a disgrace!"

I mutter that I don't want to marry and make soup for anybody, but either she doesn't hear me or she doesn't want to listen. She carries on, "You're going to pound the palm nuts so that I can peel the cassava and plantain for the fufu."

She pushes to her feet, then she removes the pot from the fire and shuffles to the sink to drain the water from the nuts. A white cloud of steam rises to the ceiling.

I want to know: "Why can't I peel the cassava, not pound the nuts?"

She laughs and turns, showing me the gap in her front teeth. "You? *Tweaa!* We would be waiting until tomorrow morning, and next thing I know, you've cut your hand. Move away. Just pound."

I want to refuse but she'll tell Papa and he will whack my bottom with a cane for disrespect. Besides, if I hurry up and finish pounding, I can sneak outside and play while the soup boils. I pound the orange-red nuts. I take care to bruise only the fleshy skins and not crush the hard shells inside. When I finish, Auntie pours hot water on them and the red juice comes out. Then I pound the roughness again. I don't like it when a blister forms on my palm.

She pokes at the fire with an iron rod and picks up the diamond-shaped fan with the long handle. Ashes fly in my face. I'm brushing off my arms when Sister Yaa and Sister Mansa walk through the kitchen. Sister Mansa is carrying a stool and the other holding a comb. They're going to plait each other's hair. I hear the crunch of their footsteps on the stones and the thud of the stool as they ready themselves. I'd rather stay with Auntie than be near Sister Yaa. Even though Auntie yells sometimes, she lets me lick the ladle when she has finished cooking. Sometimes, she shows me her gold jewels she keeps in a round red tin that has *Johnny Walker Shortbread* written on it. She even lets me try on her earrings. When I am sick, she makes garden egg soup that makes me feel warm inside. Sister Mansa too is lovely sometimes. She plays singing games with me where I have to drum while she sings. Her voice is so beautiful I call her Sister Sweet Voice in my head. Not like Sister Yaa, who is all jangle and bite.

"E-SI, come here at once!" There she goes, Sister Yaa. I don't understand why she barks out my name like that every time she wants me to do something, which is nearly all the time. At least with Auntie, she shouts only when I disobey.

I run out of the kitchen into the yard where the sisters have installed themselves. Sister Mansa's hair has been divided into several puffs that Sister Yaa will wind with black thread and gather on top of Sister Mansa's head like a stiff basket turned upside down. Sister Mansa is sitting on a low wooden stool. Her face bunches up when Sister Yaa brings the comb down and pulls. Sister Yaa couldn't be gentle if the Baby Jesus himself sat before her. I'm glad she's not plaiting my hair.

When she sees me, she says, "Look at you, insolent girl! Go to the room and bring me the hair oil." And she sucks her teeth. God blessed her with the voice of a dog and the jaws of a crocodile. That's how quickly she can snap off your head, Sister Crocodile Jaws. I know she doesn't like me because I'm my mother's daughter. Not that she needs a reason to hit or bite. When I close my eyes, I can still see the pink-red rectangles her teeth left in Sister Mansa's shoulder one night. I don't even know what they were fighting about.

I have felt the sting of her palm on my back myself. When you know someone is about to punch you, you can make your body hard so it doesn't hurt too much, but Sister Yaa likes to sneak up behind me. I'll be examining a hibiscus flower or a caterpillar in my hand and then *wham*! When I turn in hurt, her eyes narrow like a snake's and she says, *"Alatani aboa, wonnim na woka a, meku wo bia."* My Twi is good now, so I know what she's saying: "Nigerian animal, if you tell, I'll kill you well." There's something about someone hitting you for no reason that empties your head so that you stare and don't know what to do. How can she hit like an animal and look so normal?

Anyway, I never tell. What's the use? Older sisters are allowed to knock you on the head to make you behave. That's why they have titles like the Roman Catholics: Sister This, Sister That. Besides, I'm sure it's my fault. I just have to try harder to find the reason. But why does she call me a Nigerian animal? We have the same skin and feel the same mosquito bites, so why is a Nigerian an animal?

This time though, when she yells at me to fetch the hair oil, I am not upset. It's nice to escape from the ashes of the kitchen. I dash into the bedroom I now share with my sisters because I'm too old to sleep in Papa's bed. An invisible cloud of smoked fish and palm nut follows me. I love it when my sisters send me to our bedroom—when I am there alone, I can loiter in front of the mirror. Anyone can get me to fetch something from the bedroom just by adding, "You can admire yourself in the mirror while you're there." My body is changing and I watch it any chance I get.

The mirror is the height of a woman and hangs between a twin set of squat drawers. I stand in front of it, frowning at my short hair. It's too soft, unlike my sisters' that stands upright like a hedge. I pick up the wooden brush with stiff black bristles and punish my hair, beating it away from my forehead until it slants backward. Much better. I turn sideways and stick out my chest to see if my breasts have grown bigger. They have not.

I pull the straps of my dress off my shoulders and examine the two little hills. Sister Mansa told me once they would grow bigger if I allowed a termite to bite the tips. I rolled up my blouse to my chin while she held a struggling termite to each nipple. The termite stung me until I welted and burned like plantains roasting on fire. I still don't see any change. I don't know why I listened to her when she had already made me cut off my eyelashes. She said they would grow twice as long and they didn't.

I flatten my dress around me. I don't like it that I'm as straight as a sugarcane. I wonder what it feels like to have a body shaped like a guitar, like my sisters. Sometimes, my friend Marigold from school and I crumple paper into balls and add them to the lumps on our chests. Then we walk on our toes, pretending to wear high-heel shoes. We play birthing games in which I have to crawl under her dress to be born. Which I don't like because I sweat while waiting for her to groan and push me out.

Hotel Woman has a baby now because of what she did with Papa. Papa put a baby in her empty stomach. I'm the only one who knows. When Papa took me to see the baby, he didn't say out loud that I shouldn't tell anyone, but his eyes said not to, so I won't dare tell anyone. I don't want to, anyway. If I don't tell then I can pretend she isn't real. I don't mind sharing cups of Milo and stories with Kwabena, but I want Hotel Woman's baby to stay away.

Anyway, how can a baby come out of a place so tiny? I've never seen the spot. I can only feel it. Now I really want to see.

The only way to see between my legs is to lie down, but there's not enough room between the dressing mirror and the bed. I pick up the small mirror lying next to the jar of hair oil Sister Yaa is waiting for, but surely, she can wait a bit longer?

I lower my back onto the cool vinyl floor and remove my drawers. Then I draw up my knees and slip the mirror between my thighs. I gape at the ripe pawpaw color. I must be careful how I touch it, because everything seems so delicate. The door snaps open. Sister Yaa looms up. My hands attempt a quick cover-up.

"You bad child!" Sister Yaa says. My face is hot. I pray she won't raise her voice for everybody to hear but she does. "Is this what I sent you to do? I've been waiting for the oil forever. Get up!"

My bottom is cold when I pull up my drawers. My hands are shaking. Sister Yaa snatches the hair oil from the top of the drawer.

"Go to the kitchen and help, instead of being a bad child!" she says. She slaps me. Her fingers jab at my spine. My eyes feel peppery but the tears won't come.

In the kitchen, Auntie is bent over the palm-nut soup foaming on the coal pot.

"She was putting her fingers in her down-there," Sister Yaa says. "Her under-canoe!"

Auntie drops the ladle into the orange foam and stares at me. She slaps her hands together as if she is getting rid of dust. I want to sink into the earth like a beach crab.

"*Ei*, small child like you, whatever will happen when you grow up?"

Sister Yaa knows. She sticks her finger in her nose and says, "One day, the men will put it here." I don't know what *it* is but I don't want anyone putting *it* in my nose. I don't want *it* anywhere in my body.

"Fan the fire," Auntie says.

I drop onto the wooden stool beside her. I pick up the palm-frond fan and begin. We have a modern stove, yet Auntie prefers the coal pot. How I hate sitting in front of the fire flapping my wrist from side to side like a dog wagging its tail. I fan until the coal crackles and mauve tongues of flames lick the pot. Maybe if Auntie is happy, she won't punish me.

"The fire is flaming, Auntie." I scratch my head, wondering how to steal away and find my brother.

"Prepare the snails," Auntie says.

I press my lips together to prevent the angry words from falling out. Kwabena doesn't have to fan the coal pot or grind onions that make him cry. He is out somewhere while I have to stay in the kitchen and learn to cook. He has the burden of amusing himself and eating. But when I think of him with his ugly friends at school with their chewed collars, spitting and smelling funny, I'm happy I'm a girl.

After lunch I think Auntie is happy. I didn't complain once while I was working in the kitchen, even though my sisters did little more than plait their hair. Surely, she isn't going to punish me after I prepared the snails and chopped off crab claws for the soup?

I am wrong. When I see her sitting on a stool behind the grinding stone, my legs turn into mashed yam. She's got ginger in her hand. I should have gone with Papa to the bar.

The first time Auntie burned the evil out of me, I was seven. She had told me to empty the chamber pots, and I said no and called her a bloody fool. Papa always called her a bloody fool, so why not me? I shouldn't have done that. She made sure I understood that only grown-ups had the right to use bad words. But no one can do anything about what I store in my head.

I'd like to use the words now as I watch Auntie, sweat pouring down her neck. She has put the ginger on the flat grinding stone. Her fingers curl around a smaller stone and bang it on the knobby root. Small stone scrapes against large stone, crushing, crushing, crushing. Sharp smells. *Ìyá mi*, where are you?

Auntie raises her eyes to where I'm standing with my fists in my mouth, breathing fast.

"Esi, come here," she says.

My head and legs aren't working together. I don't want to go to her, but I go. The smell of ginger stings my nose. Yellow sap runs down the sides of the jagged gray stone. In the middle, the ginger forms a soggy yellow mound. My body goes hard. Sister Mansa and Sister Yaa appear from nowhere. Or have they been standing there the whole time?

"Take off your drawers," Auntie says.

I pull them down slowly, staring at the ginger.

"Turn around and bend over."

I feel screwed to the ground.

"I'll help," Sister Yaa says. She grabs my shoulders and spins me around. I shove her and she says, "Mansa, help!"

Sister Mansa puts her hands on my back and pushes until my head hangs down and my bottom points to the sky. They press my chest against my knees. I feel a cold, hard finger dig into my bottom. The ginger stings and runs into my pawpaw. Auntie feeds more and more ginger in until it feels like live coal inside me. I howl and howl. I wish Mother could appear from wherever she is and strike down Auntie, flatten Sister Yaa into skin I can stomp on. I want to pop air from my bottom into their faces.

When they let me go, I can't stop shaking and crying. I waddle to the bathroom to wash myself, and Auntie calls after me, "I hope you'll remember how it burns the next time you're tempted to touch your under-canoe, you bad girl!"

Ginger burns forever, so the cold water does little to cool me. Auntie says the punishment will help me close my legs until a man chooses me for a wife.

I want my mother. There's a pain crushing my chest and a fire in my throat. If she were here, maybe she could explain about boys and girls and my secret place. When I ask Papa, the words come out wrong and his jaw clenches and his bottom lip rolls out. When I keep at him, he asks me if I want a cup of Milo or do I want money to buy peppermint.

I don't like sad thoughts flying around in my head so in a week I forget all my problems. I find Papa in his study jingling his car keys and I start peppering him with questions about my mother. He digs into his pocket and says, "Here, do you want to buy fried yam and fish?" That's all it takes for me to drop the questions. Then he drives off.

On the way to the yam-seller's house, I can see myself carrying the hot yam in a big leaf and eating it with the freshly ground red pepper that the woman will put on it. The fish is always so crisp I can eat the crunchy head as well.

The woman who sells the yam has a nephew called Yaw.

Though he's fourteen, he doesn't mind playing with me when there are so many other customers that I have to wait. When I arrive, the queue snakes long over the yard, so I ask the girl before me to hold my place. I skip up the concrete steps to the house and pull the swinging screen door that bangs after me.

Yaw sits slanted backward on a chair in the small sitting room, listening to music from a record player.

"Hello, Esi," he says. "Come in."

I sit in the chair next to him and admire the record player, how music can flow from the pin moving through the tiny circles on the black disk.

"My uncle just bought this record," Yaw says. "Do you like it?"

"Yes." I spring up and start dancing. His eyes follow me with a sleepy smile as he snaps his fingers to the beat. When the record ends, I plop down on the linoleum. Then he puts on another one. I hum to myself and roll about, touching the round legs of the chairs. When I roll near the chair Yaw is sitting on, his legs are in my face. His shorts are white, the opposite of his skin. The hair on his legs is so curly I want to straighten it. I reach up and pull one hair.

"Hey," he says, which makes me laugh and pull more hairs. It's fun teasing him. I really like his hair. Now he is breathing fast like a person running. Then he is bent over me, sliding his fingers into my drawers, pulling them down. When I say nothing, he opens his trousers and lies on me. It makes me think of what Papa did with Hotel Woman. I want to say *Thank you, thank you*, like Papa said but it hurts the way Yaw is stretching my skin. "Stop," I say and roll away.

"Sorry." His smile is funny when he gets up.

I get up from the floor and pull down my dress.

"I'm going home now."

I forget about the fried yam.

After lunch, Sister Mansa watches me walking in the yard and gives me a questioning look. When I move away from her, I feel a pain where my left leg joins my abdomen. Out of the corner of my eye, I see her point at me and exchange whispers with Auntie.

"What is the matter with you?" Auntie calls after me in a voice made drowsy from fufu and groundnut soup. Sister Mansa gives me that look again.

"Nothing."

"Then why are you walking that way?"

"It's rheumatism," I say, because that is what Papa said once when a man asked him why he was limping.

Auntie says nothing else till after dinner when Papa drives off to visit friends and she calls my name. I open the door to their bedroom and stand there cracking my knuckles. Nothing good comes out of answering her call into that bedroom. She is sitting at the edge of the big bed, wearing nothing but a cloth wrapped around her waist.

"Come in," she says. "And close the door."

I take a couple of steps inside and pull the door shut behind me. Even from where I stand, I can smell the sharp mint of the dusting powder she dabs into her armpits after every shower. Her naked breasts are like rolled-out dough. They are so flat I'm sure she can take one and sling it around her shoulders. She raises her arm and crooks her finger at me. I don't move. Although she doesn't have any ginger at hand, I sense trouble. I don't want to cross the black-and-white chessboard tiles stretching between me and the bed.

She says in a hard voice, "Come here."

I make my feet go to her.

"Lie on the bed and take off your drawers."

My fingers shake as I do as I am told. My knees are up and clamped together. She stands and gathers my dress to my stomach.

"No," I say.

She pries my knees apart and rears back. "Aaah, Esi, what happened down there? Someone has spread you. Who did this to you?"

I don't know what to say. I don't know if spreading has anything to do with what Yaw did, and if it does, I don't want to get him in trouble. He's my friend, and I fear for him the way Auntie is shouting.

"I don't know what you mean."

She shakes her head. "Get up, get up. Come with me." She sounds so disgusted I don't know what to say. She drags me into the kitchen where Sister Crocodile Jaws has joined Sister Sweet Voice. I'm dead.

"Did you find out what is wrong with her?" Sister Sweet Voice asks.

"Her down-there is sore. Someone has spread her."

Sister Sweet Voice laughs, as if I am butter on bread. Sister Crocodile Jaws says, "No wonder she's so thin! The boys have been feeding from her!"

"Ah, Esi, why did you let that happen?" That's from Sister Sweet Voice.

I feel as if I am covered with earthworms. I want to run into the bathroom and scrub, scrub, scrub my skin off until I grow a new one, the way a snake does.

Sister Sweet Voice starts singing, only her voice isn't sweet anymore.

> *Schoolboys on a march*
> *They found a girl*
> *A stupid, stupid girl*
> *They suckled, they suckled,*
> *They sucked from her.*

Sister Crocodile Jaws says, "Disgusting girl!"

Sister Mansa says, "Shame on you!"

The Crocodile spits out, "And your mother is the daughter of a chief? *Twea kai!* Nigerian animal."

"I'll have to treat her," Auntie says.

She puts a kettle on the coal pot. When it begins to boil, she picks it up and tells me to follow her. My face feels heavy. I don't know how to cry anymore. I remember my grandfather's rambling house in Lagos, men bowing to him and women kneeling. How come in Ghana we are animals, *ìyá mi?* I have no more words in my head.

In the bathroom, Auntie pulls out the larger chamber pot, the one painted white on the inside and green on the outside. White clouds swirl up as she pours the water into it.

"Take off your drawers."

Slowly, I pull down my drawers once again. It seems I am always taking off my drawers for one thing or another and it is never pleasant.

"Sit on the chamber pot. The heat will heal your wound."

I sit on it but I have to jump up shouting. My bottom is so small it slips into the scalding water.

"Sit down," Auntie says again. "The steam is good for you. It will heal you."

"It burns, Auntie."

She settles onto a stool in front of me. "Just sit on it."

I lower my bottom slowly but I have to jump up again. My bottom is on fire. Auntie grabs the chamber pot with both hands and dumps some of the water into the tub. She must have realized the water was too close to the top and she doesn't want to burn me. The heaving in my chest lessens when I sit back down, but now it's my throat that hurts.

I sit for a long time watching water shining on my skin. The ceramic tiles look like they are sweating. Or crying large tear-drops. A weird scent like steam from meat rises to my nostrils. I wonder what is cooking and if Auntie smells it too. But she sits in front of me with her lips pressed together, holding the words in because you don't explain things to a child.

I nod off in the warmth until Papa opens the door and I jerk up. I didn't hear his Mercedes rumble into the garage.

"What is wrong?" he asks.

"She has been spread open," Auntie says. I look at Papa. His lips are tight. I know he's angry with Auntie for torturing me. He's going to yell at her, tell her what an evil woman she is. I just know it.

"You stupid girl! You good-for-nothing tramp!"

The words fly from his mouth like knives straight at me and I slump over. He storms out, slams the door as if he can't get away fast enough. I don't know what a tramp is, but I know it's an awful thing. My chest is all wood now.

At bedtime, the sisters tell me they don't want disgusting me in their bed, so I curl up on the floor with a blanket between my body and the cold tiles. A burning persists between my legs. Small dots of red glow where the cocoa skin has come off. Papa didn't give me a cup of Milo, didn't play his accordion. Now the rain is pounding the roof. Even the sky seems angry, knocking things about—*boom! boom! boom!* I want to ask God: What have I done? If a boy did something bad to me, why is it my fault? I remember the time Kwabena sat on a stool wearing shorts without drawers, with his thing lolling to the side, its mushroom top peeping out. Sister Yaa noticed it and pointed, poking Sister Mansa in the shoulder. Sister Mansa laughed. "Perhaps he has used it to eat some girl!" They slapped their thighs as if to say, "Well done!" It's not fair.

The rain is less angry now and I can hear the frogs. They sound as if they are gargling on stones. I've stayed away from them ever since Elisha told me they could turn me into a man. I'd rather be a girl in my own skin, but I don't understand why women can be meanest to girls. And why is it that when Hotel Woman lies under Papa, she makes him so happy he thanks her, but I get called a tramp for wanting to do the same with Yaw? Why does Hotel Woman get rewarded with trips to Togo and new clothes while I get ginger and a cold floor? Why do I have to keep the words in and not tell Auntie about the baby she should know about? God, tear my skin open, let my mouth hang in a scream loud enough to wake dead people!

In the morning, Auntie sends me to collect Papa's breakfast plates because he eats alone in the sitting room while everyone else eats in the kitchen. When I go to him, he gives me a sad smile. Then he opens his arms. "Come here." I run and bury my head in his chest. He says it's okay and gives me a spoonful of honey. Every drop is as sweet as his smile, but my mind is made up.

The wet grass brushes against my legs as I walk to the edge of the forest. The frogs are gargling madly. I take off my clothes except for my drawers. Then I stretch out in the mud and wait for them to change me.

CHAPTER THREE

'LL NEVER BELIEVE Elisha or anyone else again when they tell
me what will happen if I do this or that. Now I know little people
won't appear and steal me away if I whistle at night. And when
I use a pestle to pound inside an empty mortar, I know I'm not
pounding my mother's breasts. How can that happen anyway,
when I don't even know where she is? The frogs jumped on my
legs, but I am not a boy. What I am is stinging from the welts and
bumps insects left on my skin after feasting on me.

I slapped and scratched my skin all day and didn't attend church
and didn't get to play with my friends in the church compound.
Now even my eyelids are swollen. Sister Mansa says I look like a
Chinese. Nothing else has changed. The air has the same smell of
milk bush that floats in when the wind blows. The pawpaw tree is
still standing in front of our house, spreading its spattered shadow
over the tomato bushes. I am surprised I don't want to cry.

The cocks have been yelling *kokuro koo*! but I don't want to get
up and go to school. I don't want the children to call me Chinese
and ask what happened. I have never met one and I don't know if
I'll like them or not but I hate being different. It's bad enough being

a girl and a Nigerian animal without being from a land so far away they call it the Far East.

Because I slept on the floor two nights in a row, my body feels as though Sister Yaa punched me everywhere. I can hear Auntie's voice growing louder in the corridor, which means she is coming to wake me up. I close my eyes and pretend to be asleep. The door snaps open and her minty smell covers me. She shakes me roughly.

"Esi, wake up, eh. It's morning. Can't you hear the cocks crowing?" I won't answer her. I want to sleep. She shakes me more vigorously. "Wake up, lazy one!"

I roll onto my back and try to buy time. "Auntie, I want to pray."

She stops shaking me and I flip onto my stomach, rest my chin on my clasped hands, and squeeze my eyes tight. She has no choice but to leave. You can't disturb a girl praying to the Lord, especially after her badness of two days ago. I try to pray, but I don't make it past *Lord we thank you always* before my eyelids become too heavy and I fall asleep until I feel Auntie's shaking again.

"Auntie, I say I'm praying!" She leaves and I slide back into dreamland. Then drops of cold water hit my neck and tickle down my back. I sit up to find Auntie holding a cup of water, tipping it on me.

"Good, you are awake. Now, get on with your morning work."

Get on with my morning work indeed. What I really want is to kick her but I want no more fingers digging into me and burning me with ginger. I squat by the bed and peek under it. The two chamber pots are full of nose-stinging urine. Why can't we use the water closet at night? Chamber pots are fine for villagers and bush people who don't want to cross their compounds in the dark to urinate in the outhouse and have a snake bite their ankles. But our toilet is right across the corridor. It's no effort to shuffle over and release into the lovely white bowl of the water closet, yet everyone uses chamber pots and it's my job to empty them. Kwabena is nine, a year older than I was when I started on the chamber pots, but it's inferior work for a boy, so I'm stuck with it unless a baby girl comes along. Hotel Woman's baby is a girl, but there is no chance of her taking over since no one is supposed to know about her. Which is fine by me. I'm not sharing my Papa with her.

I hold my breath and empty the pots into the gutter that runs along the veranda behind the house. I allow myself a smile because Sister Crocodile Jaws is the one who is going to scrub the stinky gutter. I hope she scrapes her fingers against the grainy cement and reddens it with her blood. I take small breaths and scrub the pots with a rough bark and soap until the insides are so white in the sun they can blind you. Later the pots will be warm and I can return them under the beds so everyone can urinate in them again.

After my morning work, Sister Mansa pours warm water into a metal bucket I carry to the bathroom to wash myself. The bucket rocks and scrapes because the tub isn't flat. I wish we had hot water from the tap and didn't use aluminum buckets. You can see charcoal gray marks from the bucket scratching the white ceramic. When I wash, I have to be gentle with the loofah because of the insect bites. After bathing, it's hard wearing my peach uniform that Sister Mansa soaked in cassava starch and sizzled with the iron until the stiff pleats could cut me.

After breakfast Kwabena and I go to the sitting room to say bye to Papa and collect our pocket money so we can buy food at break time.

"Here's ten pesewas for you," Papa says and gives me two silvery five pesewas I put in my pocket. Kwabena gets ten pesewas too, which I don't think is fair. The older child is supposed to get more money, but when it comes to Kwabena and me, we are treated the same even though there are eighteen whole months between us. When we pass by the bougainvillea hedging our house, I hiss, "Do you need all your ten pesewas?"

"Yes!" He tucks his money into his pocket and I bite my lip.

We join other children on the way to school, cutting through the forest where people's footsteps have worn out a crooked red path in the grass. When we get to a small stream, we hop on wet stones, avoiding the black tadpoles wiggling in it.

The path brings us up to the grass-edged street. We loiter through Zongo where Nigerians and poorer people live away from the town. We're better than they are because, well, I don't really know. I just know that even a half-Nigerian like me is better than those who live in Zongo. If Zongo people offer you water, you're not to drink even if your throat is scratchy dry. They live in one-room aluminum houses gone crusty-brown from rust. In front of the rooms, on the dirt floor, they sell everything from needles to cooked rice. Which is good, because we don't have to go all the way to the market for the smallest thing.

We buy pencils, then kuli-kuli, a treat they make from grinding groundnuts and adding salt and pepper before frying them into circles I can wear as a necklace. Though I don't because the oil will leave dark spots on my uniform. The kuli-kuli is hot and crunchy and so delicious we chew all the way to school and I forget to be angry with Kwabena.

At school, we line up according to our classes, in front of the long building painted in two colors: cream on top and muddy red at the bottom, standing on a copper-colored earth. The headmaster faces us on the veranda while the teachers line up horizontally behind him. He is a Nigerian, but no one calls him an animal because he can make your palms burn with the whip. Everyone calls him Master.

"Attention!" he says.

Mouths shut and we stand with our chests out like soldiers, hands straight down by our sides. He leads us in singing a hymn. Then we pray to our Father which art in heaven, hallowed be His name and give us our daily bread and everything else, but Master feels the brain cannot wake up unless he drills us soldier-style: Left turn! Right Turn! About turn! By the left, mark time! Left right left right left right left right. Then the all-boys school band bangs on the drums. (It's not proper for girls to drum even if they know how.)

"By the left, forward march!"

I have to hold my arms away from my box pleats as we march around the field singing a confusing song. The second stanza goes:

> *From the land of hunger,*
> *Fainting, famished lone,*
> *Come to love and gladness,*
> *My son! My son!*
> *Welcome, wand'rer, welcome . . .*

I feel sorry for the man and the hungry son, but school is not home and Master is not Papa and I'm not hungry. No one looks hungry. Everyone has the ironed uniform and oiled legs shining in the sun. A few don't have on shoes, so thorns can pierce their feet, which may form blisters. But the children are plump, with shining white teeth. Papa says no one will go hungry in Ghana if people eat porridge from the corn we grow, instead of Corn Flakes that comes in a box and doesn't even look like corn, the way it's been singed and crisped to death.

When we enter the classroom, Teacher tells us to line up with our backs against the wall for mental arithmetic. My stomach burns like someone who ate too much pepper. You have to know the answers immediately or else. We move slowly, forming three sides of a rectangle while Teacher takes the fourth side. There is nowhere to hide.

She picks up her cane, taps it in her palm, and walks to stand in front of Doris. "What is nine times eight?" Doris doesn't answer. She doesn't know or she's too afraid. Teacher's chest grows with anger. "Your brain is dead, smelly like rotten fish!"

The cane *shwoozes* down on Doris, *kpaa! kpaa! kpaa!* and my heart jumps with the beat. They cut the cane from a special twine whittled white and so thin that when it hits you, it can open the skin. Doris shrieks, twists like a worm. I am happy my brain is not dead because Papa teaches me at home. Teacher calls me good and I don't get lashes. I'll be happy when I go home, never mind the tramp Papa called me, which I know he must be sorry for.

My friend Marigold never knows the answer, so Teacher always gives her easy questions like what is two times two. It won't do to flog the daughter of Nana Ofori-Atta II, the king of Kibi, who gave Papa acres of land to build the secondary school where Papa is the headmaster. When the bell *clang-clangs* for playtime and we tear out of the classroom into sunshine, Marigold tells me she has a secret.

"What is it?"

She puts her finger to her mouth. "Sssh!" She pulls on my arm until we are under the jacaranda tree with the violet flowers, which is where we go when we don't want others to hear us.

I bounce on my feet. "Tellmetellmetellme!"

She pulls out a folded paper from her pocket and sticks it in my face. "I got a letter from my suppy!" *Soo PEE* is the way she pronounces it. But what is she talking about?

"You don't know?"

"Marigold! Tell me!"

"It's a girl. Your girl. I mean, a suppy is . . . uhm, a special friend for playing romance."

My eyes widen. "Playing romance? How do you play romance?"

"It's all about writing love letters. Kissing even." She says it's not wrong because it's not like spreading your legs for a man who can plant a baby in your stomach. And no, Auntie won't put ginger in my pawpaw or make me sit on hot water. She's sure even my sisters have suppies.

I clasp my hands. "I want one too. I want to play romance!"

"Suppies are fine for playing romance." She folds the paper and tucks it into her chest. "But I want a boyfriend. I want to do things with boys. That's why I'm going to choose Kibi Girls next year."

"How can you find a boyfriend in a girls' school?"

She shrugs. "I don't know, but the girls at that school are famous for getting boyfriends."

My ears are ringing. I want a boy too, even if I didn't enjoy what Yaw did and it was bad. Besides, if it was so bad, why did Papa move on Hotel Woman? When the time comes for Teacher to make the list that will send us to middle schools, I'll choose Kibi Girls.

We leave the shade and join the crowd around the food-sellers who sit near the guava tree. The sizzle of plantain and cocoyam frying makes my mouth water. We buy plantains as well as gari mixed with tomato stew. Then we make our way to the field and sit on the grass where other children are playing. Our gari is delicious. I tell Marigold Nigerians eat gari too, except they make it sticky with hot water and call it eba.

"You're always talking about Nigerians," she says.

"That's because my mother is from Nigeria."

From the field, I hear the boys. "What? You're a Nigerian?" Someone takes up the chant and everyone joins in:

Alatani eee, sebɔ reba o!
Ɛy ɛ a, wɔn dodgey!

Nigerian, the leopard is coming!
Learn to dodge!

Just because when a Yoruba baby is born, a medicine man uses a knife to make cuts on the baby's cheeks is no reason for them to tease me. I don't have the marks, but they don't care. They stick out their tongues. "Did the leopard get you? *Alatani aboa*, too stupid to dodge the leopard's claws?"

I stand up to throw my gari-foto in their faces, but they run off laughing. When they are far enough, they start again, "*Alatani eee . . .*"

Before I can dart after them, Marigold grabs my arm. "Don't talk to them. They're stupid."

It's true, but what good is that to me when stupid people don't know they are stupid? They'll only go on being stupid. I won't tell anyone else that my mother is Nigerian. I don't want people making fun of me. The boys see Master's daughter coming and they disappear. No one dares tell her to run from leopards. She doesn't have any scars on her cheeks, but she has a funny name: Bintu. It sounds like Been-to, which is what people call those who have been behind the corn, which means England or America or someplace like that. I think they say that because when you stand in front of a cornfield, you can't see anything behind it. Just like you can't see America or England when you look at the horizon.

I wonder if there are Ghanaians in Nigeria and whether Nigerians sing bad songs about them. I wonder if people behind the corn make fun of Nigerians and Ghanaians over there. I don't know which is worse: being a girl or being a Nigerian.

When people call me Nigerian names, I don't like school very much and I wish I could go home to Papa, who only says I have skinny legs like a mosquito when he's angry. I know he doesn't mean it because he gives me honey to sweeten his words. Ah, here's Papa's Mercedes pulling up in front of the red hibiscus hedge. He has never come to my school except to drop us off in the mornings if he's coming in to town. I want to run and throw myself at him and kiss him everywhere.

"That's my father," I say to Marigold. The boys can call me names but I have a father with a big car. I know he has already forgotten about my being a bad girl and loves me again. I run toward the car. He gets out waving a white envelope, and crooks his finger at a girl skipping rope. He can't see me but for sure he's asking for me, so I keep running.

Wait. Why is he giving the envelope to the girl? He gets back in the car and drives off. Something doesn't smell right, just like when he gave me the tablet to sleep so he could bounce on Hotel Woman. He was hiding something from me and I'm sure he's hiding something now. I march up to the girl. "That was my father. Give me the envelope."

"The man in the Mercedes is your father?"

"Yes, the envelope is for me."

"But he said to give it to Master."

I smile to hide the hammering in my chest. "Oh, he wanted me to give it to Master. He couldn't find me, that's why he gave it to you. I'll give it to Master myself, don't worry."

She tilts her head at me. I can tell she is not sure I am telling the truth, but she wants to keep playing, so she hands over the envelope and runs off. My hands are shaking. I tear open the envelope. I skip the *Dear Sir* and greetings and—what is this I'm reading? *Some of your schoolboys spread Frederica.* He's using my English name. *Please find the boys who did it and punish them.* Boys? Now it's more than one? My face burns. I tear the letter into little pieces and fling them into the dustbin. It's not honest but I don't care. Why should I be disgraced in front of the whole school? Why should Master question me and use his cane if I don't answer? It's bad enough being a Chinese-looking Nigerian girl without the whole school thinking I'm a dirty rag because boys have spread me, whatever that means.

When Kwabena and I walk home from school, I don't tell anyone about the letter. We buy long stems of sugarcane for the walk. We rip off the yellowish green skin with our teeth and chew and suck the sweet juice before spitting out the white roughness. The street is littered with chewed sugarcane gone moldy. Kwabena kicks empty cans all the way home, ruining his shoes.

After we greet Papa, he asks me, "Did the principal call you into his office today?"

I look innocent. "No."

"He didn't speak to you?"

"No."

"Didn't he ask you any questions?"

"No."

"I see. Well. All right then, go play."

Papa drives to his office though it's only a minute's walk from home. I'm still worried he will write to Master about what boys have done to me, so as soon as I change out of my uniform, I walk out of our hedge-fence of purple bougainvillea and cross the two hundred yards to stay close to him. He won't think it strange because I do that all the time.

I say good afternoon to Peter the secretary who smiles at me. When I see Papa in his big black chair behind the desk, I wonder why people call him handsome. I think he is ugly, really, with nostrils as wide as two garages. When he is eating, his round cheeks puff out like table tennis balls. But I love his big eyes, the way they twinkle when he is smiling. He brushes his moustache every day and I like playing with his hair that is so soft it feels like cotton wool. Now he looks crisp in his white shirt and black tie. He is frowning at a paper in his hand, but when he sees me his smile is brighter than the sun.

"Ah, there you are, Esi. Did you eat well?"

"Yes, Papa." I look at the paper. "What are you doing?"

His eyes roam the paper. "Just going over something the secretary typed. It's full of mistakes. I bet you could write better." Suddenly his smile disappears. "Peter!"

"Sah!"

Peter stands near the door rubbing the sides of his khaki trousers. Papa waves the paper at him.

"This letter is full of mistakes. Monday should begin with a capital *M*."

"Yes, sah."

Papa's lower lip is almost down to his chin, he's that cross. He looks up and down the paper. "I've made corrections in red ink. I want this typed again."

Peter takes the letter and leaves quickly. Papa's voice goes soft when he speaks to me. "Would you like to write?"

"Yes, Papa!"

He slides a piece of paper to me and I begin a story about a giant Ghanaian-Nigerian girl who is going to slay those who call her *Alatani aboa* and taunt her to run from the leopard. Papa rustles papers, his glasses pressing down on his large nose. There's a knock at the door.

"Come in!"

It's Peter. "Er . . . Sah, a Mrs. K wants to see you."

"What does she want?"

"It's about her son's admission, Sah."

"Send her in."

Mrs. K waddles in with the smell of camphor, her cloth wrapped around her big bottom. She smiles. "Afternoon, Master."

"Afternoon." Papa smiles and invites her to sit. She perches on the chair beside me. Papa smiles some more. "What can I do for you?"

"Master, hmmm, it's my son."

"What about your son?"

"Master, hmmm, he didn't pass the Common Entrance Examinations."

"Oh, I see. Sorry."

She sits sighing. Papa waits. Her fingers move everywhere. She slaps her one palm faceup on top of the other, like a beggar hoping for a pesewa. "Master, if I have come, it is not for evil. I just came to beg you . . . to see if you could please admit him."

Papa smiles gently. "Well, if he didn't pass, I can't admit him into the school."

Mrs. K leans forward and presses her palms together as if she's about to pray. "But he's a good boy, Master, he knows many things. It's only because sickness took him during the examinations, otherwise he would have passed."

Papa's smile disappears. "I'm very sorry. I can't. It's not right to admit a student who failed. I have turned other people away. Let him take the examinations again next year."

"Next year? O, Master!" She goes quiet for a moment, then she digs into her bag and comes up with a calico drawstring bag. Her smile is coy as she holds it out to Papa. "Er . . . as for this one, it's just a small present for you."

Papa turns into a statue. Then he takes the bag, loosens the string, and looks inside. He looks up at her. Her smile is white with her teeth. He hurls the bag. It flies over her head and hits the waxed cement floor with a big thud. He glares out of indignant eyes. "How dare you! You think I can be bribed?" She doesn't answer. "Get out!" My shoulders hop to my ears.

She falls back in her chair, clutching her chest. Her eyes are the size of side plates. I'm afraid for her the way she's breathing and whimpering, "Ow, Master, ow! Why? Please, I just wanted to—"

Papa is on his feet, pointing to the door. "Out!"

The woman jumps up and scrambles for her money bag and is out of the office moaning, "Ow, ow. Master, why? What wrong have I done?"

I have never seen Papa shout at a woman except Auntie. With his cane he whips the backs of male students for "insubordination" but he never flogs the girls. Bribing must be a bigger crime than not knowing your multiplication tables.

Papa plops down, and when he catches me staring, he says, "It's all right, Esi. I just don't like people who think they can buy me. Stupid woman." He smiles and my shoulders drop into place. I can breathe now.

When he finishes his work, we drive into town in his Mercedes. So long as I stay close to him and make him smile, I know he won't find the anger to write to Master and ask why he hasn't replied to the letter about the boys who spread me. He whistles to the tune playing on the radio. I stand at the back, in between the two front seats, watching the coal-tarred road and belting out the words:

> There's a new world somewhere
> They call the promise land
> And I'll be there someday,
> If you are by my side.

I have the egg-under-a-hen feeling and it's good. Papa can throw things at others and cane them, but I'm the one he talks to with the soft voice, who gets to ride and sing with him. I don't need to worry about him calling me a tramp, which I'm sure he's sorry for, even though he won't say so because an adult never has to say sorry to a child.

The radio crackles. Papa fumbles with it and we hear Prime Minister Busia talking about people from other countries. He calls them aliens, which is weird because they don't have big heads and strange ears or tails. He's talking about a new law, the Alien Compliance Order.

"Papa what is Alien Compliance—"

"Sssh."

The president's voice is serious and he uses lots of big words: "It has come to the notice of the government that several aliens, both African and non-Africans, do not possess the requisite resident permit. There are also those who are engaging in business of all kinds contrary to the terms of their visiting permits. The government has accordingly directed that all aliens in the first category leave the country within fourteen days, no later than the second of December."

"What is cat—"

"Be quiet, Esi!"

Another man's voice shouts that aliens are stealing our jobs from us. He is the minister for something. "We cannot afford to feed other mouths when ours are not fed." I wonder who is hungry and when do Ghanaians put food in the mouths of aliens but Papa shushes me.

Along the road, among the trees, people are gathered under the government's wooden radio boxes wedged in the tree branches. From the box, a voice booms in Twi: *Woyɛ Alatani o, Kuruni o, aban se momfiri ɔman Ghana hanom nkɔ mo kurom.* Why should the Nigerians leave and go back to their country? And the Kuru from Liberia, what have they done wrong? It looks to me as though people from other lands have it even worse than girls.

Papa beats his palm on the steering wheel. "This is a mistake. A huge mistake. To treat fellow Africans this way. Two weeks to pack and leave, that's inhuman! Nkrumah would never have done that."

I'm afraid. "Papa, will I have to go to Nigeria?" I don't know how I'll find my mother and I don't want to leave Papa.

He gives me a tight smile and pats my knees. "No, no, Esi. You're a Ghanaian."

"But I'm Nigerian."

"You're my daughter. No one can tell you to leave."

I don't feel safe. I wonder if there is a land where no one has to be an alien, where people from different countries can live together. Just like what the preacher says about Heaven, where lions and children cuddle and antelopes ride on the backs of elephants and angels sing and people walk on streets of gold. No need to steal the gold because you don't need money, and mothers don't put ginger in a girl's under-canoe. I want a place like that on earth. I don't want to have to wait until I die from malaria or get hit by a lorry.

The Nigerians are leaving. I feel dizzy. Sounds jangle, *clack, click, bang*. I can't tell which is which. *Ngaaarrrrh* from babies! Angry metals screech and clang! Police! Boxes. Huge trucks and lorries! Long lines. Woman, I can't take all those boxes! You have to leave that one behind! But driver, I beg you, my things! Your things are not my concern! Bang! Thud! Hey, *Maame Alata*, I'll take that box for a penny! No, no! Bye then. See if you can get a better price, ha ha! Take it, take it! I'll give you ten pesewas for those plates. Ten pesewas? I sell them for twenty times that price! Can you carry them with you? Thief! God will pay you back! I love you. Please don't go! Baa-bye, I'll write always! I'll miss you! Oh God! Walk well! Go with God! Get out of here, you animals! Baa-bye, Master. No more Bintu.

The silence that follows is so loud I want to run from it.

CHAPTER FOUR

PAPA HAS BEEN in a fighting mood since the Nigerians left, and it doesn't get better when he receives a letter from my school. I'm in the yard playing soldiers with Kwabena when I hear him screeching, "Esi Agyekum, come here at once!"

I dash into the sitting room.

"What nonsense is this?" He is in an armchair beside the four-legged radiogram the size of a cupboard, waving a paper in my face. "This letter says that you are to attend Kibi Girls Middle School."

Oh, that. I had forgotten.

"Such a bad school! Why did you choose it? All those girls do is get pregnant. It's because of that school your sister Mansa's brain is dead like dried tobacco. What can they teach you?"

I have nothing to say for myself.

His finger dances in my face. "Kibi Girls can't get you into Girls High School, the best school in Africa. How will you pass the Common Entrance Examinations so you can get admission? Do you want to be useless like Mansa?"

I don't want to be useless. And I don't think Sister Mansa is useless either. She is always baking cakes or pounding fufu or scrubbing something, except when she is doing her hair. Plus, she can sew and embroider tablecloths, which she learned from Kibi Girls. But I don't say anything because I don't want to make him angry and go back to calling me names. Also, she did sing that nasty song about me.

"None of your sisters will enter university. Don't you want to go to university?"

"I do, Papa." A university must be wonderful.

"Then Kibi Girls is not for you. You need to pass the Common Entrance and get into a great school like Girls High School." It's actually Wesley Girls High, but he always leaves out the *Wesley*, as if it's the only school in the world for girls. "Most of the university girls come from there. Girls High School produced the first woman doctor and lawyer. You want a school that will get you into Girls High School so you can go to university. Not Kibi Girls with their dead-brained teachers and girls getting pregnant all over the place and amounting to nothing. You can be anything, even the first woman ambassador!"

"Yes, Papa."

"Tomorrow, I am going to see the Superintendent of Schools and ask him to change your school." And don't I want to go to Girls High School so he can tell everybody how smart his daughter is? Look at my sisters, all stuck at teacher-training institutes. They will never amount to more than elementary school teachers. I'm intelligent. I deserve to go to university. Women can go to university too. Don't I want to go?

"I do, Papa."

"Look at your sister Abena. Thoroughly cooked with intelligence, yet she ended up at a teacher-training institute because she couldn't keep out of trouble. Running off campus without permission. Boys are all she thinks about. If she went to university, she could at least teach at a secondary school, which pays better. Do you know she got herself expelled from the secondary school?"

I didn't. Nobody includes me in that kind of conversation. My eyes move in every direction.

"Ah! To teach for pennies when she could be a lawyer or an ambassador! To be called Teacher, instead of My Learnéd Friend or Your Excellency! Those are the titles I want for you. You're the only daughter left with a chance for greatness."

"Yes, Papa."

"All right." The fight leaves his body. "I'll talk to Superintendent. Go play."

My Learnéd Friend. Your Excellency. They sound lovely. Queenly. People will empty my chamber pot. But I want to be a school teacher so I can whip pupils with my cane. There has to be something great about holding a stick above children and scaring them to learn. When Kwabena and I play school, we line up rocks against the wall and ask, What is nine times six? If they can't answer, well, they can't, so I whip them all I want and feel strong. They can't cry, which is good because if they do, I'll cry too and feel like a worm. But teachers must be tough because for some, the louder you cry, the harder they hit. Now I think about it, I don't want to be a teacher and make children cry.

Auntie says there's nothing finer than a woman who can cook meals so delicious her husband will buy her all the gold she wants. Papa says he doesn't care. He wants me to go to university and become a Learnéd Friend or an Excellency. If I add "thee" and "thou" to their words, Papa and Auntie could pass for angels in the Bible.

Angel Auntie: No matter how high a woman flies, her home is down in the kitchen.

Angel Papa: Be not a secretary. Does thou want to say "yes sir" all thy life and make tea for a master? Let them call thee Madam and make tea for thee!

Papa's is the way I want to go, but I pray I get into Kibi Girls. I'll be the girl who gets to play romance and enter university.

Outside, Kwabena and I play Israelites and Philistines. In the grass, we find two kinds of seeds and line them up. The white seeds with the pretty markings are Israelites and I am David. The Philistines are wine-colored and plain, so Kwabena is Goliath. He doesn't like it but it's too bad. I draw on my catapult that I've fitted with rolled-up paper. I'm about to slay Kwabena Goliath when we catch sight of Sister Abena coming down the path.

"Sister Abena has come!" I say. I drop my catapult and run toward her. Kwabena dashes after me. Sister Mansa and Crocodile Jaws rush outside too. I get to Sister Abena first but have to stop myself from getting knocked backward by her stomach. It is hard and rounder than the biggest ball I have ever seen. She has a baby in her stomach? She did the bad thing?

She drops her two bags, panting. "Esi, *wo ho te sɛn?*"

"My . . ." The words catch in my throat and I swallow. "My body is good."

Kwabena flings himself at her. He doesn't seem to notice anything. She rubs the top of his head. Crocodile Jaws and Sister Mansa hang back, whispering the way people do at funerals, "*Akwaaba.*"

Sister Abena thanks them. She asks if Papa is home, and how is Auntie and everybody. We say the right things. Yes. Everybody is fine. Auntie is home. Papa too.

Sister Mansa and Crocodile Jaws take a bag each and we walk heavily to the house. It's so silent you can hear the suitcases swish on the grass. You can even hear the butterflies' wings and the whir of insects. Somewhere, a crow mocks us, "*Caw! Caw!*" The crunch of our feet on the gravel sounds as loud as marching soldiers. When we drop the bags in the bedroom, I can hardly breathe.

In the sitting room Papa has music going loudly, written by a man called Handel—Papa says it's not a misspelling of "handle." The woman singing sounds desperate: *I knooow tha-at myyyy rrredee-eemer liveth!* Sister Abena has to go in there and greet Papa. I think she needs a redeemer, if she is pregnant. I whisper to Kwabena to follow, but Auntie stops me. "Esi! You are too fond of adult matters. Get out of there!"

I hiss at Kwabena, "Come on!"

We dart around the back of the house to the front and skulk outside the veranda with its yellow screen. The sitting-room door that opens to the veranda is ajar, and the music has stopped.

"Sister Abena is in trouble," Kwabena says.

"Sssh, shut up so I can hear! Come on!"

We bend down, creep nearer, and drop into the ixora bush. My skin feels scratched but I don't care. I brush down the ants crawling up my legs, flick a crawlie off my arm.

Papa roars, "Who did this to you? I sent you to a teacher-training school to become a teacher, not to pick up a belly! What do they call him, the idiot?"

"They call him Samuel Adu." How can her voice be so calm?

"Adu? An Asante man? No wonder. Bush people, all of them!"

"Don't say that," Auntie says. She doesn't like it when Papa insults her people, the brave Asantes who refused to pay taxes to the British until they shipped the Asante king off to someplace behind the corn called Seychelles Island. Papa doesn't care. He is a Fante who lived by the sea where the Fantes had tea with the British and ate with forks and knives before independence. He can insult Asantes all he wants.

Papa says, "What does he do, this Samuel Adu? I want to know what kind of work the fool does!"

"Please, calm down," Auntie says.

"Adelaide, shut up or I'll slap you! Abena, answer me, what work does he do?"

"He is a lawyer."

"A lawyer?" No one speaks for a moment. "Well. At least, that is something." There's an almost smile in Papa's voice. "My Learnéd Friend. I always wanted to be a lawyer myself." There's a longer pause, then, "All right. So, when is he coming to perform the rites for you?"

"He . . . he says the baby is not his own." There's a tremor in her voice.

"What?!"

"He is denying the baby."

"He put you in the family way and now he won't be responsible?!"

Sister Abena doesn't answer.

"Tell me where he lives!"

Oh no! That's what people say when they want to beat someone.

"He, he lives in Accra."

"Two hours away? That's nothing! I will go to Accra! Just point me to his house! You see what you've done?" I know what's coming. He's going to bring up everything Sister Abena has ever done wrong. "Gone and ruined your life, that's what!"—Ah, here it is. "I send you to secondary school, you get expelled! You had to run away to see boys without permission! Final year of teacher training, you get a belly! Are your legs the highway a man passes through on his way to marry someone else? They should be the destination, not the passage, *sansa nyi*, useless tramp!"

"He promised to marry me."

"And you believed him? You bloody fool! If you weren't pregnant, I'd box your ears so hard you would faint!"

Auntie moans. There's an iron heaviness to her voice. "Oh, Abena, why did you let him eat without paying in advance?"

They go on and on. Papa makes decisions. He'll find that lawyer and show him where power lies. He'll go to the king if he has to. No, that won't do since the scoundrel lives in Accra where the

Ga Mantse is one useless king. But no one is going to make his daughter pregnant and go scot-free, you hear? He hopes Sister Abena has learned her lesson. No more passages through her legs without bride price payment, no matter if the gate is already broken, you hear? Thank God there's one daughter left who can go to university. Tramp!

I want to rush in there and hug Sister Abena. I don't care what she has done. She's the only one who met my mother when I was a baby, who told me how my smile was like my mother's and how much she liked her. Plus, Sister Abena is older than Crocodile Jaws so Crocodile Jaws has to shut up and listen to her, which pleases me to no end. When Crocodile Jaws yells at me to fetch something, Sister Abena says, "Yaa, don't shout at her like that. Why, is she your slave?" Oh, how I want to press Papa's lips together and tell him to stop tormenting my sister.

I run into the kitchen and find her sitting by the coal pot. Auntie is banging pots about, which means she is angry with Papa but can't let him have it so she is angry with the pots. Sister Mansa and Crocodile Jaws sit side by side, their heads resting on their palms. It's a strange silence when Sister Mansa isn't singing and laughing at someone. I drag a stool and sit beside Sister Abena, whose eyes are peppery red. "I'm so glad you're home." I press my cheek against her arm, stroking her moist skin. She sniffs and blows her nose into her handkerchief. Pain squeezes her face, but when she looks around at us, she tries to smile.

"Why are your faces falling apart?" she says. "Did someone die? Come on, stop this. Heh, Esi, do you want to make toffee?"

"Yes!"

"Which one do you want? Condensed milk? Coconut? Or groundnut?"

"Can we make two, coconut and groundnut cake?"

"Yes."

"I'll get the pots," Mansa says.

Even Crocodile Jaws helps. They let me stir the sugar in the pot until it turns into brown syrup. Then I stir in the grated coconut. We do the same thing for the groundnuts and soon we're singing. Sister Mansa and I sing treble, and Sister Abena does the alto in a defiant voice. Crocodile Jaws does nothing but smile. Just as well. When she sings, she slides off the notes and sounds like an accident. When we're cooking and singing like this, I think how lovely it is to have big sisters. The toffee is chewy and sweet. After we finish, they let me scrape the crunchy bits from the pot and I'm happier in the kitchen than Kwabena who is outside poking millipedes and missing out. I promise myself that when Sister Abena's baby arrives, I'll fetch for her and make sure she gets lots of rest. I don't understand why women want a passenger between their legs when it creates so much trouble.

CHAPTER FIVE

THE SUPERINTENDENT OF Schools says it's too late to remove me from the Kibi Girls list, even for the daughter of the head-master of the only secondary school in town, a man who won't take a bribe. And what's the use of doing Papa a favor when Papa won't show him the same courtesy? Papa vows the year won't end before he finds me a fine boarding school that will help me get into Girls High School. I'll have good teachers who will teach me more than how to bake a pineapple upside-down cake and embroider tablecloths.

When school opens, I put on the Kibi Girls indigo uniform trimmed in white and tighten the plastic white belt at my waist. Papa is grim when he drives me in his Mercedes, but I'm all smiles. It's the first time I'm going to a school different from Kwabena and, at twelve, I feel grown-up.

We zip through Zongo where the poor Ghanaians still live. Hens beat their wings and squawk off. Goats bleat and scamper away, dribbling black pebbly droppings like M&Ms from their bottoms.

When we get to Kibi Girls, Papa glares around the school

building that lies lazily on a slope, as if it has fallen on its back and refuses to get up. I don't think he likes the way it's crowned by a tin roof, the kind that makes rainfall sound like drums pounding. He shakes his head. "I'll send the driver to pick you up when school closes."

"I want to walk home, Papa." He doesn't know I want to walk through Zongo, watch the orange sparks fly off the blacksmith's fire, hear the screeching of metal, the *neeka-neeka-neeka* of the miller's machine, and see all the exciting things we miss when we zip by in the car. Papa searches my face and I smile.

"All right," he says. He drives off and I wave until the car disappears into the elephant grass obscuring the road.

A bell clangs. We line up on the front grass according to our classes: Forms One, Two, Three, and Four. The headmistress stands on the veranda, wearing a white uniform. She welcomes us first, then talks about our future. "You are fortunate to be in a great school like Kibi Girls. Dr. Aggrey once said, 'Educate a boy, and you educate one person, but educate a girl, and you educate a nation.' You see, a woman gives birth to children and passes her knowledge on to them. This knowledge is multiplied by her children's children and their children and so forth. Men may make women pregnant, but women are the ones who give birth."

A girl can educate a nation? A girl is important? I don't know who Dr. Aggrey is, but my chest is hot with excitement. If I get an education, I can fill a whole country with people and one of them might become the president! A girl! I don't want to be a boy anymore. Girls are special. Girls are special! I could just float right up to the sun!

At break time, I'm feeling taller, skipping around with Marigold and other special girls when I bang into a senior girl holding banana leaves. They are oily with bits of rice stuck to them, which is what she must have had for lunch, rice and probably fish stew—I can tell from the smell.

"*Kose*," I say to apologize. She is so tall I have to raise my chin to see her face. She has big eyes with thick lashes so curly they form circles.

"It's nothing," she says. "Please, can you throw these leaves away for me?"

Please. And she's smiling. Senior girls usually bark at you because it's their right to have you wait on them. *Please*. If she asked me, I'd go to the cemetery and find gold rocks for her and not even blink at ghosts.

I race to the dustbin and return just as the bell is clanging for assembly. I collide with her again, nearly knocking her down. She grabs me with both hands.

"Thank you so much," she says with laughter in her big eyes. She is thanking me!

"Don't mention it."

"What is your name?"

"Frederica." I'm using my English name because, well, everyone has one from when the British ruled and the missionaries labeled us with Christian names because our Ghanaian names were pagan.

"I'm Christabel," she says. "I'd like you to be my suppy."

A suppy? Her suppy? A girl to play romance with? My heart bangs so hard I can't speak.

"Do you like me?" she asks.

I nod quickly. "Yes!"

"Good, I'll catch you after school."

There's a sweet pain squeezing my chest. I want to write a letter to her. I can't wait to find out how to play romance. Who needs boys when girls are so special?

At our afternoon break time, instead of going outside to play or buy fried plantain and beans, Marigold and the other girls gather at my desk to help me write my letter. They buzz around like bees as I dip the metal nib of my wooden pen into the bottle of blue ink.

"You need a romantic address," Marigold says. "Something like this: *From the Sugar Mountain, Across the Milky Ocean, Between Bread, To make our lovely tea. Box of Kisses, City of love.*

I don't understand. "How will the post office deliver it?"

"You're going to send it by hand, silly you!" She's right. I write the address in my best handwriting and when I finish, someone says, "You need a greeting that will make her pay attention. The longer, the better. Make sure to put one word on each line."

Another girl thrusts a book at me. "Here's the Bible. The Song of Solomon is full of romantic words."

I don't know where to begin. Marigold snatches the Bible from my hand. "How about 'My dearest among the beauties of Jericho'?"

The beauties of Jericho? I want my suppy to be special, not one of several beauties. She finds another greeting. I love it:

My

    Dearest

        Among

           The

                Hanging

                  Gardens

                    Of

                      Babylon:

Then I follow with "The brightness of this day has given me the opportunity to pen you this, my monopolized letter. Behold, you are beautiful, behold. How graceful are your feet in slippers!" I don't know what *monopolized* means but I'm sure Christabel's feet will look pretty in slippers, in no slippers. What a good thing the Bible is! Marigold offers to deliver the letter for me. The next day Christabel replies:

> *Box of love,*
> *City of Enchantment.*
> *Date of Kisses.*
>
> *Dear Frederica,*
> *It gave me a lot of pleasure to receive your missive. I hope mine finds you in good health. I love you too. We'll see about playing romance one of these days.*
> *Love forever,*
> *Christabel*

One of these days? When, when, when? How about going to the River Birim to swim? How about inviting me to her house?

Nothing happens. When we go to the riverside, she carries me on her back like her baby, and when I get too heavy, she sets me on a rock and I am left watching her kick away with the older girls. That part of the river is too deep and I don't like swimming unless my feet can sink into the mushy sand at the bottom. When she invites me to her house that is at the parish because her father is the Presbyterian preacher, we just lie on her bed, talk, and read books. No romance. Sundays, I hang over the wooden railing of the church balcony and watch her step-pause-step-pause down the aisle, in line with other choristers. They wear black robes with white collars, and on their heads, they have black caps with tassels. They are so angel-like I wonder if I'll ever get to play romance.

CHAPTER SiX

❚ ❘ ❚❚ ❘ ❚❚ ❘ ❚ ❚❚

W HO CARES ABOUT playing romance when Sister Abena is
in trouble? Papa found the lawyer who gave her a belly,
but the Learnéd Friend was a bad friend. He said no one could
prove he was the father of the baby, that Sister Abena's gate was
already broken and others had been through the passage before
him, which made Papa yell some more. She gave birth to a baby
boy they named Akwasi because he was a boy born on Sunday.
But though everyone loves to play with the baby, she and Papa
are like two lorries banging into each other, leaving blood on the
ground.

When she says good morning to him, he snorts and looks
somewhere else, which makes her mutter under her breath, but
when he asks her to repeat what she said, she says, "I didn't say
anything." I wish I could cover her mouth so Papa doesn't hear the
defiance in her voice.

Earlier today, she heated the iron stretching-comb in the coal
pot and sizzled her hair until it straightened. Now you can smell
burnt hair as she bends to get something from the fridge that
stands in the sitting room. She is whistling, which is her way of

showing Papa that he doesn't scare her. As if in response, Papa begins his own whistling behind the newspaper. Sister Abena's whistling gets louder. The paper comes down.

"Stop whistling!" Papa says.

Sister Abena straightens up and turns toward him. The look in her eyes makes me want to urinate. How can she look out of the corner of her eyes without blinking? No one dares disrespect Papa that way.

"Look at her face," Papa says. "Get out of here, useless tramp!"

Her lips are so tight the words have to fight their way out: "I have to clean out the fridge."

Papa snorts. His lower lip rolls down and the garages of his nose widen. She bends to wipe the lower shelf, showing Papa her bottom that I'm sure he would love to flog.

"Look at your hair," he says. "Fried straight and oiled. What is the matter? Are you wanting passengers between your legs?" Sister Abena mutters something. Papa puts his paper on the side table, tilting his head to one side. "What did you say?"

"I didn't say anything."

"I thought so. Now get out of my sight!"

Sister Abena yanks out the drawer filled with tomatoes and stomps out.

I'm trying to understand, I really am. I know Sister Abena did the awful thing by getting pregnant without a husband, but Akwasi is so lovely. Papa loves him. And why is it good for Hotel Woman to have a baby without marriage—oh, I understand! Papa passed through her legs, she wasn't the destination. That's why he is angry with Sister Abena. He wants her to be smart enough to close the passage to men just like himself. He needs punishment too because he did something bad. I wonder if it would help if God whipped his bottom. I don't have time to think because a commotion begins at the front door and a man calls out *Agoo!* I recognize the scratchy voice. It belongs to Papa Kwasi Nyamekyε, Papa's older brother.

I run to the door and there he is with Papa Job, the youngest of the three brothers. They both live in our hometown Odoben and their visit is like Christmas. Papa's scowl gives way to dimples as the brothers shake hands. He yells to Auntie for drinks and I help Sister Mansa serve them. Sister Abena keeps out of sight.

The brothers sit back in the armchairs, clinking glasses of beer the color of tea with white foam on top. Sweat runs down the sides of the glasses. Papa is sipping schnapps made creamy with the milk he has poured into it. I'm standing behind his chair smiling because he is telling jokes. Everyone is roaring, trying not to spill. It's a relief to let go of the knot in my stomach from when he and Sister Abena stared down each other. Papa has his legs stretched out in front of him and is wearing just a singlet over his trousers, showing his big shoulders. Highlife music plays from the radiogram. He picks up his glass, swirls it around, and takes a sip. He licks his moustache and smiles, a really happy smile that makes me lean over to play with his cotton-wool hair. He clears his throat. "Esi, come here, come sit on my lap."

I come out from behind him and perch on his leg though I am a bit too old for that. He puts his arm around my shoulder, raising his voice. "Listen, Esi came first in her class. I tell you, she is going to pass the Common Entrance; she is going to Girls High School one day!"

Papa Kwasi burps. "Girls High School! Why, that is a wonderful school!"

Papa Job is all teeth. "You always come first in your school, Esi!" He reaches down into the folds of the cloth around his waist and brings out crumpled money. "Here, ten cedis for you. Buy yourself some toffee."

Ten cedis can buy a dress! I'm so happy. "Thank you, Papa Job!" Papa Kwasi does even better because he is older. He gives me fifteen cedis. I'm rich!

Papa grins proudly. "Do you know, she topped a class of fifty!"

They are so out of their skins everyone talks at once. Awurade! She's going to be a lawyer. My Learnéd Friend! A lawyer? She can be a doctor! Not like her sister Abena, who is a disgrace. Abena? That fine girl? Who are you calling fine girl? *Tweaa!* Oh, don't talk like that about our daughter. I'll talk about her anyway I want. You don't know what she has done, let me tell you—where is that useless girl? Abena, *sansa nyi*, come here at once!

Sister Abena drags herself in. Her face could be carved out of wood. Papa crisps up. "Look at her ugly face! Do you know what she did?"

Papa Job says, "We know she has a baby, but—"

"She ruined her life!" Papa is choking, pointing with his almost empty glass. "It's not enough she got expelled from"—he gulps—"from secondary school, she had to get pregnant by a good-for-nothing man!" The uncles tell him to calm down, but he jumps up and points to Sister Abena, still holding the glass. "Useless girl, now she's going to finish teacher training the same time as her younger sister Yaa!"

Sister Abena blurts, "So what if I got pregnant? Did I give birth to an animal?"

Papa lunges toward her but the uncles grab him by the arms, take the glass from him. Papa Job steps in front of Papa to hold him back. Papa strains over his shoulder. "Get out! Get out of my face!"

Sister Abena wants to say something but the uncles tell her to be quiet. Leave the room. She has said enough. I run after her but she tells me to leave her alone. I stand in the corridor with a trembling chin. I hate me. Now I understand why Crocodile Jaws hates me. Why not, when Papa sits me on his lap and feeds me toffee, tells everyone what a great daughter I am while he slaps the others? I am like pepper in their eyes. I want to yell at Papa but I can't because there's a soft place inside me for him. Plus, I don't want him to turn his anger on me. I go outside and sit on the ground, pulling bits of grass until Auntie calls me to come in and be useful.

When my uncles leave, a heavy silence clamps down on us. The sisters don't want me cooking with them, so Kwabena and I wander to the river until supper time. We return to find Auntie in the kitchen, spooning Papa's garden egg stew into a Pyrex bowl. She tells me to take it to the sitting room and return for the boiled plantain. I have to use a napkin because the bowl is steamy hot.

"Be careful not to drop it and break my Pyrex," Auntie says.

Papa is at the table reading, but when I put the bowl down, he says, "Take it back" in a hard voice. I know better than to disobey.

In the kitchen, Auntie glares at me. "Take it to him again."

"But he told me to bring it back."

"Return it to him."

I do.

Papa says in a dangerous voice, "Take it back."

I obey. I don't know why Auntie wants to force Papa to eat when he clearly doesn't want to. This time, she marches the bowl in herself and I follow her to see what will happen. She plops it onto the table and throws the tablecloth over it. Papa leans back with a mean mouth until she has finished. Then, with one sweep of his hand, the bowl shatters onto the floor. Stew spatters up my legs. There is glass everywhere. Auntie looks at Papa. Papa looks at me. "Esi, be careful not to walk in the glass."

Auntie bends over and carefully picks up the shards. I bend to help too but she tells me to go clean myself. I walk slowly to the kitchen, grab a rag, and wipe the stew off my legs. If I act normal, I won't shake. I sit beside Kwabena and try to eat. The sisters share a plate under a harsh silence.

I am dipping my plantain in the stew when Papa stomps in. In a voice frozen over, he throws at Sister Abena, "I can't support both a mother and a child, so one of you has to leave this house. Either you go or the child goes. Choose."

I can't swallow, but Sister Abena doesn't even blink. "Fine, I'll leave Akwasi here. I'll find a way to fend for myself. My son can't."

Inside me, I'm screaming, No, Papa! Please! He knows very well Sister Abena will leave her baby behind, which is really what he wants. Oh, Sister Abena! He just can't bear to have her around. I know that by sending her away, Papa wants to teach us not to follow her ways, but where can she go? Where will she sleep at night? I turn to Auntie. She looks wilted. No one speaks.

"Papa," I start, but he shuts the door behind him. Soon, we hear the garage door open. Then the car grinds the sand and roars him off. I feel as if I'm holding onto strings attached to everyone, strings that are too heavy and slippery for me. Mother slipped through my hands when I wasn't looking. Now I don't know how to stop Papa from cutting off Sister Abena.

When I wake up in the morning, she's gone. I dash into the sitting room to find Papa. He is sitting with his hands supporting his hanging head.

"Morning, Papa."

"Morning." His head stays down. I wait for him to say something else. He doesn't.

"Sister Abena is gone."

" . . . "

"When can she come back?"

" . . . "

Outside, crickets screech. The wind whistles. He raises his head and looks long at me. Then he drags himself up like he is very old. He touches me on the head and lumbers out to the veranda. Akwasi's crying rips the day apart. I run into the kitchen to find him plastered against Auntie's chest. I sing to him and make funny faces but he doesn't want to laugh. When she gives him the bottle, he slaps it away and sticks his thumb into his mouth. I wonder if he has the loneliness like death feeling because he wants his mother. When he falls asleep, I sit by his cot to make sure he doesn't wake up scared.

It is amazing the way water becomes smooth again after you've dropped a stone in it. Now you can't separate Papa and Akwasi. He puts Akwasi on his lap and feeds him bits of fish and laughs when Akwasi smears it on his face. When Akwasi cries, Papa yells at everyone to bring milk, bring a napkin, give him juice. Papa is happy again. There is music in the house and visitors all the time. But I wonder who takes Sister Abena food, who smiles when she walks into a room, who wipes her eyes when she cries. If she cries. When I think of her, tears heat up in my chest and bubble out of me.

Now Akwasi wants to walk. He claps his hands and we clap too. We stand in front of him and say, "*Ta taa, tu tuu*" to encourage him until he takes his first step. He takes a couple more steps and wobbles. Papa laughs. When Akwasi smiles and sways on his feet, the world is such a happy place. But a few days after taking his first step, Akwasi doesn't want to walk. When you try to give him food, he turns his face away and won't open his mouth. He doesn't want Papa to play music for him. He buries his head in Papa's shoulder and though he looks sleepy, he won't sleep. Papa is worried because he has to go to Accra for a conference and leave him behind.

After Papa drives off, the runs begin. No matter how often Auntie changes Akwasi, his bottom keeps moving, and what comes out is slimy green mush. He whimpers weakly yet breathes quickly.

After three days he is reduced to such a quiet that Auntie ties him on her back and rushes him to the clinic, but the only doctor has traveled away. The Nursing Sister gives Akwasi medicine that oozes out the side of his mouth. She shakes her head and tells Auntie to take him to Gee, a big hospital at Kumasi. It's already noon when Auntie boards the lorry for Kumasi, which is at least three hours away.

A sad loneliness wraps us when we wave them off. I miss the way Akwasi laughs and drools and grabs my nose, the way he clings to my leg and pulls himself up with a smile before grabbing the food on my plate.

After supper, we huddle around the coal pot in the yard under a black sky. I pull the cloth tighter around me to keep out the cold. Insects screech *krrrrr*. Sister Mansa tells me a story but I keep thinking of Akwasi. Then we hear dogs barking and I think he is back! I throw off the cloth, running outside. In the lane, a figure marches toward me. It's Sister Abena.

"Where is Akwasi?" she asks. There is a wild hunger in her voice. "I was sitting at school and I had this sudden burning in my stomach and so I came to see him. Where is he? I've got to hold my son."

"Akwasi is very ill," I say. "Auntie has taken him to Gee."

Crocodile Jaws thumps me on the head for opening my big mouth.

"Gee? Kumasi?" Sister Abena's eyes dart in all directions.

"Oh, it's nothing," Sister Mansa says.

"That's a lie!" I say.

Crocodile Jaws thumps me again, says I've got slippery lips and to shut up. Then she turns to Sister Abena and tells her not to mind me. "He is just a little ill, that's all."

"It's not true, he can't eat or talk—"

Sister Mansa pinches my arm, hissing, "Shut up," before

turning to smile at Sister Abena. "It's nothing serious, really. Just come inside and we'll give you something to eat."

But Sister Abena shakes her head. "I want my son! Where is he?" No one knows what to say. "I've seen real trouble. You won't believe it. Sometimes, I had no food to eat, no money to buy drawers, but at least I knew my son was well. Now he's sick, and you tell me Auntie has taken him to Gee? And you want me to eat? *Awurade Nyankopɔn!*"

"Oh, sister, don't call out God's name like that," Sister Mansa says.

"If I can't call on God, who can I call on, my father? The one who threw me out?"

"Sister, sister! Just come in and let's at least give you some water," Crocodile Jaws says. "I'm sure you're tired."

"No, I don't want water, I want my son!" It doesn't matter how late it is. She will walk even if there's no car but she's going to Kumasi to see her son. She will not let him stay in a hospital without his mother.

We watch her hurry down the path. Her arms and legs blend with the darkness, her white dress fluttering in the wind as her luggage sits on an unseen head, a ghost vanishing around the corner.

It takes two long days for Auntie and Papa to arrive separately. Papa wants to know why Auntie's arms are empty and there's no Akwasi on her back. She sighs till Papa shouts at her to talk. She pulls out a stool and sits. Her eyes are pinkish red. We gather round her.

"It was so late when I got to Gee. Akwasi was soft in my arms, not making a single sound." Her jaws move up and down as she swallows. "The doctor said Akwasi had no water in his body, but they couldn't give him any because he wouldn't wake up. So, the doctor said to give him a drip. A drip! The poor baby. They stuck needles here." Auntie points to her ankle. "I said, Akwasi, open your eyes please. They waited, listened to his heart, but the water wouldn't go in. They touched his wrist and, oh Awurade . . ."

"What did the doctor say?" Papa asks.

Auntie's lips tremble. "His pulse was too weak to drive the drip. His pulse . . . was . . . oh, Awurade . . ." She starts crying. I feel the tears burning in my own eyes even though I don't understand what she is saying.

"What happened, Adelaide?" *Adelaide*. It's a serious business when Papa calls Auntie by her name. "Adelaide?"

"He, he never woke up . . . he's dead . . . Oh! Oh!" Auntie falls on the ground. The sisters howl. Papa is a stone, like he doesn't understand anything. There's screaming coming from somewhere. From me. I run to Papa. He is shouting, "Ow! Where is Abena? Where is my daughter?" But Auntie is rolling on the ground, clawing at the stones. She cries for a long time until I fear she is going to die too. Papa and Crocodile Jaws help her to her stool and Sister Mansa brings her water but she knocks it down screaming, "Akwasiieeeee!"

They spend a long time calming her down so she can talk. Her voice is all scratched up and she gulps out her words. "The doctors asked if we could bury him. What could I say? He was already dead. I went to our family house at Kumasi and told my sisters, and my mother . . . oh God." She's crying again. "How could Akwasi die like that?"

Papa tells her in a soft voice to stop crying. He wants to know where Sister Abena is. Auntie sniffles, wiping her face with the back of her cloth. "She came to the house. I had finally managed to sleep when I heard banging on the door. At first, we panicked. How did she know? How did she come there at that time of the night? What were we going to tell her? Then she attacked the door, screeching, 'Witches! What have you done with my son? Have you fried and eaten him already? Open the door!' She was screaming so. When we opened the door . . . Oh God, she threw herself to the ground." Auntie can't go on.

"Where is she?" Papa asks. "Why isn't she with you?"

Auntie sighs. "She says she will never step foot here again. She says we killed her son. I don't know where she went."

I want to die. I don't understand anything. I don't understand God. I don't understand how Akwasi could die, how Sister Abena could be lost to us. My sister. How does she fill that empty space, like the one I feel in my stomach when I miss my mother and Papa gives me milk and Milo but I remain hungry? Now there is another hole in me, a big one for Sister Abena and Akwasi. At night, I squish against Sister Mansa but I can't sleep.

CHAPTER SEVEN

LIFE IS LIKE a rainbow. There is the blue-black of Akwasi who is dead, the purple of Sister Abena and my mother who are not dead but I can't see. The green plants that give us food, and red the color of my toffee. The dark colors force me into a corner behind the house and I don't talk to anyone. Then the sun shines. What can I do except get up, even when I don't want to?

I wish I wasn't wearing dark blue, the color of the uniform that leads me to my teacher Miss Doku with her droopy eyes and the black holes of her nostrils sprouting hair.

She sits behind her desk on the wooden platform, glaring down at us or fingering her cane, nattering. "If I were at Koforidua, I'd be eating avocados in class. Bananas. Oranges. Groundnuts. The children were always bringing me presents. You people don't know how to praise. You never bring me anything. Let me tell you, if you do something wrong, I'll cane you."

When someone is late to school or forgets her notebook or has untidy writing, Miss Doku peels her round bottom from the chair, descends from her platform, and makes the culprit open her palms. Just in case the girl hasn't already figured it out, Miss Doku explains, "I'll beat you with my right hand till it gets too tired, then I'll switch to my left hand and beat you until I can't move my arms." No one wants to annoy her.

I manage to stay out of trouble until the day she steps outside to rest her poor arms and wet her throat that has gone dry from shouting. Everybody stops studying and starts doing something wrong. You can tell Marigold is writing to her suppy from the way she keeps tilting her head to smile at what she has written. I peek over her shoulder and see a new expression: *Sweet Spirit, comfort me.* Now I want to write to Christabel. I have no paper to write with, but in front of me is a notebook belonging to Dora who has left her chair to talk to someone. I might as well take the notebook and write in it. Surely, she won't mind? I can tear out the letter after I finish. And why don't I grab her Bible as well so I can copy from the Song of Songs?

I dip my nib into the blue ink, blot the drops on felt cloth, and scrawl: *Christabel, you are the rose of Sharon. Your eyes are the pools of Hesbon by the gate of Bath Rabbim. Your nose is like the tower of Lebanon looking toward Damascus. Your navel is a rounded goblet that never lacks blended wine. Your waist—* Someone snatches the pen from my hands and there is Dora with eyes like knives cutting at me.

"That's my notebook!" The hum in the classroom stops and heads turn. "How dare you write in my notebook!"

"I, I'm sorry."

"She wrote in my notebook! I'm telling Miss Doku!"

Oh no. Everyone talks at once. Miss Doku strides in. The room goes quiet. Dora's hand shoots up. I am trembling. What is she going to say? What will Miss Doku do to me?

The room goes black, and when I open my eyes, I'm lying on my back on the floor, looking up at the frowning faces of Miss Doku and the Form Two teacher.

Form Two Teacher asks, "Is your body good, Frederica?"

I don't understand what is happening. Miss Doku tells her she was walking toward me when I fainted.

"Send for her father," someone says. They put a cup of water to my mouth and declare I've been bewitched. I don't know how you're supposed to feel when you're bewitched, but everyone knows witches are responsible for every sickness and death. The witch is always an old woman whose husband has died, because only a witch lives long after her husband has died, after she has killed him. Any woman who has weird features is a witch, like my classmate Theresa with her two rabbit teeth curving over her lower lip in a way people call kiss-me-quick, though I can't see anyone wanting to kiss her quick.

Everyone decides Theresa is the guilty one. She must have eaten off my body while I slept at night or flown up to a tree and cooked parts of me on it for her supper. I don't know how she managed that when there are no bites on me, but the cooking has to be on the one tree with no leaves. All that cooking must have harmed it and left it ashy. Theresa protests that she is not a witch and I protest too but no one listens. They think I must truly be under her spell to defend her. Marigold steps up to her. "Remove your witchery from her, you evil thing!"

They send for Papa. He yells. He wants to know what kind of school is this with witches making his daughter faint. He drives me home and gives me milk, the cure for stomachaches, sore throats, and when I don't want my supper. The next day he drives me up to a town on a mountain to see a medicine man who gives me a black drink mixed with half a bottle of beer. The drink bites into my stomach and drives me to the lavatory until everything in me comes out and washes away the witchery. I want to return to school, but Papa says no.

We are sitting at the Formica dining table sipping our night cup of Milo when he says, "I've found you a great boarding school. It's called Mmofraturo. It is a good school. Half the students at Girls High School come from Mmofraturo."

A boarding school! I'll have a shiny metal trunk, painted black with red crescents all over, a padlock and a key of my own. I'll come home acting big, like my sisters do when they go away to school and return home.

"But you have to work hard if you want to pass the Common Entrance Examination for Girls High School."

"Yes, Papa!" I throw myself on him as Milo spills everywhere and Papa laughs.

He twists around, opening letters as I dab at spatters of Milo.

Anytime a letter arrives for my sisters, Papa reads it first in case it's from a man. There is no way to prevent that because the letters come through the school's post office box. To stop Papa from knowing their goings-on, the sisters have created a secret language, which I've managed to figure out. You just add *a* to every consonant to get *ba da fa ga*. The five vowels become *1 2 3 4 5*. If a man wants to say *Darling*, he writes *Da1rala3naga*. When my sisters talk at night, I have to keep my cheeks from spreading into smiles because I don't want them to know I understand their naughty talks.

I smile at Papa but he doesn't smile back. His eyes are fastened on the paper as he sips his Milo. He is about to put the cup to his mouth when he stops midair. "Mansa! Come here at once!"

She stands in the space between Papa and me, linking her fingers respectfully behind her back. Papa's eyes burn into her. "Who is this man called Ebenezer?"

Sister Mansa blinks quickly. "He is only a friend."

Papa's head tips to the side. "Only a friend? And what is the meaning of this: 3 la4va2 ya45. What's that?"

I love you. Ha!

Sister Mansa blinks faster. "He says he sends his greetings to everyone."

"So why can't he greet in normal language? Why the numbers and gibberish?"

"I don't know."

They stare at each other. Papa pushes the letter toward her. "All right. But let me warn you, he can write in plain English or not at all. If he ever writes that nonsense again, you'll see. Then I'll find him and deal with him, you hear? With your brain as dead as dried tobacco, you should be studying, not writing to boys!"

"Yes, Papa."

He points to me. "See your little sister here? She can tell you what is sixteen times eight without counting on her fingers and toes. That's why she will go to university one day. You should be studying instead of chasing after boys!"

Her lips quiver. "Yes, Papa."

I run after her into the kitchen. She walks to the sink, twists the faucet open, and attacks the dishes, her neck moving like a turkey as she swallows hard.

I touch her arm, pushing my face into her view. "Papa shouldn't have read your letter."

"Go away, you evil witch! Leave me and let me do the dishes!"

I freeze. "Fine. But when I grow up, no one is going to read my letters."

I stalk off and plop down on the rear veranda floor. I was going to tell her the truth about what happened once, when Papa told her to go to the cupboard and fetch a tin of anything that had one pound in weight. Papa asked me if I knew the answer. I didn't, so he told me how to look for it on the side and even said what tin to get. I went to the cupboard where she knelt crying and grabbed the right tin. When she returned holding something that weighed at least two pounds, Papa said, "Dead-brain girl, even your little sister is smarter than you," which made my chest grow with happiness. Now I know Papa let me cheat just to show her up.

It's not fair. I don't know why God made Sister Mansa's brain so hard nothing can pierce through it. Every evening she sits at the kitchen table with her head hanging over her books, her legs steeped in a bucket of cold water up to her knees, which she says prevents her from sleeping. But no matter how hard she frowns at the pages, the only tests she can pass are cookery and singing, which is why they've chosen her to sing before the king on Speech Day. When Papa shouts at her, I want to make her a cup of Milo, but not when she bites my head off like she just did.

Here she is, looking at me with a brighter face. Is she sorry for shouting at me?

"Esi," she says with a nervous laugh I don't trust. "Tonight, I want to study at the boy's quarters. Will you sleep in there with me?"

I don't understand. The boy's quarters extend from the garage. That's where the houseboy is supposed to stay, but since we don't have one, Mr. Agyei, one of Papa's teachers, is staying there until he gets his own house. Even if he has traveled to his hometown for the holidays, it's not right to sleep in someone's bed without him knowing about it. That's what I tell her. She agrees. "It's just that I want to study tonight, and I don't want to disturb everyone else when I keep on the light." She smiles. "Your eyes would stay closed. Also, if you don't come with me, Papa won't let me."

Okay, I say. I really want her to pass her tests and not get yelled at.

CHAPTER EiGHT

A T BEDTIME, WHEN the yard gate bangs behind us, it feels as if we are going on an adventure. We shuffle past the padlocked garage, our arms overflowing with pillows and blankets. Sister Mansa also has a rolled-up straw mat under one arm. When we unlock the door to the boy's quarters, I immediately notice Mr. Agyei has covered his corner bed with a checkered blue sheet.

The bed looks so inviting I drop the blankets, and I'm about to dive on it when Sister Mansa grabs my arm. "Don't you know it's disrespectful to sleep on a teacher's bed?" As if I myself didn't mention it earlier. She unrolls the mat over the linoleum, in the space between the bed and writing table. Then she covers the mat with a blanket, saying we'll sleep together. Which calms me down because always when I lie beside her, the heat of her back against mine is all I need to slide into sleep.

She goes out and returns with a bucket of cold water that she sets under the table. She tells me to go to sleep, that she'll join me later. Then she plops onto the chair, steeps her feet into the bucket of water, and fixes her eyes on the dark lines of her book. I lie on the mat, watching the four blades of the ceiling fan hum and multiply until they are one blurry whir. I fall asleep.

In the middle of the night, when I wake up to use the chamber pot, I feel a cold hollow behind me where Sister Mansa's back should have been. It's dark and I'm afraid of ghosts, so I look toward the table where her head should be hanging over her book, but the chair is empty. I struggle to my feet and there she is sprawled on the bed. Except she has developed two extra legs and arms tangled together and—a head that belongs to a man? My heart pounds in my chest. Did Mr. Agyei return in the night? If so, why is he sleeping with my sister? Anger boils inside me. I want to ruin their sleep. I sit next to the four-legged tangle and pat around them. The twiggy body is not Mr. Agyei's. Sister Mansa rolls toward the wall. The man sighs, stretches out an arm, and reaches for her, still sleeping, which makes me madder. I slap his bottom, then dive down the mat before he can catch me. His breathing breaks. I lie still. Stupid man.

As soon as the hiss of his breathing steadies, I steal up to them, pinch him hard, and dive for the mat again. The bed *squeeshaws* as he turns around, and then all goes quiet. Again, I steal up to the bed but just as I'm pinching, he turns and—*yaarrrr*, it's his thing I pinch! I spring back and he jerks up. Sister Mansa twists awake, raises her head. Even in the dark I can see the angry flash of her eyes. "Go to sleep, you witch!"

I want to yell at her for her lies but the words dry up in my mouth. All I can do is slink slowly down. My abdomen hurts, I still need to urinate. I can't very well wet the mat and lie in sticky clothes, can I? I have no choice but to squat on my heels, drag out the chamber pot from under the bed on which my sister breathes with a man, and release *trrrrrrrrr* to their hearing. Afterwards my shame has nowhere to go but hide in sleep.

In the morning, I feel Sister Mansa's back against mine as if I dreamed the whole four-legged spread on the now made-up bed. No naked man with a wiggly thing in sight. Sister Mansa gives me a shy smile and says, "Please don't tell Papa, *wae*." Nothing more. I can only nod because my mouth won't open. She doesn't need to worry. Like the Hotel Woman business, I want to forget it ever happened. I am not the one who is going to tell Papa.

That's how I am still feeling when, after breakfast, Auntie calls me into the yard to treat the sore on my left leg—I got hurt when I was crossing a bridge over a stream, with Kwabena way ahead of me. When he got to the middle of the slippery plank, I was about to get on it when his weight made the end see-saw and land on my foot, scraping the skin into a sore. Just the excuse Auntie needs to play medicine woman.

Her big bottom hangs over a stool by the gutter in the yard. I sit on another stool facing her, my wounded leg stretched out. She pours steaming water into a chamber pot and breaks into it granules of "turns-red-in-water," which Papa calls potassium permanganate. As the water turns into the color of old blood, Auntie tells me it kills germs. She dips the rag into the steam, fast squeezes water out, and presses the scalding rag on my sore. The pain is white and I scratch and kick, which prompts her to yell for the sisters to come hold me down as usual. After the scalding is done, they let go. Auntie uses the soft tip of a feather to brush ground camphor-in-oil into the sore before spreading a bandage over it. Then she heaves herself up and says, "Clean up everything." She has to go to the market.

I am so angry I don't move. I listen to her slippers *slap-slap* the floor as she leaves for the bedroom. Soon after, she emerges, her head wrapped in a silk kerchief. That head will carry a cane basket of foodstuffs for preparing the afternoon meal. May her neck snap off like a dry twig! I hope she steps on broken glass!

Sister Mansa appears. Look at her, all dressed up in a flowery yellow dress, telling me she is going to visit her friend Florence. She should be going to practice her singing with the school choir for the upcoming school Speech Day, not visiting Florence to probably talk about what she did with the man last night. I hope she steps on a thorn. The gate bangs after her and here is Sister Crocodile Yaa too, dressed up to go "do my studies with a friend." That's what happens during the holidays when Papa leaves for the office. Everybody suddenly has a reason to go out. I am so angry.

I kick the chamber pot into the gutter. It lands with a bang and a huge chunk of enamel flies off. Red water splashes over everything. Good! Yes! Here's a fine kick for you too, stupid bottle of camphor oil! I kick you, miserable stools! And there! Everything in the gutter! I hate you! And you, and you, and you!

Kwabena shows his scared face from wherever he has been hiding, his mouth open wide enough to swallow an orange.

"Esi!" he gulps. "Auntie won't like that. Look at that mess."

"I don't care!"

I stomp out of the gate, and he nips at my heels. "Where are you going?"

I don't know. He trots behind me. I march past the curving street, not stopping to pluck the pink petals of roses like I usually do. I want to find Sister Mansa and tell her she's not my sister. Didn't she say she was going to Florence's house? Is it not in the same secondary school? I'll find her. I'll tell her what I think of her. And what she did with that man in bed, I'll tell her what a bad girl she is!

It takes minutes to get there. I call at the gate, and Florence opens it. Her hair is patted down into a round bush, and she has going-out shoes on but I don't see Sister Mansa anywhere.

"Where's my sister?"

Florence frowns. "Mansa is not here."

"But she said she was coming to visit you."

"*Saaa?* Maybe she will come here later but I haven't seen her today."

Fine. She will come home eventually, won't she? I'll have the chance to hurl all the sharp words I want at her. I remember to thank Florence before turning away. Kwabena pulls on my arm. "Let's go home."

I shake him off. "You go home. I am not going back when Papa is not there. I'm off to see that nice woman teacher."

"Miss Kisi! You know we aren't allowed to visit her." He reminds me of Papa's warning that she is a bad influence. A beautiful woman of marrying age who teaches and lives by herself can only be up to no good. What is so bad about her when at Papa's parties, all the men want to press her against their chests for the highlife dance? Plus, I don't want to go home to the place that is always finding ways to burn me.

Kwabena throws me an angry look. "Fine then, I'm not coming with you!" Off he goes on knobby legs.

Miss Kisi gives me toffee and lets me rub her red stick on my lips. But after a long time of watching her roll her hair on plastic tubes and trying on dresses, all the anger leaves me. I walk to Papa's office and there is Kwabena, who probably couldn't find anybody to play with. There is no smile on Papa's face and Kwabena looks at the floor.

Papa asks, "Where did you go?"

It's no use lying when surely Kwabena must have already opened his okro mouth. Papa whacks my bottom with his palm. I cry, shooting angry looks at Kwabena.

When Papa drives us home, Kwabena gets to sit in front because he is now the favorite while I'm stuck in the backseat. I pinch the back of his neck, and when he turns his head, I whip my head to glare out the window.

We get home to find Auntie in the kitchen pounding fufu by

herself. She thumps with the pestle in one hand and turns the squishy dough with the other, the pestle going *pam! pam! pam!* against the mortar.

Papa wags his finger at her. "You are too slow! From morning to noon, you still can't get the food ready?"

She raises her head to show a face shiny with sweat. "The food would be ready if I had daughters to help me." She rests the pestle on the rim of the mortar and points with her free hand. "That Esi left a mess behind, and as for the older girls, I haven't seen them since I went to the market."

Papa's hands hop to his waist, and his head jerks sideways, a bad sign. "Huh? Where are the girls again?"

"I don't know. I came home to an empty house. The choir-master came looking for Mansa because she never showed up to practice her solo." Auntie dips her hand in water, turns the fufu over, and begins pounding again, her cheeks clenched. Papa swivels on his heels and heads for the sitting room. Kwabena follows him, and since I still won't speak to him, I might as well help Auntie cook.

After lunch, Sister Crocodile slithers back home. Papa wastes no time in slapping her for studying with boys, which bothers me not a bit. Sister Mansa remains gone and I start worrying about her. At supper, the yam sands my throat. Afterward, no one has to tell me to help wash plates and sweep the floor. Now the sun has lost its heat and turned a fiery orange about to drop behind the faraway trees. On Papa's brows, a storm is gathering. After Kwabena getting me spanked, I still don't want to talk to him but this is no time for grudges. We press our chests against the rectangular bars of the corridor, whispering our worries about Sister Mansa. Finally, the gate snaps open.

Sister Mansa strolls in with Florence as if it's the most natural thing in the world. Almost at the same time, the big doors to the sitting room crash open and Papa bursts out.

"Where have you been?" he demands. He doesn't even greet Florence or ask how her body is. "I know you didn't practice with the choir!"

Sister Mansa's eyes move quickly to her friend. "I went to visit Florence."

Papa turns to the silent Florence. "Has she been with you all day long?"

Florence looks at me. I look at Florence. She knows I must have told Papa something.

"No." She swallows. "Mansa came to my house just now and asked me to walk her home."

When Papa speaks, his voice is so quiet it ices my spine. "Thank you. You may leave." As soon as the gate bangs after Florence, he tears off his heavy slipper and lunges at Sister Mansa. She runs screaming out of the house. Papa can't catch her because his legs are old.

The sky is as black as death. It's time to sleep but Sister Mansa still hasn't come home. A harsh silence hangs over the house. Only insects, who don't know any better, dare break it. I hope she isn't in the forest. At night, snakes love nothing better than to slither out of their muddy holes and they won't hesitate to bite anyone in their way. Kwabena and I make a good show of playing but we are really waiting. The boom of Papa's voice giving orders vibrates through me. He wants our two watchmen to find Sister Mansa—we have had watchmen ever since Papa fired the school accountant for getting a girl pregnant and the accountant came to his office one night waving a cutlass.

Auntie drags her body out of the kitchen and shoos us to bed. For once, I don't call her a bloody fool in my head. Without Sister

Mansa, the bed is too wide so I twist my back against the cold wall for whatever comfort I can get.

In the middle of the night, terrible howls tear me out of sleep. I sit up quickly. It's Sister Mansa. She's screaming. I whip off my cover cloth and rush to the sitting room. What I see makes me stop at the door. I can make out the top of Papa's head from behind the settee, but I almost don't recognize Sister Mansa the way her whole face is one big swelling. Her eyes have shrunken to those of a lizard and her mouth is almost as large as my fist. When I move closer, what makes me nearly topple over is the way her ankles are tied with a rope—to prevent her from running away, I'm sure. The triangle of her chest tells me her wrists are tied behind her back. Angry welts cover her upper arms, the parts I can see. She stands trembling like someone with a bad case of malaria. I turn my head to Papa, who is sitting on the settee. He smiles at me through his glasses to show how happy he is I've come to join him. An open book lies in his hands, held in place by his thumb. The cane leans against the arm of the settee. The only thing I can think of is to sit beside him and try to distract him with questions about the book he is reading but he pats my head and turns away from me.

He looks up at Sister Mansa and asks in a dangerously quiet voice. "I'm going to ask you again. Where did you go this morning?"

"I . . . I . . . was . . . er . . ." Fear has grabbed her so tightly she can't open her mouth to tell the truth. Papa lays the book on the settee and picks up the whip. I flee to bed and cover my ears, but I can hear her screeching, screeching, screeching. Papa won't stop until she tells the truth. Oh, why won't she? Please! It goes on and on. The effort it takes to hold my body rigid wears me out and I drift off. Much later, I feel her writhing beside me, sobbing hard. Papa must have stopped only when she confessed to being with a man. Papa hates lies more than anything. I lie completely still so as not to brush against her sore body, but long after she has fallen asleep, I can hear her moaning and snuffling.

First it was Sister Abena and now it's Sister Mansa. It's so hard being a girl and wanting romance with a boy while Papa has no problem passing through other women who are not his wife. I have to remind myself that girls are special and can educate a nation. When I go to a boarding school, I'll study hard. I can be the first woman ambassador and people will call me Your Excellency and not cane me if I talk to a boy. I want all girls to be somebody great so that no one will put ginger or pepper between their legs or whip them. I'll help Sister Mansa study every time even if it means she'll end up in a four-legged tangle with a man, doing what people must love so badly they'll risk getting caned for it. In my head, I beg her to stop crying so she doesn't lose her voice and won't be able to sing on Speech Day.

I HAVEN'T HEARD Sister Mansa singing in days and now Speech Day is on us. Though her welts have flattened away, it's as if she has some on the inside. At times I catch her staring at the air, jolting as if from an invisible cane, which makes me want to fetch her a cup of water or wrap her in cotton wool.

By the afternoon, the whole school is bubbling like Coca-Cola. Speech Day is the one time Nana Ofori-Atta II blesses the school with a visit, so everything must sparkle. On the entire campus, not a blade of grass juts out of place. Hedges have been whipped to attention. From the two white columns standing guard at the gates, to the farthest dormitory near the river, every building gleams with a new coat of white paint. Even the stones around the flower gardens have been brushed white.

The male students look grand in traditional white shirts that don't have collars, their huge cloth bunched up over one shoulder and looped around down to the knees, like pictures I've seen of ancient Roman senators. They have on shorts so you can see their oiled legs as they stride along to the Assembly Hall. Each girl has on a blouse gathered at the waist and an ankle-length kente cloth tied under the blouse. Sister Mansa is dressed in the same way, a real lady, if you please.

When Papa leaves the house, I wiggle into my church dress and join the students in the Assembly Hall that is the size of two church buildings, with louvers coming halfway down the sides. Because I'm the headmaster's daughter, the students make a fuss and invite me to sit near the front, as if I have the power to make Papa do something for them. Everyone is seated, and voices buzz until the organ fills the room with the first chords of "Onward Christian Soldiers." We stand up for the procession.

The choristers step-pause-step-pause down the aisle and turn right. I watch anxiously as Sister Mansa steps along, her lips working the words. They take their places, standing in rows on the side, facing stage left. In the distance, we can hear drums and horns announcing the arrival of Nana Ofori-Atta II. I am so excited I twist to the back and then to the front, not wanting to miss anything.

The teachers follow the choir, gowned in black academic robes and tasseled caps. They mount the stage and stand looking down at us. Then comes Papa, looking almost royal in his academic robe trimmed with swirls of yellow and blue. He is flanked by the assistant headmaster and another administrator called a bursar. The drumming draws closer, gets louder and louder until it explodes around us and vibrates through me.

There he is! Through the wide, open doors. His Majesty, Nana Ofori-Atta II himself, carried in a canoelike palanquin on the shoulders of eight men with glistening bare chests and ropy muscles. A huge umbrella of red brocade with gold tassels twirls above his head. He is followed by attendants and drums the size of logs carried on the heads of two men while two other men pound from behind. What a picture in gold! Gold studs on his crown, gold beads on his arms, gold on his wrists, gold, gold, gold! I wonder if those are gold threads in the kente cloth draped over his left shoulder.

They set the palanquin down with real care and the attendants take up the cries: "Nana is rising!" The ground seems to vibrate when he steps out in gold-studded slippers. Made specially for him, I'm sure. Attendants walk backwards before him, shouting, "Nana is coming! Nana, tread softly! Nana, softly!" while others follow. Slowly, majestically, he mounts the stage. Then the attendants announce, "Nana is sitting! The mighty one is sitting!" Finally, the drums cease. The microphone squeaks in embarrassment and the ceremony begins.

No wonder they call it Speech Day. I'm drowning in miles of words on "prosperity and academic excellence." A prize given to this student for something, something. Clap, clap. Speech, prize, clap, clap. Speech, prize, clap. Just when I think I'm going to pass out, they finish. Now my stomach is knotted from worrying about Sister Mansa's coming solo. The king gets up slowly to the cries of "Nana is rising! Nana is rising!" He strides to the microphone, accompanied by his linguist. It's funny, really. You can hear him clearly and yet everything he says has to be repeated by the linguist because, in public, a king can't talk directly to anyone. Horns and cheers punctuate anything the linguist repeats.

After congratulating the prizewinners, Nana praises Papa through the linguist, and then an attendant hands him a jeweled case. The linguist asks Papa to step forward if you please. A king never smiles in public but he actually smiles and shakes Papa's hand before presenting him the case. Papa opens it and out comes a huge golden jewel. Everyone gasps. When he holds it up in the sunlight streaming in, you can see it's a gold key-holder, chained to a miniature gold carriage fit for Queen Elizabeth herself. Everyone claps and shouts.

A long thank-you speech from Papa follows, and then the choir gets up to sing praises to His Majesty. I sit up straight when the organ ceases. All eyes gather on Sister Mansa as she stands before the king. In the hushed silence, her voice lifts to the sky:

Me-e ne wo-o nam a-a, mensuro-o-o!
Bi-i-ribi-a-ara nso-o nhia me-e-e!
E-efiri sɛ wadom wɔ me mu-u . . .

When I walk with you, I don't fear
And I never need anything
Because your mercy is inside me.

When her voice dies down, the silence hurts. Someone coughs, and then they erupt with clapping. I have to blink rapidly from the burning water in my eyes. That's my sister they're clapping for.

CHAPTER NiNE

S ISTER MANSA NO longer sings mean songs about me. In fact, she has made me shitɔ, a fiery pepper sauce with smoked shrimp and tomato paste, because today is the day I get to attend Mmofraturo Girls Boarding School. If I don't stick my finger into the shitɔ, it won't go bad because of the oil she used to fry it until all the water evaporated.

My trunk is filled with clothes, white bedsheets, a blanket, a mirror, soap, Vaseline, powder, and everything I need to care for myself at Mmofraturo Girls Boarding School. Apart from the black trunk with the red moon crescents, nobody goes to a boarding school without a wooden chopbox that contains provisions for when the dining hall food doesn't fill you up, or whenever you are hungry between meals. Papa has bought me cans of evaporated milk, sardines, and gari. This is what it means to be twelve and almost cresting thirteen. From now on until twenty, every age I get to will end in a teen, that realm of almost grown-up-ness!

It takes Papa and me three hours to drive to Mmofraturo. We arrive in the afternoon when the sun is a hazy yellow and the shadows are long. There are flowers in the fields, flowers along the road, and more in front of the tall building looking down on the driveway. There are sunflowers as big as my face, so warm-looking I want to hug them. Roses, hibiscus, bougainvillea, they all smile at me. Eight little houses squat in a semicircle around a circular lawn, like a village all its own. The houses are just like the ones I draw. Each has a wooden door in the middle, a window on either side—the kind you poke out and hold open with a stick—and four steps leading up to the front veranda. I want to run inside to see the girls, but Papa says we must first meet Mrs. Wilkinson, the headmistress, in her office. She is one of those Fantes, people from the coast who have British surnames. I wonder if she too thinks she is more civilized than everybody else because she had tea with the British and used butter to make fire instead of kerosene that leaves you smelling of smoke.

When we enter her office, I have to stifle a scream because she blinks from one normal-shaped eye and the other a perfect circle. The round eye waters and just stares. If she isn't a witch, I don't know who is. Her soft voice doesn't sound right, as if the softness is forced so much it's almost a whisper, "Oh, how lovely it is to have Frederica in our school. Oh, won't you please sit down. And what is this? No key-holder for her keys? Oh, no, she needs one or she might lose her keys."

"Oh," Papa says. "I didn't know. But that's no problem. Here, she can take mine."

Papa's key-holder. That pure gold, that gilded carriage forged by the palace's goldsmith, the present from Nana Ofori-Atta II. What if I lose it? What if I break it?

"No, not that one, Papa!" But he has already removed his keys and is slipping mine onto it.

Mrs. Wilkinson's eye waters some more. "Oh, your father loves you, doesn't he? It's okay, Mr. Agyekum. You can leave her here."

She seems to tremble when she calls some girls into her office. "Girls, take Frederica to House Eight. Help her with her trunk and chopbox."

Papa pats my head, saying, "You're in good hands."

Mrs. Wilkinson agrees quickly. "Don't worry, we'll take good care of her. This is a good school, a sure way to get into Wesley Girls, if she works hard."

I worry about the key-holder but Papa drives off, waving with a confident smile. Though my chest heaves, I don't cry because I don't want to be a baby. When I turn to follow the girls carrying my trunk, Mrs. Wilkinson calls me back in a voice that is no longer whispery. Her fingers wander over her polished desk, round and round.

"Erm," she says slowly, "you know, your key-holder is too precious. Someone can steal it. Let me keep it for you. Why don't you take mine? I'll keep the gold in a safe place until your father visits, and then I'll give it to him." And she smiles.

I don't want anyone stealing my father's golden carriage, so I give it to her and watch her knobby hands clasp around it. Then it's off to House Eight, my new home.

A plump girl meets us at the front veranda, her arms folded across her chest. She looks me up and down and frowns. "So, you are the new girl?"

I say yes.

"I am the house prefect. Your chore will be to sweep the front and back verandas before classes. I hope you work hard and behave yourself. I won't tolerate insubordination from you."

She and Sister Crocodile Jaws would make great friends, I'm sure. I'll do my housework well and stay away from her.

She leads me into the room I am to share with three girls. Though they are older, their smiles invite me in. The tall one in a flowery dress holds out her hands and says, "Hello! Welcome to

House Eight. I'm Sister Edna Wilkinson, I'm in Form Two." I ask if she is related to the headmistress but she says no.

"I'm not related to her either," I say and she laughs, which pushes her nose up. "I like your nose. It's as if you are inhaling the scent of a rose."

"You are so cute! And funny too. Here, let me help you make your bed."

I can't believe an older girl wants to help me make my bed. As a Form Two girl, she must be at least fourteen. My bed is easy to put together. Three flat wooden boards rest on two end beams. Then we unroll my foam mattress over and it becomes a bed that sways a bit when I sit on it. I know the boards will slide off and fall down if I wiggle too much in my sleep. I see a centipede crawling along the edge of the wall and point. Sister Edna laughs. "Ah, are you afraid of this little creature?"

"I'm not afraid! But I've never seen one inside a bedroom before."

"Just make sure you tuck in your mosquito net properly. If a hole appears in your net, mend it right away. Once, a centipede crept inside someone's ear and the doctor had to get it out."

I'll never have a hole in my net. Ever. Better still, I'll stuff my ears with cotton wool.

She finds me a spot in the trunk-and-chopbox room and tells me to let her know if I have any problems. And oh, tomorrow, Monday, rising bell is at five-thirty in the morning.

The sky is still black when the bell rings and faraway cocks crow *kokuro koo!* I hop out of bed. The toilet shares a wall with the trunk-and-chopbox room inside the little house behind the dormitory. There is no water closet, so whatever needs to be done means sitting on a wooden box with a hole over a metal bucket and letting go. I have toilet paper so I don't need the bits of newspaper in the box on the floor. A wooden crate holds sawdust, and no one needs to explain the little spade is for shoveling the sawdust to cover what solid drops into the bucket. Later, a Kru man will drag out the full bucket and empty it into a larger one he will carry on his head to an unknown place.

When I finish my business, I head for the bathhouse, one long concrete room where twenty girls splash water on themselves and wet everyone else. After washing myself, I slip into one of my five uniforms, a different color for every day of the week. Though the style is the same for everyone, the school lets us wear any color we want so we can resemble a flower garden. A breakfast of lumpy porridge follows, then we race to our classrooms in a building similar to the one at Kibi Girls. There are pairs of tables arranged in rows. When I enter, a girl called Philomena invites me to sit with her at the front. The teacher arrives and we shoot out of our seats to greet, "Good morning, Miss Darko."

"Good morning, class." Miss Darko glides to her desk while we sit. She looks very tall with her slender arms, endless legs, and a small waist. She lays her keys on the table and walks up to my desk. "You're the new girl, Frederica?"

"Yes, Miss." Although she doesn't smile, I like the way her eyes shine.

"Welcome." Then she turns to everyone. "Class, stand!" All fifty of us line up in the rows. "It's Monday morning inspection. I'm going to make sure you're grooming yourselves properly. Raise your hands and let me see your armpits."

I've never before had anyone ask to see my armpit. We point our hands to the ceiling and she marches through the rows, giving each armpit a careful inspection. "Good, good," she nods to the smooth ones. But she stops in front of one girl and we all turn to look. There is a much darker spot under her arm, which means hair growth. Miss Darko points to the spot and says, "You need to shave. A girl's armpit must be as smooth as an egg."

"Yes, Miss."

"Tomorrow, I'll check to make sure you've done it." The girl blinks shamefully.

I know Papa will approve of Miss Darko teaching us hygiene, since we are not at home where our mothers can teach us. He says a woman with good personal hygiene is the best kind, and what is the point of a man pouring juice into an unclean vessel? Still, I wish I could hide under the desk.

The armpit inspection is followed by uniform inspection. Did we iron them? Do we have seams that have come apart? It's a good thing I ironed my uniform with the coal iron. A girl with an open seam brings Miss Darko to a halt. "This isn't good. You have to sew this before it gets worse. A stitch in time saves nine, do you know that saying?"

"Yes, Miss."

"Everyone, say after me: A stitch in time saves nine."

"A stitch in time saves nine!"

Miss Darko drags the guilty girl to the front of the class and makes her sit facing us. A reel of thread with a needle embedded in it waits on the teacher's desk. The girl has to remove her uniform and begin sewing, clad only in her petticoat. It's nothing unusual for a girl to walk about with only a piece of cloth wrapped from her chest to her knees, but to have forty-nine pairs of eyes pierce you while you sit in your petticoat and they are dressed is disgraceful. The girl's face looks heavy with shame and she can't lift her eyelids. I'll sew any seam that comes apart in my uniform so I don't have to sit in front of the class in my underclothes. Not that it makes a difference, because now Miss Darko wants to inspect petticoats and drawers. I feel my skin go pimply as I raise the skirt of my dress for her.

"Some of you don't wash your petticoats well," she says. "It is supposed to be white, not cream. Put blue powder in the rinse to make the white gleam. And make sure you wash and change your drawers twice a day. Also, cut your pubic hair. One of these days, I'm going to surprise you in the bathroom. I'm sure some of you are keeping a forest down there. Keep it trimmed, like cut grass."

Miss Darko teaches us all subjects except Arithmetic, Science, and Housecraft, but her favorite is poetry. She can't get enough of it.

"It is everywhere," she says. "In songs, sermons, plays, novels. Everything." She has us reciting speeches from Hamlet, who wants to kill his uncle for poisoning Hamlet's father and marrying his mother. We act out the woe of Dr. Faustus, who learns too late the price for selling his soul to the devil. We clutch our chests and cry out, "Ah, Faustus, now hast thou but one bare hour to live, and then thou must be damn'd perpetually." Then we are murderous Macbeth shrugging off his wife's suicide: *And all our yesterdays have lighted fools the way to dusty death.* We compete to see who can recite the longest poems, and I tremble when I discover that poetry can be composed in Twi, too, like *Sɛɛ Baabi Ara Nyɛ,* and it's written by a woman:

> Akwasi broni bu ne ntoma mu a,
> ɛnyɛ Abibiman na ode nani kyerɛ?
> Obibini nso ma ne kɛtɛ so a
> Brɔman na ɔrepɛ akɔ.

> *Does he not turn his eye toward Africa?*
> *Yet when the African rolls up his mat,*
> *It's the white man's land he goes to.*
> *It's true, no place is good.*

It's true everyone wants to go behind the corn and those behind the corn want to come here! Meanwhile, people here murmur against the land, against leaders. You hear it on weekends when Papa and other parents visit. They lean against cars, pointing and shaking heads:

Can you believe it? University students can't have free education anymore, they'll be given loans!

Ein, even soldiers have lost benefits!

This will end badly, wait and see!

That idiot Busia is taking orders from the IMF!

They have devalued the cedi!

Esi, your time will be hard. God knows if you will be able to buy a bicycle, let alone a car!

Politicians, you can never trust them!

The murmurings float over the land, hum under the windows of the teachers' flats. The murmurings rise behind doors, blow over the grass. They are carried by the winds, getting angrier and angrier, but we girls skip among the flowers and play.

Saturday afternoon, Edna says to me, "Too bad you came to Mmofraturo in the middle of the term." It's rest hour and we are lying on our beds.

"Why is that?" I ask.

"You don't have a girl. All the Form One girls have girls. I cannot have you as my girl, because we are in the same house. That would be like having your sister as your girl. That is not proper."

"Ooh, you're talking about suppies." I jump to my knees. So, they do that here too! "I want one, please."

She smiles. "Don't worry, I'll find one for you. You cannot choose for yourself, it's the senior girls who choose juniors. Otherwise it would be like a girl chasing a boy instead of the other way around. Can you imagine that? A girl chasing a boy, ha ha." She rises to her feet and holds out her hand. "Come with me. I'll find a girl for you."

She holds my hand as we walk on the red gravel to House

Seven, barely ten steps away. We enter a room where several girls are sitting on two beds, talking and laughing.

"Good afternoon," Edna says. I greet them too.

"Good afternoon," the girls say.

Edna introduces me, then adds, "Frederica doesn't have a girl yet, but she's so pretty and funny I was wondering if anyone wanted to take her."

No one has ever used *pretty* to describe me. Mosquito legs aren't pretty. The girls must know that because they look at one another and shrug; they have their own girls. We leave.

No one wants a girl in House Six either. Edna drags me to House Five, same thing. Now I feel like the last tomato left on a market woman's tray after the good ones have been taken. Edna flops onto a bed and joins in the laughter of the other girls. I don't know what to do. First, I sit on an empty bed next to the happy girls. But it's tiring sitting with nothing to support my back so I let myself fall and then I roll around. Now my face is inches from a large bottom hanging over the edge of the bed next to the one I'm lying on. The buttocks are round like two soccer balls, which is funny because I know they can't be hard, can they? I reach and touch. It feels springy, ha. I want to do it again, but the owner of the bottom jerks and twists around.

"Hey!" she says. There's a smile on her face though.

My face feels warm and I'm waiting for the scolding I deserve. I have no business pinching the bottom of a girl who must be fourteen. What if she slaps my face for disrespect? She turns to Edna and says, "I want her."

My eyes widen. No scolding. Just *I want her*. Me.

Edna smiles with relief and turns to me. "Do you agree to be her girl?"

I nod yes. I just want to have a suppy.

"Her name is Sister Rose."

I'm wondering what she likes about my pinching, because I'm sure that's why she wants me. I giggle and Edna tells her, "I think she likes you. Well then. I'll leave you two alone."

The other girls tease, "Rose has a girl!" She is in Form Three and has just transferred from another boarding school. She says she hasn't wanted a girl until now, which makes me feel special though I don't know what to do or say to her.

She ties the ends of a bright colored cloth to the ends of the mosquito net to create a tent no one can see through. Then she smiles, slides in, and asks me to join her. I crawl into the tent and we lie on our sides facing each other. I've wanted to play romance for a long time, but we do nothing except speak with our smiles. And then oh sweetness, it happens. She leans closer and brushes her lips against mine. I'm playing romance, I'm playing romance! It feels so good, so featherlike I go all soft inside. She smooths my eyebrows, my cheeks, my hair. I feel the way a kitten must feel when a cat licks her. She pulls me closer and I bury my head in her pillowy chest. I take half-breaths because I'm so happy I could lie like this forever, but there goes the bell ruining everything with its *clang-clang-clang-clang.*

"That's the supper bell," Rose says. "We have to go. It's compulsory."

Rose grabs her cutlery bag, plastic plate, and cup. Then we stop at House Eight to get mine. She puts her arm around my waist and walks me to the long, rectangular dining hall standing next to House Eight. I am disappointed we can't sit together. Students have to sit according to houses.

The wooden tables are arranged along the walls, which creates a large empty space in the middle like a dance floor. Sister House Prefect is already seated at the head of our table. We Form One girls have to sit near the table tail. There are two tall aluminum pots standing in the middle of the table. Two Form Two girls serve the Sunday evening special: rice and meat stew. One pot holds the rice and the other contains brown beef stew with exactly thirteen little cuts of steamed meat no bigger than two inches, one for each girl. With an extra one for the house prefect. She deserves two cuts of meat for being already grown, but we younger ones need little. My eyes roam the edges of her plate though I know she won't give the extra meat to me. I miss the way at home Papa calls me to him and gives me the best part of the meat. Sister Senior Prefect, the prefect over all the prefects, stands in the middle of the hall and prays: "God bless the farmer, the cooker, and the eater, amen."

A thunderous *amen* goes up and I pick up my fork. Edna is sitting across from me. She forks her meat, but instead of eating it, she gives it to another Form Two girl and says, "Could you give this to Patience?" Everyone laughs because Patience is her girl. Edna explains that to show your love for your suppy, you make the ultimate sacrifice: you give her your meat. And not directly. You must always use a go-between called a *betweener*. That's good for Edna but I want to eat mine—I am hungry.

There is a sudden commotion. Girls bang their fists on tables, drum their forks on plates, and stamp their feet. They are shouting "*Yeei!*" I turn around and see a girl making her way across the wide space, heading toward our table. In her hand is a fork, its silvery teeth embedded in a large piece of meat. The drumming and *yeei*-ing grow louder. Everyone wants to see who is receiving the love. The girl swaggers toward me and shakes the meat off onto my plate. It's from Rose. Water collects in my mouth. I can't wait to sink my teeth into it.

"Do you want to send it back?" Edna asks.

"Send it back?"

"I sent Patience's back with mine. That's how you show your love."

I didn't know Patience sent her meat to Edna. This love thing costs more than I like. Why do I have to show my love by giving up the meat I badly want to eat? But everyone is looking at me and I don't want them to say what a terrible person I am. I almost choke when I ask Edna to return Rose's meat with mine. Edna dances across the room and the shouts get louder. No one is eating. Everyone wants to see who will win this eat-my-meat war. I watch Rose cover her plate with her hands and shake her head and point in my direction. I turn my head quickly and swallow the water in my mouth. I'm happy when the betweener returns with the two pieces of meat, but without asking me, Edna returns the meat again. I beg Rose in my heart, Please, don't eat my meat. Esi, you hypocrite. The meats sail back and forth until I remember that no self-respecting older girl will eat a younger person's food. I accept the meat and chew happily.

CHAPTER TEN

F RIDAY IS LOVERS' night," Edna tells me. "You get to share a bed with your girl." It's just before lights out. With our mosquito nets tucked in, I see her through a white haze. She is lying on her side facing me, her arm tucked under her head.

"Why not Saturday?" I ask.

Her teeth flash in a smile. "Saturday night is no good because we have to get up early for church service on Sunday."

"Oh, I see." I sit up, part my net, and swing my leg down.

"What are you doing?"

"Going to Rose. It's Friday."

"No, no, no!" She props herself on her elbow. "*She's* the older girl. *She* will send for you. But you must not accept to sleep with your girl the first time she asks you. You must never appear cheap. You have to learn this or one day you will be too cheap with boys."

"Really?"

"Yes. Now, lie down quickly and tuck your mosquito net around you. Someone is coming. Sssh!"

I lie down and close my eyes loosely. Through my lashes, I see a girl drifting toward my bed.

"Hello," she says, smiling. I recognize her as Diana, the be-tweener who gave me Rose's meat. Through the veil of white mosquito netting, she looks like a ghost. She bends down and says, "Frederica, Rose misses you so much that she would love it if you could come and console her with your loving company."

She must have memorized that beforehand. I want to very much, but I can't say yes and appear cheap, so I turn my back to her. "I'm sorry, I'm really tired and need to go to sleep."

"But please, Rose is sad. She can't sleep without you." Diana sounds miserable.

"Really, I can't." I cast a quick look at Edna who nods. She likes my answer.

"Please."

I turn around slowly to show I really, really, really don't want to. "I'm really sorry, but I can't. Tell her . . . maybe tomorrow."

Diana drops to her knees and begs some more.

I look at Edna. Now is the time to give in. "All right, I'll come."

I partly open my net and slide my feet into rubber slippers, not bothering to change out of my nightgown though I wear my housecoat over it. Diana puts her arm around my shoulders and guides me out of the room. I glance back and catch the flash of a smile from Edna.

Off we go crunching the gravel on the pathway while the moon throws long shadows of our bodies onto the ground. When we arrive, Rose is lying in her bed waiting. As before, she has created a tent around her mosquito net. Diana leaves and I slide in. Rose's bed smells of roses from the petals she has scattered on it. We face each other in the dark and I think, oh, we are going to play romance? I'm so excited I can't breathe. Her breath is warm on my face when she kisses me on the mouth, and her fingers are feath-erlike on my cheeks. I feel so loved I nuzzle in the warm pillows of her chest, like something fresh from the oven. She whispers, "Do you want to touch me?" I do.

I press my face in her breasts and let them massage me. I worry them with my hands. If I push them to one side, they fall back. I push them up and they fall again, ha! I wonder if there is milk in them. When my Sister Abena had a baby and her breasts swelled with too much milk, Auntie asked me to suck out the milk to relieve her pain, but she wouldn't let me swallow it because she said it would form lumps in my stomach. Now I put my mouth on Rose's nipple. Nothing comes out but it gets hard and she says *yes, please,* so I do it again. Her body is a marvelous playground for my fingers. There are hills and valleys and slides. My fingers play a racing game, over that curve, down the valley, in a tunnel, I win! Rose starts shaking. It's like an earthquake inside her. She groans and moans until she's laughing and crying, stroking my hair and telling me how lovely I am. I'm happy too though I don't know why something quaked inside her. I just love the way she is massaging me all over.

The following weekend when Papa comes to visit, I say nothing about suppies. You can't tell grown-ups everything. If you do, they'll think of ways to burn or whip you. So, you tell them only what matters to them: what you are learning at school to help you become an Excellency or Learnéd Friend. When I recite poems in English and Latin to Papa, he pulls me to his chest with "That's my daughter, thoroughly cooked with intelligence!" He lifts my chin up with his hand and says I'll be famous one day. "I'll teach you to drive," he adds while my mouth drops open. "Yes, as soon as you turn fifteen. You will be the youngest person, and a woman who drives a car!"

God, make me fifteen right now, I want to drive!

Before leaving, Papa gives me a new plastic key-holder so we can return Mrs. Wilkinson's, and she can return Papa's. But when we go to see her, she stands hovering nervously on her desk, rustling papers and whimpering, "Ow, this key-holder, eh? Where could I have put it? Ow Lord, I can't believe I have misplaced it. Ow, this is so embarrassing. It was right here in this drawer!" She opens drawers, makes a big to-do with trembling fingers. Nothing. Finally, she straightens up and says, "Let me take my time and search properly. You wait. I'll send it to you when Frederica comes home for the holidays. Greet your family for me. You're such a good father, ha ha." I open my mouth to protest but Papa says it's okay. The sun won't stop shining if he doesn't get the golden key-holder right away. He is sure Mrs. Wilkinson will give it to me to take home. He drives off in a cloud of red dust and all I can think of is how lovely it will be when I can *vroom* off with such power.

I forget about the key-holder until one day, I am crossing the veranda to House Seven and what do I see? Mrs. Wilkinson's scrawny daughter walking toward me, Papa's key-holder a golden glint in her hands! There is no way I'm going to let her walk away with it. I stand right in front of her so she has no choice but to stop, and I stick out my finger. "That's my father's!"

She says no. She took it from her mother's dresser.

"Yes, but it belongs to my father." I explain nice and long and won't take no for an answer till she removes her keys and gives me the holder. I don't wait a minute to dash back inside my dormitory, tuck it under the clothes in my trunk, and padlock it. I know I'll get into trouble for accosting the headmistress's daughter but I don't care.

Sure enough, on Sunday Mrs. Wilkinson herds us into the school chapel, something she does whenever she gets an itch to torment us with the word of God. She marches up to the pulpit and glares down at us, but it seems she's looking at only me. The words pour down with force.

"You *must* be good children. You *must* always tell the truth no matter what. You *mustn't* be bullies. If you see someone holding something that is not yours, do NOT insist that it is."

Now I know she's talking to me.

"Frederica Agyekum, step forward!"

I stand trembling before the whole school. She descends from the pulpit and lays her cane into me, punctuating each skin-splitting lash: "If. A. Child. Has. Something. Do. Not. Snatch. It. From. Her. Bad! Girl! Full of. I-don't-care-ism! I-don't-care-ism!" She flogs me blindly until I fall, but that doesn't stop her. I taste blood. I start counting. I fight the tears. I won't cry. I won't. She can't win. At last, she straightens up panting, "Get back to your seat, bad girl!"

I struggle to my feet. My body is on fire, but I'm truly full of I-don't-care-ism. She can pound me into corned beef on the cement floor. I've got my father's key-holder, you hear, Mrs. Witchyson? I won't give it back!

When it's all over and everyone leaves the chapel, Rose helps me to her dormitory and lays me on her bed, murmuring, *Poor baby. Poor baby.* She rubs oil all over my body. She tries to feed me her meat, but I can't eat. My mouth is swollen.

Every day Mrs. Wilkinson thinks of more ways to punish me. She waits until the sun has heated the coal tar on her compound to a bubbly pulp, then tells me to kneel on it. If I move because of the burning, she flogs me, so I stay on my knees until the skin peels off. I can't tell Papa because if he asks her, she will say the right things until he leaves, and then she will make me pay. When I am named Scholar of the Year, she writes in my report card: *Frederica, scholar of the year, must learn to be respectful.* Papa scolds me but I'm fine inside. She is the coward who can't ask me for the key-holder since she knows it's my father's. I won't be at Mmofraturo forever, you witch! I'll study hard and get into Wesley Girls, you hear, Witchy?

For the Common Entrance Examinations, we have to pass

Arithmetic, English, Verbal Aptitude, and Quantitative Analysis, whatever that is. Though I want to get away from Witchy, there is another reason I must pass the tests. If I don't get into Wesley Girls, Papa can't boast about my results. I'll fall from the high place he has placed me and I might as well die.

The day before the examinations, I join those trooping into the prayer room and kneel at the altar. *Dear Lord, please forgive me for the bad things I do. Forgive me for tying Helena's ear with a string in class and making everyone laugh when I was supposed to be paying attention. And for calling Mrs. Wilkinson a witch behind her back even if she's one. Forgive me for pretending to get black soil for my garden when I sneaked off to buy food in town. Please help me do so well that Wesley Girls just has to pick me. In the holy name of Jesus, Amen.*

On testing day, the bus takes us to a great hall in town where children from other schools join us. My palms moisten and my heart pounds, but I pretend it's another test at school. After the tests, we have to wait months for acceptance letters from high schools. Lumps grow in our stomachs. Each time an acceptance letter arrives, Mrs. Wilkinson calls the lucky girl into the office and gives it to her. The girl dashes out, leaps over verandas, and waves the letter in the air. Everyone runs out to hug her, shout *yeeei*, and pump fists.

Days go by and more girls run out but Mrs. Wilkinson never sends for me. Then the letters stop coming and I want to die. It fries my stomach to hear the conversations: I got into Wesley Girls. Me, I'm going to Aburi Girls. St. Louis, forever! Yaa Asantewa or I die. Hey Frederica, where are you going? Hey Miss Scholar of the Year, what happened to you?

At supper time, I don't want my food. I don't care if Rose eats my Sunday meat though she refuses. What am I going to do? Everything I eat comes out the other end. My head aches worse than splintered bones, and my neck feels hot. I lie on my bed shivering and sweating day and night. I am sure I passed the examinations. Something has to be wrong. I am going to Wesley Girls even if I don't have a letter. I just know it. Surely a letter has come for me and someone has forgotten to give it to me. Maybe the post office lost it. That's it! I'll roll off the bed. I'll run across verandas shouting "*Yeei!*"

My body believes the lies, grows strong. I leap, I leap!

Everyone comes out *yeei*-ing. No one notices I'm not waving a white paper. I believe it when I shout, "I'm going to Wesley Girls!" What is wrong with me? What if there is really no letter? It doesn't matter. I'm going to Wesley Girls. I AM!

Saturday. Mrs. Wilkinson sends for me and I wonder what I've done wrong. I have lost so much weight I am a walking coat hanger. I enter the office and—Papa! He is waving a letter. All his teeth are showing. He says, "You put your home address on the form instead of Mmofraturo's. You're going to Girls High School!" I pitch forward and he catches me before I fall.

When I open my eyes, I'm lying on my back in a four-poster bed, in a dark room only a witch could have put together. Smoke spirals out of a burning incense stick propped up against a plate on a black dresser. The smoke forms a snakelike shadow on the gray wall. Bottles of lotions, perfume, and Sloan's Liniment crowd the top of the dresser. And cans of powder. The incense, mingled with the smells of spice and old clothes, makes me want to vomit. A huge wardrobe faces the bed and, oh no, Mrs. Wilkinson's normal eye is smiling at me, coming at me. She has a steaming enamel bowl in her hand. Now I can smell *apɔnkye nkrakra*, light soup with goat meat. I want to sit up but I can't. I shout, "Papa!"

"Esi," he says and here he is in my view.

Ah Papa! Tears sting my eyes. He sits by my side, touches my forehead. Papa, oh Papa! He tells me I fainted. Mrs. Wilkinson parrots him but I keep my eyes on Papa. "Is it true, Papa? Am I going to Wesley Girls?"

"Yes. You did well, Esi. You are going to Girls High School."

"Wonderful news!" Mrs. Wilkinson says, still holding the bowl. "Just wonderful! We just have to make sure you are strong and well. Here, have some soup, my dear." Her dear? I'm really going to throw up. A chair scrapes against the wooden floor. She sits facing me and I can't believe she is holding a spoon to my mouth. It's all I can do not to knock down the bowl and send the soup splashing over her the way Papa does when he is angry with Auntie. I shake my head. *I don't want your soup, you ugly witch!*

"Come now, Esi." Papa says. "And don't shake your head. It's not polite to use your head to answer a grown-up."

I'll use my head all I want. "I'm not hungry."

Papa gives Witchy a smile of embarrassment. "Well, I guess she is still not well."

She sits back and drops the spoon into the bowl with perfect concern on her face. "Hm, I think so too." The chair creaks when she gets up, and her slippers slap the wooden floor as she walks to the door and calls her maid to come take the soup away.

Behind her back, I whisper to Papa that I want to go home. I've already passed the Common Entrance. Papa nods thoughtfully. When Mrs. Wilkinson returns, he says if it's all right by her, he would like to take me home to see a doctor.

Mrs. Wilkinson's lips tremble and her good eye goes hard but she can't do anything. She touches the red part of her lower lip. "Well, it would have been lovely to wait until the end of the school year. Frederica, don't you want to wait to finish with your friends?"

I shake my head and Papa gives me the warning look.

"Well, then," Mrs. Wilkinson says. "I'll get some girls to pack her things for her."

As soon as she leaves the room, I tell Papa about the key-holder.

"Oh," he says. "Is that so?" He stands up and shoves his hands into his pockets. I'm waiting for the explosion. "I see." He takes a couple steps, looks at the floor. "Okay. Well, you have the key-holder in your hands. We'll leave it at that."

"But Papa—"

"Look, you have passed your Common Entrance. You're leaving, no? It's not good to shame your elders. What is a little key-holder?"

I wish someone could close my mouth for me because I can't. Papa fights about Sister Abena, fights with Auntie, throws a money bag at a briber, but he won't stand up and tell Mrs. Wilkinson what an evil woman she is for trying to steal from him. He won't embarrass her. He tells me one must always respect authority. We must pretend nothing happened. I must not let her lose face. If he weren't my father, I would throw something at him.

Mrs. Wilkinson comes back and Papa actually smiles. Smiles! "Oh, thank you for keeping the key-holder safe. Esi says you returned it."

Such a blinding lie. She clasps her hands together in holiness. "Oh, Frederica is such a joy! We will miss her cheerful spirit." She sounds as if she's about to break into hallelujahs. She'll miss my cheerful spirit indeed. It's all I can do not to suck my teeth at her, show her the highest disrespect.

They both leave for the teachers' flats so Papa can thank Miss Darko for being a great teacher. It's okay to thank Miss Darko but Mrs. Wilkinson deserves to kneel on coal tar bubbling in the sun, not to walk beside Papa as they smile and nod at each other like the best of friends.

Rose and Edna come up to see me. Rose rushes in and hugs me and I can't stop my lips from trembling and the tears from spilling out.

"Oh, my darling," Rose says, "so you're leaving me." She tries to make a funny face, like a baby sulking. Her big eyes are so pretty and I love her fuzzy hair. I put my head in her lap, sobbing as she soothes me. "Ssssh, don't cry. Don't worry, we'll write always. And I'll come visit you at Wesley Girls." I don't know how that can be when she's going to Yaa Asantewa in Kumasi and I'm going to be in Cape Coast, which is more than four hours' drive away.

"I'll miss you too," Edna says. "I love you. If you weren't in the same house with me, you would have been my girl, not hers."

"You watch yourself," Rose says. They laugh and I have to smile.

Papa returns too soon. They help me down the stairs and Rose slips a letter in my hand, whispering, "I will love you always." If only Mrs. Wilkinson the crow would fly away, find some tree and perch on it forever, then I could stay at Mmofraturo and cuddle next to Rose for the rest of the year. There's a pain in my chest like when Mother crushed me to her and cried.

As we pull away, I see Rose and Edna standing and waving beside Witchy Wilkinson, all of them turning gray through my watery eyes.

CHAPTER ELEVEN

I N THE QUIET of the sitting room at home, I lie flat on my stomach and rest my cheek on the floor. The thin carpet is new. Green, flecked with black. That's what happens when you go away to a boarding school. Nothing stays the same. Like Papa.

He is the sand under me when I wade in the River Birim. There are moments when the riverbed is solid and I know where to step. Other times there's a sudden dip and I have to struggle to stay upright so I don't gulp water. I've been at home for more than a week now, but I still don't want to smile at him because he didn't stand up to Witchy.

The world is gone mad too. While we were studying and playing at school, the murmuring of the people got so loud it exploded into action. Days ago, Papa was reading on the veranda when he came tearing in. "Adelaide! Adelaide! Where is that woman?" Before I could spring to my feet and run for her, Auntie panted into the sitting room.

"There has been a coup!" Papa said. When Auntie asked what's that, he slammed the newspaper on the center table. "C-o-u-p,

coup! Coup d'état. French. Soldiers have taken over the country!"
He shouted so loudly the sisters rushed in, asking what was wrong.

"There has been a coup!" I said. "Soldiers."

"*Ei*, Awurade," Sister Yaa said.

"Ghana *ooo*, Ghana, *ein*?" Auntie said.

Papa rushed to the radiogram. There was a hiss and a crackle,
and then a man's voice broke through in that click-clack way English people talk: "This is the BBC." The broadcaster click-clacked
about the coup, how Dr. Busia was in London receiving treatment
when soldiers took over the presidential castle.

"Ow, Awurade, see?" Sister Mansa said in a pitying voice.
"You're not even allowed to get sick."

Kwabena too burst in.

"Ssh!" I said.

Papa whispered there was a coup, a blow that knocked off
Busia. I crawled closer to the radio. The BBC man said to listen
to the leader of the coup talking about the new order. Another
hiss and a voice barked over, "I, Lieutenant Colonel Ignatius Kutu
Acheampong, will not stand idle and let incompetent people ruin
our nation."

Papa snorted. "Here we go, an ignoramus of a soldier taking
over the country."

"What kind of name at all is Ignatius?" Auntie grumbled.

"*Ein?*" Papa said. "What proud Asante names his child Ignatius?"

Kwabena giggled. "And Kutu, that means a pot."

"You know what?" Papa nodded several times. "One can turn
over a pot."

My tongue turned into cement. Colonel Acheampong gargled
on about the new regime, how it "will save Ghana from economic
depression and oppression!" On and on he growled. Papa turned
off the radio in disgust, got into his car, and peeled off. Auntie

sighed and slid into the kitchen as if she just wanted to mind her own business. The sisters disappeared. To distract ourselves, Kwabena and I decided to venture into town, but the streets were strangely quiet with people going about their selling and buying and talking in clumps.

Now we have a new government, the National Redemption Council. Didn't the four generals in the Nkrumah coup call themselves the National Liberation Council? Liberation, redemption, same thing in the *Advanced Learners Dictionary* Papa gave me. They'll save us from "oppression and repression."

The radio does nothing but blare the Colonel Redeemer's speeches: "*Yɛntua!*" We won't pay! We won't pay back the millions we owe to foreign governments and the IMF. "*Yɛntua!*" He says he will raise the value of the cedi so we can buy more with it. And how dare that IMF tell us what to do with our own money? It's all Nkrumah and Busia's fault anyway, says he. Well he, I can imagine him punching his chest, he, Ignatius Acheampong, won't let the WEST bully us. We're going to feed ourselves—you hear? That's the new motto: Operation Feed Yourself! Everyone, take to the farms! The radio reports even university professors have picked up their hoes and are digging away. Yes, we'll have corn coming out of ears, just wait.

It seems to me people are like dried leaves on a tree. One minute you are hanging high, then the wind blows and down you fall. Meanwhile the tree keeps standing. The sun still rises pink and purple, sets the trees on fire, sits directly over my head at noon so I have no shadow, and sinks in the evening. Women go to the market, quarrel over prices, carry their cane baskets of cassava, plantain, whatnots, and return home to cook the afternoon and evening meals. Men lean back in their chairs with their legs stretched out, sipping beer and yelling what's taking so long for the food to cook. These are the thoughts that make my body so heavy I remain on the carpet, blinking at its black flecks. I can't read because when I do, the words jump around and I keep reading the same sentence over again.

When I hear Papa's car grind to a stop on the gravel, I arrange my face into stone. He crunches in, banging the screen door after him. He stops, looking at me.

"Esi." His voice is soft. *"Ete sɛn?"*

I'm supposed to say *"Bɔkɔɔ,"* but things are not fine. I mumble that I don't know. I can't bring myself to look him in the face. He sinks into the couch and crooks his finger. "Come here, why this sour face?"

I push myself heavily up. "Everything is . . . is falling. Nothing stays up." I don't want to cry but the tears won't stay dammed behind my eyes.

"It's the coup, isn't it?" My silence spurs him on. "Stupid soldiers! Here." He hands me a handkerchief. "Stop crying, stop crying. Do you want Milo?"

"No." What use is Milo? Sweetness on the tongue can't fool me anymore, I'm too old for that.

He looks at me for a moment and makes up his mind about something. He lifts his voice, "Adelaide! Adelaide!" Auntie drags herself in, looking annoyed, probably wondering what she has done wrong that Papa should shout for her and waste cooking time. Instead of Papa talking to her, he raises his voice some more, "Herh, Mansa! Yaa! Kwabena! Come here, all of you!"

Sisters Mansa and Yaa wedge in the doorway, worry lines on their foreheads. I can tell they're also wondering if they've done something wrong. Kwabena pushes between them and stumbles in.

"What is it?" Auntie asks carefully.

"I'm tired of the gloom around here," Papa says. "The coup is nothing. Ghana is fine. You're miserable for nothing. Look, I'm taking you all to Accra. You'll see for yourself. There's nothing for your stomachs to burn about."

I drop Papa's handkerchief. "Accra?" Suddenly I am laughing and crying. In fact, I could burst into a thousand pieces. Kwabena and I squeal. We grab each other's arms and jump around the room. "Let's go, let's go!"

I've been to Accra many times with Papa. Each time we left to return home, I had an urge to grab the steering wheel and turn it around. I love everything about Accra—its crowds, the newness of the streets, and the confident way women flounce their skirts. Some even drive cars! Accra, I can't wait. My sisters would love to go, too. I can tell from their smiles and the way they dislodge themselves from the doorway and now enter fully. Even Auntie is smiling though she says she'd better hurry up and cook foods to store in the fridge if we're leaving early.

It's early in the morning. I am sporting a long skirt and a show-your-stomach blouse that Sister Crocodile keeps frowning at. If the sisters want to impress city people with their church clothes that's fine, but I want people to see me as a big girl. Kwabena looks sharp in a coat over a pair of shorts. He even has on a bow-tie. If Akwasi were alive, would he also have on a coat? Oh, Sister Abena, if only she were here! Her Royal Highness hasn't been home and can't join us. Which is just as well. Kwabena and I get squashed in the backseat between Sister Crocodile and Sister Mansa, what with Auntie enjoying a rare front-seat honor, her afro wig almost touching the ceiling of the Mercedes. She has on enough powder to choke a pig with its scent, and I don't know who told her powder around the neck was a fine thing. When it gets steamy, the powder will form rings around her neck.

Yippity bumpity. We bounce past towns full of rusty roofs and church steeples poking out from the greenery, villages with mud dwellings and thatched roofs standing on clearings of red earth. Along the sides of the road, people walk in a single file to avoid stepping on grass or getting bitten by snakes. Now a man in an old singlet with a cutlass in his hand, now a woman carrying a bundle of firewood or a bucket of water on her head plus a baby tied on her back, now children straying onto the road and dodging cars. The sun heats the air so I can't hold up my head. Though I don't want to, I fall asleep on Sister Mansa's shoulder and don't wake up until I hear shouting.

We're high in the mountains, weaving through the town of Aburi, just forty minutes to Accra. I suck in thin, crisp air. The rolling hills scallop in alternate rows, from a golden green in the sun and to a darker green until they are a bluish gray mist at the horizon. You can see the valley dipping, and beautiful villas hanging by mountainsides. I look to the right and gasp.

"It's beautiful, isn't it?" Papa says, smiling at me through the rearview mirror. The sign says Aburi Botanical Gardens. The land is such a thick green you can't tell mango from orange. Papa tells us that inside the garden there are spices growing: vanilla, nutmeg, cardamom, and more. You can smell them. Sister Mansa complains she's cold but for once, I agree with Sister Yaa, who says to keep the windows down.

"Can we go there, Papa?" Kwabena asks.

Papa shakes his head. "There's nothing there you haven't seen before. It's only because scientists have gathered them into a small space that you're impressed."

We leave the garden behind and cruise past a walled, palace-looking complex with two guards boxed in roofed structures on each side of the white gate. In the distance, you can see the four-story palace rising above smaller houses. Auntie wants to know who lives in such a grand place. Papa says it's Peduase Lodge, which Nkrumah built for himself but never got to live in before those "infernal bullies called soldiers ousted him." Then he goes on about the Biafra war in Nigeria and the Aburi Accord. Sister Mansa groans softly so Papa can't hear.

I ask, "What's an accord?"

The crocodile sister pinches my arm, hissing, "Don't you know better than to question Papa and subject us to an on-the-spot history lesson?" Papa tells us how the Nigerian leaders met here but the talks failed to prevent that terrible war and how it went here and went there and so forth. I dare not ask any more questions as we zigzag down the mountain where the air is warmer.

In Accra, Papa weaves along Beach Road near Teshie, a fishing neighborhood right outside Accra. There is no disturbance of any kind here. Just a lazy lapping of seawater shining like glass. Wrapped in the smell of fish, we stare at buildings blistered with peeling paint and shacks struggling to stay upright. As the buildings give way to coconut trees, Papa tosses his arm out at the frothing waves. "This is how I used to drive all the way to Nigeria, the sea to my right and the land to my left." A scene flashes in my head . . . Papa driving with me in the car, falling asleep behind the steering wheel . . . but wait, what's that? A whitewashed wall to our left. A big sign: ARMY HEADQUARTERS. A network of gray buildings on cut grass. Soldiers with machine guns standing on either side of the X metal gates. How scary they look! And . . . what's that on the beach, far out there on a hill? Four rectangular stakes the height of a man. The black shapes painted on them could pass for shadows of men. Not far from the stakes, there is a wooden wall opposite, with holes in it.

I sit up. "Papa, what's that?"

Papa's jaw hardens. "The firing squad."

Kwabena blinks. "What's a firing squad?"

Auntie twists around, frowning. "Ah, you children. You ask too many questions!"

Papa sighs, giving me quick looks in the rearview mirror. "I'm afraid it's where soldiers shoot men condemned to die. I didn't know they would have this set up. But as you can see, no one is getting killed or anything. It's probably just there for target practice." He points. "You see the stakes? Normally they tie the men to them and then soldiers stand behind that wall facing them. There is usually a tent to hide them. They poke their guns through the hole and fire. But as you can see, things are calm."

Kwabena's eyes pop. "Is the tent so that the men can't see who is shooting at them?"

Papa nods with a sigh. "They tie hoods over the heads of those going to be killed anyway."

"But why?" Sister Mansa asks. "Why would they kill anyone?"

"Enemies of the state. Don't worry. I don't remember the last time anyone got killed that way."

Silence has gripped us all. Auntie turns around and dresses me down with her eyes. Sister Crocodile nips at my ear, "Why do you always have to stir the pot? Why can't you be quiet?"

Shut up! I dig my elbow into her. "Sorry," I say with a straight face. My stomach roils over. I picture a man tied to a stake, his feet digging into the mushy sand. A man like Papa who has a child like me. He stands tied up while someone he can't see shoots and makes his blood flow into the sand. What awful secrets the sea must wash away. I can't breathe. A wave rises in my chest, higher and higher. Papa glances at me through the rearview mirror and says quickly, "Did I tell you I once saw Maame Water at the beach?"

I blink. "You saw a mermaid? A real Maame Water?"

"Yes, a real Maame Water. She talked to me." He's not smiling. Surely, he won't make up something like this?

"She talked to you! In Twi?"

"That's right. In Twi."

I stare at him. "What did she say? Tell me!"

He laughs. "I can't tell you."

"Why not?"

"She made me promise to tell someone only at midnight."

I think for a minute. "If I stay awake until midnight, will you tell me?"

"Yes."

I bet he thinks I can't keep my eyes open until midnight. I *will* stay up.

"I'm hungry," Auntie snaps. "Can we stop for lunch?"

It's fine by all of us. Papa heads back downtown and herds us into the Ambassador Hotel with its red carpet and crystal lighting. Waiters in white shirts and black bowties serve us what he orders. The meat is a flat round affair, and when I cut it, blood seeps out.

"That's steak," says Papa, "the white man's food. Go on, eat." He points with his knife. "It's good to try different things."

I don't want to eat this bloody meat that draws up water from my stomach and makes me want to vomit. Plus, the white lumps called potatoes taste nothing like yam. They don't have the hint of sweetness or the thickness, and they look disgusting sitting in bloodied sauce. Sister Yaa mutters no wonder white people look so sickly. Auntie asks in a disgusted voice, "Don't they have Ghanaian food?"

Papa shakes his head as if he can't believe what he has to put up with. He gives her the "You must overcome your bush ways" speech but Auntie shakes her head firmly.

Papa puts down his fork and dabs at his lips with the white cotton napkin. "Adelaide, do you want to remain an ignoramus all your life?"

Auntie's nervous laugh is a firm no. He sighs and asks the waiter to take the food away and bring us whatever we want. Then he picks up his fork and knife, saws into his bloody meat, and sops up the pinked sauce with his potatoes. We don't mind waiting, and when they finally serve us, we wash our hands in the warm, soapy water before diving into our banku and grilled tilapia. The pepper sears my tongue, just the way I like it.

Back in the car, we drive around the Black Star Square by the sea. I gasp at the circular fountain with its rim of gold-green hedge and red flowers. I wonder if it's possible for someone to pole-vault over the tall arch framed against the sea. Behind it, you can see a curved row of Ghanaian flags flapping in the wind. A concrete monument with thick columns bridges the road dividing the square, a black star on top. The words etched below the star declare:

AD 1957
FREEDOM AND JUSTICE

Freedom and Justice, I repeat to myself. For me, it means girls should be free to play football and drums. No one should smear ginger or pepper in their under-canoe if they touch themselves, but it's like making soup for your family. Someone wants more salt, someone wants less. Someone likes pepper. Someone doesn't. Sigh. If I were alone with Papa, I'd share my mind and he'd say, "You're too precocious," but there would be pride in his voice. I can't say anything right now because I don't want Sister Yaa to pinch me again.

From Black Star Square, we drive to the impossibly clogged Makola Market. Papa wants us to see it because "it is the epi-center of trade in Ghana." There are a handful of men who own shops but what you see are mostly women. Big women with shiny faces under large hats woven from dried palm fronds. Big women shading themselves under huge, multicolored umbrellas. Women who look strong, who laugh like they could take on an army, who don't have Auntie's yielding personality. Their stores spill onto the streets and it's impossible to pass.

"Hmm . . ." Papa murmurs. "We should have parked somewhere else and walked."

There is so much energy! My head whips from side to side. Endless columns of fabrics, piles of bedsheets, rows of shiny aluminum pots, radios on shelves, pyramids of oranges. You want toffee? Dolls? Live snails? Smoked meat? Just wave at someone and your car is surrounded. Sellers jostle, shout, and shove things at you. Mats cover the sidewalks with more displays and women bending down to examine them. I want to be like the women, fingering a cotton print, trying on a pair of high heels, or turning my head from side to side, to see how my earrings dangle.

"All of Accra must shop here," Auntie says, paying for doughnuts. She passes some to the back and we tear into them. She glances at Papa. "Can I get some material to sew some dresses?"

"No," Papa says crossly. "I am not going to stop in the middle of this madness for you to go look at some cloth. Just look at this jam! People, carts, bicycles. Do you really want me to stop here?"

Auntie shakes her head forlornly. We can only look and move forward, inches at a time, which is fine by me. I just love watching these strong women. After forever, we peel out of the market. It feels good when the car picks up speed and the cool air rushes in.

One by one, we fall asleep, while poor Papa drives alone with his thoughts. The last thing I remember is the radio playing "Jesus Is a Soul Man." The next moment, Sister Mansa is shaking my shoulders. I rub my eyes. The sky is black, except for the stars that sprinkle over and the lights around the circular lawn and . . . I sit up straight. Mendskrom! We're at Mendskrom Hotel, the same hotel where Papa bounced on top of the waitress! Oh, Awurade. I steal a glance at Auntie's side view. Her jaw is still. Does she know about Hotel Woman?

WE'VE EATEN OUR supper by the fountain though I was too tired to eat much. Hotel Woman was nowhere in sight and Auntie obviously knows nothing. Apparently, no one does except me. Now I'm wide awake. If I stay up until midnight, Papa will tell me the Maame Water's story.

The same little room-houses slumber around the lawn. My sisters, Kwabena, and I get one for ourselves while Papa and Auntie have their own. The sisters declare themselves hammered by a headache and decide to sleep right away. Like me, Kwabena doesn't want to go to bed so we skip out to look for Papa in their room, but we find Auntie alone who asks me to help open her zipper. Why do they put zippers on the back of women's dresses, anyway?

After helping Auntie, I tug at Kwabena's arm and we drift outside. Ah, there is Papa! I scrunch up my skirt and run toward him. He is talking to someone, sitting with a woman on a bench. Someone I know . . . Hotel Woman! I stop, screwed into place. I have to keep Kwabena from finding out. I pull on his arm. "Stop! Can't you see he is talking matters with someone? He'll shout us off."

"Oh," Kwabena says. "What do we do then?"

"Er, let's sit on this bench. Right here." It's not too close for Papa to order us to go sleep, but not too far away for us to make sure he doesn't disappear to do what I am sure they shouldn't with Auntie right here in the same hotel. Anyway, we can still get him to tell us the Maame Water story at midnight. Kwabena says okay. He is just happy we can stay up late without anybody yelling at us. But it's hard to just sit talking, so we start chasing each other around the fountain. We forget about Papa and have a great time falling down and laughing. There are hardly any other guests in the hotel because it's so far from town. No one pays us any attention. Papa is too busy murmuring anyway and . . . stop!

He is gone. So is the woman. It's quiet and all lights are off in the rooms. The only light comes from the bulbs winking over the tiny verandas and the lampposts standing around the circle.

"It's too creepy," Kwabena whispers. "Let's go to sleep too."

"No, Papa promised me the Maame Water story!"

"Fine, I'm going."

Typical. Just like him to leave me hanging. "Coward!" I call after him. He doesn't even look back.

Alone, I walk to Papa and Auntie's room and rap with my knuckles. There is no answer. I turn the door handle and it opens. Auntie lies on her back, snoring by herself, a splash of light on her rising and falling breasts. Papa is nowhere. I close the door softly and drift back to the circle. My shadow is long and ghostly. I'm afraid of ghosts. Think, Esi, think!

A little far off to the left lies a white, one-story dormitory style building. Papa once told me it housed waiters and waitresses who chose to live at the hotel. What if the woman lives there? What if Papa went to her room? It's not disrespectful to interrupt them, is it? She is not his wife, is she? Auntie would probably thank me. In fact, I should interrupt them.

I walk to the first door and knock. No one answers. I try the second door.

"Who is it?" Her voice, Hotel Woman!

"It's Esi," I say, really respectfully. "Please, I'm looking for my father."

There is whispering, creaking, and shuffling of feet, and then the door opens into a room lit by a naked yellow bulb dangling from the ceiling. She stands in the doorway, wrapped in a cloth up to her chest. She has one hand on the hinge and another holding the door open. When I duck under her arm and step into the room, there is just a bed. Papa is nowhere in sight. Then, just as I'm turning around, I spy his big fingers curved around the door handle at the back. I look and oh no! I whip away. Think fast. You can't shame him. You have to pretend you didn't see him naked, pressed backward into the dark, one hand covering his ding-dong-ding, his passenger.

Keeping my jaws still, I whirl around to face the woman. She mustn't know I can now see Papa's trousers and shirt hanging on the bed board, shoes on the floor. "Where is Papa?" For an answer, she takes my hand, turns the light off, and pulls me outside. Bathed in the veranda light, I can't see into the blackened room, which is fine by me.

She lances into a nonstop chatter, grinning like a buffoon: "Ei, Esi, so you passed the Common Entrance, hee hee! You're going to Wesley Girls, wonderful. Your father says you're brilliant, you can talk politics even, ha ha. One day, you'll be a lawyer, *ein?* Maybe I'll come to you if I have problems and you'll take care of me, hee hee!"

I want to smack the smile off her face, hiss at her, "You bloody fool! Can't you tell he's just passing through you? You are not the destination, idiot!" I can only hope she can mind-read.

She darts looks over her shoulder as she rambles on. After a final glance, she tells me I can come in, and hey presto, here is Papa fully clothed, sitting on the bed, pulling his sock on. I amaze myself at how well I can act. "Papa!" I burst out joyfully. "Where were you? I looked in this room but you weren't here!"

He looks up from his ankle, smiling like a naughty boy. "Magic. I fell from the ceiling."

He actually thinks I'm that stupid? Fine. He taught me with Witchy Wilkinson, didn't he? I can play my part. I let my voice sound puzzled. "But where did you go?"

"We went to eat the white man's food." He winks at her, licking his lip. She giggles.

Idiot. With just the right touch of baby in my voice, I whine, "But why didn't you take me?"

He laughs and pushes to his feet, tugging at his trousers. "You said you hated white man's food, remember?"

I pull a spoiled child's lip. "Yes. But I wouldn't have minded."

"Is that so? Next time, then." *She* giggles some more. In my head, I'm sucking my teeth at her. He finishes his toilet, picks up his keys, says "See you tomorrow" to her, and tells me let's go.

"Good night," she calls after us.

I don't respond. My cheeks are burning with the shame of what I saw. I'm getting good at this, creating cupboards in my mind where I lock up scenes that threaten to shred me to pieces. Hotel Woman. Mother at the airport. Shut it out, shut it out! There, see me smile. See me walk beside my father, see me keep silent until we get to the benches around the lawn. I stop and look up at him, going for the safer subject. "Can you tell me the Maame Water story?"

He shoves his hands into his pockets, avoiding my eyes. "You should have reminded me exactly at midnight. Now it's too late. Next time."

I stare at him stepping ahead of me, wondering what would happen if I threw a stone at him. I would get slaps on my buttocks so hard my eyes would burn. I have no choice but to match my steps to his, watching our long, stilt shadows lead us along the concrete walkway while he whistles a tune to fill the silence.

CHAPTER TWELVE

W HAT CAN I do about the happenings at Mendskrom Hotel?
I have better things to think about: Wesley Girls. At last,
I get to attend the great Wesley Girls High School. Do you hear
that? Wesley Girls! Already I can do the slogan: *We don't brag
because we know we are good. We're gonna walk on you like we walk
on wood.* Wey Gey Hey, here I come!

The road to Cape Coast runs along the beach. Miles and
miles of seawater like a silvery sheet roll along with Papa and
me. The blue sky could pass for a painting with black shadows of
fishermen rowing their canoes in it. I love how the coconut trees
lean toward the sea, like tall ladies with slender waists and wind-
blown fronds brushing against the sky. There are women sitting
on benches along the road, behind tables painted red, blue—
all colors, with rows of kenkey arranged on them. Bible verses
painted on the sides of the tables remind us to thank God and
fear Him: Ezekiel 4:17. Trust in God. Psalm 91. The Lord is my
shield. The verses are good juju that keep away evil spirits and
bring lots of buyers.

"Girls High School is on the outskirts," Papa says, "so we're going to bypass the town." That means we won't get to see the castles where the Portuguese and British locked up slaves before shipping them to lands behind the corn, which is just too bad. Someday I hope I get to see the forts and find out what happened to those who got put to sea.

We turn off the main road and there it is on the right, a green signboard with yellow letters: WESLEY GIRLS HIGH SCHOOL. A high school perched high on a hill. I could stretch out on the black tarred road and kiss it!

Papa drives up between the trees and takes me to paradise. At the top, straight ahead, you can see the school chapel, a giant cross rising from its airy white tower. Bungalows snuggle under leaves in the valley. I want to curl up under the shady trees, skip over the hedges and hedges of lanes. Papa says the headmistress is called Miss Garnett, that she is a British missionary making Christians of everyone, which is silly because everyone knows God. Awurade is only one of the many names for God. As soon as Papa turns off the engine, I jump out.

We find the school office on the ground floor of a gray-and-white building. Miss Garnett rises from behind her desk to meet us. I think she must be too busy with sinners because her hair needs combing the way it's tousled around her round baby face. I love how her blue eyes sparkle through her spectacles, but I wonder how she can get a spoon inside her mouth. It's narrower than a baby's, as if God just slit an opening and forgot to mold lips.

She and Papa greet and shake hands. They know each other from some headmasters' conference.

"This is Frederica," she says and I wonder how she can know my name already.

Sister Mansa says white people smell like raw chicken, but Miss Garnett smells fine to me. She is a pinkish wonder sprinkled with little brown spots, from too much sun, I think. She says I will be in Block K, which is also called Compton House, and won't we please follow her outside.

She points to a beautiful hall with nothing but round pillars for the side walls, and spiral steps coiling against one end. You can see the stage, a real one with velvet drapes. I want to run and wrap myself around the white pillars, leap on the stage, and shout *To be or not to be*. Miss Garnett points, that's the Assembly Hall, and the low, gray buildings lined behind it are the classrooms. Papa wants to know how many girls are in the school.

"About six hundred," she says. "We've got ninety-nine in each form, with thirty-three girls in each class. And then we have Lower and Upper Sixth-Formers."

"That's a lot of girls!" I blurt out before I remember I am not supposed to say something when grown-ups are talking, but Miss Garnett smiles and says it's true. I can tell she is not in the least like Witchy Wilkinson.

She points out the tall buildings to the right and left of the chapel. "We have seven houses of residence, four on this side. Compton House, where you're going to be, is behind the chapel. It is one of the three new blocks. Just reverse and follow the road to the right."

We drive past white, one-story bungalows in the valley, past the three floors of the science laboratory building, and arrive at a little roundabout where Compton House stands with the two other houses. How grand the slate green and white buildings look! No dusty roads here.

The parking area is jammed with cars and students. Boys in frayed shorts and torn shirts rush to our car and scuffle with one another like football players, shouting, "Me! Me! Pick me! See, I'm strong! I can help you with your box!" Papa says they must have come from a nearby village to make money. He picks two boys to help us.

They carry my trunk up the two flights of stairs to my dormitory on the second floor. From the landing, you can see rolling hills as far as the horizon. A lane hedged with hibiscus runs between the house and the chapel. And look, on the pawpaw trees behind the hedge, monkeys swing from branches! Look at one eating the fruit right off the tree!

Papa laughs and tells me to come on. We cross the landing and push through swinging doors that open to my dormitory, a huge, windy room. Leaves from trees flutter in through the open windows that have no netting, which is fine because everyone has a mosquito net. There are twenty-four beds against the walls, twelve on each side. We have wardrobes and drawers, so I don't have to live out of my trunk like I did at Mmofraturo. I choose a bed near the end of the room.

On the beds, girls loll around in nightgowns and bathrobes. Papa takes one look and says he'll wait downstairs.

The dormitory is full of Been-tos. Been to London. Been to New York. Been to Canada. Back downstairs, they say Bye Daddy and Bye Mummy to their parents, not Bye Papa and Bye Maame. When it's time for Papa to leave, I too say Bye Daddy so I can sound like the Been-tos but Papa says, "Daddy? Where did you get that nonsense from?" Sometimes I wonder if Papa has wood in his head. I don't mind that much when he leaves. Besides, I'm getting used to saying bye to him. I've already been to a boarding school and I'm not afraid.

The good thing about arriving on Friday is we have the weekend to get to know our dormitory mates. Some Been-tos have surnames like Grant, Quist, and Vanderpuye. Some already know one another from having attended expensive international schools with names like Christ the King and Morning Star Preparatory. They roll around on their beds moaning about the things they miss—*Oh, how I wish I could have hot dogs and sausages. What about ham-beggars! I want ken-tacky fried chicken.* They want to stroll along Piccadilly Street and feed pigeons in Trafalgar Square and buy doughnuts in Brooklyn and Los Angeles. You can tell they live on butter and milk the way their cheeks glow and their skins look soft as dew. When you have never stepped behind the corn and you hear things like that, you feel a longing for things you didn't know you needed. The way I imagine ken-tacky fried chicken brings water into my mouth, but hot dogs? I tell them I'd rather chew glass than eat dog meat or beg for ham, whatever that is. When the girls hear that, there is a gasp, and then they are falling with laughter. One girl points at me, shaking so hard she's choking. "Oh, my! She, she thinks hot dog is dog meat!" Everyone hurries to explain. "Hot dog, it's just a name! You've never had one? I mean, really. Even if you haven't, haven't you seen any films?"

They dab their eyes. I know they think of me as a bush girl. Eurydice has skin the color of papaya and curly hair like a doll. She sits with her legs crossed in a *W* and wants to know why my lips are so thick. I don't understand because my lips are like my mother's and Papa's and I've never known anything wrong with them. Eurydice turns to the others. "Her eyes are so Chinese, and black like a prostitute." I know what a prostitute is and I don't like the Chinese bit. Now all eyes are stuck on me and there is nowhere to hide when I need to change into my nightgown. Everyone feels the need to tell me how my skinny legs could be mistaken for cassava sticks, and why are my breasts growing so high they're almost at shoulder level. I wish they would talk about something else.

Eurydice, whose skin must be mixed with a white person's, says, "If you look at her from the back you'd never know she was a girl, what a small bottom she has!" She comes over and squints at my hair. "Look at her hair, so fluffy and light, you can see through it, like cobwebs." She reaches for some strands. "Well, the hair is very soft, almost like quality hair, but without the silky curls." Hair of no quality is the Ghanaian-looking hair curled like the dried seeds of pawpaw. Quality hair is the silky kind that looks like someone's blood is mixed with Europeans. I'm frozen. Now everyone wants to feel my hair. A Form Two girl reaches for white powder, sprinkles some on my hair and says it might as well look like cobwebs because that's what it feels like.

I unfreeze and swat the powder away and I'm glad she gets powder in her eye. "Don't you touch me again!" I snap. They laugh and tell me not to be so touchy, such stupid words from people touching me. I guess that's the way it goes everywhere, people who have to be better than others. Here it's the Been-tos, who spend their holidays behind the corn, who have quality hair, whose skins are soft like ripe fruit, who call their parents Daddy and Mummy. It's all so stupid.

"So, you call your father Papa?" Daisy wants to know.

I snap a *yes* at her.

"Well"—she dimples helpfully—"you could pronounce it Papa like the Italians, not the Ghanaian way, Pa-a-pa. That's too *saeto* you know, like the bush people."

I can see Daisy is the kind Papa calls an ignoramus, a Ghanaian who thinks foreigners are better. *Papa.* In Twi, if you pronounce it in different ways you get a different word but it's always good. If you raise the tone and say it like you're hitting the same musical note you get *pápá*, meaning good, which the pastor says only God can claim for himself. Papa is like God even if he isn't always good. If you lower the tone and say it like you're hitting the same base note, you get *papa*, a fan to cool you off when you're too hot. And you can fan the coal pot for the food we eat so we can grow. Papa is like that to me. There's another word, *patapaa*, which is using force to get what you need. Papa is an expert at that too, except when Witchy Wilkinson steals from him. The Been-tos can take their daddying and mummying and go burn the sea for all I care.

"I call my father Papa too," Akosua says. "He insists on it."

We're going to be best friends, I know it.

The truth is most of the girls are like Akosua. They may even be Been-tos, but they choose not to make announcements about tacky fried chicken and whatnots. In fact, they are starting a trend, shedding off their foreign names. Maud, Gladness, and Gladys are giving way to Nana Yaa, Maame Akua, and Oparebea. They go about their business quietly. So why is it that the unkind moments are the ones you remember?

When the bell clangs for lights out, I slide inside my mosquito net, squirming from the Been-tos' sharp words. I know it's foolish of me but I'm miserable that I'm ugly with my fluffy hair, skinny legs, dark eyes, and cheeks that sit too high on the bones. But wasn't Papa proud when I passed the Common Entrance? That's right. The girls may say ugly things about my body but what's in my head is more important. No one will make fun of me in the classroom, they'll see!

Monday morning, the rising bell clangs us up at five-thirty. We wash ourselves with cold water from our buckets because the pipes don't run, then we dress up and do our chores. But instead of breakfast, we have chapel. I have never heard of worshiping God before you've filled your stomach.

We troop into the chapel and slide in wooden pews. Miss Garnett reads from the Bible but fried eggs and bread float before my eyes. The music teacher plays the piano and we sing from the Methodist Hymn Book. We pray and then it's off to class on empty stomachs, but you won't hear me complaining because I'm in the great school of Wesley Girls and I can't wait to learn everything. We break the fast after two periods, then we have four more classes until the twelve-o'clock break when we drift into the dining hall for warm, sweet bread or bananas and groundnuts, and then we get to play outside for twenty minutes. After that, we have two more periods before the lunch bell rings at one-thirty.

From Form One to Form Three, we will study all subjects, even Needlework, Cookery, and Commerce. Then in Form Four, we will choose seven to nine subjects and study them for two years. At the end of Form Five, we will sit for the General Certificate of Education Ordinary Level Examinations (GCE O Levels). If we do well, we will attend two years of Sixth Form before taking the GCE Advanced Level Examinations (A Levels) so we can enter the university.

We have a different teacher for each subject, not like Mmofraturo where Miss Darko taught everything except Science and Housecraft. In Literature, we learn how Elizabeth Barrett of Wimpole Street ran off to marry Robert Browning, who was seven years younger, which sets us dying with laughter. That would never happen in Ghana. A man must marry a woman who is several years younger, otherwise who will take care of him when his wife dies and leaves him? Though I wonder why no one worries about who will take care of the woman when her husband dies. In fact, often people declare her a witch for living longer than her husband.

What is really strange about the Barretts is their father won't let any of his daughters marry, as though he wants them to replace their poor dead mother who used to fear him in the bedroom. Unlike Elizabeth, her siblings were born in fear, says Papa Barrett, which makes me shudder. Hotel Woman begged Papa for it, and I've heard him laugh with Auntie when they shut the door to the spare bedroom. And Papa wants my sisters married, especially Her Royal Highness, since she is the oldest. Anytime she comes home Papa hounds her, "Who is your man? When are you getting married? A woman's glory is her husband." Sister Crocodile Yaa too isn't married and has to endure Papa's questioning. I don't know which is worse—Papa Barrett, who won't let his daughters marry, or a man who can't get his daughters married fast enough. I'm glad that when it comes to me, Papa only talks about the great things I can do in my future.

We also read books from the African Writers series. Now I know there are books written by people not from behind the corn, who write about African people. Chinua Achebe, Wole Soyinka, Ayi Kwei Armah, especially Ama Ata Aidoo, who actually graduated from Wesley Girls!

In Religious Knowledge Mr. Kobb has us reading about the lineage of King David, the ancestor of Jesus, and it has my head swimming. It goes like this: A lady named Naomi had two sons who married foreign women, which in itself was disobeying God because the Israelites were not supposed to marry foreigners, though I don't really understand why, since God created those foreigners in the first place and everything He created is good. Now, when Naomi's sons died, one of the daughters-in-law decided to return to her people. Ruth the Moabitess chose to stay with Naomi. But a woman needs a husband, so Naomi plotted to marry her off to a relative, an uncle named Boaz, which is okay because the women of Auntie's people marry their uncles and disgusting stuff like that. To get Boaz to notice Ruth, Naomi told her to go gather what the laborers left behind after harvesting the grain, and at nighttime, to lie at his feet. It is gross considering Boaz had been working in the farm all day and had dirty feet even if he rinsed them—I don't believe they had soap. Ruth obeyed, and here is the confusing part: the Bible says Boaz went into Ruth.

Vida Ayitey raises her hand. "Mr. Kobb, I don't understand. How can Boaz go into Ruth?"

"Well, he . . . ah, he didn't exactly go into her."

"But that's what the Bible says."

"He . . . ah, you see, uhm . . . it's just a manner of speaking."

I get it immediately. I can tell others are getting it too because we are falling off our seats laughing. The oil on Mr. Kobb's sweating face is enough to rub on a baby's bottom. Vida still doesn't understand.

"Mr. Kobb, how can a man go into a woman?"

"Look . . . uh, I mean . . . it happens. It can . . . happen."

"How? Mr. Kobb, can you show us how Boaz went into Ruth?"

"Aah, I can't show you!"

"Mr. Kobb, but why? Why can't you show us how Boaz went into Ruth?"

We're howling and Mr. Kobb turns blacker than coal. Finally, he tells her to go find a Ga Bible that says things directly. She does. Mr. Kobb commands her to read. She clears her throat: "And Boaz fucked Ruth . . . Mr. Kobb, what does fuck mean?"

We're weeping.

Mr. Kobb bangs on his desk. "Ask your mother. Let's move on." She's going to get ginger in her bottom for sure.

The word *mother* feels like a needle puncturing my chest. Apart from the first day of school when they helped us settle in, fathers are not allowed into our dormitories. While beds creak with the weight of mummies laughing with their daughters like sisters, Papa and I remain downstairs in the parking lot with the mosquitoes and the chauffeurs who drove the mummies' Jaguars. Mummies bring home-cooked meals like fufu and chicken soup or jollof rice with lamb to share with everyone. Papa brings me a car trunk full of coconuts and oranges. Coconuts. Who in the world will think to bring coconuts to a teenager in a boarding school? It's all I can do to stop myself from screaming.

I give six oranges to each girl and still I have too many. The gardener breaks the coconuts for us and I give him the rest for his family. The girls say, "Your father must really believe in oranges and coconuts. We can eat this forever." Shameful sweat collects under my armpits. I want crabs and snails swimming in palm-nut soup. I want rock buns, pineapple cake, sweetened condensed milk toffee, not bloody coconuts and oranges. I want my mother. I want her to sit on my bed looking pretty. I want her to braid my hair, rub my back, and giggle with me like a sister.

"Where is Mother?" I ask Papa.

He blinks away, digs into both pockets. "How many times have I told you? You know she's in Nigeria."

"But why can't she come here?"

"Look, she is busy. I told you before, she's a businesswoman."

"So why can't I go see her?

"She travels a lot . . . sometimes she's in London, Las Palmas. She never knows where she's going to be. Look, I've told you, why don't you write to her?"

My dear mother,

I miss you so much it hurts. Why haven't you ever come to see me since I came to Ghana? Why haven't you sent for me? I'm in a boarding school. Did you know that? Kwabena is also getting ready to go to a secondary school.

Here at school mothers bring their daughters food but Papa can't because he doesn't know how to cook and Auntie doesn't send me anything. I suspect it is because Papa never tells her when he's coming to visit me. He does things like that. He gets up, washes himself, and announces he is off to someplace and no one dares make him wait. I know he wasn't that way with you. I remember how angry you got the day he knocked down his dinner, how you threatened to leave and he begged you to stay, how you danced together.

The girls in my dormitory feel sorry for me. They say I'm ugly though Papa says it isn't true but I don't believe him. I

*wish you could braid my hair and sit on my bed and scratch my
back to sleep the way you used to. I remember everything.*

*Please, please, write to me. Or come visit me. If you're
too busy, Papa says I can come to Nigeria and visit you. But
please write and send me your latest picture.*

Tons of love,
Esi

I draw and color flowers on the envelope and address it to the
address Papa gave me:

2 Rosamond Street
Surulere
Near Moshalashi Bus Stop
Lagos, Nigeria

CHAPTER THIRTEEN

'VE GIVEN MOTHER'S letter to the office. I know they will post it, but I don't know if she'll respond. I just don't understand how she could leave me for so long and not write to me. Doesn't she want her only daughter? I once heard Papa tell a friend that having daughters is sometimes better than having sons. Sons go off to plant new families. Once they do, they become closer to their wives' relatives, but daughters remain attached.

Her Royal Highness truly sticks by us, which is why she sends Papa money to help pay for my school fees from the money she makes teaching at St. Monica's Secondary School at Mampong. To show I am grateful, Papa tells me I should spend Christmas holidays with her. I don't like it that her tight lips squeeze out words like *Wash the dishes. Your hair is untidy.* So, whenever she comes home and I see those lips move in my direction, I suddenly need to go to the bathroom or fetch Papa some water. But the last time she was home, she told Crocodile Jaws never to call me a Nigerian animal again, just like Sister Abena did. So, it's no problem to visit her. When Christmas holidays arrive, I climb into a wooden truck that rocks me for hours along the rutted road to Mampong.

"You're welcome," says Sister Royal with a smile. The deep lines crawling from her nose to the sides of her mouth look like cracks in the ground when the sun has baked it too dry. I wonder if her blood is drying up. That's what Papa says happens when a woman doesn't get married. He says Sister Royal has no business being the spinster teacher of a Catholic school, a spinster who is not a nun. A woman's glory is her husband, says he. Without a husband, you're nothing, and even a bad husband is better than spinsterhood. How I hate the word *spinster*. It sounds ugly, like spit landing on cement.

Her Royal Highness shows me to her bedroom and I push my bag under the double bed. There is another room but no grown-up will let her younger sister sleep in a room all by herself. Everyone knows that nighttime is scary, what with ghosts and evil spirits roaming around.

She leads me into the kitchen, and while we eat, she asks me the usual grown-up questions: How is school? Am I studying? After supper, she tells me to wash myself unless I want to sleep on the floor. She means no evil by it. You get dusty just walking outside.

In the morning, I find her in the kitchen hovering over a steaming pot of corn porridge bubbling on the stove.

"Good morning," I say.

"Morning," she says into the pot. She scoops up some porridge with an aluminum ladle and blows the steam away from her face.

"Sister, do you like teaching?"

"Yes." She blows into the ladle again, puts a drop on her palm and tastes it. People must have had her in mind when they said to save your breath to cool your porridge; it's clear she would rather not talk. She spoons some for me, drops two cubes of sugar into it, and tops it with creamy swirls of evaporated milk. Then we put our bowls on the waxed cement floor, sit on low wooden stools across from each other, and eat in silence, if you don't count the occasional slurp. The real fun is when I go outside and find children my age to play with.

That's how it goes for many days: sweep the kitchen, eat, and go out to play while Sister finds clothes to fold or goes to the market or marks students' papers. Then we cook, eat, and sleep. It's not her fault she grew up with Auntie, who probably made sure she never had a moment of play so she could grow up to be a good woman like the one in Proverbs 31 of the Bible. The one who worked so hard to make money that all her husband did was sit at the gate and chat with other men and praise his wife for being the best.

After a week, while we are eating our lunch of boiled plantains with cocoyam-leaf stew, I'm swallowing a morsel when I feel water dribbling into my drawers, which is strange because I don't have the grabbing in my abdomen that says I need to urinate. I steal a glance at Her Royal Highness but I have nothing to fear. Her royal eyes are fixed firmly on her food.

"I'm going to the toilet," I say.

In the toilet, I pull down my drawers and—oh, Awurade, a bloodstain has formed a red hibiscus in it. My knees turn into mashed yam. Where did the blood come from? There is no cut on me.

I sit on the toilet and wait to see if more blood will come out so I can discover where it came from. Nothing happens and then I think, oh, no! It's because of my sneaking mirrors between my legs. Or I have a terrible disease and I'm going to die. My hand trembles. I wipe myself and struggle to hold it together before joining my sister, but the dribbling happens again. I dash back into the toilet. More blood. I pull and pull on the toilet paper, make a thick wad and stick it into my drawers.

All day I use up so much paper that when Her Royal Highness

goes in, she comes out snapping, "How come the toilet paper is going so fast? Don't be wasteful."

In the middle of the night, I get up to use the bathroom again. The wad of toilet paper is soft and red, so I make a bigger one and when I flush, I don't check to make sure it has disappeared. The next morning Her Royal Highness shakes me. "Esi, you've made life and you didn't tell me!"

Made life? What is that? It sounds so awful I'm quivering under the sheet. She marches to a chest of drawers, pulls out a plastic packet, and tosses it onto the bed. "This is what you should be using instead of all the toilet paper. And you should have flushed it properly." She swivels on her heels and leaves for places unknown. There is no doubt about it, I'm going to be doomed. I'm bad. I can't tell Papa in case he gets angry like he did when Auntie said someone had spread me.

On the packet, the word *Pads* is printed. I pick it up, squeeze its softness. Then I tear it open. There are white pads, thick, stacked in a neat row like mattresses for dolls. Studying the picture on the packet, I decide the sticky part should be against my pawpaw. When I try to remove it, the hairs stick to the glue. I howl as I peel it off. I finally figure out how to use it. I am so ashamed I don't go out to play. The dribbling lasts for days before stopping, but when I return to school, it comes again. After that, it's every month. When it happens, I stay in my bed until everyone has washed and left for breakfast before getting up so no one notices me. I'm sure they only have to look at me to see sin plastered all over me. I am so miserable that in class, when I look at the board, the words swim.

I am in the dormitory, talking to my friend Akosua who calls her father Papa and whose mother is the Chief Nursing Officer of Ghana. Akosua has to know something about diseases. I sit on her bed carefully as if protecting a raw egg between my thighs. I tell her about making life and her eyes open wide. "You mean you've had your period?"

I must look like a stupid fish the way I'm staring with my mouth open. To me a period is the time we have a class.

"But that's so normal! Don't you know?" She whips out pencil and paper, folds her legs into a *W*, and starts drawing. "It's normal. See?" She points to an oval. "This is one ovary, where the eggs are stored. Every month, it releases an egg, and the womb forms a bed for the life that is coming. The egg travels inside this tube here, the fallopian tube, all the way to the womb. When there is no boy's tadpole to make a baby, the bed bleeds out."

For a moment, I stare at her. How come I'm only now noticing how her big eyes sparkle, how beautifully black her skin is? Making life! That's why they call it so. I'm like a hen laying an egg inside me. The egg needs a nest, which my body builds in case a baby forms, and when there is no baby, the nest just breaks down. What a woman's body can do! It's a marvel! I leap up and land on the cement floor laughing so hard I'm choking. There is everything right with me, not wrong. Everything wonderful and miraculous. My body is a source of life. Blood of life, not dirty blood! How alive everything is. The birds are prettier, the hibiscus flowers redder. I love even the insects. I like me. Hello, Esi, I'm so happy to know you!

At night in my bed I get to know me better. I feel the calabash shape of my breasts and wonder how a child will feel eating from them. I grab one with both hands and strain my neck, stretching out my tongue until it touches the nipple. The skin is rough, with a slightly salty taste, but it tickles, and oh the ticklishness feels so good. *Mmmm*, I do it again and again until I am squirming. My restless fingers wander down my stomach to the fuzz below my navel. The curls are tight, so I draw them out to see how long the strands really are. I think what lies below is a girl apart from me.

She has hair, a nose, big cheeks, and a long mouth that's hungry for sure the way it's drooling. I name her "Little Esi" and make a little braid. I'll put little beads on it, I promise. But she's drooling more and more so I pacify her with my finger. She likes that and there's a hot itch that makes me move faster. The faster I move, the hotter and sweeter the itch and the harder I have to move, and then something painfully sweet is boiling and quaking so hard I'm groaning though I'm supposed to be quiet in bed. It's wonderful, I'm wonderful! I fall into a deep, deep sleep and wake up happy. I must do it again at night, I must.

The next day, I press my secret between my legs and hum. The Housecraft teacher tells us about menstruation and puberty rites, how older women teach girls who have made life to be beautiful. To develop a straight back, a girl balances a bucket of water on her head while climbing up a hill in rubber slippers, something I can never do without sloshing water all over me. And she must eat a boiled egg without chewing it or risk not being able to get pregnant when she gets married, because the egg represents her future children. Chewing it is the same as a hen breaking open an egg before it has hatched, and a woman without children might as well be a spinster. I'm sure the girls tell lies, because how do you swallow a boiled egg without chewing it, without choking? And if those girls become women, won't they know the lie before asking their daughters to eat an egg without chewing it? Being a grown-up must be tiring, always carrying lies.

The only thing I care about is the sweet quaking, which I bring on every night. I own only two drawers that I save for when I make life, so when I go to class I have nothing under my uniform, and when I sit on the wooden chair and shift around, Little Esi's nose rubs against the chair and burns so sweetly I have to wait for everyone to leave so I can do the quaking. Also, I can't help looking at the front of the male teachers' trousers and wishing I could see them naked. This goes on all the time until a friend invites me to join the Celestial Melodies singers. These are boys and girls who have been born again because they invited Jesus to live in their hearts as their personal savior. If witches can take over someone's body and make her do evil things, then surely Jesus can enter several people's hearts at the same time. Once that happens, the person never has to worry about going to hell. I tell Jesus to move in, and I join the Celestial Melodies. This means I may not commit the sin of "lasciviousness," which I suspect includes what I do with my finger at night, but never mind.

Saturdays, when boys from other schools come visiting, the boys have to sit on the wall in front of the school office, but the Celestial Melodies boys are allowed to join us in the chapel to make a joyful noise unto the Lord. No Celestial Melodies singer will do something as terrible as be caught behind a bush, smooching with a boy. We sing that soon and very soon we're going to see the King, for we are strangers here in this world full of sin where Satan is the king. We are filthy black with sin but we've been cleansed and are now as white as snow. I've never seen snow and my skin has the same chocolate color, so I have to think I'm white on the inside even if I'm dark on the outside. When we sing in churches and other schools, people say what a joy it is that such young women love God, praise the Lord. All the boys want to be friends because the girls are beautiful and will make good wives, if you don't count me.

The problem with Celestial Melodies is we have to fast every Tuesday from when we wake up until lunchtime at one-thirty. After two periods of English and Math on an empty stomach, we can't join the other girls in the dining hall to slurp our breakfast porridge. Instead we huddle together in the Prayer Room the way the apostles did when they waited for the Holy Spirit to drop tongues of fire on their heads.

I don't want any fire to fall on my head even if the apostles didn't get singed, and I'd rather not babble in strange tongues no one understands. I know it happened in the Bible but I don't see how it can happen today when the Holy Spirit already came and left Holiness on earth, but the leader says if you don't have the least of the gifts of the Holy Spirit then what does that make you? The girls screech *hamdala toe-balla-hamdalalalaa!* They tear the air to pieces with voices raised to terrorize the devil, who is responsible for all sins including fornication, which seems to me like what Boaz did when he went into Ruth, though to be fair, he married her. I asked Mr. Kobb how Christ could descend from a fornicating woman, but he says the marriage was sealed when Boaz went into Ruth. So how come it's a sin when someone does the same thing without a marriage ceremony?

I can't screech *haamdala toebala* but I desperately want God to keep the devil away from me, keep me from sneaking into the dining hall at noon to stuff bread in my cheeks, which forces me to keep my jaw still when I pass a Celestial Melodies singer who is also holding her jaw still from the food tucked inside her cheeks (I caught someone). Liars, all of us. God keep me from digging into Little Esi's throat to rub the ticklish itch that ends in sweet quaking. I cry and pray for forgiveness but I can't control my sins. When I search, I can't find anything in the Bible that tells me what to do.

One day before we pray, a Form Five girl jumps up and shouts that she has a prophecy. She hoists her spectacles high on her round nose, points her finger with authority. "I had a terrible vision last night. One of us"—she tries not to choke—". . . oh Jesus, one of us, is going to die!" The air is gone from the room. She pounces on: "You know who you are! Though you keep asking forgiveness, YOU have been sinning repeatedly! Thus says the Lord: YOU are going to die." Her voice trembles from the feeling. Oh God, she is talking about me. My gorging on bread instead of fasting. My dancing. My pacifying finger between my legs. I'm going to die.

Everyone shreds the air with prayers but I'm a stone. The floor vibrates, windows rattle, lions growl, hyenas shriek, monkeys cackle, and fires rage. *HARRRRAAAAMBA—SANDALALALA-MAMBA!* Cease your wicked ways *AARRRR!* Before the Angel of Death smites you *AARRRH!*

I almost urinate. I squeeze my eyes tight so I don't go blind from the sword the Angel of Death is surely bringing down to split my head in two. After forever, the groaning and tongues bubble down. Slowly, I unfold myself and crack open one eye. The waxed cement floor is spattered with tears and maybe saliva. I know my eyes must be as red as the others' from crying. Dare I breathe? The angel has passed over me. Phew. But I know he hasn't finished with me. He can get me in my sleep, in the bathroom, when I'm alone in the classroom or library.

When we creep out, we avoid looking at one another. I certainly don't want my sin to show. Forget rejoicing about making life. It's death I'm making now. When I return to class the teacher asks me why I'm crying but I can't tell her, so she sends me to the school nurse who gives me pills to make me sleep. After siesta I go to the library and discover the word *masturbation* in a book but it doesn't say whether it's wrong or right. And there is nothing like concentrating on not doing something to make you want to do it. At night I pray not to make the quake, but the more I pray, the more ticklish the itch grows and the faster I have to rub—oh why does sin have to be so deeply, wetly sweet? If it weren't, nobody would commit it. Why couldn't God make sins of the body hurt? No one needs to tell you to stay away from fire, unless you fall accidentally into a coal pot like when Crocodile Jaws pushed

Sister Mansa into one and the angry red coal ate away her skin. You know you'll burn. But sinful quaking feels so heavenly it blots out hell. I don't see how the other girls never do anything wrong, how people can get visions and know without a doubt someone is going to die for her sins. What is the use of having Jesus live in my heart if I can't be as white as the snow I've never seen anyway? To tell the truth, I don't know if I'll like such whiteness even if I feel terrible after I've dirtied myself with my finger. The dirt is delicious.

My misery hangs around for weeks but the Angel of Death doesn't smite me. Now I'm wondering if it's possible for God to forgive me. I have to find someone older in Christ than me for help. There is a Celestial Melodies singer whose face is smoother than a baby's, with quality baby hair curling round her face. Surely, she is sinless and God will listen to her if she begs on my behalf.

We sit in the sun, on the footbridge that links Block M to Block L, and lean side by side against the whitewashed wall. Even if my voice shakes, I have to tell the hard truth, not wrap the words in cotton wool. I'll use the word I found in the dictionary. "Sister, I've been, ah . . . masturbating and I can't stop doing it. I pray, I really do but . . . I'm so sorry. I know I'm supposed to die but do you think God can forgive me?"

She smiles sweetly and says I was right to come to her. "If we confess our sins, He is faithful and just to forgive us and to cleanse us of all unrighteousness."

I can't believe how easy it is, how lovingly she looks at me. We clasp our hands together in prayer. She lifts her sweet voice, "Oh God our Father, you say we have not because we ask not, so we come to you today to ask you to please forgive Frederica, oh Lord. Help her to resist the devil, and the devil will flee from her." She comes against the stronghold of the devil and principalities and hosts. She invokes a hedge of protection around me, oh Lord. She prays long with passion and I feel free from sin as an iron hedge of holiness clasps about me.

I thank and thank her. I'll never sin again, *yeei*! I spring up, turn to go, then she stops me.

"Frederica, what is masturbation?"

My mouth flies open. She prayed for me when she didn't have the faintest idea what she was praying for? My eyes drop when I explain.

"I see," she says and turns her face to the trees straight ahead of her. I know I've shocked her. Now I know her prayers are of no use and there's no help for me.

I never want to be a Celestial Melodies singer again. I don't need more reminders of my coming death. I might as well laugh with my friends and stop starving at breakfast and worrying about the ticklish itch I can't and won't stop relieving.

I feel even better when an airmail letter arrives in the mail for me. The handwriting is all rounded like a woman's and oh, Awurade, it's from 2 Rosamond Street, Lagos.

My mother.

My dear Esi,

I am so sorry to have been away from you for so long. I'm glad to hear you are doing so well at school. I'm very proud of you and your brother. So are your Grandpa, Grandma, Auntie Biggie, and all the others.

I've been very busy traveling the world over for business, but I promise you'll see me soon. You'll never have to worry about anyone making fun of you at school again. I've told your father to let you come to Nigeria for the long vacation. I can't wait to see you.

There are things you'll understand when you grow up but

for now, I want you to know I love you very much. I miss you
too. I can't wait for you to come here. Everyone misses you.
    All my love,
    Mother

She loves me! Let the sky open because I'm so big I can't fit on earth. My mother is no ordinary person. She is a businesswoman who's always behind the corn, you hear? Las Palmas, London, and Paris, are you listening? She'll bring me dresses and food galore. When she visits and braids my hair and we laugh and hug, everyone will want to be me, you'll see. Who needs Celestial Melodies singers when you've got your own mother? I fold the letter and put it under my pillow the way I'd store a Bible.

CHAPTER FOURTEEN

GREET YOUR GRANDPA for me," Papa says at the airport. I wrap my hands around him because I can't believe he is letting us fly to Nigeria to see our mother for the Christmas holidays.

Papa turns to my brother. "Kwabena, take care of your sister."

"Papa, I'm older than he is!"

"But I'm a boy," Kwabena says smugly. "Come on, let's go."

"Don't even think about acting all tough," I hiss. "I can still beat you."

He smiles and I kick him. Still he smiles, so maddening.

An open bus drives us to the plane and we climb in. Only one hour and we'll be in Lagos!

I wonder if Mother will recognize me. I'm probably almost as tall as she is. We can be like sisters! My stomach feels as if someone is whisking eggs inside it. I have to hold on to the seat in front of me, which causes a bespectacled man to turn around, scowling through the gap between the seats. I give him a sorry smile and grab my knees.

With Sister Abena gone, Sister Mansa disappearing and never wanting to be with me, and Auntie perpetually steeped in the steam of the kitchen, I've had no grown woman to talk to or share mutual hair-braiding with. (Crocodile Sister doesn't count.) My hunger for Mother feels so sharp I can't stop myself from squeezing Kwabena's hand tightly. I can tell he too is excited because rapid puffs of air blow out of his mouth. The hour-long flight seems like a year. When the plane touches down, we leap up, never mind the air hostess warning to wait for the plane to come to a complete stop.

I hold on to the top of the seat as the plane lurches and the giant fans whir to a stop. When they let us out, we run down the stairs. They direct us to the arrival hall and oh Awurade, here they are! Grandpa, Grandma, uncles and aunties. I know them because they have the same long face and slanted eyes like my mother. I recognize my aunt that everyone calls Auntie Biggie. She is as big as ever. I can't see my mother yet, but I know she's hiding behind them. Any moment now she'll jump out and grab me. I'm lifted, hugged, kissed. I look around but I don't see her. I am about to choke.

"*Ìyá mi dà?*"

Auntie Biggie swallows my face in her bosom. "Oh my darling, your mother is not here . . . Oh no, don't cry . . . *ó ti tó*, it's okay, sssh . . . listen—"

"NOooOhooOhohohoooOOOh!" I'm choking on lace, fingers entangled in lace—

"—she had to fly to London on business, but she'll be here next time. Don't cry, oh, please, enough!"

"Why did she leave when she knew we were coming?" Kwabena sounds angry.

"She didn't know."

I wrestle out of Auntie Biggie's arms to look at my grandfather, who has taken an interest in the ceiling. "But she knew, didn't you tell her? You said she'd be here, you promised!"

He looks down at me with pain. "We didn't tell her, because we didn't want her to be disappointed in case you didn't come. One time your father said you were coming, and when you didn't, she cried. Please, don't cry. Sshhh."

The Angel of Death might as well take his sword to my chest because I want to die. It's my fault. Why did I have to tell her we were coming to Nigeria? Why did I hurt her?

Grandma says, "*Oya*, let us go. People are staring." That sets me off bawling again and everyone says, "*Ó ti tó, ó ti tó*, don't cry, you hear?" I wish I had never written to my mother. I wish she had never written back.

Everyone ignores Kwabena because he is a boy and doesn't need to be pampered. I'm the only one who notices how quiet he has grown.

Auntie Biggie takes me shopping. Auntie Yetunde takes me shopping. Grandma feeds me nonstop but all the food and dresses in the world can't turn into Mother. When I return to school I'll have to lie some more and tell everyone my mother is coming to see me. The girls will smile and nod, which is fine by me. They won't know when I cry inside my mosquito net.

GRANDPA VOWED THAT the next time I flew to Nigeria Mother would be there or he was not Chief Ademola. Mother herself swore she would be there, in yet another letter. Once again, I flew to Nigeria only to have her absence stab me in the stomach, which set me running. Running away from the pain. I flew past the sellers along the road, dodging cars and getting yelled at by drivers and standers-by until Grandpa's driver caught up with me. I kicked and punched but they wrestled me to the ground.

Now I'm fourteen and I run everywhere. When I run nothing can grab and punch me. I've stopped thinking about my mother.

I leap over hedges and sprint to class, trot to church, streak to the dining hall, to the library. Everyone says I should take part in this year's track and field but I don't know that I can.

It's a hot Saturday when we gather down the field for the inter-houses' competition. I try to cool down under a tree with my friends, squeezing and sucking peeled oranges for the juice. My house, Compton House, isn't doing badly. Already my friend Esther has destroyed the hundred- and two-hundred-meter records. A man puts his mouth to a yellow plastic cone and yells, "Competitors for the four hundred meters flat, report to the starting line!"

Girls trot to the white painted line on the grass and pace up and down with the narrowed eyes of animals about to pounce on prey. They're wearing their Physical Training uniforms: green shorts held by elastic at the waist and topped with a white cotton blouse. No one appears for Compton House. The man calls again, looking round to see if anyone is coming.

"How come no one is competing for us?" I ask.

Esther spits out orange seeds and licks her lips. "Four hundred meters is not easy. You need speed plus stamina, that's why even I don't want to do it."

I don't see why my house should come in last just because no one wants to run. Why don't I run? I'm always running anyway. All I need is to finish the race so we don't disgrace ourselves. I tell her, "If I had my PT uniform I'd run for Compton House."

Esther's brows shoot up. "Is that all you need? That's no problem. You can wear mine." She drops her orange into the dustbin under the tree and wipes her mouth with the back of her hand.

"But how can I change?"

She points behind the tree and says, "Let's do it over there."

We exchange clothes quickly while she yells to the field, "Wait, Compton House is coming!"

Necks stretch. Compton House girls see me trotting to the field in the green shorts and white top and they giggle, *Frederica doing the four hundred? Can she do it?*

I don't care what they say and I don't care about the grass pricking my bare feet.

The announcer shouts, "Competitors, get to your marks!"

I drop to one knee on the prickly grass and place both hands behind the whitewashed line.

"Set!"

Poom! Run, Esi, run. Feel the wind. No one can get you. You've got power. Halfway round the field. What? Runners are slowing down? I pass one, then another. Everyone is shouting, *Go! Go, Baby Jet!* I go baby jet go, pass everyone, eat up the distance until there is nothing but the white sewing thread stretched out in front of me. I run through it and keep going until someone catches me. It's a new record for the school and suddenly everyone wants to be my friend. They want to sit beside me at the dining table and oh, you're really pretty, you know. Maybe you're straight like sugar-cane but your hair is so soft. I lap up the admiration. Now I want to try everything there is.

It's lights out and I'm stretched out in my net but I can't sleep because I still want to go baby go and fly baby fly and oooh, the hot itch is on. I slide my finger deep inside. I make the quake three times but my body won't quiet down, I'm full of power. The moon throws a ghostly light on my mosquito net and for the first time in more than a year I let my mother enter my mind. How I wish she could have seen me fly around the field and receive the gold medal they took back after the ceremony because they have to use it again next year. Now I don't want to forget her, but when I concentrate on her face and soft arms, I feel nothing.

She is gone. My mother is dead.

How could I not have known before? It's the only thing that

makes sense. The feeling is so strong it pulls all the energy from me and I fall into a deep sleep. Mother floats to me dressed in white. Her eyes are soft and she gives me such a peaceful look that I understand she wants me to be the same. In one hand she holds open a newspaper, pointing at her picture. The letters *O-B-I-T-U-A-R-Y* stand on top. Then we're at the earth behind my grandfather's house and I immediately understand that the mound is where she is buried.

I jerk up crying only to find I'm in my mosquito net, on my wooden bed with the foam mattress at Wesley Girls. No! Sister Mansa says the dead sometimes return to take those they love with them to the other world. I want Mother to take me with her, talk to me, touch me. I know it's against the rules to get out of bed, but I don't care. I jump out and shuffle into rubber slippers.

A gray mist hangs on the trees and flowers. Insects protest and an owl hoots but I'm not afraid. My feet crunch dry leaves. I skirt around the chapel, past the Houses, and run down to the cornfields toward the gate. I stand between rows of ghostly cornstalks and call out, "*Ìyá mi!* Mother!" The skittle of lizards and crawlies makes me jump. Even if there could be a snake, I must find her.

A light is coming at me, she's coming for me! I've got to get to her. Run, Esi, run. The light is growing brighter. Now there are voices and . . . all the air comes out of me. I'm looking into the pink face of Miss Garnett, surrounded by the dark faces of my dormitory mates.

"I'm looking for my mother," I pant. "She's dead." Miss Garnett shakes her head sadly. She wants to know how I got the news. "Mother told me." I can tell she thinks I've become unhinged the way she says *Yes dear* so I lie, "I received a letter from a relative in Nigeria."

Miss Garnett wraps her arms around me and lets me cry into her cotton housecoat. She leads me into her house and puts me to sleep in her visitor's room. In the morning, she makes me scrambled eggs and tells me I don't have to attend classes. Then she sends condolences to Papa and Grandpa.

Grandpa fires back. "Who says Esi's mother is dead? That is not true. It must be some enemies of mine who want to create trouble and cause my granddaughter pain." He could pass for a politician on the radio.

I'm tired. What is this fuss about my mother anyway? In Literature, we are studying *Tell Freedom*, about four-year-old Peter Abrahams in apartheid South Africa who has to live with an aunt when his father dies and his mother has to work as a housemaid. The aunt can't even protect him when a white man has him flogged for daring to defend himself against three white boys who knocked him down because he had the nerve to say his father was as good as theirs. Even reuniting with his mother brings little comfort. She has scalded one side of her body from falling into a tub of boiling water, and her white masters have fired her because she is now useless. As for school, Peter can forget about it because he's too poor. What's more, a black South African can only learn Afrikaans, a language no one else in the world understands. In a film Miss Garnett showed us, we saw children in Soweto gunned down because they wanted to study in English. We saw graves laid out like the teeth of a giant zipper. The children were wrapped in cloth and dumped into the rectangular holes, no coffins to speak of.

Here I am in a good boarding school with a father who buys me books by the box, a headmistress and teachers who can't stuff my head enough with knowledge. I have food in my stomach and am never cold for the want of a sleeping cloth. I don't have to live with rich relatives and wash their plates, sweep their rooms, and get beaten for nothing. I don't have to leave school to sell groundnuts and bananas on the street the way some children do. So what if Auntie never sends me home-cooked food or thinks to buy me new drawers or a brassiere? My body feels freer with fewer clothes anyway.

Grandpa insists in his letter that Mother is alive. If I come to Nigeria, I'll see her. Miss Garnett joins in the clamor. "Your grandfather wrote to me," she insists. "You know I would tell you if she were dead." Papa adds his voice: she's alive. It sounds like the resurrection of Jesus, angels singing, "She's aliiiiiiive!"

The letters fly back and forth. I tell my Grandpa: "If my mother is really alive then I want her to be at the airport when we get to Lagos." Kwabena writes to Grandpa and threatens to kill himself if Mother isn't at the airport.

Now the long vacation is here and it's time to see Mother, but before we fly to Nigeria, we have to go home to Swedru. Normally Papa picks me up for the holidays, but not this time. He is an examiner for the West African Examinations Council, which means he gets to stay in a hotel for a month marking papers while waitresses bring him tea and cake in his room.

Our house in Swedru stands facing a narrow street whose edges have eroded into jagged scallops revealing the coppery earth beneath. Downstairs, there is a huge room Auntie wants to use as a store to sell things, plus two bedrooms. The kitchen and bathroom are in a separate structure behind the house. There is a sitting room upstairs, three bedrooms, plus Papa's study. When he isn't at home, I go into the study to find a piece of him. I love to smell his musty books and rifle through the files he keeps on us children. I sink into his black leather chair, which is so big I feel small. The thick file lies on the table. I examine my report cards, even those from Mmofraturo where Witchy Wilkinson wrote: Frederica, scholar of the year, *MUST* learn to be respectful, not bully others by taking what doesn't belong to her. *May you develop a twisted mouth, Witchy!*

The afternoon drags on as I rifle through Papa's papers. Auntie lies snoring in the bedroom topless, the fan blowing on her flat breasts. Sister Mansa is off to town to visit a friend, she says. I hope she isn't in a four-legged tangle on a bed with a boy just because Papa isn't around. He will return in two weeks, same time as Kwabena. Then Kwabena and I will fly to Lagos to meet our mother, oh, I don't know if my heart can stand the joy. Miss Garnett says Grandpa gave his word and I know Grandpa would never lie to her and she would never lie to me. *Ìyá mi!* We'll go shopping. I'll let her pick out the material for my bellbottoms. I'll sleep in her bed and make her scratch my back until I fall asleep even if I'm too old for that. We have some catching up to do.

I continue poking through the file. Maybe I'll take my report cards to show Mother what a good student I am. I'll tell her all about Witchy Wilkinson and I know she'll be angry for me. Also in the file are airmail letter cards with Grandpa's sweeping cursive on them. I turn each one over and put it aside because unlike Papa I never read letters not addressed to me. As I turn one over, two words at the top stop me: *late mother*. Some poor child's mother has died. Just this once, I want to find out whose mother is dead. I can send a card to make the person feel better. I turn the paper over again so I can read the sentence from the beginning and . . . what is this I'm reading?

Esi and Kwabena have been writing to their late mother again.

Late mother? My mother? I was right? Slow down, Esi. Chew the words one morsel at a time. Everything is quiet. The whole world has stopped moving, except the grandfather clock going *tick tock tick tock*. They won't lie to me? To Miss Garnett? Surely not Grandpa? Not Papa? I'm outside of my body, watching me.

I go through each letter and the facts arrange themselves. Mother died when I was nine years old, of something called a brain aneurysm. I'll look it up in the dictionary. THEY didn't want me to know, so they had to exchange letters to keep their stories straight: Should we tell Esi her mother is in Zimbabwe? No, we need a new location. Australia is too far. Auntie Biggie will write and pretend it's her mother. She'll know what to say.

Those letters, Mother never wrote them.

I can't get up because I can't feel my legs. But it's all right. I'm not going anywhere. Not to Nigeria, anyway. I'll have to write to Kwabena. He should know the truth. I'll include Grandpa's letters in the envelope. Kwabena will get that faraway look in his eyes. He'll not talk for a while and everyone will say what a good boy he is for not making trouble, unlike me. They won't know how difficult it is for him to find the words. Outside, across the street, the biscuit-seller is singing that God is the one who speaks for her. She is lucky.

In the evening, Papa returns from Accra. I don't run to the car to hug him or get his slippers or fetch him water or beg to scratch his back, no. I am in my bed. He goes into his room and calls, "Esi!"

I must answer even if I don't want to because he is my father.

When someone is ashamed, people say his eyes are dead. Papa's eyes are certainly dead the way they keep falling to his black shoes, so polished they reflect the light. He loosens his tie, and then removes his shoes and leans against the wooden headboard.

He pats the spot beside him and says, "Come on, sit down."

I sit at the edge of the bed, far from him, as close to the door as possible. I'd rather hug a porcupine than sit beside him. His eyes wake up long enough to meet mine. "I have something to tell you . . . Your mother is dead."

At last.

"I wanted to tell you, but your grandfather . . . he wanted to protect you . . . thought you were too young. You were only nine . . ."

The words are out.

The truth has flattened down the lies, the way skin goes flat when a boil lets out the pus in it. I feel relieved, almost. I have no

words. Just numbness. Death rides gently on the soft voices floating up from the kitchen, the whir of the grandfather clock as it
strikes eight, the cars humming past our house. I'm hunched over,
hugging myself, unable to look away from Papa whose eyes have
died again and fallen to his feet. I don't know if my tears are flowing because Mother is dead or because he and everyone lied to me.
I can only blink away the gray haze so I can continue to see Papa
and rock forwards and backwards. Something has broken between
us. And yet, everything is strangely the same.

He is all I've got.

The anger comes in the morning. When Auntie asks me to
wash the frying pan after frying eggs, I storm into the yard and
throw the pan onto the cement floor. Sister Mansa darts out after
me. The screen door bangs behind her. Bang, bang, responds my
heart.

"What's wrong with you?" she asks.

"My mother is dead, leave me alone!"

"What?" For a moment, she is quiet. Then her eyes narrow.
"How do you know that?"

"Papa told me." I rub soap into the sponge and attack the pan.

"Oh Esi, *kose, wae.*" She's offering comfort, saying things I
don't want to listen to. She falls silent. I can tell she doesn't know
what to do because I am not crying and not talking. She goes into
the kitchen, whispering something to Auntie.

"Ow!" Auntie rushes out. "Ow, Esi, sorry, sorry. *Kose!*" I know
she wants to be kind, but I can't bear to talk to anyone. I run
upstairs to my room, slam the door shut, bawling. They follow
me, sitting, patting me, talking, soothing. They're giving me all
the love they have inside them, but I can't stand it. I lie facedown
and scream into my pillow. Papa rushes in too. I pound my fists,
howling with the pain in my heart. The pain travels to my head
and hammers it.

"Give her Tylenol," Papa says. Sister Mansa runs out and returns with two tablets and a glass of water that Auntie puts to my lips. Though I don't want to, I flip over. The tablets sand my throat.

Auntie sits on the bed, speaking in a soft voice. "It's okay. Cry all you want. Ssh, it hurts, I know. But remember Akwasi? Your mother is taking care of him for us now. They are with the ancestors now. Ssh, it's okay. You go on and cry, my child. You will feel better. Don't mind anybody. She needs to cry it out." For once, Papa is silent, standing there like a pillar while Auntie soothes me with wise words. I imagine Mother holding Akwasi's hand. He must be a big boy now, if life continues after death, in the land of our ancestors. I try to smile, even as the tears continue to wet my neck. *Ìyá mi!*

Auntie turns and looks up at Papa. "Dee," she says in a firm, clear voice. A voice I have never before heard falls out of her throat. "She needs to go to Nigeria. She needs to see her mother's people. She needs to mourn and heal with them."

CHAPTER FiFTEEN

FOR WEEKS AFTER Papa told me about my mother's death, I lay in bed, shivering under my blanket only to throw it off, sweating. Auntie sat beside my bed, feeding me soups. Papa made me Milo, but each time he came into the bedroom, I turned my head away from him. He'd stand by the door, not knowing what to do. Sometimes I wanted to sit and read with him like I used to. Other times, I couldn't bear to share the same air with him. I spent more and more time alone in my room reading. I'd read until the words blurred into a gray mist, then I'd fling the book across the room as loud sobs shook my body. School became my escape. But now, the pain has subsided into a dull ache I can live with. I am happy Papa listened to Auntie and let me come to Nigeria. I chose to wait for the long vacation one year later so I could spend more time in Nigeria.

"We were just talking about your clothes," says Auntie Yetunde, who is married to Uncle Bola, my mother's brother.

I stand in the doorway smiling at her. She is sitting on her bed, rubbing Nivea cream on her bare breasts. Hers is more than a bedroom. Because Grandpa's house has only one big parlor, if someone visits you, you can expect to feel several pairs of eyes peering at you through the louvers, children running in, the television jabbering. The bedroom is the only place to entertain privately. That's why Auntie Yetunde's bed is decorated with a flowery sheet and matching pillowcases. Two chests of drawers hug the wall on the left. A Sanyo radio cassette player is playing Fela's music, while the television fights to be heard. She has managed to squeeze in a refrigerator as well as an armchair. Between the drawers and the bed, there is just enough room to roll out a small mattress for her children at bedtime, which makes me wonder if the children hear their parents slapping against each other at night, if they get confused as to what is really going on.

It's funny how I don't mind the rotten smell that blows in now and then from the gutter below the pink-curtained window. The love in this room smells good enough to blow away the bad.

"Ah, ah, don't stand at the door like that." That's from Auntie Biggie, the one who wrote me letters and pretended she was my mother. She could pass for a queen the way a huge gele sits on top of her head. You could doze off behind her in church and the pastor would never catch on. Every morning, after drenching herself in perfume and wrapping glittery lace around her body, she commands her driver to take her from Victoria Island through three hours of go-slow traffic to Grandpa's house in Surulere. Just to fuss over what I ate for breakfast. As I gulp on perfume and get scratched by her lace wrapper, I know she loves me like the daughter she never had, which is why she lied to me about my mother. When you can get inside a person's heart and feel why she did hurtful things, it is easy to forgive. Besides, I am tired of anger. It takes too much energy.

She sits spilling over the armchair at the foot of the bed. When she heaves herself out and swallows my body in a hug, I think I wouldn't mind having her for a mattress. Past the lace, she is that comfortable, and her nickname Biggie suits her. I sit on the bed and she bends to peck my lips. If Auntie and my sisters could see me, they would fall on the ground and die from the sin. The thought makes me giggle and I peck her back. Kissing Auntie Biggie makes me feel I have something of my mother with me. They came out of the same body. Auntie Biggie has six boys but no daughter. I can be her daughter and she can be my mother.

"When you smile, you look just like your mother," Taye says, sitting beside me to put her arm around my shoulder. "Just like your mother!" Taye is the youngest of the trio and Grandpa's daughter by his fourth wife. I don't see why I should call her auntie when she is only four years older than I am. "Your mother was special. She treated everyone well, even the groundnut-sellers by the roadside."

"True," Auntie Biggie says to the others. "Esi behaves a lot like her mother." She settles back into the armchair and flashes her gold tooth at me. "But she doesn't dress as well. Your mother, when she stepped on the street, everyone stopped to look at her."

"What is wrong with my clothes?" I want very much to dress like my mother.

"De poor child," Auntie Yetunde says, shaking her head. "She doesn't even know."

I love her deep masculine voice, and the way she says *de* for *the*, but I'm confused. "I don't understand."

"Have you seen what de Lagosian girls are wearing?" she says. "Your clothes are not just old-fashioned, they are old. We don't want you to look like a pauper, *jo*! Look at Taye, how she dresses."

Taye smiles proudly. She has on a silvery lace wrapper, and her long legs perch on black-and-white platform shoes. She could be on the cover of *The Mirror*.

"Esi, you are a young sisi now, hee hee!" Auntie Biggie says. "Look at you with the big breasts." She reaches over and weighs my bosom in her hand. "Ah, my niece should look like a princess. A beautiful princess."

Taye raises jeweled fingers to her chin and says, "You know, sometimes she looks like a Negress."

"What's a Negress?" I ask.

"Negress . . . that's the female form of Negro, a black American. Have you seen how beautiful they look in that *Ebony* magazine?"

I don't know how I can look like the Negresses with their huge afros when my fluffy hair obeys the wind and looks as if I wrestled with someone.

Auntie Yetunde laughs, slapping cream on her arms. "Sisi Esi! Come on, get up and let's look at you."

I get up. They don't seem to notice I have mosquito legs and arms. They say nothing about my Chinese eyes and bony cheeks. Come to think of it, Auntie Biggie has the same Chinese eyes and narrow face.

"Let's get you some fine clothes," Taye says.

"That's right," Auntie Biggie says. "We are taking you shopping."

The door opens and Grandma pokes her almost bald head in. She wants to know what I want to eat. I am not used to people asking me what I want for breakfast, lunch, and supper, so I have to think for a moment. "I want eba and ewedu."

She shakes her head. "Ah, ah, you had that yesterday. Don't you want rice and stew?"

"No, Grandma."

"Okay ooh. What of supper?"

"Can I have dodo and akara?" I can never eat enough of fried plantain and the fried, spicy bean paste that we call kose in Ghana.

Auntie Biggie throws her arm out. "No need to worry about food. We're going shopping. If she gets hungry, we can buy her something."

"*Ó da*." Grandma smiles. "I'll send for dodo anyway." She closes the door behind her.

I wouldn't mind if I never went back to Ghana and Papa moved here so I can eat anything I want. Here, when we eat chicken, Grandma doesn't give me the lower legs with the toenails sticking out in all directions and nothing but gristle on it, which is what Auntie believes is best for growing children. In Nigeria, I get the real meat. Also, my aunties can decide how to spend money, not like Auntie, who has to ask Papa for money to buy onions. Auntie Biggie's husband owns a shoe factory and she has the right to his money. Plus she has her own money Grandpa gave her when she got married. Auntie Yetunde boasts that she makes more money than my uncle: "I make his one-month pay in a day!" She sells Afro Sheen products to traders so women can straighten or Jerry-curl their hair the way the Negresses do in America. I am not sure I like that, to be honest. Taye is headed for the university, after which she will earn as much money as her boyfriend. I want to be like them when I'm full-grown—have money of my own, not ask for money like a child asks for pocket money.

The three aunties take me shopping. I think of them as *auntsketeers* the way they haggle with the sellers and are ready to fight anyone who cheats them. They throw away my copper earrings, fasten gold chains around my neck, and slide three gold bangles on each of my wrists. I worry about losing the gold, but I like how the bangles clink when I move my arms. I stand in front of the *auntsketeers* in my white lace blouse, red bellbottoms, and platform shoes the color of curry. Five and a half inches high, I love it!

"Now you can look beautiful when you go to de cinema with your boyfriend," Auntie Yetunde says. How easily the bad words slide out of her mouth. Papa would be angry to hear her talking like that.

"I don't have a boyfriend."

"You wait," Auntie Biggie says, "you'll get one, a fine man who will marry you."

"Ah no," Taye says. "I won't allow it. She is too young!"

Auntie Yetunde waves her off. "No, she's not. Let me tell you about my . . ."

"Can I go outside?" I don't want to talk about marriage. I want to clump around the street in my new height.

"Of course, my dear!" Auntie Biggie says.

I clop onto the corridor where Kwabena is bouncing a ball. His eyes fly open. "You look so silly!" I push him and stumble. Platform shoes aren't fun when you want to chase your brother and hit him. I think I'll save them for when I go to parties.

My favorite thing to do after supper is follow Taye around as she entertains men who can't get enough of admiring her copper-colored skin, and the confident way she throws her head back and laughs. When she does that, you can see how lovely her neck is, how it's slender like a flower's stem.

One night, I find her standing, facing three men sitting on the low wall of the downstairs veranda that looks out onto Rosamond Street. Lights from ground-level stores glow pink, blue, yellow, and green. Music blares. When she sees me, she calls, "Esi, come and greet!"

The men laugh, swigging from bottles of Guinness. I don't know how they can stand to swallow the black foamy drink— Uncle Bola let me taste it once. It was so bitter I spat it out.

The man in the middle has his shirt unbuttoned to show the hair on his chest, which makes me want to touch it though I don't do such things ever since Yaw tried to push inside me and Auntie made me sit on hot water. I only like to look.

"This is Esi, my niece," Taye says with her arm around my shoulder. I shake hands from right to left like I'm supposed to, but the man in the middle swallows my hand in his and won't let go. I don't know what to do. Taye laughs. "Meet Kayode. He lives here, in the room facing the back stairs."

If only he'll let go of my hand instead of curving his finger into my palm and stroking it in that ticklish manner boys do when they like a girl for other things than playing Ludo. I should be angry but a hot itch grows in my armpit and it's hard to breathe when I look at his big eyes. Mine grow weak and fall to the cracked cement floor.

"She is beautiful," he says. "Hey, come on, look up. Look at me . . ."

I don't want to.

"I'm going to marry you, little girl."

The men laugh, and one says, "Hey, Hijacker, lay off the small girl!"

"Go way you," Kayode says. "I'm going to marry her."

I pull my hand away and run off as their laughter follows me.

That's how it goes after that. Whenever I see Kayode and he says, "Hello, my wife," I run away. He tries to catch me and I laugh when he can't. Sometimes he looks so pitiful I let him catch up to me and buy me Coca-Cola from the bar on the ground floor. On days he doesn't chase me, I get a hollow feeling in my stomach and I look for him. Sometimes I wait on the balcony and watch him walk down the street. I like how his chest and small waist make him resemble a triangle on long legs. I no longer mind when he calls me his wife.

"Do you have a writing pad?" I ask Taye because Kayode's face keeps sliding onto the television and I don't want to watch *Village Headmaster*.

"Yes," she says, her eyes still fixed on the screen.

"Can I have it? I want to write a letter."

She turns to me. "Do you want to write to your father?"

"Uhm, yes."

"Wait a minute." I smile as she clumps down the corridor on her high heels. She returns and hands me a writing pad with flowers swirling at the corners.

I sit at the dining table and begin a letter to Kayode, calling him darling. I pause for a moment, chewing the end of my pen, because I no longer want to write biblical words. After thinking hard, I string my own words together, a fine work of poetry. Then I fold the letter carefully and slip out.

Taye calls after me. "Don't you want an envelope?"

I pretend not to hear and race downstairs to wait for Kayode. As soon as I see him step out of a taxi, I run and push the letter into his hand and run back upstairs to the parlor.

"What happened to your letter?" Taye asks. "Do you want me to post it for you?"

"Erm . . . no." Why can't she leave me alone? I must hole up somewhere. "I'll be back in a minute," I say. The bathroom is a good place. No one will bother me there unless someone needs to go badly. I slip in there and sit on the toilet, watching a spider moving slowly across the ceramic tiles. I remain there until I am sure Kayode has already read my letter. I wash my hands and open the door. I tip-toe through the corridor, escaping Taye, who is still watching the show. Down the stairs I go.

Ah, there he is, facing two friends, my letter unfolded in his hand. The way his mouth is moving, he must be reading it to them. Why are they laughing? He turns his head and sees me.

"That's my wife!" He is laughing. Laughing at me. My cheeks grow heavy with shame. I try to run back upstairs but he catches me by the waist, from behind. I'm so upset I am shaking. He turns me to face him, still laughing. "Hey, what's wrong?"

"You and your friends," I sniffle. "You are laughing at me."

He is trying to hold his cheeks together, but the laughter

continues to escape him. "Well, your letter was er, original . . . uhm . . . Love is like music in heaven, eh?" My ears burn with anger. I try to pull away, but he holds on. "You will remember me in your dreams? Send me kisses by air transmission? I like that."

"Leave me alone. You think I'm a little girl, but I'm not, I'm grown!"

His eyes tease me. "How old are you?"

"I am sixteen." Well, it will be true. Eventually.

"Sixteen?" He pulls back. The laughter disappears. "I thought you were younger."

"Well, you're wrong!" The way he looks at me makes me tremble, and I feel dizzy when he lifts my chin up with his finger.

"All this time? You're sixteen? I've been wanting to . . . I mean . . ." He looks into my eyes for a long time. Then he bends down and brushes his lips against mine. It is very different from kissing Rose at Mmofraturo because somehow, he gets my mouth to open and I taste his spicy tongue. I press closer.

"Take it easy, girl." He laughs softly. "Here, this is how it's done."

I follow his movements, forgetting where I am. I'm roaming hotly in his mouth when a voice shouts, "Esi!"

Oh no. I jerk away. Taye has both hands on her hips, and fiery eyes. "What are you doing?"

"Kissing," Kayode says as if he can't believe she would ask such a question. "Leave us alone, Taye, she's my girlfriend now."

Taye pulls on my arm, pushes herself between us and turns to Kayode. "She's too young for you! Do you know how old she is?"

"Yes. She's sixteen. That's old enough."

Taye turns around to me. "Esi, I need you to go upstairs and get me my hand lotion."

"But—"

"It's okay, Esi," Kayode says. "Don't be disrespectful."

The floor has turned into sand under me, I stumble away. I manage to take the steps two at a time, find the lotion, and hurry back but already Kayode has his arms crossed over his chest, and the smile is gone from his eyes.

"How old are you, Esi?" he asks in a schoolteacher's voice.

I whisper, "Fourteen . . . But I'm going to be fifteen in two months."

"You are fourteen?" He covers his open mouth with his hand and all I can do is nod my shame. He shakes his head. "You lied to me. My God, you are too young! I cannot believe it, I am almost nineteen! I've been fooling around with a little girl! I'm sorry, but it is over." He brushes his palms against each other to make his point.

I am desperate. "It's not against the law?"

"What law? It's not against our laws. It's *my* law. Sixteen is my limit. You're too young." He turns away from me. Taye puts her arm around me, which is the last thing I want from her. I shake her off and run.

"It's for your own good, Esi!" she calls after me.

For my own good? Why do things done for my good have to hurt? I want to be miles away from both of them. I dart to the back of the house and crawl under the concrete staircase. I heave and gasp until I think I am going to die.

After my tears dry up, I crawl out, brushing the cobwebs off my arms and legs. I drag myself upstairs to find Auntie Biggie sitting in the cane couch on the balcony.

"Ah, there you are!" She flashes the gold tooth. "I was waiting to say bye to you before going home." I don't want to talk to her, but when I try to walk past her, she grabs my wrist. "Taye told me what happened. Don't mind that girl. Embarrassing you like that, ah, ah? You are young, yes, but it's all right to like men. You're developing, ha." I drop onto the couch and she squishes me deliciously against her, then kisses the top of my head. I move closer.

We stay like that for a while and it feels so safe that I ask the question I couldn't put to Papa. "Auntie Biggie, why didn't Mother come with Kwabena and me when we first went to Ghana? She cried so hard on the plane."

Auntie Biggie frowns, "You remember?"

"Yes. She didn't want us to leave her."

She sighs, stroking my hair. "Hmm, it's a bit complicated. You know, she was in Ghana with you. Before your brother Kwabena was born." I sit up because I didn't know. She nods slowly. "After Kwabena was born, she brought you both to Lagos for a visit. But she got ill, you see. And your Grandpa didn't want her to return to Ghana. The doctors kept admitting her to the hospital." She stops to search my face. "Do you really want to know?"

"I do."

Her arm around me goes slack, maybe from the weight of sadness. "She had a vein in her brain that blew up, kind of like a balloon. No one knew until it was too late. That's what killed her. The vein burst open and leaked blood and she died, right there in the hospital." In the soft light, her eyes shimmer with tears. I know mine shimmer too.

I touch her cheek. "I really like you, Auntie Biggie."

She laughs and squishes me again as her tears roll down. "It's more like love. You are my daughter now." I brush my eyes with the back of my hand. We have no more need for words, just the sweetness of it.

The next day Grandpa takes Kwabena and me to our home-town Abeokuta for a week, which is all it takes to make me realize I won't die if I don't see Kayode again. But when we return, Taye tells me we have been invited to his niece's birthday party.

"Kayode's niece?" I ask. "A children's party? I don't want to go."

"We all have to go," she says, spraying perfume behind her ears. "He is family."

"What?"

"Didn't you know? His aunt is one of your Grandpa's wives, so if we don't go it won't look good."

"He is not related by blood?"

"No."

Good. I would rather eat worms than have Kayode as family. Not that it matters, since he doesn't want me. Grandpa's driver drops us off at a street packed with so many cars it's almost impossible to pass through. The guests fall into two groups: adults and children. No one is in between like Kwabena and me. The way Taye flutters over to Auntie Yetunde and the other women, laughing and touching arms, you'd think she was as old as they. Kwabena and I have no choice but to join the children, mostly ten years and younger. Anyway, there is music playing, so I might as well dance away my troubles. Kwabena sits on the window ledge smiling at me.

"Come and let's dance," I say.

He shakes his head. "You know I don't like to dance."

Someone pokes me in the arm and I turn. It's my eight-year-old cousin Fidelia with the permanent pinkeye from the dust in the air or something.

"Uncle Kayode is calling you," she says.

I don't want to see *Uncle* Kayode. I don't need another scolding for having lied to him. I ignore her but she keeps pulling on my arm until I finally ask where he is.

"There," she points to the open door and turns to go, as if I'm supposed to follow her. Fine. I might as well find out what he wants and get it over and done with. I follow her and she stops in front of a door opposite. I take a deep breath and open it.

Kayode is sitting on the bed, leaning sideways against the wooden headboard. When he sees me, his teeth flash like the moon at night.

"Sit down," he says, patting the spot next to him.

I sit carefully, far from him.

He clears his throat and draws circles on the bed with his palm. I want him to give me the scolding and finish with it, but he seems to have trouble getting the words out. He opens his mouth, closes it and opens again. "You know . . . hmm. I—I don't know what you are doing to me. You are much too young, and yet . . . I don't know how to say this. Erm . . . I have fallen in love with you. I ought to have my head examined . . . I am in love with a fourteen-year-old, even if going on fifteen. Do you understand what I am saying to you?"

"I think so." His words bounce round my head, not quite penetrating.

"I'm going to wait for you to grow up."

"What does that mean?"

"I want to marry you when you grow up."

"Really?" I have never wanted to marry, but I want him.

"Come here," he says, arms open like wings. I hesitate. "Don't be afraid . . . I mean it. Come on. Please."

I uncoil myself and go to him as the wings close around me. His lips press warmly against my forehead. After a breathy silence, I ask. "Why do they call you Hijacker?"

He smiles. "Well, they say I like girls."

I frown. "I don't understand."

He pulls me tighter to him and sighs. "I never fell in love before. I used to look at my friends making fools of themselves over girls and think, I am incapable of love. So, I'd have a girl for a short time and lose interest just like that." He snaps his fingers. "I only knew how to talk a girl into being with me. But you? You're in my head all the time. I have never felt this way about any girl before. You're barely up to my shoulders!" He shakes his head. "Have you ever had a period?"

"Yes, many times."

"Oh my God, you are so young! I have to wait for you to grow up."

"But can we kiss, like before?"

"Oh yes, oh yes."

He urges my mouth open and I taste his spicy tongue again. I don't understand how the most disgusting thing in the world, another person's saliva, can taste like something you thirst for, how a man's hard bones can make you press closer and closer until you just want to melt into him and have him melt into you. But he says I'm too young to have his passenger, so we groan in desperation and when he pulls away there is a dark patch in front of his trousers. We're both so hungry for it but he insists he wants to wait until I'm older.

"Believe me, it's hard for me," he says in a thick voice.

I beg and beg but he still says no, stroking my cheek. "I want you to meet my sister one day," he says, stroking my cheek.

"You have a sister?"

"Yes, and brothers too. An older sister and three younger brothers."

My eyes fly open. "Where are they? How come you don't live with them?"

"My sister lives with her husband."

"What about your brothers?"

"They live with my father and their mother in Ilorin, another town."

"But where is your mother?"

"She died when I was five." He nods at my surprise. "You and I have a lot in common, you know. I know about your mother. Except I left my father's house when I was sixteen."

"Why?" I prop myself on my elbow. I can't imagine being on my own a year from now. "Was your father's wife wicked?"

He laughs, leaning in to kiss my lips. "No, not at all. She was my mother too." He shrugs comfortably. "It's not uncommon for boys to be on their own. We weren't rich, you know. I left home because I wanted to help take care of my brothers. I work in customs at the airport and I send them money every month." He pauses and then gives me a teasing smile. "I think that's why I liked girls a lot. They were the softness I needed to take off the hard edges of life. But I never wanted to attach myself. Until now."

I feel like warm bread. "Is it because I'm a virgin?"

He shakes his head, his brows coming together. "Not really. I think it's because you're raw. You see these Lagos girls? Most of them are about money. It's like a game. They play hard to get, we men pay hard to get them. Once, a girlfriend and I were waiting for a taxi when a man in a BMW stopped and asked her if she wanted a ride. She went with him."

"No!"

"Yes," he nods with irony. "But you, you haven't learned their ways yet. You're natural." He smiles, smoothing my brows. "You know, I laughed at your letter, but it touched me. You're like a person with no skin. Everything shows. You beg me to enter you, because you feel pleasure. It's intoxicating." The way he's looking at me makes me wet between my legs.

"What will happen when I go back to Ghana? I have only four days left."

He kisses my nose. "I'll write you every day."

I push against him, rubbing my legs together.

CHAPTER SiXTEEN

■ ■ ■ ■ ■ ■ ■ ■

K AYODE AND I sneak in kisses any chance we get and I want to
die when it's time to return to Ghana. The hot itch is like a
fever in my blood. Now I understand why Sister Mansa will risk
getting beaten just to relieve it. I don't understand why Auntie
Biggie hasn't returned to her husband in a week. She sleeps in
Grandma's room. Every morning, I run to knock on the door.
Though she always has a smile and kiss for me, she remains in
bed, sometimes until noon.

"Why don't you ever go home these days, Auntie Biggie?" I am
sitting on the edge of the bed, her hip warm against me.

She sighs, looking at her fingernails. "It's my husband. He
brought another woman to the house."

"What?!"

She is talking to her fingers. "I caught them."

"How could he do that?"

She smiles suddenly and looks at me. "I don't want to talk
about it. Now, what do you want to do today?"

"Well, I need to go and shop for provisions for school, but your
husband . . ."

"I don't want to talk about him, you hear?" My heart jumps. She has never shouted at me before. I don't know what to say. She smiles suddenly and her voice softens. "What is this about provisions? You want to shop for school?"

My heart calms down. "Yes." I won't bring up her husband again.

"Then let me go and bathe so we can go."

Bathe. She hasn't been doing much of that lately. Her normally perfumed smell has been replaced by a sour odor, the smell of curdled milk. I don't understand how she can spend so much time in bed, but I'm so relieved she is willing to get up that I focus on my shopping. Besides, I need provisions for school. In Ghana, prices have jumped off the roof, thanks to Acheampong's commandment that sayeth thou shalt not import any foreign goods.

I tell Auntie Biggie this includes what boarding school students need to survive at school: cans of corned beef, sardines, mackerel, luncheon meat. Acheampong's sermon, Operation Feed Yourself, blares daily from radios but no one listens anymore. By-force price controls have caused market women to hide their goods under their beds. They sell only to those who agree to pay higher and higher prices. We have a new word for that in Ghana: *kalabule*. Acheampong is too busy squashing monthly attempted coups to bother. Nsawam Prison is bursting with hundreds of political prisoners.

Though the food at Wesley Girls is better than at Mmofraturo, they give you barely enough to fill a mouse's belly. For yam, you get one slice plus a teaspoonful of tomato gravy so the yam doesn't sand your throat, plus a small piece of fish fried so hard it jumps off your plate when you try to cut it. The fish has earned the name agama lizard for its appearance. On days we eat plantain, it's the size of a banana. The beans are tasty though, never mind the weevils. You eat and thank God for the protein. Every meal is accompanied by a slice of overly sour kenkey that you'll save for later, if you're wise, because the hours between siesta and supper can be long. If you've run out of provisions, soaking the kenkey in a bowl of sugared water and adding canned milk, if you have it, can go a long way. Before every meal, I usually drink lots of water to fill my stomach.

This is just too much for Auntie Biggie. She packs my suitcases with tins of milk and sardines, Lux soap, Omo powder for washing my clothes. Auntie Yetunde supplies two jars of Afro Sheen pomade for my hair and Nivea to soften my skin. Grandma presents me with a twenty-karat gold-bead necklace that used to belong to my mother, and Taye gives me a bottle of Opium perfume. Kwabena gets his provisions too, plus new shoes and clothes. We also receive twenty naira each. It's as if we're leaving Nigeria and never coming back. Oh, those snobbish Been-tos at school—they should just wait. They'll admire my platform shoes and bellbottoms. I, too, am a Been-to. I've been to Nigeria, ha!

When we get to the airport in Ghana, no one bothers us at customs. I can let out my breath. After all, we have nothing to declare. The lady customs officer just uses a blue chalk to mark our suitcases to show we've been cleared, and it's off to the street to catch a taxi. Papa wrote to us that he has to attend a conference and can't pick us up. We have to take a taxi to the Ambassador Hotel where he is staying. We're not afraid because Ghanaian children can travel by themselves and no one will bother us.

At the curb, we hail a taxi, and just as we're loading our luggage into the trunk, I see a traffic policeman walking toward us. Why has he stopped waving and whistling to let pedestrians cross the road? Kwabena and the driver keep loading but I draw myself up to watch the policeman. *Crunch, crunch, crunch* he marches in his black cap, blue uniform with metal buttons glinting in the late afternoon sun. His skinny shadow leads him toward us. He crunches past me and points at our luggage. "Do you own all this?"

I turn to face him, chin raised in confidence. "Yes."

He licks his lip and I see the greed in his eyes when he tells us to open our bags.

"Why?" I ask.

He nods insistently, pointing. "Just open them."

Kwabena starts to unload but I say, "No, Kwabena, don't you dare!"

The driver doesn't know what to do, so he stands waiting. He knows he can always charge us more money for taking up his time. I don't care. I'd rather pay more money to him than give a bribe to the policeman. I've never paid one and don't intend to ever. I give the policeman the full glare of my fury. "You want us to open our suitcases so you can steal from us? No. We've been through customs." I point at the bags. "Do you see this mark? And this? This means we've been cleared. If you want provisions you can go to Nigeria and buy your own, but you won't steal from us!"

I can tell he isn't used to people refusing him and he doesn't know what to do. Ghanaian police don't carry guns, so I'm not afraid. He wags his finger in warning. "If you don't open your bags, I will arrest you."

"Arrest me! Take me to the police station!" I lug the last suitcase in and slam down the trunk lid. Kwabena has been standing quietly in his usual way of wishing I wouldn't cause such a to-do. If it were up to him he'd open the suitcases and be done with it but I tell him to get in, we're leaving. He sits beside the driver, who cranks up the engine. I get in the back behind Kwabena but before I can pull the door shut, the policeman grabs the handle, tells me to scoot over, and tells the driver to take us to the airport police station.

"Oh no," I say. "You are not getting a ride from me! You want to arrest me? Fine! I'll meet you at the police station. But this is *my* taxi. *I'm* paying for it, and I am not giving you a ride! You can hitchhike all the way, you hear?" I slam the door in his face and tell the driver to take us to the police station, yelling through the window, "Shame on you, stealing from children!"

The policeman sees another policeman on a motorbike, whistles for him, and hops on the back. That's how we are escorted down the avenue fringed with trees painted white from the roots to the stem. At the main road, we turn right, past the yellow police barracks with windows trimmed in dark blue, and then another right turn into the dusty red compound of the tiny, one-story police station. I tear out of the car, scattering chickens scratching for food. They squawk in protest. Kwabena hurries after me while the driver waits outside. The motorbike *vrooms* to a stop and the policeman hops off.

Inside the police station, a lone policewoman sits behind the wooden counter. She frowns. "What's the matter?"

I am so angry I talk like someone with asthma. "This . . . this man! He wants . . . he wants to bully us!"

"Take your time, lady," she says.

I breathe, swallowing. "We, we went through customs and when we were leaving the airport, he asked us to open our suitcases! He wants to steal from us! I won't let him!"

Her big breasts heave. "Young lady, I tell you, take your time."

The policeman gives her an earful about my refusing to obey and general disrespect.

"I don't trust him!"

The policewoman tells me to take it easy. "First of all, we're going to look inside your suitcases."

"I don't mind, Madam, I just don't want to be bullied." Why don't I throw in a "Do you know who I am?" That scares people, because for all they know you're related to General Somebody. But stop. She seems fair. Don't annoy her.

She asks us to bring in the suitcases, that she'll inspect them herself. Kwabena goes out and lugs them in, onto the cement floor.

She heaves up and walks out from behind the counter. She looks smart in her blue uniform: pencil skirt and matching jacket with the same metallic buttons as her male counterpart. I like the cap perched on her curly hair. She bends from the waist and starts rifling through the bags. It's getting dusky now, and as there's no electricity, we have to content ourselves with what pale light falls in from the open shutters. Finally, she straightens up, gives the policeman a pained look. "I have to say there is nothing here but personal effects. Provisions and toiletries."

Before I can throw him a smug smile, she turns to me. "Young lady, let me give you some advice. Even if you have gone through customs, any policeman can stop you. Even if you feel you haven't committed any crime." The policeman nods importantly as she explains further. "If he thinks there is something suspicious, he can ask you to open your bag. Next time, don't be so disrespectful."

I simmer down. After all, I have won. No one stole from us.

When we get back into the taxi, the driver is all smiles. "*Ei*, small lady, you are tough *ooo*. I tell you, this is what is going on in Ghana these days. Bribery is the only way to get anything."

Now that it's over, I'm actually shaking. I don't know if Papa will pat me on the head and smile because I refused to pay a bribe, or yell at me for getting arrested. It's best to say nothing. Kwabena agrees.

CHAPTER SEVENTEEN

A T SCHOOL THE happiest time is after supper, just before prep time when we receive letters. Kayode writes every week, even before I reply. I have so many letters that when I go home for Easter holidays, I pile them in the bottom of my trunk. The letters from others, I slide into a drawer by the dressing mirror. But now Papa has taken to snooping around the room I share with Sister Mansa and Crocodile Yaa, who is home for the holidays.

Anytime I go downstairs to bathe, I return to find him moving things on the dresser, lifting the mattress, or standing with his hand to his mouth as if he has lost something. I clutch my housecoat tightly around me. When he sees me, he stands straight, blinks quickly, clears his throat, and says, "All right. I see you need to get dressed." I close the door, not so hard as to have him yell at me, but loud enough to let him guess I'm not happy.

This morning, I come up the stairs after my bath and stop to glance at him. Good, he is slumped in his armchair by the radiogram. His one pop record is playing *Who do you think you are, Mr. Big Stuff?* Which is really a question I want to put to him. I look away quickly, cross the sitting room, and turn for the bedroom before he can ask me questions. Like why do my slippers slap loudly on the floor when I walk? Why do I have my hair flowing like a bride, and God almighty, hasn't he told me to wear a brassiere? I could tell him I am angry because he lied about my mother or because he didn't teach me how to drive on my birthday like he promised—he has suddenly decided it's not fair for me to drive when my older sisters can't—but I don't understand my own self. Sometimes I feel as if there's an insect under my dress biting me and I want to slap something. The air in our house has grown thicker and harder to suck in. I can't wait to return to school.

I'm struggling with the zipper on the back of my dress when Papa yells my name in that you're-in-trouble voice, "Esi Agyekum, you come here this instant!" I go out to find him sitting with opened letters and envelopes scattered on his lap, which I didn't notice earlier. He gives me the wagging finger. "You've become a very bad girl. You've been receiving letters from boys."

I'm too stricken to answer. It has been years since he called me a tramp. He picks up a card edged with flowers. "Who is Stephen? Why does he sign your birthday card with love?"

That sets my heart banging in my chest. "How dare you read my letters! He is just a friend! Someone I met at a voluntary work camp in Cape Coast!"

My fury stops him for a moment. Then he drops the card into his lap and holds up a letter in my face. "And your cousin Kweku? How could your own cousin call you darling?"

"He calls me all sorts of things! What is wrong with that? Why do you have to think dirty things?"

He is struck silent.

I stumble over the coffee table as I run to my room. I yank at the drawer holding the rest of my letters. It's stuck. I shake, yank until it bumps out and hits my foot. The pain makes me angrier. I lift the drawer with both hands, rush out, and turn it over his lap, shaking out letters. Somewhere a shrill voice warns me I'm going too far, but the rage bangs in my chest. "You want more letters? Read them! Read them all!" Letters fly off his lap, slide onto the linoleum. I fall on my knees, grab them, and throw them onto his lap. They keep falling and I keep tossing them up until I'm shaking and sobbing. Papa doesn't speak. My anger is so big I don't know what to do with it, so I run and throw myself on the bed. My sisters come crashing through the door.

"Esi, have you no respect?" Sister Mansa says. "Your own father, and you talk to him that way?"

Sister Crocodile Jaws sucks her teeth and spits out, "Bad child! The trouble with you is you're spoiled, rotten as a fart. What you need is someone to whip you with a cane and teach you wisdom!" She slaps the side of her thigh to show me.

I spring up to my knees, fists clenched. "Give me lashes? Let's see you try, Sister. I'm not so little now. You touch me and I'll fight you back, you hear?"

"Disrespectful child. You think your eyes are open to civilization? One day your eyes will open so wide you'll wish a goat good morning, like a mad person!"

"I'd rather greet a goat than talk to you!"

She shakes her head, raises her hand to my face. I'm ready. If she hits me, I'll hit her back. She looks at me for a long time, then her hand drops to her side and she stomps out of the room. Sister Mansa puts her hand to her open mouth. She stares, then shakes her head. "*Ei!* Esi? Is that how you are?"

I turn my back to her. She leaves without closing the door, so I get up and slam it.

I sit at the edge of the bed. My feet *tap-tap-tap-tap* the polished red floor. I close and open my fists. I punch the bed. Get up. Sit down. The frogs should have changed me into a man, really. Women are so disloyal! No one cares that I may have stopped Papa from reading their letters. The only thing they can see is my disrespect. At Wesley Girls we've been learning about the women's liberation movement, how women in America and England behind the corn are fighting to be treated the same way as people treat men. I know what is fair. If Papa won't open Kwabena's letters then he shouldn't open mine or my sisters'. But how can I fight when my sisters are part of the problem, when girls join forces with men?

No man ever grabs a girl to smear ginger or pepper in her pawpaw or make her bottom cook on steaming water. No man in Nigeria or anywhere else pins a girl down and uses a razor blade to saw off her clitoris, that sweet stump in her vagina to please a man. I learned about that too at school. No Chinese man crushes his daughter's feet with a stone, folds them under, and ties them up so the daughter can stumble about to make a man feel stronger. It's always a female. Why do we women act as if men are so frail we need to hurt ourselves to make them look strong? And look at how Auntie always gives the best meat to Papa and gives us the bones? Then they get angry when Papa gives me more meat. Oh, I'm so tired of it all!

Long after I have simmered down, I'm surprised by the clear ticking of the grandfather clock. Papa's music has stopped but he hasn't changed the record. I creep out of the bedroom and see him still sitting where I left him with my letters all around him. His head hangs down. He looks collapsed, as if someone crushed his bones. Now I want to fall on my knees and beg him to forgive me for being such a horrible daughter. But I can't find the words. I can do nothing but slink back into my bedroom and shut the door with a hushed click.

CHAPTER EiGHTEEN

WANT TO BE a good daughter. Pour Papa a glass of ice water to cool his tongue. Beg to scratch the itch off his back. For Auntie, I want to be the girl who fans the coal pot while singing, and clap my hands at the thought of grinding pepper on the stone. But it's hard when I watch how she allows Papa to squash her down.

Every morning after we wash the breakfast plates, she asks him for money so she can walk to the market and get what we need to cook the afternoon and evening meals. She crunches up the stairs and makes a good show of straightening up the tablecloth while her eyes move to Papa and the table like the grandfather clock's pendulum. Papa's face stays hidden behind his newspaper. Auntie's entrance disturbs him little more than the air around him. Her mouth twitches into different shapes before it makes the sound, "*Eee.*" It's supposed to be *dee*, like dearie or darling that Papa insists she call him, but she can't urge the word out of her mouth, so she winds up with *eee*. Which she repeats a little louder because Papa won't answer. She tugs at her cloth, rubs it.

"What is it?" Papa says without turning his head.

"I—I am going to the market."

The newspaper lowers. "I see. You need money."

"Yes." Auntie's face is that of a schoolchild standing before a teacher wielding a cane.

He shifts to his side, digs around in his pocket, and comes up with some bills.

"It's, it's not enough," Auntie says in her eight-year-old voice.

Papa delivers the lesson: "You have to know how to manage money. You are too wasteful. Do you think I own a money tree?" On and on. Finally, he pulls a few more notes out of his pocket. When she thanks him, the only thing missing is the schoolgirl's curtsy. I give him a biting look because I know he hands out money to any stranger who asks him the same way I give toffee to little children who knock on our door at Christmas.

Auntie has been trying to make money for herself like any self-respecting Asante woman. Was it not Yaa Asantewa, an Asante princess, who led male soldiers into battle against the British? The only problem is Auntie has as much luck for making money as a tomato. At Kibi, she sewed children's clothes to sell, but people bought them on loan and never paid her. Now she has been running a store in the large room downstairs facing the street. Again, people buy and promise to pay later, and then they stay away. She has no choice but to go out chasing those who owe her.

One day she leaves the house for town and comes home laughing, which makes Papa twitch the way a teacher does when students seem too rowdy. Surely, she has been up to something bad. He is in one of the moods that fall on him when he gets tired from sitting upstairs while we wash his handkerchiefs, polish his shoes, and take him his meals. When that happens, he descends mightily down the stairs. The bottom step is as near to the kitchen as he can come without the risk of turning into a *kɔtɔbenkum*, a man who acts like a woman.

Now he rests his elbows on the banister under the shade of

the aluminum roof covering the staircase. From the coolness of his shelter, he cuts his eyes around to make sure everyone is busy washing plates or something. That's my cue to go hide in the library, the two rooms by the store he has filled with books, a settee, and two armchairs for Kwabena and me. The library, which I like to think of as mine alone because I'm the only one who uses it, has become pepper in my sisters' eyes because it leaves us with only the three bedrooms plus the study upstairs. I am too spoiled, they think, especially because it's where I hide when I don't want to grind something in the kitchen.

I want to disappear into the library, but the way Auntie is dragging a stool to the middle of the compound, right under Papa's angry face, troubles me, so I wait. Through the kitchen's screen door, I can see my sisters banging pots about in an attempt to look busy.

Auntie settles comfortably on her stool, unzips her bag, straightens crumpled cedi notes, and counts them into her lap. A smile dances around her lips.

"I saw Mr. Asare at Bom Dwen," she says into her lap though she's talking to Papa. "He says I should greet you for him."

If she could see the way Papa's mouth is twitching, she wouldn't sit there calmly counting her money. Oh no, here it comes. Down he flies, bends, and slaps her cheek, *kpaa*! Her head jerks up. There is a child's hurt look in her watery eyes, and her palm lifts to her cheek.

Papa pants with rage. "Bom Dwen? A bar? What were you doing there? Have you seen me ever go sit and drink at that place?"

Auntie's chin quivers. She tries to explain. "I never go there. I only went to collect a debt."

"How did someone at Bom Dwen come to owe you money, unless you went there?" Up flies his hand and whacks her other cheek. Colonel Ignatius could be holding a gun to my chest, I don't care. I rush and shove myself between them. I'm nose to chin with Papa since he never made it up to five feet and I am five three.

"How dare you hit her!" Papa rears back from my words as if I've hit him. "What has she done so terrible you have to hit her? She is not your slave! Don't you hit her again or . . . or else!" I don't know what or else, but I know if he lifts his hand again, he'd have to knock me down. We stare at each other, two animals ready to charge. Sweat runs down from my armpits. Suddenly, he turns and goes up, his slippers crunching the concrete steps. The screen door at the top slams after him.

I turn around to the cowering Auntie whose chin rests in both hands. I bend down and put my arms around her, a first time for me. "Why do you just sit there and receive his slaps? Why don't you protest? If my husband hits me, I'll not stand for it!"

She shrinks farther into her chair and mumbles, "A man who hits me, I don't respect him." Now I want to slap her myself. Disrespecting someone when he doesn't have an inkling of the disrespect is useless. She should tell it to him. Tell him she won't take it anymore, but all she says is "It is nothing, I just won't mind him" and stares at the air. I don't know what to do. You'd think she wasn't the woman who took charge when I found out Mother had died. While Papa stood there looking useless, she was the one who made him send me and Kwabena to Nigeria. How can she now wilt like that?

From behind me, Sister Mansa comes out of the kitchen. She puts her hand on my shoulder and I turn, ready to snap at her, but the way she is smiling at me feels better than honey oozing down my throat.

SOMETHING IS WRONG with Sister Mansa. She sits on the kitchen stool with her hand supporting her cheek and her mouth shut. When I ask her what's wrong, she won't tell me. She won't eat, won't smile, won't do anything until Papa sticks his head out of the upstairs bedroom window and bellows, "Mansa, come here!" Without answering, she jumps to her feet and runs up the stairs, so I race after her.

Papa is holding a white paper, obviously an open letter. His lips become one line when he sees me. He tells Mansa to follow him to the balcony. I hover near the door. Papa leans over the balcony with the paper in his hand. Sister Mansa stands a little behind him, away from slapping distance.

"What is this letter you have written me?" he asks. "Is it true? You have a man who wants to marry you?"

Sister Mansa is shaking but she says, "Papa, please, yes."

Papa turns around, a meditative look on his face. "Why, that is good news. A woman's glory is her husband. If you have found a man, then it's very good news." You can tell Sister Mansa can't believe it the way her eyes are round. Papa tells her to have the man's family come see him. She still doesn't move. Papa has to repeat himself before she says Yes, Papa.

I don't believe it myself. I run down to the kitchen to wait for her. As soon as she comes downstairs, I attack her. "You're getting married?"

"Yes." Her body has quieted down now.

"But why?"

"Why not? I'm not going to the university. I don't have your brain. I never passed the Common Entrance, and Papa won't let me go to a catering school. He says he won't pay for me to learn to cook when I can cook at home. I have nothing to do except stay in that kiosk in front of the house selling lotto tickets. Everyone knows that's work for someone who couldn't finish school, oh, the shame! If I don't get married, I won't have any glory." She drags a stool and sinks onto it. "And there is another reason: I'm with child."

"What? You're pregnant?"

She nods.

"What? Who . . . who did it?"

"He lives down the road. Haven't you seen me walking with him? He's the one I've been visiting when you can't find me." She allows herself a smile.

My head hurts. It's true I have seen her walking with a man whenever Papa travels but did she have to open her legs for him? "Why did you let him inside you?"

"What do you think? A girl gets lonely." That smile again.

"But . . . Are you sure he is a good man?"

"Yes. He is an S.U. man, you know, Scripture Union."

"A born-again Christian! And he slept with you before coming to perform the rights for you?"

She laughs up at me. "Oh, Esi, you *paa*, you have these ideas. It's Wesley Girls that has confused you. Anyway, can you imagine what would happen if Papa found out I was pregnant without marriage? Now he won't mind when my stomach grows round."

I pinch my lips together because I know she is right. She tells me the man lives at Benso, which is such a tiny village people have to go to the one pipe stand to pump water into buckets they carry on their heads for use at home. I want to see this man who has entered my sister, who is going to remove her from home. From me.

I get my chance when, after our lunch, he comes to visit because Sister Mansa sent for him. From the side, his head could be a question mark sitting on top of the body moving up the stairs to face Papa. I know I should like how his eyes shine like black glass, how white his teeth flash when he turns to smile at me, but I fold my arms over my chest and refuse to return his smile. I know Papa will have Sister Mansa serve him beer and rejoice at her coming glory. The best thing is to waylay him so I can get answers to the question mark of his head. I hang around the front of the house waiting.

It's a good thing Sister Mansa now wants to appear the un-touched girl by not accompanying him outside, because as soon as he emerges alone, I get so close to his face he has to back up against the wall of Auntie's store.

"Why did you give my sister a belly?"

The question mark stiffens. His mouth opens in a nervous smile and I see how his teeth are so crowded some get out of line.

"It's normal, isn't it, for a man and a woman?" That's what he says to me.

"But you're supposed to be a Christian. Isn't fornication a sin?"

His arms fold over his chest and the smile fades. "Look, you're young. This isn't your business."

"Yes, it is! She is my sister, and you made her sin. Fornication is a sin!" My arms are rigid and I'm trying not to stamp my foot. I don't like that I'm being a Pharisee. Kayode and I did everything except him penetrating me but I can't help it.

"I know what the Bible says," he explains calmly, "but we have our own tradition. What if the woman can't birth a child after you marry her? Sometimes the worry about the ceremony can stop her from getting pregnant. This way, she's set. Many women are usu-ally three months pregnant before the wedding, you know."

I shake my head. "But, don't you love her?"

"Of course, I do."

"So why should it matter if she can birth or not birth?"

He laughs. "You're young, so you don't understand. Listen, I've got to go home now. We can talk some more later."

And he walks off.

Hey, Mister, I want to talk some more now, not later. I'm so tired of everyone clucking on about how I'm too young to understand anything. If they would make sense to me, I would understand.

I hurry after him and stick to his side. I pour into his ears how much I hate hypocrisy. "Because that's what you are, a hypocrite.

Just like all grown-ups! They tell you to behave a certain way and you find out that no one believes what they tell you!"

We get into a lively debate as we drift past goats bleating, hens pecking, and women washing by the side of the narrow road. We descend down a hill and turn onto a muddy path before landing in a house crowned with a rusty tin roof. Only a little better than a house in Zongo. It is a thick square around earth sprouting weeds, where women are cooking on coal pots. He leads me into a room the size of a pantry and tells me it's all he has—other tenants occupy the other rooms. Though his room is neat with a white sheet on the hard-looking bed, I stand in the middle and glance around. "Where is the bathroom? Where is the kitchen?"

He gestures outside. "We cook outside. We wash in a common bathhouse."

I blink. "You share a bathroom with other people?" Here is what's strange. If Kayode lived here I wouldn't care, and I shouldn't look down on anybody, but I feel a heat rise in my chest when I picture Sister Mansa in a tin bathhouse with a bucket, where strangers wash themselves. "My sister is not going to live in this house, you hear? She will not leave us!"

I run all the way home, shut myself in the bedroom.

CHAPTER NiNETEEN

T HEY MARRIED WHILE I was at school and I came home to
find the question mark living with us, and because they need
their own space, I have lost my library. It could be worse. Sister
Mansa could move away the way Sister Crocodile has. Not that
I'm missing the latter.

Sister Mansa gave birth to a baby boy and when he was three
months old, the family had an outdooring ceremony to introduce
the baby to the community. My new brother slid his arm around
my waist and we moved to the music by Prince Nico thumping from
Papa's radiogram, telling a woman not to cry if she can't have a
baby:

> If you no get pikin, make you no cry because you no get am
> If you get pikin, make you no laugh the people wey no get,
> God's time is the best, opportunity knocks but once in this
> wo-or-or-or-ld.

And when I danced with other men, Kwabena, now a born-
again Christian himself, gripped the balcony banister behind me

and prayed loudly above the music: "Oh God, make her stop! Make her stop her sinful ways!"

I won't stop, and I won't tell Papa about my sinful ways with Kayode until I'm ready to get married. Papa says the word for a lady, *akatasia*, means *kata wo ho sie*. Cover to hide yourself. No keeping company with boys for no reason, and no loitering on the street unless you have business being there. Well, I don't want to cover myself and hide from Kayode. I'd rather uncover for him, but he won't break my passage because he says I'm still young at sixteen, even if I have passed my O Level exams. He carries me over muddy puddles. He fries plantains for me and washes my clothes and doesn't mind when his friends laugh that he is a fool over a girl. Because of that I stay away from other men. That's what I tell Auntie Yetunde when I go to Nigeria and Auntie Biggie is in bed as usual.

"You are too faithful," Auntie Yetunde says. She is dressed in a traditional buba top with a wide, oval neckline and big, airy sleeves like bells. She fusses with her head kerchief, saying, "When I met your uncle, I was seeing five other men."

Five men! She stands in front of the mirror, going over her cheeks with a powder puff. When she smiles, her teeth are white and even. But five men?

"I thought you were a virgin when you met Uncle Bola."

"Yes, I was." She draws purple lipstick over her meaty lips. "I said I was seeing five other men. I didn't say I was sleeping with them." She presses her lips together and rolls them forward and backward with a smack. "Ask your uncle, I was a vargin." That's the way she speaks. *Thirsty* is *tharsty* and *first* is *farst*.

"But it's not right to go to the cinema or the seaside with another man." I stand behind her so she can witness my horror from the mirror. "I don't want to sleep with any man."

"You can go out with men without sleeping with them. Is that not what you are doing with Kayode?"

"But he is different. What if the men want to have my body as a thank-you-for-taking-me-out? I won't like that."

Her big eyes laugh at me in the mirror.

"Then you will tease them. You will promise, but you don't give." She shrugs and the buba slides off her shoulder. "You can play with them a little bit. Do you remember de young man who came here for his supply of Afro Sheen? He wants to take you to de cinema. Why don't you go with him? You want to get to know other men before you marry. By de way, you are still a vargin?"

"Yes."

She turns to stare as if I've turned into a creature she doesn't recognize. "What is wrong with you?"

"I'm afraid." Wesley Girls has taught me that sex belongs only in marriage because that's what God says, and also you can get pregnant.

"So? Use contraceptives, you know abo't that, don't you?" She marches to her wooden dresser and produces a box of pills. "This, this is Ovum Tharty. This is what you should be using." She tosses the box onto the bed, reaches for a bottle of perfume, and dabs at her ears and neck.

"So, how come you have eight children when you wanted only four? This Ovum Thirty must not be good."

She shrugs. "I forget to take de pills sometimes."

"Well then, why don't you just stop doing it with Uncle Bola?"

A loud cackle erupts from her. "You try it an' tell me if you can stop."

When she slips her sunglasses on her tiny nose, an amazed smile spreads over her face, as if she can't believe her own loveliness. "Hello dear!" she says to her reflection. Then she slings her purse over her shoulder, grabs her keys, and says, "I'm off to de store in Lagos. Have fun."

Oh Awurade, what Papa would say if he could hear her!

I find Kayode downstairs in his room. He is dressed to go out and is reaching for his briefcase. Without wasting time, I tell him. "I want to go to the cinema tomorrow with Auntie Yetunde's client."

He stands still and the smile vanishes from his face. "You want to go to the cinema."

"Yes."

"Fine. I'll take you myself." The briefcase is now on the floor.

"But I thought you were traveling to visit your family tomorrow."

"The trip is off. You want to go to the cinema? I will take you myself. You're not going with another man, you hear?"

"But he asked Auntie Yetunde if he could take me out."

"Listen, you don't know men. I know you've probably kissed other men in Ghana. I've intentionally never questioned you. I felt you needed to satisfy some curiosity. But you're not fourteen anymore. You're sixteen. You're growing. You can't just go out with any man who asks you. This man, do you even know him?"

I laugh. "I don't. He's like a shadow. I don't even remember what he looks like."

Kayode sits down on the bed, his hand over his heart. "I thought you were attracted to him."

"I'm attracted to you," I say, touching his hair.

He catches my hand and pulls me onto his lap. "I'm jealous, that's the truth. I can't stand the thought of another man touching you."

"So why won't you enter me? Auntie Yetunde has been talking to me about contraceptives."

He laughs, pressing his lips on my forehead. "You're too young for sex."

But the fever is raging within me and I don't know how much longer I can wait.

AFTER THE O LEVELS, I do two years of Sixth Form, studying French, English Literature, and Economics. Only a few weeks to go and if I pass the A Levels, I'll graduate and enter the university. I write to Kayode that I don't want to be an ambassador just to have people call me Excellency. It's madness to do anything involving heads of state when said heads can be removed by soldiers whenever they feel like it. What's more, anytime someone takes over the government, that person sacks everyone from their positions and replaces them with his own people. I don't want someone to kick me out of office. So much has happened in Ghana it's enough to make me dizzy. Scary new words slap our ears daily: Runaway inflation. Failed price control. Black market. Corruption. Smuggling of gold, cocoa. All manner of evil running rampant.

Acheampong tried every trick: reshuffle the cabinet, bring in the commanders of all the military services, even the Inspector General of police. That illustrious regime deserved a new name, the Supreme Military Council. Redemption was laid aside. People rolled their eyes as they continued to line up for milk and soap. Acheampong promoted himself to General and another inspiration hit him: Form yet another new government! Brilliant, truly inspired, a Union Government to include a farmer, a lawyer, a shoemaker, soldiers, every entity! A government "of the people, for the people, and by the people"!

Yawn.

We listened to news of university students' riots, the strikes of professionals and hey presto, General Ignatius Kutu the pot was overturned like Papa said. Enter the Supreme Military Council II, and the purge went on. In the end, like a runner out of his last breath, the SMC II flung itself down, lifted the ban on political parties, and set a date for elections come June 1979.

Now people are campaigning with a frenzy. Even General Afrifa of the Nkrumah coup has roused himself from his farm to stand for something. I'm not in a hurry to enter this adult world where people are always ready to knock someone down. I keep my mind on my books.

My friend Akosua has invited me to travel home with her and spend two weeks in Accra. We plan to have a grand time. We'll taste our first glass of wine and learn to ride horses on the beach. Maybe we'll even experience the darkened cave of a disco for the first time and dance without a teacher watching. After that, I'll go home, then hop on the plane to see my Kayode. I can't wait for that. Maybe he'll go into me this time.

A day before my final paper, we're dancing around the dormitory in our drawers when a man's voice shatters the music on the radio: *This is Flight Lieutenant Jerry John Rawlings.*

He has taken over the country.

We huddle around the radio, not understanding this man with the foreign name and English accent ranting at us to be calm. The more he yells about calmness, the higher the waves rise inside me. No one has a clue what or who a flight lieutenant is.

The radio goes silent. We wait in clusters, biting our nails. A different voice pants out of the radio, "This is General . . . Everything is under control!" I didn't catch the name, but the coup has been stopped. Rawlings is going to be court-martialed. Phew. But wait! Sounds of rapid-fire crackers. Rawlings is back on the radio. He repeats, he has taken over. He repeats, we should stay calm. And then silence.

In the evening, we learn he has failed, been caught, and thrown into prison. But three days later, junior officers break him out of prison. Exit the Supreme Military Council number two, enter the Armed Forces Revolutionary Council, the AFRC. The young and the discontents have taken over. Rawlings, the Junior Jesus, has arisen to drive out the money-changers and greedy ones from the temple of Ghana's economy. *Whack, whack!* Down with the rich! Down with corruption! Down with poverty! Papa fires a panicky letter to me. Don't go with Akosua to Accra, he says. Soldiers are ransacking shops, roughing up people.

CHAPTER TWENTY

HOLLOW. AT HOME, on the balcony and hollow. The *vroom*ing of cars below, laughter from the roadside biscuit-seller and her buyers—all slide off me. I wonder what it feels like to be a corpse on a table, like the one they lay out in the dusty red compound to wail over. The same compound where they hold concert parties. The see-saw of life. I should have listened to Papa.

The balcony door claps shut behind me. I jump and whirl around, heart pounding. It's Papa stepping back from me, calling my name.

"Sorry," I mumble.

"It has been a week and you're still jumping," he says. "Didn't I tell you not to go to Accra?" His voice is hard, yet his eyes are soft. I know one part of him wants to hurl me over the balcony while the other wants to make me Milo like he used to, even if that has lost its magic. I have nothing to say for myself because he is right. He sighs. "Well, I am going to Bom Dwen. Do you want to come?" I tell him no thank you very much, sir. Sipping Pepsi in the sun at the outdoor bar won't erase what I saw in Accra.

Here at Swedru, our house stands on the fringe, in an area

that is more village than town. Ours is the only story building looking down on the rust-covered roofs of smaller houses squatting around the graveled clearing. There is no commotion in this place except for people squawking at the water pump, jostling for position, their metal buckets scraping the concrete. Such a sharp departure from Accra.

When I got there with Akosua, Accra shivered under a nervous fear. Armored tankers rumbled down the streets for no reason I could see. Food was scarce. You could buy the usual roasted plantains and groundnuts by the road, but people flung off their sleeping cloths while the sky was still black to line up for kenkey and yam. When Akosua and I decided to visit Makola Market, her mother lifted her voice so high it could be heard from the street. *Do you see these headlines?* She slapped newspaper after newspaper on the center table. *Daily Graphic, Ghanaian Times, The Mirror.* Bold headlines screamed, **Get Market Queens Off Our Backs! We'll Kill Hoarding! Army-Student Team Impounds Fish!** *The market is not safe; do you hear me? Don't go out at night, there's a curfew, do you hear?*

We tried to hear her. We tried until a lieutenant announced on the radio that Makola women had until six a.m. to collect all "nonperishable" wares from the market, that only food could be sold.

I said to Akosua, "How can the women get their things when they can't go out?" We were in bed, facing each other under a scratchy blanket that I had pushed down to my waist. Both of my hands supported my cheek on the pillow.

"It's on purpose," she whispered. "They want to make things hard for them."

We whispered back and forth, imagining the different scenes that would play out. Finally, we got the idea to sneak into the market to witness things for ourselves.

The sky still bore the smudged brown of dirty cotton wool

when we climbed out of the window and stopped a taxi. The driver, already sweating, said, "You girls are mad! Haven't you heard the news?" We told him we had and to just take us and stop shouting. "Fine," he said, peeling away from the roadside. "I'll get you to High Street and you can walk the rest of the way. I am not an idiot. I am not going to the market."

At High Street, he gripped the wheel and urged us to get out so he could drive off. We crossed the street and melted into crowds of women pushing toward the disk of the market. They grumbled in confusion and anger.

They tell us not to sell food at night! Sister, is it my fault I can't sell in the afternoon?

Don't mind them! Do they know what bribe we have to pay to get corn? If we sell at price control, we will get nothing!

What about the price of the bus, do they think about that?

Did you hear about the woman they shot? They removed her baby from her back, then they killed her for hoarding!

We pushed forward, others hemming us from behind, pressing on all sides. The smell of old cloth, camphor, and mint made me dizzy. Akosua said we could squeeze out of the crowd and return home if I wanted but I said no. Might as well forge ahead. Suddenly, we could go no farther. Cries of *why* and *what's going on* rose up. Stretching my neck in between shoulders, I noticed ropes barring the entrance to the market. Soldiers pointed guns, stepping forward. Nowhere to run.

The soldiers shouted, "Halt! Go back!"

There was shoving and pushing but no one tried to run away. This was Ghana, and these were women, mothers and grandmothers after all, in a land where everyone respected old age. No one believed anything bad would happen. A woman who appeared to be sixty pushed ahead, asking, "How are we supposed to get our wares? Please, give us way and let us pass." But a soldier shouted,

"Hey woman, where are you going?" and *wham*, the whip cut across her face and slammed her to the ground. I froze.

"Hold her down!" other soldiers yelled. They ripped off her blouse. She screamed. A soldier yanked out the rolled-up cedi notes tucked into her brassiere. Another tore at her cloth and rolled her onto her stomach, the better to strip her. Then they pulled off her drawers, the ultimate shaming of an older woman, revealing dimply buttocks. "You filthy hoarder! I'll teach you a lesson you'll never forget." The whipping began. Shock froze my mouth. Women shrieked, beating their way to escape. Arms tore at me as people pushed past me. An elbow caught my cheek. I was shoved about, separated from Akosua. Others surged forward shouting, as if to take on the soldiers. Sounds tore the air. *Boom-boom!* Like firecrackers.

Soldiers everywhere. Soldiers in tankers. Soldiers with sticks. Soldiers moving goods. And men, men who seldom sold at Makola. Rushing sideways like crabs, they hefted refrigerators, loaded them into trucks. They pulled out columns of textiles. They piled on pots and pans. Then an explosion ripped my ears. Thugs, women. Both fell. The earth rose and became thick dust. Then I was running, screaming and crashing into Akosua.

My mind retains nothing of the aftermath. Nothing of the scolding we probably received. Nothing of the journey back home. Nothing, except a fear of sudden noises and raging questions in my head. Why are market women blamed for shortages when rows of men higher up press down on them to pay bribes? Why is there no shame in attacking older women? Why is it that even a female journalist asks only that women not be stripped naked and flogged publicly? Why doesn't she question their assumed guilt? Those strong women, reduced to mush, their stores reduced to ashes and dust. I want to wipe their faces. I want to rub oil on their bodies and wrap them in silk.

Now home at Swedru, I smile at the woman trader across the street whose thatched-roof shed boasts of the usual biscuits, soap, milk, sugar, and essentials. This is a woman who once gave me gifts and begged to be my friend. It shames me that I wanted to spit at her for asking if I would spread myself open for her husband. Her actual words were "My husband wants to eat you." While I was wondering if she was sick in the brain, she added, "I know you must be a virgin, but don't be afraid. I swear to you, my husband's thing is very little." And just in case I wasn't convinced, she curved her forefinger to meet her thumb in a circle to represent a woman's hole. Then slid her other forefinger into the circle and moved it in and out, explaining, "When he enters me there's a lot of space around it, just like this. I can hardly feel him move inside me. It won't hurt, believe me." The madness of a woman begging a girl to sleep with her husband. Now I understand her desperation. She knew her husband wanted a younger, firmer girl, so she chose me rather than watch her husband choose a stranger she couldn't control, a rival who could steal him. In a land where soldiers can shoot women for growing money, what's a woman to do? This is why the things that used to shred my nerves now leave me calm.

Take Auntie for one, her large bottom always spread on the low kitchen stool as she stirs something steaming in an aluminum pot. I don't flick her off with my hand anymore. Sister Mansa is now a younger version of Auntie, banging pots around, doing her best to stop her son from getting too close to the crackling coal pot. Meanwhile her husband is invisible, but I can hear him whistling in their sitting room that used to be my library. Such an irritation. Such a strange relief that some things remain the same. In our split life, women occupy the kitchen while a man rules from the sitting room. *Where are the oranges? Adelaide, you are too slow! Bush woman!*

At least Auntie never has to feel the sting of Papa's hand on her cheek again. Not when I'm around. Not since I told him he had no right to do that. Otherwise no revolution has touched home, except in me. Now I sit downstairs in the kitchen and gladly fan the coal pot for Auntie, which makes her pat me on the shoulder. Sister Mansa smiles at me when I grind tomatoes on the stone for her. If I help Auntie and Sister Mansa, it's not because I accept my low position. It's because we are the same. We grow breasts and have mouths between our legs that can bleed. I want them to know I am with them.

There is a soft place inside me for Papa too, so I sit upstairs beside him in his kingdom, reading and hearing him grumble about the news. I'm the roving ambassador between downstairs and upstairs, softening his messages to Auntie, *I can help you gouge the seeds from the orange and take it to him, he has almost finished his fufu,* and covering for her when the soup is long coming, *That was a tough cut of meat the butcher gave her, it's not her fault.*

Some days, I watch the black-and-white television Papa has installed in the sitting room. Though I try, I can't tear my eyes from the army tanks rumbling on chains down the streets of Accra, soldiers rigid behind the big guns on top, the monarchs of all they survey. University students, laborers, clerks—every person who has felt cheated—raise placards, screaming as the soldiers roll by: "Let the blood flow!" "Vengeance for the shortages of food!" But it's not women they want this time. They want past leaders to pay.

One day, he materializes on the screen, Junior Jesus himself. Scrawny as a giant ant. In dark glasses, uniformed and capped. He stands on a platform at the Black Stars Square with Ghana flags blowing in the sea breeze. The crowd boils around as he growls, shouting louder than when Ghana beat Nigeria at football. He rouses them with a fiery speech and they scream again, "Let the blood flow! Firing squad for nation wreckers!" They punctuate his words with "J.J.! J.J.! Junior Jesus!" Despite the wickedness of Makola, a dart of excitement flames in me. This man who is not much older than a university boy, ruling the nation. Maybe a woman can rule one day.

Papa sits forward in his favorite chair, smiling and rubbing his hands, eyes fastened on the screen. "We have tried Nkrumah-ism, Busia-ism, Unigov. Maybe this one will work. Rawlings will clean house and give us a fresh start." He doesn't believe any blood will flow. He is almost childlike, shifting his bottom from side to side. He turns to me from where I'm resting my elbows on the settee and says, "Come, scratch my back for me." I slide behind him, curving my fingers over his bare skin. There are dips of muscle and smooth blubber. He guides me with "Higher . . . yes, that's it . . . *mmm* . . . a little to the left . . . yes, thank you . . . now move down . . . no . . . yes, right there, ah thank you! Your mother used to do that for me, wonderful woman! She even used to comb my hair, did you know that?"

I scratch with daughterly pride, only half listening to J.J.'s shouts because Papa is pleased with me. And then Junior Jesus declares some people have been tried and convicted of corruption. Acheampong and the border guard commander, Major General Utuka, will be executed by firing squad in the morning. In public. My fingers freeze. Papa leans away from me, jaws opening and closing fishlike. The crowd roars, "J.J.! J.J.!"

I whisper, "The firing squad at Teshie?"

Papa nods.

I stumble to my room and fling myself facedown. *Please, God, no.* I don't want anyone to die. Someone's father. Someone's husband. Sadness has taste, like quinine oozing down my throat. This Jesus isn't the resurrection and the life. He is the crucifixion and the dead.

In the morning, the BBC tells the tale. An army convoy including an ambulance sped to the beach where sandbags had been piled high behind the stakes we saw when Papa took us to Accra. Acheampong and Utuka were blindfolded and tied to the stakes at chest level and ankles. Then soldiers entered the tents and there followed a rapid series of popping sounds. The condemned slumped forward, their blood staining the sand red. What was the point of the ambulance? Just to carry the dead?

The people, ah, the people. The many-headed hydra. They have satisfied their thirst for blood. They let flow the blood of six more commanders, including General Afrifa of the Nkrumah coup who had the foolhardiness to remain visible. Rawlings said he actually tried to stem the blood flow, but he had aroused the hydra's lust and risked being gobbled himself. So, he gave in, like Pontius Pilate before the crucifixion of the Christ. But did he have to fly over the firing squad afterwards, wiggling the wings of his plane to the cheers of "J.J.! J.J.!"?

June 1979, bloodiest month in the history of Ghana, has ended.

Junior Jesus allowed elections to proceed, just as the SMC II had scheduled. Now he says there will be no more firing squads. We have a president who will be sworn in within three months. But J.J. will be watching, he warns, ready to step in if the government doesn't fill our pockets with money. We can watch out for his second coming, just like the Christ.

Now I know. The firing squad is not a place. It is the men who enter the open-ended tents and open fire. I can't think of a better time to escape Ghana. I am desperate for Nigeria. I want to get away from death and suckle life from Kayode.

CHAPTER TWENTY-ONE

A H, AH, MOVE away, *jo!*" says the rice-seller. "Do you want to fall in the soup?"

She is not happy Kayode and I are wrapped around each other, standing right next to her meat stew bubbling on the coal pot that she calls soup, blocking it from the view of potential buyers.

"Sorry!" I say, but still I cling to Kayode. I've been impatient all day because Grandma and Auntie Biggie met me at the airport, which meant I had to wait for him to return from work. I am desperate for pleasure. I want to erase the violation of the Makola women's bodies, the humiliation of all female bodies, starting with my own. This body of mine deserves goodness. I don't want it gingered, flogged, or torn apart. I want it stroked, massaged, licked, and worshipped. I want it thrilled into frenzied, frothing pleasure.

Kayode pulls me to the low wall enclosing the front veranda, facing the pharmacy's pink lights. I pay no mind to the street corner where small stores stick together like giant pigeonholes, each with a different color light, setting off rainbow hues. Despite the loud music blaring from a bar, Kayode's heartbeat is loudest in my ear. He sits as I face him, his hard thighs pressing me.

"You've grown taller," Kayode says though my head still fits under his chin. He rocks me from side to side, murmuring my name. I press into him and nibble his neck.

"Have you eaten?" he asks.

I tell him I haven't, so he buys me rice and stew from the rice-seller, who now smiles. I love her peppery stew and the pinkish brown northern rice she uses. Kayode leads me to his room at the bottom of the outside stairs. I sit on the bed while he kneels before me, spoon-feeding me. After only a few bites we're both full and just look at each other.

There is a reason why when a man lies with a woman, we say in Twi he is eating her. *I* say both the man and woman eat each other. He pulls my feet onto his lap and gives each toe such a thorough kneading my muscles go to sleep and I can't raise my feet. He rubs my insteps, making my knees fall apart like overcooked crab, making me moan for more. He presses his warm lips on my ankles and eats his way up my legs until he is giving my clit delicate flicks with his tongue. I urge him on, bucking against him. He raises himself and presses his lips to mine. Tasting my own saltiness is glorious. "Please," I say, "don't tell me I'm too young."

His breath is hot. "By God, you're not, you're ready."

When he steps out of his trousers and supporters, I thrill at the stiffness between his legs. Though it is perpendicular to the wall and rears up with spasms, I am not afraid. He guides himself with one hand, pushing in a little at a time, stopping to ask if I'm okay, as if I would say no to this sweetness. I've heard the first time is supposed to hurt. He's supposed to feel a barrier and tear through it, but there is none. Maybe it's from my sprinting. Maybe it's from the times I've pacified with my finger. I don't know. All I feel is this okro smoothness as he sinks into me until he can go no farther. Bone against bone, hair against hair, slowly at first, and then faster. There's a desperation to his plunging, as if he wants to go back to the beginning of man from whence he came. Back to birth, back to life. I'm just as desperate in my gorging on him, squeezing him deeper. So this is how Boaz went into Ruth? I raise my hips higher, feed harder, sink my fingers into his buttocks and then I'm convulsing around him, roiling, screaming life.

Long afterwards, he props himself on one elbow and looks down at me, shaking his head. "You . . . *mm, mm, mm* . . ." He reaches between my legs, stroking the hair. "I can't wait for you to finish schooling so we can be together all the time."

"Me too," I whisper. "Why didn't I think of applying to the University of Lagos?"

He nibbles at my nipple and says not to worry. I'm worth waiting for and we'll make the best of the holidays. Papa doesn't have to know I've done it and when we get married, he will say *Thank you God.*

Days and nights, we feed each other. I luxuriate in the untamed rawness of our hunger, the way he grabs my hips and drives in. The innocence. It doesn't matter if I happen to be looking out the window, he can lift my dress from the back and let himself in, I'm ever ready, grinding against him as he bends his knees and pushes up, though it's hard keeping my face straight and holding still when Grandma walks by and exchanges long greetings. As soon as she leaves, we resume.

When we are not in bed, we spend evenings wandering around the city, visiting Fela's shrine. We take taxis to the bowl-shaped National Theater to giggle at a Nigerian play or a Goldie Hawn film. We splash in the sea and eat fried shrimp in restaurants. Sometimes he takes me shopping. When I wear a halter top, one look at the exposed curve of breast makes his crotch swell, which makes me so hungry we have to look for the nearest private corner.

I hardly spend time with my aunties now. Besides, Auntie Biggie spends more and more time in bed, growing bigger, hardly changing clothes. Whenever I wake up, I knock on her door and throw myself in her arms, as if to shoot her with some of my energy. Her face clouds up when I try to get her to talk about her husband, so I kiss her, take in her sour smell, make polite conversation until I can sneak downstairs to Kayode. Kwabena has ceased to exist altogether. Only this feeding exists. My hair has thickened. My skin is shinier. My eyes sparkle, and my breasts keep swelling.

Kayode and I carry on living inside and around each other until one night, toward the end of the holidays, Uncle Bola comes downstairs and knocks on the door.

"Esi," he barks like an army general, "we want to talk to you. Come upstairs now."

I enter the parlor. Grandma sits rigid on the couch. Grandpa is slumped in an armchair, supporting his drooped head with withered hands. They have even managed to fetch my Uncle Yomi from Idioro, someone I seldom see because the family is not happy he married a prostitute. He and Bola, looking like twins, stand with arms folded across their chests. I can tell they are cross the way their sharp noses stab the air. Auntie Biggie is stuffed in her chair but her Chinese eyes have no smile for me. Kwabena is perched on the arm of the couch, looking like the angel he's not.

"Esi, we want to talk to you about your behavior with Kayode," Uncle Bola says.

"You cannot marry him," Auntie Biggie says. Just like her to get straight to the point. "He is not the man for you."

My mouth flies open. "Why can't I marry him?"

"Because he is related to you, that is why! How can you marry your own relative?"

"But we're not related by blood!"

"It matters not," Auntie Yetunde says. "His aunt is your grandfather's wife and your granny's rival. That would be a slap in our faces."

"I can't believe what you are saying, Aunt Yetunde, you of all people!"

She rolls her big eyes away.

"Besides, he is a nobody," Auntie Biggie says.

"What do you mean he's a nobody? He's a human being. He loves me, and I love him."

"He has no money."

"He has enough for me!"

Auntie Biggie sucks her teeth like someone who wants to get rid of a bitter taste. "What is love, when you can have money?"

"We cannot let you marry him," Auntie Yetunde says. "You cannot even marry someone who lives on de same street with you, let alone your relative. That is Yoruba culture. If that barbarity goes on in Ghana, fine. But not here, ah, ah!"

"But you never said anything before! I have been with him for years. I told you my secrets, you never said a word!"

"That is because we thought it was a childish thing that would end," Auntie Biggie spits out. "But now you are sleeping with him. You spend nights with him as if you were married. It is a disgrace! I didn't want to hurt your feelings. But now, you have gone too far. It is one thing to sleep with him, who cares if you have some fun? But you cannot marry him."

"Fun? Is that what you call it? I love him."

"Love? What rubbish! Money helps love last longer, believe me!"

"I am going to marry him and there is nothing you can do about it!"

"Yomi, say something," Uncle Bola says. Uncle Yomi shrugs and looks away, which makes me want to hug him. Uncle Bola pulls his pointy beard. "Esi, how can you be so stubborn?" He turns to Kwabena. "Is she always like this? Does she behave like this in Ghana?" Kwabena looks down and shakes his head as if he can't believe it himself, the pleaser!

"You cannot marry him!" Auntie Biggie says.

"I can and will!"

Her voice goes very quiet. "If you do, then you will have no family. The next time I see you, don't let me call you a bastard." With that, she squeezes herself out of the chair and jiggles out the door.

I am stunned into silence. A bastard? If you're a bastard, you have no family. Auntie Biggie is disowning me? No one is saying anything. They agree with her? Why do I have to give up one person to keep another? I'm burning with so much fury I could turn to ashes. Uncle Bola shakes his head and sweeps out of the room as if he's had all he can take from me. Auntie Yetunde gets up, glares at me, and hurries after her husband. Uncle Yomi shrugs and leaves too. Grandpa drags himself out of his chair. He totters to me and touches me lightly on the arm. I can tell *he* still loves me; he doesn't need words. He turns and makes for his room.

"Esi, what you are doing, it is not good, oh!" Grandma says.

"And what you're doing is not fair! It's not fair!"

I run downstairs to Kayode, throw myself on his thighs, sobbing. Grandma comes down to the bottom of the stairs. "Esi! Esi!"

Leave me alone!

"Kayode!"

Kayode eases me off and goes out to meet her.

"Talk to her," I hear Grandma say. "We're sending her back to Ghana tomorrow." Then she fires off rapid Yoruba that I don't understand. Kayode doesn't say a word, but I'm sure she is insulting him. When he comes back into the room, his jaw is set. I sob louder.

"Ssh, don't cry," he says. "No one is going to tear us apart. Listen, listen."

I sit up, still sniffling. "But I don't want them to hate you."

He laughs, sucking his teeth. "I don't care. I've been on my own all this time, never needed anyone. What about you? You know what this means, don't you? They will disown you."

"What do I care? I will marry you, only you!"

He throws his arms around me and pulls me tight. "No one is going to hurt you. I swear I will always love you. Always."

The following day, Grandma and Auntie Biggie accompany both Kwabena and me to the airport. He is acting so saintly I could box him. *Yes, Auntie. Yes, Grandma. Oh, thank you. Sorry about Esi.* That's how it goes on in the taxi and at the airport. When we say goodbye, Grandma wishes me a safe journey, but Auntie Biggie only spits out, "Useless girl!" She doesn't even look at me. Tears burn my eyes but I force them back. I'll look straight ahead as if I don't care. I hoist up my nose and walk away.

The officer stamps our passports and we're walking into the lounge to wait for the plane when I see him, Kayode, waiting for me! Of course he is, he has an airport pass. He opens his arms and I bury my head in his shirt as the sobs shake me.

"It is all right, Esi," he says. "Ssh, don't cry." He pulls back to look at me, wiping my tears with his thumbs. "Our love is strong, we can withstand anything. I will write to you every week."

"I will write too," I say in a trembling voice.

He kisses the top of my nose and smiles. "We both know you are not a very good correspondent."

"I mean it this time, I swear!"

"Okay." He takes out his handkerchief and gently dabs at my cheeks, urging me to smile. As I look into his steady eyes, I believe him. Nothing will separate us.

Back in Ghana, I settle into university life and though I try, I can't forget the quarrel with my Nigerian family. I go to class but I don't want to hear what the lecturer has to say about Jean-Paul Sartre and how everything is meaningless, how I am worth the same as a table because the table and I do nothing more than "exist." I don't care about Pablo Neruda's poems, and that weird Juan Ramón Jiménez taking walks and talking to his donkey Platero that he loves so much I am convinced he has lost his brain.

Kayode and I write letters for two months, three months. But it's no longer anger I feel toward my Nigerian family. What if I've lost Auntie Biggie forever? Am I really disowned? That means I'm not related to her. I'm a stranger to the family. I don't have a mother. I don't exist. No one will take part in my marriage. If I have children one day, the family won't know them. I might as well be dead. No! I want to see her. I can't toss off my family like rags. Grandma, I'm sorry. Uncle, forgive me. I pick up a paper.

Dearest Kayode,

I am very sad to write you this letter. I'm so sorry. I love you very much, but I can't lose my family. I don't know how to live without them. So, I have to choose. I'm so sorry. I know I'm crushing your heart. Mine is crushed too, but we have to break up because I can't marry you. I'm so sorry. Please forgive me.

Yours forever,

Esi

How do you say goodbye to half of yourself? You fold up with pain. You don't eat. You shrink inside your clothes. The days are long, nights are longer. Every movement hurts and draws tears from you. You learn to wait through the days. You learn to bear the weeks, then months. You wait for Christmas, the season to grab desperately at joy.

I have to go to Nigeria. I have to see Auntie Biggie, make things right. Oh, she'll be so surprised. She'll swallow me in her fat arms and wave my *sorry*s away with a kiss on the lips. I am desperate for her love. Hold on, Auntie Biggie, I'm coming.

A few days before Christmas, a Lagos taxi bumps me to Grandpa's house. Auntie Biggie, I can't wait to smell her. I pick up my bag and run up the stairs. Little cousin Fidelia is alone on the balcony.

"Hello!" I say. "Where is Grandma?"

"She dey inside," she says in pidgin English.

"And Auntie Biggie, she dey inside too?"

"No, she don die." Her round eyes add nothing and I don't understand pidgin well.

"Oh, she didn't die. Was she sick?"

"No," she shakes her head, locks eyes with me. "She don die."

"Okay, so she didn't die! Where *is* she?" I want to shake her.

"She don die."

An unseen bird is flapping its wings inside me. I drop my bag and run shouting through the corridor, "Grandma! Grandma!"

She rolls slowly out of her room, like her body is too heavy for her. Her face could be a relief map the way it's lined everywhere. Lines I've never seen before.

I shriek. "Where is Auntie Biggie? Where is she?"

She stops, then raises her hands to the sky. "Esi . . . she's dead, Esi."

"Noooo!" I tear at her. "Auntie Biggieee! Auntie! Mother!"

They shush me. I scream and scream. She doesn't answer.

She never will again.

Grandma tells me Auntie Biggie swallowed a fistful of sleeping tablets because she was sad. She says it's not my fault, but I don't believe her. It's my fault. I broke up with Kayode and yet Auntie Biggie died anyway. Why didn't I listen? If only . . . oh, Auntie. I close my eyes. I see her heave out of her white Mercedes as before. I see myself run to her. I feel her scratchy lace on my face. I smell her perfume. I feel her kiss on my lips. And sobs shake me all over.

CHAPTER TWENTY-TWO

TAYE SAYS SHE believes in miracles because I am a different person now. She is right. For the rest of the holidays, I behaved. If Auntie Yetunde told me not to talk to this man or that man, I didn't. If Grandma took my hand when we crossed the road, I didn't swat her hand away and shout that I knew how to cross a road. I never argued with anyone. It was easy not to see Kayode because he had traveled to visit his family. Now that I'm back at the university, I'll do more than want. I *will* be good. I will be a good granddaughter. A good niece. A good daughter. I will not fight. I'll keep angry words from flying out at Papa, even when he shows up on campus and makes me want to fall into a hole in the ground.

He turns up weekly at the porters' lodge, and when they ask him for my name, he rears back, indignant. "Don't you know my daughter? That small girl, don't you know her? Cooked with intelligence. Like fire." Everyone laughs at me, asking if my father thinks I'm the only important girl at the university.

If he can't find me, he has no problem installing himself in the armchair of anyone he imagines is my friend and unloading on them: "I wanted her to study law, not languages. Or even medicine. She had very good marks in the sciences, you know. Let me tell you, she is thoroughly cooked with intelligence . . ."

One time, we had no electricity. Some of us girls were standing on the veranda peering into the darkness when, from the bathroom, someone shrieked, "There is a man in the bathroom!" followed by a deep voice blubbering, "Pardon me, pardon me." There arose sounds of metal buckets toppling and water splashing. Girls tore out of the bathroom clutching towels. And there was Papa stumbling out, blubbering some more, "Sorry, I was looking for my daughter."

If he can't find me, he must knock on every door, hunt for anyone from Wesley Girls who will tell him where I am. That's how one day he arrives at the hairdresser with two of his friends, all three dressed in suits and ties. The sight of a room full of girls with heads under dryers doesn't faze him. He stands in the open doorway, talking loudly enough to reach God.

"Ah, there you are, I've been looking everywhere for you!" Everyone stops talking to listen. I wish he'd leave, but his legs take root. "I just returned from Osu Castle."

The presidential castle? What was he doing there? The second coming of the savior Junior Jesus is here. It happened so fast I am still trying to catch up. After only three months in power, President Limann violated probation in people's eyes, so Junior Jesus arose from the grave of retirement and knocked him off. But there are murmurings that the CIA is not happy with J.J. cozying up to Cuba, Gadhafi, and every entity on the LEFT. For his part, J.J. says he doesn't care about left or right, only about whether his stomach is empty. The masses are thrilled with his new regime, the Provisional National Defense Council, and his "power to the people" speeches. People say he's so humble he'll sit down with a coconut-seller and share a beer or marijuana. If you have a grievance, tell it to Junior Jesus and he'll save you. But he is purging with a vengeance all the evil ones plotting against him. Oh, he has kept his promise all right. No more firing squads. People simply disappear. Why is Papa going near that man?

"I went there to report a crime," he says importantly while his friends nod their support. "You remember that scoundrel I paid to repair my radiogram?"

I have only vague fragments in my head, but I nod, hoping he'll get on with it and leave.

"He disappeared with it. No one knows where he is. So, I've reported him."

"That's right," his friends chorus.

I can't believe how Papa thinks it's the responsibility of a head of state to deal with the theft of someone's radiogram. Please, God, make him stop talking.

"The guards didn't let me in to see Rawlings, but they promised to take action. They will arrest him, I'm sure." He digs his hands into his pockets with satisfaction. "Ah, yes, it's a new world. A good one. These young officers are going to clean the country of corruption. Starting with that thief!"

Dance, Ghana, dance! Have you forgotten? Soldiers stripped market women old enough to have wiped the soldiers' bottoms. They shot them even. They are razing off women's hair with broken glass and turning scalps red with blood, just because the women have straightened their hair with "Western imperialist products." Soldiers are seizing dollars and pounds sterling. They are chopping off the penises of their enemies. Oh, yes, rejoice, Ghana, rejoice, for your savior is come! It reminds me of when we studied Shakespeare's *Coriolanus* at Wesley Girls, how the plebeians spread their cloths on the ground for Coriolanus to walk on until the tribunes persuaded them he was evil. How quickly the plebeians took to the streets jubilating when he was banished only to regret it later. Politicians suck your blood and spit out promises that spin you round and round until you hallucinate about a land where everyone's stomach will be stuffed with food. Sure, J.J. is not responsible for every evil act committed by the soldiers, but obviously he can't control his people. Papa himself taught me not to trust. Has he forgotten?

He stands there smiling until he sees I'm not going to open my mouth. Then he clears his throat. "All right. I'm leaving. Here is some money for you." He digs into his pockets, fumbles around, and comes up with air. Anyone can see he has no money. He turns to his friend on the right. "Brother, let me see you for a minute." They turn their backs and huddle together. There is urgent whispering and shuffling as banknotes pass between them. Papa turns to face me with a big grin. He digs his hand into his pocket and it's a miracle, "Here, twenty cedis, just for you!" My ears are so hot they could burn the hairdresser's hands. Twenty cedis today will buy little more than groundnuts and bananas. Does he have to show off such an amount? Must he do this here at a university full of students whose parents have money to send them behind the corn for holidays?

When he leaves, the silence is so painful I want to scream. Then the hairdresser giggles and says, "Old men. Aren't they funny?" Everyone laughs. I laugh too and suddenly everyone is talking and sharing stories and I thank God they have forgotten me.

But not everything at the university makes me want to hide in the library behind the biggest book I can find. I shine in my classes and attract many friends. In the university there are no bells to jerk you up at five-thirty in the morning. No need to go to chapel for early morning prayers. You sleep when you want, eat when you want. Boys can come to your room to visit, except they must leave by ten at night when the gates close.

Some boys' feet lead them to our rooms because they know the girls cook better food than what you get in the cafeteria. It doesn't bother me, I never cook anyway. My roommate Charity is forever cooking meat stew or something on the balcony, and boys always happen to drop by when we are about to eat, especially her brother. He shuffles in with at least three friends who gobble our food and never buy us any.

Here they are, four of them, their bellies round with the yam and stew made with luncheon meat from a can. It's not enough that they have stuffed themselves. They must sit around telling stories about how when they were in London they saw this film or that film. One of them brags about a house he moved into after his soldier friends seized it from a rich family. The family had to flee, ha ha. It's all I can do not to spit on him. I fling myself across the bed and drift into sleep.

Voices bounce off the walls and suddenly I hear a deep one I've never heard before. I open my eyes and think, Is that Michael Jackson's brother? He is just like the pictures I've seen of the Jackson brothers: tall, topped with a bushy afro. Except he is almost too beautiful, his cheeks bridged by a fountain-pen nose, and eyes with thick lashes. When I sit up, I recognize him as a man I've seen in a play on television. Though he is as handsome as sin, his dimpled smile is shy.

"I'm Rudolph, from the drama school," he says. "I'm directing a play for my final year. I wonder if you girls could come and audition." He has seen and admired Charity in a play she did for television when she was a child. We say yes.

The mimosas have on their orange-red flowers when we walk down the main university avenue to the School of Performing Arts. After we sit under a tree and read, Rudolph gives me the main female role, a Japanese woman who is so crazy in love with a man who won't reciprocate that she has to resort to tricks and pleas to get his attention. I don't mind acting the part, it's just a story, but no girl should acquire a stomachache for a man who doesn't care about her pain. When we rehearse, Rudolph gives me shy smiles and brushes against me any chance he gets. As for me, I have trouble keeping my eyes away from the thick hair on his chest.

On the day of the play, he borrows a kimono from the Japanese Embassy and takes me backstage to show me how to wear it. He turns around so I can take off my dress and wrap the kimono around me, but I can't help the heat from spreading through me because he is near. When I finish, he inspects me and says, "The Japanese woman warns that you must be very careful. You have to put the left flap over the right. It's very important because something bad could happen to you if you don't do it right."

But I forget to wear the kimono the right way for the play. After I run off the stage crying because the man still won't love me, I go down the stairs and step into the dark night to breathe in the smell of overgrown grass. That's when a sharp pain stabs my ankle. I yelp and there is a scorpion disappearing into the grass, its black tail curled up. Everyone rushes out.

"Oh, no, it must be the kimono," Rudolph says. "You wore it the wrong way." I don't believe him, but who am I to complain when he carries me in his big arms and hails a taxi for the hospital? The faint sweat on him only makes me hide my head in his neck.

At the hospital the doctor jabs me with a needle, and Rudolph carries me back to the waiting taxi and all the way to my room. He puts me to bed and sits holding my hand until I fall asleep. The next evening when he asks me to go eat dinner with him, I say yes. Boys buy dinner for girls all the time and it doesn't mean anything. Still, my heart bangs in my chest as I sit across from him in a room full of murmurings and clinking glasses.

"You know, you're very easy to talk to," he says. I tell him I talk too much, that my sisters call me the Ghana Broadcasting Corporation, that I forget to think before speaking. He smiles. "I like that," he says, then he points his fork at me. "But I notice you never wear lipstick."

Oh no. I don't want him noticing my lips. My hand goes over my mouth as I try to explain, "At Wesley Girls they made fun of my lips, even Charity who was in the same dormitory. She says my lips look like a . . . a vagina. People say my eyes are too dark, like I'm wearing kohl, and I could pass for a prostitute."

His brows gather in an angry *V*. "That's not true! You look foxy, but that's not a bad thing. Show off those thick lips. Put on lipstick, lip gloss, whatever you like. And stop trying to hide yourself under those huge shirts—is that your father's?"

He has caught me. I am wearing Papa's shirt, something I've been doing because of people saying I could pass for a boy. I tell him I want to hide my sugarcane lines.

He laughs, pointing with his fork. "Let me tell you, you are no sugarcane. You're a guitar girl now."

My face heats up and I dig my fork into my jollof rice.

After dinner, it's the most natural thing to walk with him to his room. We go at each other with kisses and touches, but what is this? Why is his organ not so strong? It's not easy to gain entrance with a weak thing no matter how hard you push, so he spills his water without full penetration. After that he grows softer and smaller and no amount of pulling and pushing will rouse him. All he can say is I love you, I'm sorry, it will be better next time. Then his eyes close and his nose turns into a car engine.

I roll out of bed and stand staring at him. There has to be a way to get him going. I mean, come on! I bend down to look at his penis, now a big worm lolling on black grass. Hello, wake up, I whisper. It's funny, really, this thing that looks drunk and passed out. I push it this way and that, shake it, but it refuses to rise. I put my mouth to its salty stickiness, but it remains soft. I straighten up and gaze at the mirror above the table by his bed. My lids are heavy, my lips puffy and panting with hunger. Sigh. I lie down on my back beside the sleeping man, blinking at the pink gecko crawling on the ceiling, stroking my hair down below. I am so hungry for it. I slip in two fingers and close my eyes, remembering Kayode.

CHAPTER TWENTY-THREE

W E GOT LUCKY the first time and I didn't get pregnant. Now he is bent over me guiding himself into me with one hand. This time I ask him, "Can you wear something?" After our first time, Kayode always did.

"Ah no," he pants. "That rubber is a wall against pleasure."

"Then I must take the pill."

He pulls back. "Why do you want to take the pill? Are you interested in someone else?"

"No, I'm not interested in anyone but . . ."

"Well, then, no pill for you, okay? You won't be unfaithful if you don't have the pill. Unfaithful women are the ones who need something so they don't give birth to another man's child."

"Unfaithful? What are you talking about? Are you saying I'm going to sleep with another man?"

"Uhm, sorry, I didn't mean it that way."

I flop over to face the wall.

"I'm just scared of losing you," he says in a coaxing voice. "You're so beautiful. And you do know what they say about the pill, don't you?"

I whip around. "What?"

"Many women can't have children after using it."

I'm silenced for a moment. Indeed, I've not only heard the rumors, I once met a woman who told me the pill prevented her from birthing a child, after she had used it for years. Many older people warn girls who want to remain fertile to avoid family planning clinics. "So, what do we do? I don't want to get pregnant."

"Look, if you like, we can use Emko. The tablet will dissolve into foam and kill any sperm. I've got one. Let me get it."

Emko, eh? Good, because I'm starved, dying to have him sink into me and . . . oh no, he has unloaded already. No, no, no! I dig my nails into his buttocks. Anything, come on. But nothing. He slips out, giving me the look of a puppy who has urinated in the house.

It's not his fault, is it? If I say the wrong thing, he's going to feel even more puppy-sorry. I smile, then I feel something flat and solid between my legs. When I pick it up, I see half of the Emko tablet didn't dissolve. Fear shakes me. "You said it would dissolve!"

"Shh, please, please, don't worry," he says, covering me with his hairy chest. He wipes my eyes and shushes me some more. He tells me the half that melted will do the job. And it's my fault, anyway. He has never met a woman so hot to the touch that even her father must want her. I don't know if I should slap or kiss him.

"Here, let me take care of you." He wiggles down between my legs and strokes me with the tip of his tongue. Still upset, I ignore him at first. But his tongue darts around the sweet stump of my clit. Then the pleasure builds and I say yes, oh yes! But it's like hors d'oeuvres before the main meal. I'm a man's girl. I need the insistent thrusts, the softness around the hard. I press down on his head. "Push your tongue inside."

He obliges me and I imagine it's Kayode's hardness. I buck against him, the painfully sweet convulsions seizing me. He kisses me, thrilled he has brought me to such joyful tears, not knowing it's for Kayode I am crying.

At the end of the month, I don't make life. At first, I don't believe it, but when two weeks go by with no red spots, I tell Rudolph I'm late. We're sitting on the stone wall in front of the Department of Modern Languages. He is struck silent for a long time, kicking his feet away and back to the stone. Then he says, "Okay."

"Okay what?"

"An abortion . . . why are you crying?"

I don't make sense to myself. I want to finish university and find out what I can do. What's more, I don't want to watch Papa's face turn stormy when I tell him I am pregnant, even if Rudolph will marry me. And yet I don't want an abortion, a word people whisper with the same horror as an encounter with the devil himself. I don't want to anger God, who might send a lightning bolt to strike me—I heard a preacher say that at the Presbyterian church at Kibi. I can't strip off my upbringing like an ill-fitting dress. I look at Rudolph's profile that Sister Mansa described as noble. Ridiculously, he's smiling. "I can't have an abortion," I tell him, pulling at the grass. "It's wrong."

His smile freezes. "It's just a ball of cells. You have such old-fashioned ideas. It's foolish to have children when we're both students."

"True, but . . ."

"I want to go to Hollywood and try my luck. I want to win an Oscar. It's the biggest award an actor can get in America! You can't do it from here." He hops down and takes my hands in both of his. "Let's go to America together, you and me. You're beautiful, you'll make it."

I don't want to go to America for any Oscar, whoever or whatever that is. I just want to finish school and become . . . a journalist. Or run a school for orphans. But even as the tears now trickle down my cheeks, I know I'll have an abortion because I can't have a baby. I don't want to suffer like Sister Abena, get stuck in some place away from home, begging for money to buy drawers, or have a baby who might die because I can't take care of it, not to mention the whispers that will follow me when I walk about—*look at that girl, she got pregnant without a husband.*

Oh, I'm going mad thinking about it. Abortion is against the law. If you get caught, you'll get locked up in prison. Most of the time it's not the performer of the abortion who gets punished, except when the girl dies. And no doctor in a government hospital will do it. At least, not openly. Because private clinics cost more than a student can put together, I've heard stories that will singe your hair.

People concoct a brew from the blue powder used to brighten white clothes, poisoning not just the baby but sometimes the mother too. Women guzzle entire bottles of whiskey that poison the blood and kill the baby. Also, people know the womb will vomit out anything foreign, so a metal coat hanger can be pulled apart and threaded into the womb to ransack it. Infections abound, punctures open, and death swoops in to claim the souls. No, mister, I will not risk my life.

"We will do things properly," he says in a soothing voice. "I promise you, there will be no back-of-the house operation. Listen, we'll go to a doctor. Or a clinic. There are even medical students who can do it." I taste the salt of the tears running into my mouth as he presses me against his hairy chest. "Don't worry, darling. I'll take care of you."

Inside me, I feel so much activity I could be bubbles in a pot of soup, swelling upward, bursting and falling to the bottom only to swell up again.

"I don't want to decide now," I say. "I want to go home first."

He kisses my cheeks. "Okay, but we can't wait too long. If

you like, we can both go home to visit our families, spend Easter. When we return to campus, we'll do it, okay?"

I say nothing.

As the bus bounces me on my way to Swedru, signboards of sellers whiz by as usual: JESUS SAVES HAIR DRESSING SALON. IN GOD WE TRUST MOTOR WORKS. God is everywhere. I breathe Him, drink Him, eat Him, only to turn around and exhale Him, urinate Him, and excrete Him. That's the way faith feels, ever shifting, ever transforming itself. I need space to breathe and forget, though I can't really, because while a man can walk away from a baby, a woman carries it wherever she goes. Only she feels the secret pulsating within.

When I get home, Sister Mansa is sitting on a stool in the cemented yard, plucking the feathers off a cock. Chicken in the middle of the week? There must be an important visitor. She is all smiles, and a sheen of sweat covers her face. She wipes her brow with the back of her wrist and says, "Esi, *akwaaba!*"

"*Yaa anua. Ei*, is the chicken for me?"

She laughs. "No. You won't believe who is upstairs."

"Ooooh tell me, who?" I love visitors. They always make a fuss over me and give me money or something. I could use some happiness.

"I won't tell you. You go upstairs and greet Papa. You'll find out. Let me pluck this chicken before the water gets too cold."

When I race up the stairs and throw the door open, I don't believe what I'm seeing. Papa is sitting in his chair sipping beer. Music blares. A man in a political suit reclines in another chair, but the chair beside him is occupied by the last person I expect to see. I just stand there with my mouth open. It's Sister Abena.

"Esi, how is your body?" she says. I can't speak. She laughs. "Why, did your tongue flip over?"

"Sister!" I throw myself at her. "I've missed you!" She presses me against her and I could die from joy. I know I'm too old but I want to sit on her lap and bury my head in her neck. I'm so happy she isn't dead. She came back!

"Esi," she makes me sit up straight. "I want you to greet my husband, James Quarcoe." I turn to face Mr. Quarcoe, who is smiling at me. I get up and shake his hands like I'm supposed to. I tell him *akwaaba*.

"*Yaa anua*," he responds. I've gained another brother. I can't believe Sister Abena and Papa are sitting together talking and laughing.

"He is a chartered accountant," Papa wants me to know. His dimples are on full display.

I'm just happy my sister is home. I touch her afro wig, admire her white bellbottoms and matching platform shoes. Her earrings are so big I could pass my wrists through them. When I smooth her blouse, I feel the hardness of her round belly.

"You are pregnant?"

"Yes," she says. She can't stop smiling.

Papa leaves off talking to Mr. Quarcoe and wags his finger at her. "I hope you've learned your lesson. You almost ruined your womb with abortions. If it weren't for the doctor, you would be barren." So, Papa has been in touch with her all this time! Mr. Quarcoe stops smiling. Sister Abena's eyes are watery because Papa's words have knifed her. "You're lucky you've found a man to marry you. I hope you learn to be humble. A woman's glory is her husband. Now that your man has lifted you out of disgrace, you better be quiet and respect him, you hear?" He turns to Mr. Quarcoe. "If she misbehaves, just let me know."

Mr. Quarcoe's lips stretch tightly. Sister Abena gets up and asks me if I want to go downstairs with her. I follow her quietly. At the top of the stairs, she stops to search my face. I'm trying not to cry.

"Esi, sometimes, it's just better to shut your mouth. He is our father and we have to show him respect."

I am ready to protest when I remember how I defied everyone and Auntie Biggie died.

"Yes, Sister." I wonder if this is what happens when your childhood disappears. A child howls and protests every indignity, but as she grows, her voice hushes. I'm not sure how to retain the strength of my own voice.

"Do you miss Akwasi?"

"I do, Esi. I'll never stop missing him. But we have to let him go. I think he would be happy that Papa and I are talking again. Papa told me he was sorry. He loved Akwasi. That's one thing I am absolutely sure of."

"Yes. He loved him. But why does he have to bring up your past in front of your new husband?"

She sighs. "He can't help himself, you know." She touches my cheek. "Let's not forget, I did have an abortion. You see, he thinks he is doing the right thing. He wants to teach me a lesson the way you train a puppy. When it soils the floor of your house, you grab it by the scruff of its neck and rub its nose into its feces until it learns not to do its business again."

"That's not true, the dog continues to do its business. It just learns to do it outside the home!"

"Yes, you're right."

Well then. I guess that is the answer. You do what you have to do and keep it outside of everyone. Even yourself.

SHE LIES ON the table. A shaft of light from the sun cuts through the window above her head and sears her nose. The nurse is powerfully built: big breasts straining against the white apron of her uniform, legs planted like trees, made to withstand struggling patients. In her hand, she holds up a giant syringe. The girl's legs tremble from being open so wide the cold air enters her. She is relieved she can't see anything because of the white sheet over her thighs.

The nurse bends down and reaches under the sheet.

The girl whimpers, "Aren't you going to give me anesthesia?" Tears burn the corners of her eyes, run down into her ears.

The nurse's bosom heaves. "What anesthesia? We don't do that here. We don't have any. Now keep your legs open."

The pumping begins. Maybe if she concentrates on the nurse's shoulder, the hard beauty of that shoulder moving in a powerful rhythm, maybe it won't hurt as much. She bites the back of her hand, muffling her screaming as the nurse pumps piffum piffum piffum . . .

"It's over." The nurse straightens up, withdrawing a steel kidney bowl from under the sheet. Blood streaks from the bowl's edges.

The girl strains her neck upward, whispers, "Can I see?" She wants to know if those were really twins the nurse said she was carrying.

The nurse frowns. "There is nothing to see. It's . . . nothing."

"I must see."

She looks into the bowl and screams. Everything is ground up, like minced meat. The nurse drops the bowl on the table and pins her down.

When the sea crashes on the sand, it washes away claw marks left by people scratching the sand together and the footmarks of those trampling on it. All is smooth again. The sand forgets. So it is with the girl. In time, she forgets.

CHAPTER TWENTY-FOUR

F OR HIS FULL-LENGTH PLAY, Rudolph has chosen a play he won't let me act in. We are swallowing morsels of fufu at a chop bar called Don't Mind Your Wife, which is an invitation for a man to come eat when he wants to show his wife she can't punish him by refusing to cook, a place to eat cheaply. On the dusty earth, you can see a scalloped line of ants carrying white clumps of what must be cassava. Two sweaty men pound the squishy dough in a wooden mortar, while the woman-owner dips her hand in water and turns the dough over in a deft rhythm: *Puhm!* flip, *puhm!* flip, *puhm!* flip.

"Why can't I act in your play?" I ask as a tiny river of soup trickles down my arm that I lick off like a dog licking its paw. It's not easy to use your fingers as a spoon. I can tell he wants more time to think up an answer by the way he fishes out goat meat from his soup, bites into it and rips off the smoky skin, the part people call coat. Then he sucks on each finger with loud smacks. I wait him out, letting my hand dangle over my earthenware bowl to stop the soup from trickling down my elbow.

"It's a part for a bush girl," he says, rolling out his tongue to lick the soup from his bottom lip. "I don't want people to think you're one of them."

"Is the character an evil person?"

"No." He cups his fingers, scoops up soup, and slurps his pleasure. I wish he'd stop enjoying himself long enough to actually look at me.

"She doesn't poison someone's food?"

His brows come together in surprise as he turns to me. "No."

"So why can't I play her?"

"I told you. She's a bush girl. People will think you're bush too."

"That makes no sense. When you act in a play, all you're doing is telling a story. You animate the playwright's words. I don't care if any ignoramus calls me a bush person."

Rudolph's chin stiffens and he stops eating, which tells me he's not going to change his mind. I wave off the fly looping around my fingers and tear at my fufu.

RUDOLPH INVITES MANY girls to read the play but he is left shaking his head because no one will do. In the end he has no choice but to ask me. When I read the play, I have to cover my mouth with excitement, because in parts, the girl Kyeiwa and I could be the same person.

On the day of the performance, the folding metal chairs squeak, the room buzzes with spectators, mostly university students. One can hear rustlings of paper from people fanning themselves with the programs. Rudolph tells me Mr. Bediako, the playwright and TV producer, is sitting in the middle of the front so I must act my best.

The black velvet curtains pull apart to reveal my mother, a woman with a tomato-ripe body. She is smiling at her tenant Christopher in the manner a woman shouldn't toward a man young enough to be her son. She reaches out to touch his shoulder. When he slides out of her reach, she corners and pounces on him the way I imagine Potiphar's wife in the Bible pounced on poor Joseph who had been sold into slavery. Christopher pushes Mother off and sends her flying across the stage so that she lands on her bottom. She scrambles to her feet, stamps about and calls him a fool, but when I step into the scene holding a comb, her body stills. She pretends to be talking about mangoes.

"Remember," her finger dances at him, "if you don't pluck the mango when it's ripe, someone else will." Christopher stands staring until she says, "What are you waiting for? Go away and let me plait this girl's hair!"

After he rushes off, she takes my shoulders in both hands, pushes me down onto a stool, and breathes hot air down the back of my neck. With the pick she claws at my scalp and yanks away. When I protest, she hisses *oh shut up* and her fingers pinch my back in a way that would make Sister Crocodile cheer. "And don't forget, you okro mouth," Mother says. "If anyone asks, you are my sister, not my daughter, you hear?" She has been telling me that ever since I was old enough to understand words. She won't get a husband if men know the truth, do I hear?

When my hair has been pulled so tight my eyes feel peppery, she sends me into Christopher's room to collect buckets belonging to her. If he won't be nice, she won't allow him to use her bucket to fetch water for his bath. He can walk to the market and buy his own.

The curtains close and open again to reveal Christopher's room. He lies on his bed with his arms and legs spread out like a star. I ask him why he won't go to the office where he works as a messenger.

"Occupy yourself with your own problems," he tells me, but I very much want to occupy myself with his. Suddenly the scene rolls me straight back to my afternoon with Yaw, the yam-seller's nephew, when I pulled the hairs on his legs and he tried to push himself into me. Somehow Christopher merges into Yaw, whose mouth remains padlocked no matter how much I tug with my questions. I sing and dance around. I unwrap the scarf from my head and wave it about. He springs to his feet. He grabs at my shoulders. I try to move but he clamps down harder on my shoulders, which sets me yelling, "What are you doing?"

"I'm going to teach you facts," he pants, "hard facts!"

The stage goes black and he lets go. I lunge for a bucket in the corner, ready to attack him. But he hisses at me. "We're supposed to be fighting. Quick!" He knocks buckets about. I do too. The audience howls with laughter. Someone yells, "*Ɔtwea! Akɔlaa bɔne!*" *Serves you right! Bad child.* So that is how things are? A child is responsible when a grown-up forces himself on her? I am so angry I hit Christopher on the head with the bucket. Just then, the lights come on.

Christopher is buttoning up his trousers and I cry, not only because I'm supposed to but out of boiling rage. People jump to their feet, pump their fists, and *yeei* the way they do when a football player scores a goal. I almost hurl a bucket at them.

In the next scene Christopher is roasting on fire because he won't do something illegal his master wants, and somehow the master has him thrown into jail. Which is where I show up seven months after we knocked about the buckets in his room. Now my belly is round with the baby that is in it. I grab the prison bars, yell through them that he has to marry me. I won't take no for an answer. In my head I imagine spitting at him through the bars, not carrying on loudly, "You took the land by force and planted in it, now you have to claim the farm and the harvest!" I hate the reduction of a woman to soil. To have his peace, he agrees. The prison guard reads from the Bible and declares us married.

Well, I won't be forced to marry Rudolph, who doesn't want a baby anyway. I just have to find a way not to get pregnant. I've read there are doctors who insert a squiggly metal called an IUD into a woman's womb to prevent a baby from growing in there. I'll give it a try. Rudolph doesn't need to know.

When the play ends, the playwright comes up on the stage to shake my hand.

"You couldn't have played Kyeiwa better!" He turns his bearded face up to Rudolph's. "I think you have found the one you were looking for."

Rudolph says yes.

After the playwright leaves, I ask him, "What did he mean by you found the one you were looking for?"

Rudolph stares into the air. "Before I met you, I had decided to stay away from girls."

"Why?"

"The girls I had before . . . they didn't give me enough." He starts picking up the scattered scripts from off the backstage floor as if wanting to forget. When I ask him to explain, he straightens up and just repeats, "They didn't give me enough." He stares into the air for a moment. "You are different. You give everything."

Well, I don't know about giving everything, but what I want this minute is for him to give *me* everything. I've just acted in a scene with a man who hurt the girl I played. It seems fitting I should experience pleasure instead. Now that the others are out- side packing things, what if . . . ? I lean against a table by the wall and give him a flirty smile.

"Are you crazy?" he says, but a glint sparks in his eyes and his breath quickens. He drops to his knees, raises my dress, and in- sinuates his tongue. I moan what I want, stroking his head, urging him on. My legs give way and I pull him down with me. This is delicious. I wish he possessed several tongues: one to suck each toe, one for each breast, one for my navel, one for . . . Oh! I wrap my legs around his neck and buck into glory.

Monday after the play, I visit the family planning center near the university. To my surprise, the women waiting on wooden benches are either mothers cradling newborn babies on their laps or women with the round belly of someone about to birth a baby. There isn't a single young person in view. They throw me looks that say I'm a tramp, a useless girl.

The clinic consists of just a large room with rows of benches similar to those in a village church. A chunky nurse sits behind a table in front, with a window to her right. When it's my turn, I sit on the hard chair across from her. She peers curiously at me through her glasses, lacing her fingers. "What is the matter?"

I shift uncomfortably, cracking my knuckles. "Erm, I just wanted to ask if you could please give me something so I don't get pregnant, a contraceptive."

"How old are you?"

"I'm almost eighteen."

Her fingers come apart. "You look fifteen. I thought you were in secondary school."

"No, I'm a student at Legon."

She gives me a knowing smile. "Small girl like you. So, you are enjoying, eh?"

My face turns heavy with shame the way it did when I was little and Sister Yaa caught me with the mirror between my legs. Still, I forge on, "I . . . I . . . could you give me the IUD, please."

She cocks her head sharply. "IUD? Do you know what it does to women? It kills!" She points to the picture of a springy-looking thing on the wall behind her. "Do you want this metal rusting inside you? Do you want it to pierce your womb and turn it into a sieve?"

"No," I say in a guilty child's voice.

"Did you know the IUD is just an abortion? It doesn't stop pregnancy. You get pregnant, but the baby can't stay in your womb because there's something in it. Sometimes the baby manages to survive inside and comes out with the metal half embedded in its bottom. Is that what you want, you bad girl?"

"No, but . . . I don't want to get pregnant."

"Why don't you use condoms? Or Emko? Or better still, why don't you keep your legs folded together and focus on your studies? I'm sure your parents want you to do just that."

I swallow. "But . . . I don't understand. Look, is there a doctor I can talk to?"

"What doctor? Are you challenging me?"

I shake my head quickly, "No, I just felt a doctor would . . ."

"Listen, young lady, I've been working here for a long time. If you don't believe me, ask these women. I know what I'm talking about!"

The women, too, raise their voices. They know someone who has died from family planning. Do I know what I'm doing? Do my parents know what I'm doing? Children of today, no respect for tradition, no morals at all.

I flee.

RUDOLPH WON'T WEAR a rubber and I don't trust that foam business, so he comes up with an idea. If I let him penetrate me, he swears he'll pull out before spilling; he knows how to do that. He guarantees nothing will swim and dissolve the walls of my egg. I want to give it a try, not just for my sake but also for his. Because he too gives everything. He is so kind I sometimes want to soak his feet in warm soapy water, dry them, and massage oil onto each toe. Especially when, four days after the play, I wake up with the shakes.

My teeth rattle so hard I chatter like a monkey. No number of scratchy blankets he piles on thaws the ice in me. I try to lift my head off the pillow but the pain knocks me back down. He pushes the blankets aside and lays an icy hand on my forehead. "Awurade, you're burning! You have to go to the hospital."

"O-k-k-k-kay," I manage. He helps me out of bed, tucks the ends of a blanket into the neckline of my dress. The weight of his arm around my shoulder almost hurts. Though I'm a lump of ice, my breath forces itself out in hot, sour puffs. Slowly, we make our way down the cemented steps. Outside, Rudolph snaps his fingers and hisses *"Ssspss! Ssspss!"* until a rusty yellow and red taxi creaks to a stop in front of us. The car's engine *putts-putts* while charcoal-colored smoke puffs out from the exhaust.

At the hospital, a nurse in a green uniform and white apron shakes a slim thermometer before slipping its coldness under my tongue, warning me not to bite into it. When she takes it out, she frowns at the thin silver line in the glass and says my temperature is 103 degrees. Rudolph wails, "You're really sick." After a patient comes out of the consulting room, the nurse ushers us in to see the doctor, causing the people waiting on benches to complain loudly that they too are people.

The doctor spends only a short time looking into my mouth and feeling around my head. Everyone knows that when you have the shakes and a hot head, malaria has caught you. I don't understand why English people say, "I have caught malaria." No sane person would catch a disease. The doctor scrawls on my card and hands it to Rudolph. Then he calls for the nurse, who smacks my bare bottom so I don't feel the needle when she injects me with chloroquine. Then we head for the prescription area where they give me bitter white tablets.

Back in his room, Rudolph lays me in bed and piles on the blankets. He sits by me, dips a towel in cold water, and presses it on my forehead. I sink into sleep, rising only to beg for the oranges he can't give me enough of. The orange-seller has cut out cones from the tops so I can squeeze and suck the juice. When I sweat, Rudolph changes the sheets and gently eases my arms through a fresh dress. He goes to the market and returns with smoked fish, tomatoes, and eggplant. On the hotplate he keeps under his bed, he makes soup, which is the only thing I can eat without vomiting. Then he sits sponging me, anxiety forming pleats between his eyebrows.

At night he curls up around me, trying to keep me warm. I am so weak it feels as if I will die. I wonder if Mother is watching me from wherever she is and waiting for me. But after one week, I wake up to find the heavy pain has seeped out of my head and I can lift it.

When I smile, Rudolph's eyes moisten.

"You've been so ill." He is choking on the words. "I thought you were going to leave me."

He worries so much I feel like a newly hatched bird he wants to wrap in cotton wool.

Less than a month after my illness, when I tell him I want to run for my hall in the athletic competition, his brows gather. "You are not going to run, you hear? You've just recovered. What if you collapse?"

Not going to run? I have to smile. No one can stop me from running. As soon as he leaves for the School of Performing Arts, I pull on my PT shorts and head for the field. The relay is about to start and they need someone to run the first leg. It's no problem, I say.

When the gun goes off, I pump my legs and arms with all my energy but we lose. I sit on the prickly grass right in the middle of the field, smiling shamefully at the girl who ran the second leg.

"You are fast," she pants.

"Not fast enough," I say, struggling to my feet and brushing the grass off my bottom. A man in a black-and-white tracksuit stands staring at me out of unblinking eyes. "Who is that man, and why is he looking at me that way?"

"That's the coach."

"He must not be happy, the way he is staring."

He comes straight to me and says without blinking, "I want you to be on the school team." The university is going to Nigeria for bilateral games with the University of Ibadan. Would I like to go?

"Yes," I say. Nigeria! I haven't been back since that terrible day when my cousin uttered those words that almost dissolved my bones. Auntie Biggie is gone, but I still have Auntie Yetunde, Taye, and Grandma.

When Rudolph returns and sees me lying in bed wearing my uniform, he drops down beside me. "You ran, didn't you?"

"Yes. And you know what? I'm now on the school team. We're going to Nigeria in a month to compete with Ibadan!"

He shakes his head. "You're naughty, you know that?" But there's a smile on his face. He wants to know if I've hurt myself because I'm lying in bed.

"My legs are a bit wobbly," I confess. He heaves himself up and makes for the door. I wonder if he is angry. "Where are you going?"

"To make you some soup. If you're going to win the gold medal, you need to be strong."

I get up and wrap myself around his waist. He lays me gently on the bed, a plea on his face. I hesitate, and then I nod. He enters with reverence, with gratitude.

BOTH FISTS IN her mouth, the girl lies on her back and watches the rhythm of the nurse's shoulder. She no longer asks to look inside the bowl.

CHAPTER TWENTY-FIVE

TOMORROW WE GO to Nigeria," Coachito says. He is a man who has no use for a lot of words. If he needs you to run, he just snaps his fingers and you know what he wants. It's funny that people call him Coachito, because from my Spanish class I know it should mean Little Coach. He is our head coach and anything but little, with his big shoulders, round face, and round eyes, almost like Papa's. The one we call Coach, a lecturer at the law school, is really the assistant coach. Now, that's a man whose lips can never stay still, so Coachito turns it over to him to pump us up. We are sitting with propped knees on the grass, slapping mosquitoes on our arms.

Coach waves vigorous hands, saying, "They think they're better than us because they're taller and bigger. Let me tell you." He looks slowly from face to face. "We can beat them. We have the best sprinters. Just because they now have oil money doesn't mean we can't show them who is superior."

We jump. "That's right! We're better!"

Although Nigerians and Ghanaians are now friendly, when it comes to sports, the two countries treat each other like two women wanting the same man. In Nigeria, if Ghana beats Nigeria at soccer, buses get turned over and set on fire. When Nigeria beats Ghana, there is much hurling of insults from Ghanaians, never mind that everyone wants to go to Nigeria because it is now a rich country.

"Last year our only weakness was the girls' relay," Coach says. "We had only three fast runners, but now we've added Esi, who will give us a good start." His smile pushes his fleshy cheeks so high up they almost force his eyes to close. My face is hot because everyone is smiling at me. "The relay will be the final event on Saturday afternoon. Last year they beat us. This year, they will see where power lies! Am I lying, girls?"

We shout, "No, Coach!"

I had better not fail to win for the team.

"And now, for your special allowance, follow me." We follow him into the sports office where he counts out two hundred cedis for each athlete. Two hundred cedis! Oh, the things I'll buy! I can travel to Lagos. Better still, I could get off the bus at Lagos and join the team on Saturday morning. When everyone disperses, I linger behind.

"Coach," I say, "I am half-Nigerian."

"So I hear." Up close, I can see the tiny black holes pocking his face.

"Please, when we get to Lagos, if you would permit, I'd like to get off the bus to visit my family." His smile dims. I explain quickly, "If I stay there Friday night, I can take an early bus to Ibadan."

He looks up at the yellowing sky for a moment before sighing at me. I know what he is thinking. It's not every day a person gets to visit relatives in another country, and family can't be ignored. Finally, he says, "So long as you are there by ten in the morning, that should be fine."

Nigeria! Nigeria!

We travel on the bus all Thursday night and arrive in Lagos on Friday morning with the go-slow traffic when everyone is going to work. The din of cars and people almost shatters my ears and jolts my heart. The road we're on runs four times the size of the biggest road in Ghana, and our helpless driver takes a wrong turn. Confused, he stops astride two lanes, fueling more honks and screams from drivers and walkers alike. Yellow letters on the side of our long green bus spell UNIVERSITY OF GHANA. Anyone can see we are visitors in the country, yet a policeman thinks nothing of yanking our door open, jumping in, and flinging his whip on our driver who begs repeatedly, "Sorry, please! I made a mistake, I'm sorry!" The driver clings to the steering wheel and we shout until the policeman gets off. No one is going anywhere with all the confused traffic, so I jump off and hail a taxi to Grandpa's house.

When Grandma sees me, she lifts her hands to the ceiling and says, "*Oluwa Segun.*" God is great. Wiping her wet eyes with the corner of her cloth, she asks me what I want to eat. I tell her I'm only half awake and can't eat a morsel of anything. Auntie Yetunde is so happy she crushes me to her chest and kisses me on my lips, which reminds me of Auntie Biggie and it's all I can do not to blubber.

"Ah, ah, come. Come inside," Auntie Yetunde says and drags me into the bedroom where my uncle lies snoring next to a larva of a baby, so new its wet-looking hair seems glued to the scalp. I look from the baby to Auntie Yetunde's beaming face and she gives me the naughty smile. "Yes, we have another one." Ovum Thirty has failed as usual; she has birthed her ninth child.

We don't mention Auntie Biggie, but she is very much in the room, coloring the sad-happy way we look at and hug each other.

"Where is Taye?" I ask.

"At the University of Ibadan."

"That's where we're having our games! But I thought she was married?"

"Who says you cannot go to the university just because you have a husband? I would go myself if I didn't have nine children." She laughs, then catches me yawning. "*Oya*, lie down by your uncle. I am going to bathe the baby anyway." She lifts the curled-up baby and I lie down, pressing my cheeks on the warm spot, not bothering to remove my skirt and blouse. My uncle rolls away, still breathing heavily.

I sleep until I feel someone shaking my shoulders.

"Look at you," Auntie Yetunde smiles. "You slept like a python with a full belly."

I sit up in the now empty bed, rubbing my eyes to look out the window. The sun has disappeared, leaving brown smudges in the sky. I might as well lie down and close my eyes again.

"You have to eat, ah, ah!" Auntie Yetunde says. "I went to de store and came back a long time ago. Now your uncle has gone out. He got tired of waiting for you to open your eyes." She asks if I'd like to walk to the bus stop and buy dodo, fried plantain. The older children can watch the baby.

Grandma, who must spend her time listening behind doors, steps in. "You are going out?"

"Just to de bus stop," Auntie Yetunde says. Grandma looks disappointed, so I fling my arms around her and tell her we'll be back soon. I'll eat what she has cooked. It's hard for her to understand how I can eat fried plantain on the street and still come home and stuff myself with her eba and okro.

When Auntie Yetunde and I walk downstairs, past the room where Kayode and I took care of each other so well, something sharp wedges in my throat. Outside, the air feels as thick as if we're inside someone's breath. We pick our way through the different sellers who have settled on mats and stools. A cacophony of music blares from the pigeonholes of stores lining the street. The whole time I'm thinking of Kayode, but I hold in the words until they burst out of me.

"Where is he?" I burst out.

"Kayode?" She shrugs. "He moved out. He said he couldn't live here anymore. It's still his room though."

I study the curve of her cheeks and lips but they tell me nothing. She could be discussing the weather the way the words slide easily out of her mouth, the way she bears down on the crowds like she owns the street. I can't explain to myself why I think or say nothing about Rudolph, why I feel as if something is crushing my chest and my legs can't go on. Finally, I say, "Can we go back home?"

"Why?" She frowns. "What is wrong?"

"Nothing. I'm just tired."

"Don't you want dodo?"

"I . . . I'm not that hungry."

She puts her arm around my shoulder and we start back home. When we get upstairs, I tell her to go inside, I want to lean on the balcony. What I really want is to eat away this huge time I have on my hands. I watch drivers who won't make way for others, people shouting and the different dramas playing down the street. I walk to the concrete railing, but my legs feel wobbly. It's no use standing there being miserable. I might as well go inside and let Grandma stuff me with whatever she has cooked. I turn around and am about to go in when I see him.

I stand absolutely still like a pillar. I don't believe my eyes. I remain a statue until he is standing so close I can almost feel the warmth of his chest. His face is all sharp angles, but his eyes hold the same unblinking stare, except the fire has dimmed.

"So, it's true," Kayode says in a cracked voice. "Your aunt

came to see me while you were sleeping. She said you were here but I didn't believe it."

"Just for the night." I wish my voice wouldn't sound like someone with a fishbone stuck in her throat. I swallow. "I leave for Ibadan in the morning to join my team. I have to run the relay tomorrow . . . we can't lose."

He says nothing. I have so much to say, such as how sorry I am, how I wish I could make him smile. But I can't open my mouth. We remain rooted in one boiling circle of air until slowly, he reaches for my hand and strokes it. Such a small gesture, but that's all it takes for my body to remember. I wonder if he is remembering too, if it's the reason he is breathing fast and swallowing, if that's why he is pulling me close.

"Can we talk downstairs?" he whispers.

I nod and follow him. The street might as well be a temple, compared with the activity in my chest. In his room, he tells me to sit down on the bed and then kneels in front of me. I can't look at him. I don't want to stab him with the guilt of Rudolph. I don't want him to know so much has happened, some good, some so ugly they must remain hidden the way we tuck a urine-filled chamber pot under a flowery bedsheet. He takes me by the chin, forces me to look at him. He shakes his head slowly and whispers, "I've missed you."

I've missed him too, I say, and that's the truth.

We talk in halts and starts. When so much has happened between a boy and a girl, when two bodies have seared so against each other, it's impossible to remove the branding. It's the most natural thing in the world when he peels off my blouse and sees what hunger lies below. I don't want to give in but I'm home and he's home and that's all I know. He enters me and I welcome his marvelous hardness, his durability. He gives it to me from on top.

He turns me over on my stomach, puts a pillow beneath me and pushes in from behind. He sits on my chest and thrusts between my breasts as I flick his hardness with my tongue, then he throws my leg onto his shoulder and explodes, feeding my body and soul as I convulse, over and over again. How I love this purity, the honesty of our need.

But when it's over, instead of the fullness, I feel the gouge of Auntie Biggie's words: I'm a useless girl and she don die because I couldn't stay away from Kayode.

I roll out from under him. He's got happiness written all over his face.

"I am so happy you came back, *iyawo mi!*" he says.

He is calling me his wife, oh Awurade.

"We can be together now. Always. I'll visit you in Ghana and . . . why are you shaking your head? Why do you look as if you're going to cry?"

I swallow, whispering, "Sorry, Kayode. I can't marry you. We can't do this again."

"Why?" The hurt in his voice burns my chest.

"Auntie Biggie," I say, as if that's all the explanation there is.

He sits up, passes his hands over his eyes as if to shut out pain. His bushy head hangs down. Finally, he turns to look at me. "Do you know she came to see me the night before she died?"

I spring up. "Auntie Biggie talked to you? Really?"

He nods heavily. "She told me she was sorry for disowning you. She missed you, you know, she was very sad. We talked for a long time and I told her you loved her. Before she went back upstairs, she asked me to forgive her. She said I could marry you."

"So it's true! She died because of me. It's my fault."

"It's not true, Esi."

"Yes, she died because I loved you too much, oh God."

"Don't say that."

I can't help myself. If only Auntie Biggie could yell at me, punish me instead of lying forever silenced in the earth. I could wrestle her for standing in my way and refusing to let me pass, but when she lies crumpled on the ground, my arms and legs feel broken. I don't know how to step over her and continue happily on my way.

I get up to dress and Kayode grabs me by the wrist. "You're walking away from me? Where is that girl I fell in love with? Where is the Esi who could spit in a king's eye? You're going to give up on us? Just like that? You're using me? You think I haven't figured you've got a man in Ghana?" His eyes hold a fury I have never seen before.

"No, no. I love you, I'm not using you."

He shakes his head with a sneer. "And that man in Ghana, you love him too?"

"It's not the same. I care about him, yes, but . . ."

"Does he know you the way I do? Does he understand you?"

I'm crying. "Please, Kayode!"

"Your aunt forgave us, but you, you won't come back to me!" I open my mouth and taste my tears. I can't speak. He grabs my waist and pulls me onto his lap, putting his mouth on my nipples. "Does he touch you like this?" He's almost rough. "Does he nibble you like this?"

I groan, wishing I weren't responding to him again.

"He doesn't, does he?' He searches my face desperately. "Tell me you don't want me."

I shake my head. Tears run down his face. "Tell me you . . ."

He falls on the bed with me. There's a desperation to his thrusting, as if to imprint himself inside me. Despite my protests, I raise my hips to meet him. This is the last, what I have left, this night when we eat each other for the very last time. My mouth opens in a soundless moan, as if I'm gathering all the breath in me for one final pleasure. He shouts my name. Then from deep within, I yield to the groan. Maybe people can hear us from upstairs. Maybe the pope himself can hear me. I am lost in a marsh, roiling, moving, moving, not stopping for a long time. Just drowning, sinking into depths unknown before.

Morning comes. I disentangle myself from him and get up from the bed. He lies on his back, watching me. Not saying a word. I don't know which is worse: his desperation or this loud silence.

"I'm going upstairs to bathe," I whisper, feeling his liquid trickle down my thighs. I can smell its nuttiness. As I struggle into my clothes, it feels as if I'm putting on a shroud. My throat burns.

He says nothing until I am dressed. "Can I take you to the bus stop later?"

"You want to take me?"

He gives me a bitter smile. "What do you think? Just because you're leaving me doesn't mean I have left you."

"Oh Kayode, I . . ."

"I know! You can't be with me. I'm still going to see you off. Okay? Unless you don't want that."

"I want you to," I say quickly. I can't inflict any more hurt on him.

After bathing, I apologize to Grandma and eat her eba and okro for breakfast, which makes her smile. That's what I want to see, a smile on everyone's face. I even search for Auntie Yetunde's smile to see if it's all right for Kayode to take me to the bus stop.

Here we are next to a long, yellow bus, full of shouting passengers. I'm ready to leave for Ibadan. Kayode says nothing, but his jaws are tight. His eyes remain dimmed, almost hard. Good. I will not weaken him with tears. I hug him tightly, then I pull back to study his face, those eyes that still make me weak, that jaw moving with words he holds in, that throat with the pokey bone, the curls of hair on his upper lip I'd love to lick. He nods repeatedly, giving me a lasting look. Then he reaches behind him and removes my arms from his waist.

"Take care," I say, but he says nothing. The driver toots his horn.

Slowly, I climb into a window seat so I can see him. He slides both hands deep into the pockets of his khaki trousers and it's all I can do not to reach out and touch the *V* of hair showing above his white shirt.

"Take good care of yourself," he says without a smile and steps back from the bus.

"I will write," I say lamely.

"Don't." His voice is cold.

I nod because it's better I don't speak. I have lost him. When the bus chugs off, I wave with frantic brightness, watching him grow smaller, his khaki trousers and shirt blurring into the crowd. He doesn't wave back. I swallow the pain in my throat.

I am ready to run for my school. That's one thing no one will ever take from me. If Nigeria thinks they will snatch the gold medal, they are wrong. I'll run so fast my heart will explode. If that happens, I'll welcome it. Maybe then, the sharp pains in my stomach will cease. *Oh, Kayode. Auntie Biggie.* The tears are warm on my cheeks.

The bus rocks me all the way to Ibadan. With my bag slung over my shoulder, I ask for directions and head straight for the field. I know the heat events were completed yesterday evening. Today are the finals, and then come the relays. I can't wait.

I find my team but no one smiles at me. They turn away when I say good morning. Coachito comes straight at me. "Where were you?" The anger in his voice knocks me backward. Why doesn't he know Coach gave me permission?

"I was in Lagos."

"What were you doing in Lagos? You were supposed to be here, not in Lagos!"

I shake my head in confusion. "But I asked Coach and he said I could stay in Lagos for the night." Coach is standing behind him. I don't know why he won't speak up. I point at him. "You can ask Coach here, I asked him before I went to Lagos. Coach, didn't I ask you for permission?" But Coach's eyes have fallen to his feet and won't look up. "Coach, I asked you, didn't I?" He is digging into the grass with his white sneakers.

Coachito is so angry he can barely breathe out the words. "The Nigerians changed the program. We were to run the relay this morning! Because you weren't here, we couldn't run. They won by default. We brought you for the relay and you weren't here!"

"But how could they change the program just like that?"

"That's neither here nor there. You missed your event!" He marches off as if he is too angry for words. Coach remains, still digging into the grass. I draw closer and stick my head under his nose so he has to look at me.

"Coach? You gave me permission!"

He nods, but whatever he is feeling is not strong enough to force his mouth open to defend me. I can hear the other athletes complaining loudly. Do I think I'm better than anyone else? I used the team. This trip was nothing but an excuse for me to visit my family. Am I the only one who has family? I took their money for no reason. On and on. Now I don't dare go looking for Auntie Taye, who is on this very campus. No one wants to talk or stand near me.

Supper time, we eat at the university cafeteria where I sit with the Nigerian students because my teammates are still angry. While I'm eating, Coachito marches up to me and asks me to step outside with him. He wastes no time in getting to the point. "We brought you here for the relay and you didn't run. Therefore, you need to give back the allowance we gave you, simple and short."

I have no choice but to do just that. I've lost Auntie Biggie. I've lost Kayode. This is nothing.

On the return journey to Ghana, no one talks to me. When I get to Rudolph's room, I bury my head in his shirt and cry.

"Sssh," he comforts me. "Don't mind them, I'm here."

I don't tell him about my night with Kayode. I can't hurt him too. This is one burden I'll carry alone.

CHAPTER TWENTY-SIX

WANT TO GO to Nigeria," Rudolph tells me from the window-sill of my room where he is perched, strumming his guitar. He has finished his university degree and wants to go abroad. He is fed up with the *kalabule* that has returned with a vengeance in Ghana: hoarding, smuggling, runaway inflation. I don't know why we bother importing corned beef or fish from a can when there are cows everywhere and plenty of fish in the sea. Anyway, Nigeria needs teachers and skilled workers, which is why he wants to go there.

"There is no future for me here as an actor," he says. "No one respects artists, but in Nigeria, I can act for a living, even write. Look at Wole Soyinka, who won the Nobel Prize."

It's true. Nigerians have their bowl of a National Theater and even produced a film called *Bisi, Daughter of the River*. In Ghana, Kaakaaku players set up stages on dusty street corners where anybody passing can stop for a laugh. But no one has to pay them. If you want to show your thanks, you put whatever amount of money you want in an offering bowl they place nearby. Even actors on television don't get paid much. Only the producer has a respectable salary. We never got paid for Rudolph's play we did on television. No one feeds a family by acting in plays. I tell Rudolph I understand.

"I want to go and make money so that when you finish university, I'll be already settled and we can get married," he says.

Ever since he took me for his girl, we've been walking down the path toward marriage, the direction to follow when you have a boyfriend. Everyone knows that. Yet picturing the destination makes my stomach drop. I say, "I thought you wanted to go to Hollywood and become an actor."

He smiles. "Yes, one day, when I have enough money for the airplane and everything. But for now, Nigeria is the only place I can work. We can get engaged, Esi. Then when you finish schooling, we'll marry. We will have a big wedding in a church."

I don't want to marry until I've finished the university, but getting engaged is different, isn't it? An engagement is just a promise. If a girl realizes she has made a mistake, she can always un-engage, can't she? So I say yes, and Rudolph plucks at the guitar strings, singing:

> Long ago-o-o-o,
> high on a mountain in Mexico-o-o-o,
> lived a young shepherd boy Angelo-o-o-o-o,
> who met a young girl and he loved her so-o-o-o . . .
> Rich was she-e-e-e, came from a very high family-y-y . . .

He croons songs like that though we sprouted from the same kind of soil. His father used to teach, mine used to run a school. We are both blessed with fathers who don't have too much money. At any rate, I don't mind him going to Nigeria. When you have a boyfriend who wants to work hard for the future, you let him go. He has heard about a resident theater company at the University of

Ibadan, that same university where I missed the relay, and wants to try his luck.

I say okay and, within a week, he climbs into a bus bound for a six-hour journey to Nigeria.

Rudolph is not the only one shaking the dust off his feet for another land. All the brain is draining out of Ghana into everywhere else in the world. I'm not surprised when I travel home and Sister Mansa tells me her husband has found work in Zimbabwe. She will join him as soon as he sends for her. Zimbabwe is rich and recently free from apartheid, and what with its president being married to a Ghanaian, we the in-laws are flocking there in droves.

Her Royal Highness too has left Ghana to teach in Nigeria, and Kwabena has enrolled himself in the University of Lagos. He didn't even tell me, I had to find out from Papa! And honestly, did he really have to leave? At least students in Ghana receive loans from the government. How is he going to pay for his tuition in Nigeria? He is a squirrel, that one; he hides his future. And did Sister Abena and her husband have to move to northern Ghana, which might as well be a foreign country? It's a four-day journey just to get there, including a ferry ride across the Volta River. When it's working, that is. Meanwhile Sister Crocodile got married while I was at school and has moved with her husband to another town.

Now it's just Papa, Auntie, Sister Mansa, and me in the house, plus a new maid Auntie clucks at to empty the chamber pots, fan the coal pot, and set the table. After lunch, Papa and I are sitting side by side in our armchairs as he licks his finger to turn a page of the *Daily Graphic*. It's no wonder his hair is so gray—there is much to complain about these days.

"Can you believe this fool?" When he uses the word *fool* without specifying a name, you know he is insulting Junior Jesus. Four circular spots mark the linoleum where the radiogram is still missing, which to Papa is a sign of extreme incompetence because J.J. failed to find the man who stole it. "The IMF tells him to devalue the cedi and he does. Now he says the government will no longer give loans to university students. The cheek of it! This bloody fool takes orders from other countries, countries that help their own people with education!"

He thrusts the paper at me and grabs his sweating glass of whiskey, which has left a ring of water on the wooden table. I start reading and there it is. No loans for students. I sigh. I know I'll manage. My sisters will help with my education, it's the tradition. But students whose parents struggle to find milk for porridge may not be able to continue schooling.

Over the radio, a journalist describes the Student Resistance Council's fury: *We would continue to struggle till all the remnants of the obnoxious antiworker and antistudent policies imposed by the IMF and World Bank puppets have been dismantled!*

Why the conditional "would," and how Coriolanus-like as usual. These are the same people who hid Rawlings on campus, screamed for blood, and dubbed him Junior Jesus. Now the same mouths that cried *Hosannas* to Junior Jesus are crying *Crucify him!* I almost feel sorry for the man. Even his own cabinet is grumbling at him for turning away from the LEFT.

The radio announces further that the SRC has declared an *aluta* against J.J. and his government. I think *aluta* is a corruption of *El Lute* in Spanish, or the Fight in English, the nickname for that Che Guevara character who helped turn governments upside down in Latin America, which is what the students want to do to the Provisional National Defense Council.

Daily radio reports blare on about how the students in Accra are running through the streets holding signboards, whacking the air with sticks, chanting *Aluta continua!* J.J. orders soldiers to scatter the rebels with tear gas. He yells that students are rioting because they have too much time on their hands. He has had it. Students have to become a productive "task force." They have to help construct roads, build bridges. They will learn how hard life is and think twice before rioting again. Soldiers round up students, forcing them to pick up spades. I am thinking I should probably go hide in Nigeria when a letter arrives from Rudolph.

Darling Esi,

It's been too long since I saw you. Really, a month feels like a year.

I miss your laughter. I miss you curling inside my arms at night.

Fortunately, I got what I wanted. I'm an actor with the resident theater at the University of Ibadan. You're right about the town being huge. It's bigger than Lagos. I have also found a place to rent not far from the university. I have missed you terribly. I will be arriving in a week to fetch you. Let's meet at Volta Hall in the evening.

I will be miserable until I see you.

All my love,

Rudolph

Papa doesn't know Rudolph exists. Ever since the fracas over my letters from boys, I don't tell him anything. If I say I am going to visit Rudolph, he'll ask how dare I go to a man's house when the man hasn't performed rites for me. He'll call me a useless tramp, so I tell him I want to visit my Nigerian family.

The appointed day, I travel to Accra and head for the university. The taxi turns right to Volta Hall, and there he is, Rudolph, sitting on the steps. I run to him.

"I've missed you," he says, squeezing my bottom.

We spend the night at the university guesthouse and wake

up at six in the morning to catch a taxi into Accra station, near Makola Market. Though we can't see the market, a smoky, acrid smell blows over us, bringing up the horrors of the day soldiers destroyed it. I breathe easier when we join two others at the back of a Peugeot 505 for the ride to the Ghana-Togo border at Aflao. The rainy season has eaten away at the road, leaving such large potholes that it is almost noon when we arrive at the border.

The immigration office is little more than a kiosk facing the street, a mere two minutes' stroll from the border crossing. Beyond the border lies Lome, the coastal capital of Togo. No wall separates the two countries, just two gatelike openings with a few yards of no-man's-land between them. On both sides of the border, a row of taxis lines the road, Ghanaian taxis versus Togolese ones. Under umbrellas and hats, women fry doughnuts and fish. We ignore the delicious smells because first we must enter immigration and get our passports stamped.

Two immigration officers sit behind a long wooden table. One could pass for a grandfather while the other one grins like a fresh recruit, happy to be in charge, a pencil tucked behind his ear like a carpenter. I smile at him, and his eyes twinkle. "Yes?"

I hand him my passport. "We're going into Togo."

He flicks open pages and shakes his head, handing me back my passport. "I am sorry, you cannot cross the border."

He is not looking for a bribe, is he? I stop smiling and cock my head sideways. "Why can't we cross into Togo?"

"It's not us, lady," he says, waving away a fly as his partner nods. "It's the Togolese. Our side is open, but they won't let you into their side."

"But why not?" Rudolph says. "We've always had open borders between Togo and Ghana. Why have they closed their side?"

"They say we don't have democracy, because of Rawlings's coup. They're afraid we Ghanaians will infect them with our rebels."

"I don't believe it!" I say.

"It's not only Togo, lady. If you go west, you'll find Ivory Coast won't let Ghanaians cross."

"But so many people have relatives in Togo," Rudolph says.

I add my piece. "I'm sure people still cross every day. I mean, the Ewes in Ghana and those in Togo are the same." If it weren't for the French and British carving them up, the Ewes would be one people, not French-speaking Ewes and Ghanaians speaking the same language speckled with English. And what is this rule-for-life mentality anyway? President Eyadéma of Togo, President Houphouët-Boigny of Ivory Coast, both refusing to hand over power. No wonder they're pissing in their pants with fear and won't let us pass.

Rudolph gives me a look to be quiet. He begs them. He explains that he needs to get back to Nigeria where he works. And please, don't they know how hard it is for a man to function without his wife to cook for him? I frown at him but the older officer looks moved. He points at me. "That's your wife?"

"Yes," Rudolph says with a straight face. "I just came back for her."

They grow quiet.

"There's a way," the old guard says quietly. "You can travel farther north to Hohoe and then cross the border. It's easier from there. It's still dangerous though."

Rudolph and I look at each other. "Are you okay with that, my beauty?" he asks. "You can go back home, you know."

What kind of girlfriend leaves her man to face hardship alone? "I'm coming with you," I say firmly. He gives me a proud smile. We ask how far Hohoe is from Lome and they tell us about eighty-five miles.

"It's going to take a long time," Rudolph says. "I bet the roads are not good."

The old guard nods. "In fact, you may have to spend the night."

"Spend the night? But we don't know anyone there!" I say.

"I'll help you," he says. "When you get there, ask for Mr. Te-makloe. He is my cousin. Tell him I sent you. He'll give you a place to stay."

"Thank you, thank you," Rudolph says, shaking his hand. I also say thank you, tearing up. This is the kind of senseless generosity I love about Ghanaians.

About one in the afternoon, we find a wooden truck bound for Hohoe. Rudolph gives me a hand as I grab the side pole, stick my foot in the triangular hole, and hoist myself in. I blow into my blouse, dabbing at the sweat trickling down my temples. Rudolph's shirt is beginning to form dark spots from sweating. Sellers surround the truck, tempting us with food on trays or arranged in glass containers: steamed corn on the cob, fried shrimp, clams, snails, fish, bushmeat, not to mention fruits and groundnuts. We opt for bananas and the nuts. There are also cold drinks for sale.

"Would you like some Fanta?" Rudolph asks.

There's nothing I'd like better than chilled soda dancing down my throat, but I don't want to later beg the driver to let me squat in the bush and urinate, so I decline. We shift to the end of the middle row of the truck. This is the kind of truck people call a bone-shaker, a wooden shell on a flatbed, furnished with slabs of wooden benches. I pray we don't hit potholes or we'll bounce up like basketballs.

Our traveling companions are mostly of the working-class variety, plus women shushing restless babies or sucking the juice from peeled oranges. As I listen to the buzzing around me, I feel a sudden dip in my stomach. Every person on the bus is Ewe. Rudolph and I are Fantes. There are rumors that because J.J. is Ewe, they have taken to killing non-Ewes. Even before the coup, people always accused Ewes of being more tribalistic than other ethnic groups, and now they've supposedly turned murderous. Usually I swat away such rumors the way I do flies. I have never met a single Ewe person I didn't want to sit with and share Coca-Cola. Plus, wasn't that fatherly border guard Ewe? And yet my heart thuds. I have never ventured deep into Ewe territory. What if the rumors are true? What if when we drive through a stretch of forest, they pull us down and hack off our heads with cutlasses?

There are more than twenty of them and only two of us. Plus, I don't understand their language. Hardly anyone else does. Really, they seem to belong to Togo where almost everyone speaks Ewe or Mina, which sound the same to me. For all I know, our traveling companions are plotting against us. Beyond a few words I've picked up over the years, I can make nothing of their language beyond *gbagbana gbna, gbagbana gbna*, like a bottle swallowing water. I whisper to Rudolph, "You know Ewe people are supposed to be killers, don't you?" He nods but his profile remains undisturbed. "Listen, I'm going to speak the few Ewe words I know so they're aware we understand them."

His shoulders shake with giggles. "You are mad."

"No," I hiss. "I'm serious. You never know."

As we swelter in the heat waiting for the driver, I roll my eyes in annoyance and say, *"Nuke dzor!"* (What is going on?) No one pays attention to me. They carry on, *gbagbana gbna gbna*. When they laugh at an apparent joke, I throw my head back and cackle too, complete with thigh slapping and eye wiping. Rudolph shakes his head helplessly. When we talk to each other, we whisper in English, not in Fante, and I make sure to adopt a singsong Ewe accent. However, as we bounce along our way, I'm struck by the kindness of my fellow travelers. Someone offers me a piece of fried cassava dipped in pepper and I accept, saying *"Apke!"* But I'm still wary, so every now and then, I blurt *medekuku!* (please) to no one in particular and *fiafitor!* (thief!) to Rudolph whose jaws quiver with suppressed laughter. Behind me, I feel a pull at my braid and a feathery pat on the back of my neck. I twist around. It's a baby pushing to her feet on her mother's lap, reaching for me as the mother secures her in the crook of one arm. At the same time, the mother is trying to feed fingers of fried cocoyam to a child sitting next to her. When I smile, the baby's cheeks fold away in delight, two lower teeth glistening in a pool of drool. I whisper, "*Va mi dzo*," and hold out my hand. The mother allows her to fall into my arms. I hug her soft, warm body. She smells of sour milk. *Mmm* . . . lovely. I shrug off Rudolph's teasing smile. And I don't care that her drool leaves dark spots on my blouse, that she grabs my nose, yanks at my hair, like Akwasi did.

We're barely forty-five minutes into our journey, rounding a bend obstructed by elephant grass, when a whistle tears through the air. The driver brakes, sending us flying off our seats. When we gather ourselves, they come into view. Soldiers. Green uniforms. Long guns pointing. Striding powerfully toward us in their black boots. They fan around the truck and take their time glaring from row to row, studying our faces. I twist to look at the baby. Good. She's asleep on her mother's lap. My heart jumps about. Are they looking for runaway university students?

After a long time, one of them nods at the driver and we take off. My body sags with relief. Everyone talks at once. Rudolph and I look at each other. This journey is more dangerous than we thought.

Every thirty minutes or so, we get stopped while grim-faced soldiers with guns drawn inspect the truck. I wave at the mother and children when they get off at a village. I'm getting more and more nervous. Each time, Rudolph squeezes my shoulder, whispering, "Don't worry." I no longer shout Ewe words. We're in this together.

About four o'clock, we're entering a large village when soldiers stop us again. These ones bear the appearance of settlers, unlike roadside soldiers in the middle of nowhere. They are behaving like people who live there. Apart from the three who approach us, I notice four of them lolling in front of a kiosk, quaffing what must be palm wine from calabashes. A few feet away, two others are relaxing on a bench, smoking under the shade of a mango tree. There is something different about this bunch. They look less disciplined and have bloodshot eyes.

They stomp about the truck. "Everybody, get out! Get out!"

"I think they're going to search us," Rudolph whispers. I know he has nairas, and soldiers have been seizing foreign currency as contraband. Makola women got beaten for that offense.

"Give me your money," I hiss urgently. He reaches into his pocket, shoves a wad of notes into my hand. I roll them fast and ball my fist.

When we climb down, a soldier barks, "Stand in line! Form horizontal lines! Face the grass!" Rudolph and I stand in the third line from the front, hoping they'll get tired and less vigilant by the time they get to us. I also know the best way to hide money is not to try too hard, so I keep the money in my hand.

A soldier begins searching us, row by row. When he gets to our row, he says, "Now, everybody, hands up!"

I wish I were wearing a brassiere. I could have tucked the money in it. The soldier slides to face me. He is so close I can smell his sweat and smoky-druggy breath. My heart goes crazy. I have to appear calm. I stretch up my empty hand and yawn, pretending to scratch my back with the other. He is looking me up and down. Quick, avoid his eyes! I drop my hand, slip it behind me and quickly transfer the money. I raise the now empty other hand, arranging my face into a bored expression. Then I let the hand holding the money hang by my side. I try to maintain a steady breathing. He moves on. Oh God! Breathe, breathe.

The soldier burrows his hand into the pocket of the man to my right and brings up a balled-up paper. When he opens it, all I can see are dried leaves, but the others know what it is because they gasp.

"Look at this!" the soldier says, displaying it for all to bear witness. "Do you see this?" he asks with bulging eyes and flared nostrils, walking from one end to another. No one says anything, but the other soldiers gather round excitedly. "This is *wee!*" Marijuana. "Do you know the penalty for possessing *wee*?" The culprit just hangs his head. They shove him. They punch him. Then a soldier raises his stick, knocks him down. The women moan in sympathy. My heart pounds in anger.

"How cruel," I mutter through clenched teeth. I want to snatch the stick and hit the soldier on the head.

Rudolph grabs my wrist. "Please, Esi, I'm begging you, be quiet."

"It's inhuman!"

"I know, but please, don't lose your temper." His grip on my hand is so tight I wince from the pain. The soldiers look gleeful, as though they've won the lotto. They take turns slapping the man. They strip him of his shirt. Then they order us to get back in the truck. I start crying. Rudolph presses me against him. "Sssh, control yourself, please. I beg you."

I try to twist away but his grip frustrates me. "How can we leave him behind? What will they do to him?"

"I don't know, but he's going to be all right, I'm sure. Sssh . . ."

"They hurt the Makola women, they shot at them!"

"I know, but this is different. They won't kill him."

The driver slides behind the wheel, gives impatient toots on his horn. "Come on! I'll leave you behind, you hear?"

Rudolph drags me up into the truck. He puts his arm around me and tells me not to look, but I shrug him off. I don't want to be spared, I need to see this. The victim kneels under the tree, his wrists tied behind him. A soldier approaches, a gleam in his eyes. He wields a cutlass, testing its weight. He is not going to cut him, is he? No, he's about to hit him with the flat side. Another soldier grabs his colleague to hold him back, laughing. As the truck pulls away, I keep my head twisted so I can watch, as if by merely watching I'm preventing something more sinister. The last thing I see is the soldier raise the knife above the victim's back. They won't kill him, I promise myself fiercely. I *have* to believe that or tear at my cheeks.

CHAPTER TWENTY-SEVEN

OHOE GREETS US with deceitful delight, a small town gathered on a lush plateau. The setting sun has turned the vegetation into a golden green that makes it hard to believe we've witnessed cruelty only hours before. We have no problem finding Mr. Temakloe's two-level house. A young girl takes us up a side staircase to an upstairs veranda and knocks on the front door.

A tall, blubbery man in a singlet and black shorts opens the door. His eyes are warm.

"Good evening, sir," Rudolph says. The man returns the greetings with a smile, tells us he is Mr. Temakloe. We explain our presence.

"Oh, Mr. Lawluvi sent you? Oh, you're welcome. Come in, come in."

He ushers us into his gleaming sitting room. He calls his wife Rosina to meet us. She insists we have to eat something. It seems the most natural thing to have us in their home, discussing our trip to Nigeria. They serve us a delicious meal of rice and fish stew and give us a lovely room to sleep in, promising to help us cross the border. Such unbelievable kindness. If I ever hear one nasty word about Ewes again, I'll slap the speaker.

In the morning, after a breakfast of eggs, porridge, and bread slathered yellow with margarine, Mr. Temakloe leans forward in his chair and says, "I have found two young boys who will take you through the forest into Kpalime in Togo. You just have to give them a little money." We tell him we have no problem with that.

Not wanting to look Ghanaian, I choose a Nigerian outfit Grandma gave me. Thanks to the Europeans carving out countries with disregard for ethnic groups, there are Yorubas in Benin and even Togo. I slip a buba over my head and slide my arms into its long, bell sleeves. Then I tie my wrapper tightly around my waist, making sure to keep the length mid-calf. The current fashion is ankle-length, but I'm going to walk through the forest, so I need to make it easier on myself. The material is white lace with large holes, bound to keep me cool. I complete my ensemble with low black pumps. Rudolph is in brown trousers and a dark blue shirt. He could pass for any West African national anyway, because of his indistinct features.

Mr. Temakloe accompanies us to immigration, which is little more than a shed. There, we get our passports stamped without questions. A few yards beyond, we meet the boys, who appear to be fourteen or fifteen. Mr. Temakloe explains that border guards don't bother locals because many are farmers whose lands spill across borders. Besides, they have relatives on both sides. I look the boys over. They are skinny and short, wearing brown, torn shirts like farm boys, dark green shorts, and brown rubber slippers. We pay them first because Mr. Temakloe says things will move rapidly when we get to Togo. There will be no time for goodbyes.

Rudolph shakes hands with him. "Thank you very much, sir."

"I will never forget your kindness," I say, hugging him, but he hasn't finished.

"It's at least a ten-mile walk," he says. "You may have to spend the night in Kpalime." He too has a cousin over there with whom we can stay the night. "Just ask for Mr. Nutsuga when you get to the station. Someone will show you to his house."

I am without words. Ewes have got to be the nicest people I have ever met.

My heart is going *krrpoom krrpoom krrpoom*, but I'm ready. Rudolph smiles and takes my hand. One boy heaves my suitcase onto his head while the other carries Rudolph's smaller bag on his. They explain the plan: we'll walk in one line. The one carrying Rudolph's bag will lead the way, followed by Rudolph, then me. The other boy will bring up the rear.

"Are you ready?" Mr. Temakloe asks.

I nod and Rudolph says yes, squeezing my hand.

Mr. Temakloe raises his palm in a blessing. "Go with God." And we set out on a muddy path that swallows us into the forest's dark canopy.

SWISH, SWISH, SWISH, we march through the thick, moist under-growth of creeping plants and pregnant leaves. Why did I wear white? Everything and everyone is dark brown or green. I might as well shout, "Here I am, come arrest me!" And why did I wear heels? They're only two inches high, but pumps are not for walk-ing on a dirt path overgrown with tall, wet grass sprouting every which way. Rudolph looks back at me and I smile to show him I can do it.

The path twists under the canopy. From above, a spattering of sunlight plays hide-and-seek with us, mocking us because we can never catch it. As we cut through bamboo, I worry more and more about my white lace. Also, the wrapper keeps coming apart and I have to tie it again and again. And my ankles are beginning to hurt.

Swish, swish, swish. How long has it been since we started? I can't tell because now we can barely glimpse the sun through the cluster of leaves high above us. Confidence, Esi! You are an athlete. You are baby jet. Now I'm striding with my chest out, ignoring the cawing of birds. This is wonderful, really. Look at the magnificent trees, so large their roots rise three feet above ground. We could easily sit on them to rest if we wanted. As for the tree trunks, it would take about ten men to join hands around each base. Underneath, you can see an endless blanket of fallen leaves in various stages of returning to dust. Some dark green, some brown. I'm feeling like singing when suddenly the leaves rise into the shapes of men.

Soldiers in camouflage. Oh, Awurade. How were we supposed to see them?

One barks, "Stop!"

My stomach flips over. We stand absolutely still. They crunch up to us, all eight of them. The one who shouted is obviously their leader. He is the age of someone's father. I hope he can rope the younger ones back.

His hands go to his waist as he asks in Twi, "Where are you going?" There is something a bit reassuring about his dialect. He is obviously Akuapem, a people so polite that even when they want to insult you, they ask for permission: "I beg to say you're an animal."

Rudolph replies, "We are going to Nigeria, sir. We're just traveling through Togo."

"Then why are you sneaking through the forest?"

I clear my throat and address him even more nicely, "Papa, please, we tried to cross the border, but though they stamped our passports, we were told we couldn't cross."

He rolls his eyes at his companions, who say nothing. Then he holds out his hand. "Show me your passports." Rudolph reaches into his wallet and hands him our passports. The soldier flips through both and looks up at us. "Well, you've cleared Ghana's immigration." Then he turns to the others. "We see no problem here, do we?" They draw closer to peer at the passports too. He shrugs at them. "Ah well, we don't have a problem? They haven't broken any Ghanaian laws. Let's allow them to go then, eh?" The soldiers nod, though a couple glare as if they've been robbed of an opportunity to smack us around. He hands us back our passports and wags a fatherly finger. "Be careful not to get caught, you hear? Togolese soldiers are shooting Ghanaians on sight. They're even riding motorbikes through the forest. They know people are crossing on foot, so look carefully, you hear?"

I gasp. Togolese shooting Ghanaians? We're supposed to be like the European Economic Community. We are part of ECOWAS, the Economic Community of West African States. We're supposed to have open borders! If Rawlings has staged a coup, why are we ordinary citizens being punished? What could we possibly do to hurt the Togolese government? Why can't they just stick to refusing to recognize J.J. and leave us out of it?

Papa-soldier shakes his head pitifully at me. "You should have worn something dark. Because of your white lace, we spotted you from far away."

Now I feel even more stupid about it. But what can I do? I'm surrounded by men. There is nowhere to hide and change.

"Well, good luck and take care," he says, leading his men away. They lie down and blend into leaves again.

Please, God, don't let the Togolese catch us.

Swish, swish, swish we stride. Anytime we see a clearing ahead, the leading boy turns around and puts his finger to his mouth to indicate we should be quiet. Then he whispers, "Wait with my brother." He sets the suitcase down and walks casually ahead by himself. He looks all around until he gets to the next cluster of bamboo. When it's safe, he whistles softly and the other brother tells us to run fast to the bamboo. I hitch up my wrapper and sprint for it as Rudolph runs, holding his bag. Then we resume walking with pounding hearts.

About noon, my throat feels dry. The boys tell us there is a river ahead we can drink from. When we get to the bank, I look doubtfully at the gurgling water, fretting about germs. I've never before drunk water that wasn't pipe-borne. But the boys tell us if we don't drink, we're going to have a hard time of it. They bend down and scoop with their palms. Rudolph follows suit. Well, it's a rushing stream and looks clear. If the boys can drink, then I'd better drink too. Not too much though. I don't want to have to stop to urinate. A man can whip out his penis and arc his water in any direction, but I have to find a place to squat and risk something biting my bottom.

After quenching our thirst, we are walking by more bamboo when we hear a hum. A motorbike. My heart jumps into my throat. We dive into the bamboo. The boys crouch to cover my whiteness. We're all squatting, holding our breaths. The hum grows louder, closer. Oh God. It's upon us! The bike *vrooms*, vibrates on the ground. It's a Togolese guard, leaning forward in his khaki uniform and cap. He flies by us, only a few yards away, without seeing us. We wait for the hum to fade, and when we finally get up, my legs are shaking. Absurdly, I giggle and Rudolph smiles nervously. Phew. That was rather close.

After walking all day and facing one more close call, we hear faint voices and the hum of vehicles in the distance. The boys tell us this is it. In fact, we're so close to the border we can see a tower to our right that reminds me of a picture I saw of a tower by the Berlin Wall, though this one is Lilliputian by comparison. Through the window, I spy the outline of an armed guard but luckily his face is turned toward Ghana. The boys tell us this is the most dangerous part of our journey: getting us into the clear and into a taxi.

We hide behind a thick bamboo cluster not far from the dirt road. Through an opening in the elephant grass, we glimpse the occasional car and border guard on motorbike. The boys have to execute the plan with perfect timing. One has to find a taxi going to the border that will agree to return with room for two passengers plus luggage. Then when the taxi gets back, we have to be ready to make a run for it. The sun is on its downward journey and shadows have lengthened. I slap a mosquito on my neck.

The leading boy leaves us with the luggage and ambles toward the edge of the road, hiding behind the tall grass. Though taxis drone by, he can't stop them because each time, a border guard *vrooms* along on a motorbike. My heart keeps jumping. Will this ever end?

Here comes a taxi. No guards. The boy slips out into the open and the taxi stops. He leans into the window, exchanges hurried words with the driver, and then the taxi speeds off. The boy runs back and explains, "When the driver comes back, he will slow down and wait to make sure there is no border guard in sight. When he toots, you will run to the car."

Rudolph and I look at each other. I bite my fist anxiously. We could get caught and imprisoned. Or shot. Oh, Awurade. How much longer? Breathe, Esi, breathe.

Here's the taxi! It creaks to a stop with the engine running and the back door open.

"Now!" the boys hiss. We dash out. I hit my ankle against the step. No matter. Quick, dive in! We squeeze in beside two other people. The boys throw our bags into the unlocked trunk and off the taxi zooms. We're giddy with relief.

But it's not over. After a couple of miles, we run into a police barrier. They are searching through cars for Ghanaians. I'm really getting tired of worrying. When the policeman leans into our taxi, I roll my eyes and sigh. *"Nuke dzor!"* It's no act this time; I'm angry and want to know what the big problem is. I stare out the window until the policeman taps the side of our taxi and tells the driver to move on. We are free. Kpalime at last!

The driver takes us to the station and indeed we have no trouble finding Mr. Temakloe's cousin just before dark. It's the same wonderful hospitality. They feed us, give us a nice place to sleep, and the next day, we doze off in a bus that rattles all the way down to Lome. We have completed a long, hairpin trip just to reach the same town yards from the border we had tried to cross two days ago.

Togo is a narrow slice of land. From the Ghana-Togo border to the Togo-Benin border is a mere thirty-five-minute ride in a taxi. No one makes a fuss over our Ghanaian passports. The sleepy-eyed guard, slouching in a chair, simply holds out his hand and says, "One naira." I am about to complain when Rudolph fishes out two naira and throws them into his hand.

Benin is not much bigger. It takes only forty-five minutes to cross the country to the Benin-Nigeria border at Badagri. From there, it's another ninety minutes in a taxi before we reach Lagos. At every stop, we have to give a naira to a soldier.

Because I don't want to take the chance of running into Kayode, I suggest we push ahead to Ibadan, arriving a little before sunset. The journey has taken us three days, compared with a plane ride from Accra to Lagos that would have lasted only an hour. But I'm relieved. We're in Nigeria, at long, long last.

I am so tired I barely register the crowds at Ibadan. Rudolph hails a taxi that bumps us over a muddy road with rocks poking out. We arrive at a building about a mile from the University of Ibadan, a house standing tall and aloof in a cranky neighborhood of small houses. It is the size of a secondary school dormitory. We enter through a corridor and turn into a large room to the right.

"My pay is not high," Rudolph says with a modest smile, "so this is all I can afford."

I smile back to show I don't mind where he lives. When he un-locks the door, I am so drained I just crumble onto the bed and I barely feel it when he peels off my sandals.

The next day I wake up to Yoruba voices yelling from outside. Rectangles of orange light slide through the louvers and splash the bed. My eyes travel round the room. The important things are here: a wooden table with two chairs to the right of the door, and a dresser with a mirror on the left. A couch hugs the wall near the foot of the bed. There are even blue tie-dye curtains billowing from the windows above the headboard.

"You're awake," Rudolph says, rolling over to peck my lips. "Well, what do you think of the place?"

I smile. "It's lovely. So where do you cook?"

He gives me an apologetic smile. "There is a kitchen at the end of the corridor. We have to share it with the other tenants."

"When we lived at the university, we shared with so many others, didn't we? I don't care about any of that."

He pulls me on top of him. "You're special."

FOR THREE WEEKS, I walk with him to work and watch him re-hearse. Then we eat lunch at the university or a chop bar before walking back home. We play music or I help him learn his lines. Most of the time, I read. Life rolls on this way until the day Auntie Yetunde forwards a letter from Papa.

I tear open the flaps of the airmail letter card and flop onto my back to read. Rudolph stretches sideways beside me, propped on his elbow and stroking my braids with his free hand. Papa's cursive swims before me because I don't believe the words floating across the blue paper: *Mr. Frempong has asked for your hand in mar-riage to his son Rudolph, and I have accepted. From now on, you must not be seen in the company of any other man.*

I twist to face Rudolph. "Your father has already been to see Papa?"

His hand stops moving. "We talked about it, didn't we?"

I try to explain. "We said we would marry one day. That's different from your father going to see Papa with a bottle of schnapps to knock on the marriage door."

"Am I not the man?" he says, mashing his forehead in exasperation. "Am I not the one to decide? You were coming to visit me. What kind of man has a woman come live at his house without ceremony?"

"But I'm just spending holidays here, not living with you. I thought we would both decide when your father could go see Papa."

He goes quiet for a while. "Why are you acting this way?"

"It feels as if . . . as if I don't have any say. And I don't like being told I must not be seen in the company of any other man. What about my friends? What if I want to run for the university again?"

He gathers me to his hairy chest. "Oh, no, don't worry. You can run all you want. And knocking on the door is only an engagement, remember? We're not marrying. I still have to go to Hollywood to earn that Oscar."

I have to smile. "Yes, you go on and get your Oscar."

I write to Papa, and the ceremony is set for December, the month of the Harmattan, when the dry winds from the Sahara blow southward and crack the skin. I am nineteen.

CHAPTER TWENTY-EiGHT

T ODAY IS MY engagement. There is something thrilling about bringing a man into Papa's house without trembling with fear. He will look from Rudolph to me and know without a doubt that I've done more than kiss, and he will actually smile. This must be why people get married, to experience this sense of ultimate approval. I mean, Sister Yaa came all the way from Takoradi yesterday because of me, and she hugged me. She hugged me!

By this time, I'm sure Rudolph has put together the requirements for engaging a girl: a gold ring, a sewing machine, and a trunk full of beautiful Ghanaian print cloth. I can't wait to slip the cool jewel with a precious stone onto my finger, but the rest I can do without. I can't believe anyone would give me a sewing machine, considering the only time I quarreled with Sister Abena was when, as payment for making me a dress, she made me hem clothes she made for people. Not to mention Needlework was my least favorite subject at Wesley Girls.

I know Rudolph has laid money aside to pay the *akonta sekan,* the brother-in-law's knife fee. This is to repay my brother for his years of protecting me from harm, even though Kwabena hasn't been around lately. In fact, I haven't laid eyes on him in two years, and he hasn't deigned to respond to my letters. Not that he has ever protected me. When he was in secondary school, I heard from him only when he ran out of money and wanted some of mine.

No engagement is complete without a Bible for the girl, which is usually bound in white leather, with gold lettering on the cover. Even the edges are trimmed with gold, and God himself seems to fashion the pages that are as delicate as onion skin. In addition to the Bible, Rudolph must bring boxes of strong drinks for the ceremony, which must have God frowning. The Bible and booze, ha. And he shouldn't forget the most important thing: money to compensate Papa for what Papa has spent on me since I slid out of my mother's womb. It sets my teeth on edge to think about it. How do you price the caring of a child? What is the cost of bathing a baby and putting your nipple to her mouth? What about the times Papa let me sleep in his bed when I was raging with malaria, when he begged God to heal me? Or when he used a cutlass to carve a cup out of a coconut shell because I asked him to?

Auntie says there is a good reason for insisting on a huge sum from the man. When a man spends a lot of money on his woman, he will treat her like a jewel. Hmm, but a jewel can't speak, can it? A jewel gets treasured in a box, taken out and admired and replaced when not in use. On the other hand, it can also mean a man won't mistreat something he had to work so hard to get, right? Anyway, Papa says I am not for sale, so Rudolph can bring any respectable amount. Which is the reason Uncle Papa Kwasi isn't happy.

After showering, I'm about to go upstairs to get dressed when he sweeps into our compound before anyone else arrives. He wishes me a curt good afternoon and turns swiftly for the stairs. I hurry after him, trying to keep up with this old man pounding up the stairs like a soldier. He bangs the screen door after him and waves away my welcome with "Where is your father?"

"He is washing himself."

"Fine then, I'll talk to you." He sits forward in an armchair, throwing his massive cloth over his shoulder with angry energy. "I'm not happy you're getting engaged like this. I wish that man wasn't coming to perform rites for you today. Why can't he wait for you to finish school? And I told your father, you're worth more because the man is getting an educated girl. And you"—he wags his finger at me—"I hear you refused the sewing machine. Fine, ask for a car. An educated woman should get a car!"

I could say I don't want to feel like a cow you bargain over at the market, but what's the use? He won't listen, so I just smile. Since Auntie Biggie's death, I challenge only outsiders, not those I love. I fetch him a glass of water and dash into the bedroom to get dressed.

I wiggle into a red dress fitted at the top and gathered at the waist so tightly the skirt flares out. Then I sit on the bed, painting my nails red to match. After I finish, I lean back with my fingers spread out and keep my feet in my white slippers. Rudolph's eyes will pop out when he sees me looking so pretty.

The door snaps open. It's Auntie.

"What do you think you're doing, sitting around being useless?" she says. She is breathing fast, which means there is much cooking to be done, and even if Sister Mansa is here and Sister Yaa has come home for the occasion, she still needs me. So much for feeling like a princess.

"My fingernails aren't dry yet."

"Your nails? *Tweaa!* Hurry up and come downstairs before your in-laws arrive!"

"They are not my in—"

"Esi, just come on." She stands with her hand curved over the bronze doorknob. "You have to show them you know how to cook, not sit there looking like a hibiscus." It's clear she won't leave unless I get up and follow her. A murmuring starts up in my chest but I squelch it and shuffle down the stairs after her.

In the steamy kitchen, my sisters are grinding and stirring away. They give me knowing smiles and ask me if I am excited, but before I can answer, Auntie grabs a huge basin of rice and points her chin at a stool. "Take that and come with me."

"Where are we going?" I ask, but she is already pushing past me, kicking the door open with her foot.

"You are going to sit in front of the store—that way your in-laws can see you working when they arrive. You have to pick the stones out of the rice. You know how the farmers don't clean it properly."

"Outside? Why do I need to show people I'm working?"

"Just keep quiet and come, ah! You talk too much!"

I follow her through the store, around the wooden counter, and through the double doors to the front of the house. She crosses the shaded veranda into the sun and sets the basin on a short table she has placed there for that purpose. She tells me to sit behind it, facing the road. The murmuring in my chest is growing so loudly she must surely hear it. I grit my teeth and set the stool on the dusty red gravel. The biscuit-seller who wanted her husband to eat me waves from behind her table and yells for the world to hear, "I hear you are getting engaged! Long life on your head!"

"Thank you," I say with a foolish grin and look away lest she bring up her husband.

Here I am up to my elbows in a huge basin of uncooked rice, flicking stones out for the world to see. Forget about looking beautiful. All I can do is remember not to stir the dust around my sandaled feet, to protect my newly painted nails. Trucks and cars hum by. Some slow down for passengers to gape. Men hanging from the sides of trucks whistle at me and I roll out my lips at them. The sun burns my arms that are white with rice powder, and that's how Rudolph finds me when he arrives with his family in a yellow-and-green taxi.

When he steps out, something delicious squeezes my heart. He is showing full respect here, in well-ironed black trousers and a blue shirt. His black shoes are so shiny you can see the gravel mirrored on them. No wonder a woman selling boiled eggs on a tray is staring with her mouth open.

"Hello." His dimples are extra defined, like the bass clefs on a musical staff.

I say hello too and stand up to greet his parents. I can't believe how much he resembles his father, though age has practically curved Mr. Frempong's back into a *C*. He has the same bushy hair as Rudolph's, except you'd think he used a comb dipped in white paint to comb his hair, he has that much gray. Mrs. Frempong stands almost as tall as the mister, with a child's smile and puppy brown eyes.

"Good afternoon," Mr. Frempong says. On this hot afternoon, he is dressed in a black suit and mopping his forehead with a white handkerchief. He holds out his hand, and I'm about to take it when I remember mine is powdered white from the rice, so I just stand there with a foolish smile pasted on my face. Before I can say anything else, the screen door upstairs opens and claps shut. I lift my chin to see Papa standing on the balcony, dressed in a white shirt and brown trousers.

"Oh, Mr. Frempong, welcome!" Papa waves his arm. "Come on upstairs!" He points to the side staircase, and up they go. I long to go upstairs too, sit with them and feel the coolness of Coca-Cola tingling down my throat, but that will have to wait. Besides, I might as well do a good job cleaning the rice because I don't want anyone chewing stones.

After finishing, I carry the bowl into the kitchen to find it buzzing. Auntie is stirring the chicken stew on the coal pot. Sister Mansa is cutting orange circles of carrots on a table, and Sister Yaa is measuring flour to make banana fritters. The steam has given a moist shine to everyone's arms.

"Esi, you have to cook the rice," Auntie says. "It is important that you work well so you don't disgrace us."

After that, it's more of the same:

"Esi, make sure you don't burn the banana fritters."

"Esi, take the tray upstairs."

"Esi, we need more ice!"

"Esi, bring more stew!"

"Esi, what is taking you so long?"

I lean against the wooden cupboard in the kitchen. I haven't even spoken to Rudolph yet, and my stomach is protesting from hunger.

"When does the ceremony begin?" I ask.

"It has already started," Sister Mansa says.

"What? How can they do it without me?"

"You are not supposed to be there," Sister Yaa says. "Your duty is to make sure the guests have enough food and drinks."

Rudolph can be present because he is a man and a guest in our home. An engagement is a pact between two families, not individuals.

"You know," Sister Mansa says, "in other homes the girl is treated like a princess for the day, but you know how colonial our family is, no progress here."

"Stop encouraging her," Crocodile Yaa says. "She is spoilt enough."

I turn away from her. I'm really getting hungry and angry. I could pinch some chicken to eat, but someone might ask me to take something upstairs and I'd be forced to swallow quickly and run. I'd rather wait for them to finish upstairs before eating.

After a long time, Papa calls me into the living room. Here they are, the happy ones, sitting on the brown sofa and armchairs, moon-shaped smiles gleaming white at me. Why should I smile? My stomach is empty while theirs are full. You can tell by the chicken bones they have cracked and sucked till the pieces have dried white.

Papa Kwasi asks if Rudolph is the man for me and I say yes.

"This is your husband now," Papa says, patting Rudolph on the shoulder. "Look at the beautiful ring he has bought you."

The whole situation feels unreal, as if I'm floating on a cloud above them and their voices are coming from far away. Papa Kwasi rises, loosens the large cloth from his shoulder, rolls it down, and twists it around his waist, revealing the gray and black hair on his bosomy chest. His stomach is round and movable from all the whiskey he has poured into it over the years. He picks up the bottle of schnapps and fills a glass. The center table squeaks against the linoleum as someone pulls the table to make room. Ah, the libation.

He pours a drop of schnapps onto the linoleum, invoking the names of the ancestors. After each name, he adds a drop. "Here is a drink." But he doesn't call out my mother's name, and when he mentions "Auntie Adelaide, the woman who gave birth to her," I want to snatch the glass from his hand. I love Auntie, but why do they have to lie to the ancestors, who must surely know the truth? Why pretend my mother never pushed me out of her body? If she is watching, isn't she sad that she is not worth more than the ground we stand on? On he goes in his scratchy voice, "Ancestors, we are gathered here because a man has chosen your daughter for a bride. This is a happy day indeed. We ask you to bless their union and give them joy."

Amen, everyone says. I swallow the burning in my throat.

"Keep the evil one far away from them."

Amen!

"And let her give birth, give birth, and give birth until she has thirty!"

Amen! Amen! Well said!

Then he pours the rest of the schnapps onto the linoleum.

He is supposed to have done this outside so the drink would sink into the earth, into the ancestors' mouths. Now, the ancestors can't drink it and I have to wipe the floor before someone slips and falls. And thirty children? Everyone talks at once. Papa shakes my arm, "Clear the dishes, Esi."

Rudolph's eyes tell me he feels sorry but I look away. I snatch the plates from the table and let them *clatter-clatter* onto the tray. *Thirty children.* I can see myself, waist stretched wide, shiny, tributaries of scars on my hanging stomach and ironed-out breasts, cooking forever, thirty children running around my legs like ants.

I finish clattering the dishes and stomp downstairs and next thing I know, Rudolph and his parents are saying goodbye and I'm left staring at their taxi creaking and disappearing down the hill.

BACK ON CAMPUS, every girl wants to be me. They say, "You're so lucky to be engaged." They ask me to show them my ring and I stick out my hand to reveal the gold band set with onyx, even though I don't like the stone, the color of death. I told Rudolph beforehand but he chose that anyway. Also, it's too big so I have to take it off when I wash myself, otherwise it will slip off of my finger and gurgle with the foamy water into the drain. I told him my finger was the size of his little finger but he bought a bigger ring because he didn't believe I knew the size of my own finger.

I find out from my friends that Sister Mansa is right, my engagement was not the usual way. Girls do get treated like a princess though they do a ceremonial serving of their in-laws. Mine was the way it was because Auntie is old enough to be my grandmother and things were different when she was a young girl getting engaged herself. I shake off my frustration and bask in the envy of my friends, and when Easter holidays arrive, I travel home. I can't wait to see everyone who will come home for the festivities, especially Sister Abena and my new brother. On Palm Sunday we'll dance on the streets to brass band music, waving palm branches. On Good Friday we'll go to church to enjoy the haunting, melodious harmony. On Easter Sunday the choir will sing glorious songs about the risen Christ and then we will go home and throw a big party and dance and dance because no one has to work on Easter Monday.

As soon as I step into the sitting room, Papa asks, "What are you doing here?" No welcome home, Esi. He just sits in his favorite chair by the radio, an open book in his hand.

"It's Easter holidays," I remind him, thinking he is getting old and forgetful. As I walk over to greet him properly, he pulls back farther into the chair.

"You ought to be with your husband. You don't belong here anymore."

It's my turn to step back. "But I am only engaged."

He drops the book into his lap and wags his finger. "A traditional engagement is marriage. This is not the white man's silly idea of engagement where you can give the ring back whenever you feel like it."

"But we haven't had a wedding!"

He shakes his head emphatically. "Rudolph can give you a wedding anytime, but once he has brought the drinks and the ring and performed the rites, you have to live with him as his wife."

I can't believe what an ignoramus I've turned out to be, thinking I am married only if I dress up in a white gown and say "I do" in a church. Now Papa is pushing me out the door as if I'm not his daughter anymore, as if I now belong to another family. Tears burn my eyes and then I let out loud sobs but he won't listen. He tells me he will buy my ticket himself and send me to go live with Rudolph in Nigeria. When I keep sniffling, he says, "Grow up! Marriage is a good thing for a female. If you wait to finish university, men will be afraid of you. No man wants an overeducated woman who will give him a headache with arguments. Now you will have a secure future no matter how educated you get. I tell you, a woman's glory is her husband."

CHAPTER TWENTY-NiNE

ALLAAAAAAH HU AKBAR!" That's the watchman for Rudolph's building, yawning and shouting at the same time. He has apparently decided the only place to sleep is behind our window. The shouting is followed by a long silence during which I suspect he's dozing off, and then, just when I think he has truly fallen asleep, he starts again. This is what wakes me up at five every morning, unlike Rudolph. Dogs yelp and cocks crow but he snores undisturbed on his side of the bed. We have been engaged, or I should say, betrothed, for nearly seven months, and yet this place doesn't feel like home. I pull my pillow over my ear and manage to drift off. When I wake up, the room is bathed in sunshine. Car horns blare from the street. There are the usual shouts from the landlady upstairs, calling her son Abel to fetch one thing or the other. Rudolph sits at the edge of the bed smiling at me. He is dressed already in a light green shirt tucked into black trousers.

He rubs my thigh through the bedsheet. "I was about to wake you up. I want you to come with me to work today."

"Why?" I have taken to remaining behind, reading, writing,

and walking until he gets back. I no longer wish to spend my days just watching him rehearse. I am creating space to live.

"I want you to meet somebody." His voice quickens. "I think you'll like him. He is a lot like you."

"Who is he?" I've never seen him bring such energy into an introduction. He can't stay still the way he rubs my thigh one moment and scratches his knee the next.

"He's a graduate student. I met him when I first came to Ibadan. We've become good friends, he's my Nigerian brother, I tell you." I'm suddenly alert, wondering where his thoughts are going. "Look, I just don't like you staying here by yourself reading."

"So?" I am sitting up now.

"You could spend time with him. He plays the guitar like me, and loves reading."

"Why would I go spend my time with a man I don't know?" It's not unusual for a Ghanaian man to ask a friend to squire his girl-friend, but not his so-called wife, one she doesn't even know. Also, there is a saying in Ghana that asking a Nigerian man to keep your woman company is like asking a cat to watch your fish dry. Not a wise thing to do. "I don't like this," I say.

"Come on, it's just for today. That way I don't have to come home right after. We could go eat at a chop bar or the cafeteria. We could visit friends, or go to a bar."

"Hmmm." I am studying my curved fingers, flicking thumb-nail against fingernails.

He pushes heavily to his feet, his head hanging. "I'm just trying to make you happy. You don't talk as much as you used to. Your eyes hold secrets you don't share."

I have no energy for a debate as to why I don't talk or smile or eat enough. "Okay," I say. "I'll come meet him—don't look so happy. I don't want to stay with a stranger for three hours while you work. I'll greet him, talk to him a bit, and then I'm leaving, okay?"

"Okay."

"What's his name?"

He smiles eagerly. "Taiwo. You'll really like him!"

An hour later, we are walking along a veranda on the first floor of Tafawa Balewa Hall for postgraduate students. Rudolph explains that Taiwo is studying eighteenth-century literature. At the end of a cemented veranda with wooden railings, he raps his knuckle on the door. What am I doing in this ridiculous situation, as if I need someone to keep me company? I should leave. This is silly. I'm about to turn around when the door opens. A twiggy man pops out, a child's gleam in his eyes.

"Rudolph!" he says. "And this beautiful one must be Esi!"

Rudolph smiles proudly. "This is Esi indeed."

"Good morning," I say without smiling.

"Come in, ah-ah, welcome!"

His energy is so infectious I find myself smiling. We step into a large room with a desk at the far end. The rest of the room is cluttered with books. Books in bookcases lining the walls, books stacked on the floor near the bed, books propping up a guitar. He plops on the chair and pats the bed. "Sit here, it's more comfortable." Rudolph and I sit side by side. Taiwo turns to me. "So, you speak Yoruba?"

"A little."

Rudolph jumps in, "A little? She speaks it well, that was her first language!"

"That's true," I say. "But I've forgotten a lot. My father moved me to Ghana when I was little."

Taiwo leans toward me and says in a teasing voice, "Ṣé dáada ni?"

I laugh. "Everyone understands that. M'owà. I'm doing well."

Rudolph pushes to his feet, turning to me. "Can I leave you two? I have to go to work."

For some reason, I feel so grateful I leap up and throw my arms around his neck. "Walk well," I say.

Taiwo and I have fun. He teaches me Yoruba endearments to use for Rudolph. We debate on whether Chinua Achebe's Chief Nanga was really a man of the people. We sing. I teach him a Ghanaian song and he strums on his guitar. Something about him makes me kick off my slippers, tucking my feet comfortably under me. When he's not looking, I catch myself staring at the definition of thigh muscle in his trousers. Awurade, I want to knead them. Stop it, Esi, you are engaged. Yes, but look at those fingers. Stop it, just stop it. When I get up to run my hands over the books in his bookcase, he lays down his guitar and follows me. I can almost feel his breath on my neck as he apologizes for the dust and invites me to wash my hands in a basin and sit again on the bed. It seems minutes when Rudolph returns.

Taiwo jumps up to pump his hands. "She is fantastic. You are so lucky!" Rudolph smiles with pride and slips his arm around my waist, but a cup of sadness runs over me, a feeling that eases when Rudolph invites him to join us at a chop bar.

At the chop bar, the men compete to take care of me, pouring iced water for me, giving me more and more meat. Taiwo laughs a lot. Sometimes, it seems his smiles are private, just for me, causing my cheeks to warm up. The next day, when Rudolph suggests I stay again at Taiwo's I say yes eagerly. I am in trouble. Heat is growing between us, like hot bread from the oven that melts butter on contact.

Taiwo takes to holding my hand longer when I greet him, putting his arm around my waist unnecessarily. It ends with me feeling his hot breath on my cheek as he drops a peck on it. How long before his lips land on mine? If they do . . . No! This is madness. I must stop spending time alone with him.

Two weeks of Taiwo convince me even more firmly that I have to stay away. I am losing the morality battle. One morning, I stay in bed and refuse to get up.

"Why don't you want to come to the university with me and stay with Taiwo?" Rudolph asks. His eyes hold a hint of frustration.

I can't tell him the truth. Instead I say, "Don't make me spend time with him. It's, it's not right."

He is standing over me as I lie on my back, twisting the edge of the cotton bedsheet around my forefinger. "Come on, Esi, I just can't bear the thought of you slipping back into your aloneness. You've been so much livelier of late."

"Look, I'll go for a walk or something. In fact, I'll visit the landlady. Do you know what a good cook she is? I'm going to learn how to make Yoruba dishes. That's it. I'm going to stay with her today."

He goes quiet, arms folded across his chest. "Has Taiwo offended you? Has he done something to make you dislike him?"

"Oh no, he is always so kind to me!"

He thinks for a minute. "You find him boring? Is that it?"

Don't you see it? I shake my head. "Far from it! He is . . . interesting. Very."

"Then what's the problem?"

Oh, Awurade. "Nothing, it's just . . . look . . . I just don't want to."

"Did you tell him you wouldn't come today?"

My voice drops. "No. I told him to expect me."

"Then he might be offended, don't you think? You know your Yoruba people, how easily they can take offense."

I nod.

"Look, if you like, you can go today and then give him an excuse or something that you can't visit him tomorrow."

Sigh, sigh, sigh. Why can't Rudolph rip the curtain from his eyes and behold that I am the one I'm fighting?

"Okay," I say.

My heart bangs all the way to Tafawa Balewa Hall. Rudolph and I part ways in front of the building. Taiwo lets me in. There are no words. When he probes my mouth with his tongue, I say to myself, it's just a kiss. I'll only taste him. But when I do, I can't have enough. And then he is peeling off my blouse, a rush of air prickling my nipples. I promise myself I'll enjoy only a few caresses. He puts his mouth on my breast and it feels so good a hiss of air sucks through my teeth. Clothes fly off, and when the rubber stretches taut over his stiffness, I melt into the safe danger. I know it's wrong and I want to stop but oh the way he drives into me. It's been so long. Just this once, I say to myself, opening wide, heels planted on the bed. I sink my fingertips into his buttocks and grind him until I'm screaming with the unbearable sweetness. I can't have this again after today, so I might as well gorge on it. I roll on top of him and tell him to lie still. I sink slowly, feeling every ripple of muscle, every tingle of vein. Anchoring my hands on his chest, I close my eyes and abandon myself. I climb, climb, climb, head thrown back, soaring deliciously, soaring above shooting lava.

IN THE EVENING, guilt dries me up. When Rudolph slides down below my waist, I press my sore legs together, shaking my head no. He raises his head to ask what's wrong. I say nothing.

"Tell me," he says.

"It's nothing." I can't look at him.

"Come on, Esi. Something is wrong."

The wrongness presses on me, so I open my mouth. "I slept with Taiwo."

Four words. Four quick jabs of spearing truth. He lies crumpled at the foot of the bed.

"I am sorry," I say, crushed to see him so flattened.

He remains silent, sorrowful eyes fixed on me. I can hear the tenant across the corridor moving things, opening and closing a drawer. The landlady yells at her son to come here at once or else. Outside, a dog yelps.

"I am sorry," I repeat helplessly.

Finally, his voice cracks. "I forgive you."

"Huh?"

"It's not your fault. He must have forced you."

I jerk up. He forgives me? Just like that? I don't want forgiveness. I want truth untangled and laid out straight between us so we can find our direction, not this jumbled, choking knot of forgiveness and kindness. He knows me. He knows there is no way Taiwo forced me and all he wants is to forgive me?

"Can we talk about this?"

"No." His mouth is set in a line, his arms over his chest. "We won't talk about this again and we won't see him again. We won't ever mention his name again."

I take in a sharp breath. Is this what bleakness lies ahead? I can just open my legs to anyone and he'll forgive me? Is this the messy future, carcasses of wrongdoing buried in cupboards until the stench chokes us both? No acknowledgment of betrayal and our shared responsibility? I shake my head. "We need to talk."

"No." He heaves himself up to snuggle up to me, slipping his arm around my shoulder so my head rests on his chest. "I forgive you. Let's go to sleep."

I am stunned into silence. How does he manage such oblivion?

I hear him slide into sleep, the steady rhythm of his breath blowing puffs down my head. I fling his hand from my shoulder and roll away, creating space between us.

We forge ahead in our dishonest union. His forgiving kindness grates my skin each night he tongues me desperately, checking my face to see if I'm pleased. Maybe that's the point. You heave kindness on the other, piling on the guilt. I feel guilt's weight in the dimness of his eyes, the way he seems shorter, smaller, like hands pressed around my neck, squeezing. It's unbearable. One day, when he pleads for entrance as if to rebuild himself, I give in.

"I'll pull out in time," he whispers. "I promise."

SIX WEEKS AFTER. A breakfast of boiled yam and fried eggs steams on a chair facing the couch we're sitting on. We eat silently. I can hear every squishy swallow from him. The yam slides uneasily down my throat like fishbone and I have to keep drinking water to push it down. He looks sideways at me as if wanting to ask me a question but he doesn't.

The breakfast over, I remove my engagement ring before wrapping a housecoat around me so I can go wash the dishes in the kitchen without the ring sliding down the drain. Then I return to our room and put them away before leaving to wash myself. The whole time I ignore Rudolph's eyes.

In the bathroom, the cold spray from the shower stings my nipples, and when I pass the loofah over them, they burn. They have been this way for weeks. My breasts are hard like unripe mango, with the skin pulled so tightly it shines. I can't deny it any longer. I am pregnant.

My chest rises and rises and rises until I am gasping, shaking with the effort of holding in the sobs because I don't want anyone to hear me. I slide on my back, down the ceramic wall, and the salt of my tears runs into my mouth. I should be strong like leather, used to skinning, but I feel as tender as raw liver. I can't shrug it off any longer and pretend it's happening to someone else.

I am disappearing. Each shaving of my womb is a violent wave that rips off a piece of my body and washes it away in a red-blood ocean. Shame on you, Esi! All your big talk. You challenge Papa. You scorn Auntie. Yet look at what you've become: a person who can't stand up for herself and use contraceptives. A person riddled with guilt. Why do you act as if Rudolph is a king you must obey? What is wrong with you?

By the time I come out of the bathroom, Rudolph is not in the room. I throw on a dress and sink onto the couch. I reach for a tissue. My fingers shred and reshred it. I hear the door open but I don't raise my head. I tear, tear, tear at the tissue until I am clawing at my own fingers.

He sinks down carefully beside me, whispering, "What's wrong?" I hear the fear in his voice, but I think of the last time when he promised to pull out before spilling, how I let his quivering weight press me down as I moved, trying to feel some of what he was feeling. But he cried from deep inside his throat, "*Ouuh Esi, I'm pouring it in!*" No, I said. I shook my head, the heels of my hands pushing at his chest, but already his warm liquid was squirting. How I slapped him as he went limp and slipped out. How he wiped my tears, sorrying, sorrying, sorrying. How I pushed him off and stumbled to the bathroom and turned on the shower. Now here he is, Mr. Concern himself. I could choke from the anger bubbling in my chest.

"What's wrong?" he asks again.

"I'm pregnant! You promised not to spill but you did! Now I'm pregnant!" His hands reach out for me but I slap them. "Leave me alone, you hear? Let's just get it over and done with!"

The taxi bounces us to a house in a neighborhood that seems

thrown together with broken plates and scrap metal. The room with its bare cement floors and peeling paint presses around me. This time it's a man in spectacles, a medical student from the university, Rudolph's friend. He tells Rudolph to wait outside. Then he makes me lie on the iron bed standing in the middle of the room. He is reaching for the shiny, sharp instruments in the aluminum bowl. I squeeze my eyes shut. No use asking for the ever-absent anesthesia.

The man's wrist moves in and out, scraping my insides. Blood. I feel its warmth flow down between my buttocks and creep up my spine. Scrapes, scrapes, scrapes. I shriek like an animal being slaughtered. Rudolph rushes in to hold me. My nails dig into him.

"I'm sorry," he says, "I'm sorry!"

I shriek louder. "Don't you sorry me!"

At home, I move slowly, knife pains in my abdomen. I curl into a caterpillar on the bed. The tears flow over my nose onto the pillow. I wish my mother were alive so she could wrap her body around me, so I won't feel reduced to a slab of meat on a butcher's table. I hate myself for being a wimp. When I was a child and they held me down and pushed ginger into my bottom, I was helpless, but now I'm bigger. What's my excuse? Or is it because of the pain I endured in childhood? When a girl's tenderness has been scalded and gingered, it's easy to slide into acceptance of pain. Still, I could shake my own shoulders.

Am I any better than my friend's older sister whose husband pushed abortions instead of contraceptives, which turned her womb into one big scar? Later, when no baby would take root in her, the husband left her for a fresher woman. What if my womb also becomes one big scar? Such a deceptive fruit of a marriage, good on the outside but rotten on the inside. Spitting it out isn't as simple as me throwing my things in a suitcase and jumping on a bus. Like the betrothal, it involves parental negotiation.

As soon as I am strong enough, I travel to Ghana to see Papa and tell him about the abortions. He springs up from his chair, knocks his glasses to the floor. He roars, "When Rudolph comes to Ghana, I'll meet with his family. He'll see where power lies! No one is going to destroy my daughter!" I can see him grabbing Rudolph by the throat, people trying to pull him off. It's too bad I won't be there to witness it, because I have to fly to Senegal for my year abroad at the University of Dakar. By the time I return for my final year, I won't be anybody's wife.

CHAPTER THIRTY

■ ■ ■■ ■ ■ ■ ■ ■ ■ ■

T HIS IS IT. I'm on a Ghana Airways plane with fourteen giddy Ghanaian students, flying to Dakar, capital of Senegal. Already I've pushed Rudolph into the recesses of my mind. It's a veritable bus ride in the sky, this flight. We are looping up and down the Gulf of Guinea, unloading and picking up passengers. Abidjan, Monrovia, Freetown, Conakry, Bangui, before hopping up the coast to Dakar. I'm going to live in a foreign country for a whole year, speaking only French. No Rudolph!

It's nighttime when we land, so all I notice is the white foam of the sea following us as the bus weaves along the coast to the girls' hostel. Outside the wire fence, men and women stroll along the baobab-lined avenue wearing long, flowing robes. When we step down, our feet sink into soft white sand that covers the land, so loose and dry it rolls off your ankles without dirtying them much. The only problem is when the wind blows, the sand whips you in the face and your saliva gets crunchy. I've never seen a land with so few trees. The baobabs squatting along the avenues have few leaves, which is not surprising because we are in the Sahel, on the fringe of the Sahara Desert.

At the Cité Claudel, the girls' hostel, the *directrice* allots us our rooms. Each of us has to share with a Senegalese or another French-speaker. "Here is the rule, *vous avez compris?*" she tells us. There are to be no males in the dormitories at any time whatsoever. This is a Muslim country. There are morals to uphold. Boys may sit on the whitewashed wall circling the roundabout with flowers in the middle. Only in the daytime, mind you. After hours, they may stand at the gate or talk with you through the grill in the fence, but not inside. "If you break this rule, you will be expelled from the cité, *vous comprenez?*" We say *Oui, Madame*. Rudolph is far away in Nigeria, may he remain there forever. He won't visit and I've vowed not to run around with another man until the engagement is dissolved.

The next day, the Ghanaian ambassador arrives to welcome us. He rolls out of a gleaming black Mercedes, twinkles at us through his thick glasses, and tells us to be good girls. He promises to show us around Dakar and invites us to his residence to meet the Ghanaian community. We will see him often because we have to go to the embassy once a month to receive our allowance. He says we should call him H.E., short for His Excellency. His body is not so excellent though. He is so round that a giant could use him for a football. But it warms my chest to have a stand-in father.

We are walking H.E. to his car when a girl in blue jeans, a white T-shirt, and a baseball cap saunters toward us. She could pass for a Lebanese the way her skin is lighter than an anthill and her curly hair flows under the cap. She clutches the handle of a radio cassette player.

A girl who has evidently met her previously whispers, "She's a Ghanaian, a half-caste who has come to join us from England. Her name is Sally."

Half-white. That explains her papaya-colored skin and curls. She shakes hands with H.E. and we exchange introductions. H.E. tells her she's one of us and to join us for visits to his residence.

"All right," Sally says in a lovely British voice, then her face brightens. "Hey, I'm going to the beach. Would any of you girls like to come?" The girls murmur no and shift away from her. Obviously, they don't want to go to the beach in a strange country with this half-caste girl who wears jeans like those who have lived for too long in the Western world, who probably smokes *wee*. That's the way people think of half-caste girls. Because of the assumption that a woman who has a baby with a white man will open her legs for any man, it stands to reason that a girl born to such a woman will be wide-legged too. Well, I am itching to know more about her. I don't want to go around Dakar with clumps of girls who are too afraid to try anything.

"I'll come with you," I say.

H.E. pulls me aside and lances into an urgent whisper, "Don't follow that girl. She looks like a bad influence." I smile and nod politely, but as soon as he leaves, I hop on the bus with her.

"So," I ask, "where are we going?"

"Ngor Island," she says with an eager smile. "It's so cool, it's the tiniest island. You're going to love it!"

A dart of pleasure shoots through me. I love the reggae she's playing on her radio cassette. Third World, she says. I wish she'd turn down the volume though. It doesn't seem polite. "Do you think we should maybe turn down our music?"

She looks around with surprise. "No. We're not disturbing anyone. They're probably enjoying it."

It's true, no one looks particularly upset, just curious. I pick out a woman with a long chewing stick and whisper to Sally how disgusting to clean one's teeth in front of the world. Peggy explains that Senegalese women chew sticks to show off their teeth. "Notice their dark gums? They dye them deliberately, to contrast with the whiteness of their teeth."

My eyes widen. "Come again?"

She smiles. "Beauty is important to Senegalese women, I tell you. Most likely she has to compete with other wives for her husband's attention, so she has to look her best at all times. See that gorgeous lady by the window, the one with the transparent boubou? For all you know she's a maid."

"No!"

"Yeah." She nods. "Even a maid looks like a model. They take pride in their appearance."

I'm surprised at how much she has learned in such a short time.

The bus rolls along the beach road they call La Corniche. When the bus attendant says "Ouakam, Ouakam," Sally tells me that is our stop. We get off and make our way to the beach.

Oh, the water lapping at my feet! I love how the island sits in the distance like a rugged ship. To get there, we pay 250 francs and sit inside one of the wooden canoes painted every color. When the canoe is full, two men with blue-black skin yank a rope, and the canoe roars and cuts through the water to Ngor.

As soon as we peel off our clothes and press our bottoms into the sand, young men with uncombed hair and baggy Senegalese trousers approach us. "You wan buy necklace? Try dis skirt?" They have cow horn necklaces and bracelets, brass toe rings, and wooden sculptures. When they hear Sally's radio cassette player blaring reggae, they ask, "You from Jamaica?" They sit with us, rambling on about Jah and One Love and Haile Selassie. They admire how we are not snobbish like the *cheep cheep*, people who want to be more French than the French themselves. And isn't it nice to find girls on their own in Senegal, not like other girls who always have a man with them and you can't even talk to them. They go on until they realize we aren't buying.

When they leave, I remove my engagement ring, put it inside my bag so it doesn't fall into the sea. We flop around in the waves and splash each other until we tire of it. Sally wants to be coffee-colored like me, she says, so she lies down and I rub oil on her back so she can toast herself while I sweat under a towel, getting blacker anyway. We swap stories about ourselves. Her mother was a Ghanaian teacher, but when her British father took them behind the corn to England, he ended up leaving her because having a dark wife made life difficult. Which is why she has come to Dakar to study French instead of going to France. She doesn't want to have anything to do with white people. "I wish I could be whole-dark like you, not half of anything," she says.

"But you're beautiful with your papaya skin," I tell her. "And I wish I could travel like you've done and not worry about sitting on a beach with a man." But I can tell she doesn't agree, the way her mouth turns into a line. She'd rather talk about Bob Marley and Haile Selassie, which is fine by me.

Later, we stroll to a restaurant near where the sea crashes against the black rocks. We sit on white chairs around a table, under a straw umbrella. We sink our teeth into brochettes of lobster grilled fresh from the sea, and when I taste my first glass of wine, I groan with pleasure. The way it heats through my throat and tingles down my body makes me want to shed my skin. Oh, the wind on my neck. Oh, the heat of the wine and the heat of the sun! Oh, the freedom!

Sally and I talk and talk. When the sun starts losing its heat, she reaches down into her bag and draws out crumbly leaves from a tiny plastic bag.

"What's that?"

She gives me an amused smile. "You don't know? You're funny." Carefully, she lines the crumbs on a rectangular piece of paper, and then rolls it up until it resembles a cigarette, and lights it. "Want some?" she asks.

"What kind of cigarette is that? I don't smoke anyway."

"Marijuana."

Wee!

She tells me there's nothing to it. Lots of people in England do it. And in Jamaica where she has been. Even here in Senegal. She got it from the boys on the beach. My heart is pounding with fear and excitement. I am sitting with a girl who not only smokes cigarettes but *wee*, that forbidden thing. She puts it to her mouth and drags on it until it glows red and her eyes narrow from the smoke. I'm staring so hard she asks me again if I don't want to try it. I tell her no. At Wesley Girls I learned *wee* is a drug and drugs will possess you like an evil spirit and eat away your brain. I won't do it. She shrugs and puffs away, singing with the reggae on her radio: *Don't worry about a thing, 'cause every little thing gonna be all right* . . . I feel the same, that somehow everything will be all right, that this entanglement with Rudolph will unravel.

As the sun turns orange and slides down behind the coconut trees, Sally giggles, points at me, and says that I am getting some *wee* inside me anyway because I am laughing so hard and dancing around the crackling bonfire. Maybe she's right, but I think it's because I have never felt so free in my life, so lovely, so powerful. Listen to the French rolling off tongues, and the staccato cadence of Wolof! I can say, *Na nga def?* How are you? *Mangi fi rekk.* I'm fine and *Jere jef.* Thank you.

I wish my sisters could experience this sense of freedom too. I feel even more so when a week later, a letter arrives from Sister Mansa.

My dear Esi,

I miss you very much.

Now that we are so far from home in Zimbabwe, my husband has changed. He lies with other women and even brings them home and I have to sleep with my daughter while he groans on top of another woman. When I complain, he punches me and bangs my head against the wall. I tried to tell Papa but he says I must have done something wrong. I don't know what to do.

I have news about Sister Abena too. She hasn't changed. She won't humble herself for Mr. Quarcoe. She asked him to wash her drawers, can you believe that? How can a woman ask a man to wash her drawers? It is disgusting. Well, she says that if she has to wash the starch out of a man's supporters, she doesn't see why he can't wash her drawers. And she dared to ask him to help pound fufu because she didn't want blisters on her palm. She said she didn't see why she had to pound with one hand and turn with the other while he sat sipping beer with his friends. As if that isn't enough, she challenged him in front of his friends. He was so angry he tried to throw her out the window, but she bit him hard in the arm.

When she left him and came home, Papa said it was her fault because she was disrespectful. She says she doesn't care. She has left Mr. Quarcoe and is living by herself with her daughter. She has rented a room in Accra and teaches at a primary school.

At least, Sister Abena has work, just like Sister Yaa, but me? I can't work because my husband won't let me. As you know, I never finished school and he refused to let me attend even a typing school. I don't have any skill. God didn't give me the same brain He gave you. I have to stay married, otherwise what will happen to me? Besides, Papa won't let me come back home.

Please pray for me.

Your loving sister,

Mansa

I want to find that man. How dare he hit my sister! Not allowing her to work. Taking her to a foreign country and maltreating her. As for Papa, there has to be a mistake. Maybe Sister Mansa didn't explain things properly? How could he not take her side? Didn't he support me when I told him about Rudolph? Didn't he promise to confront him and give him back the bride price? If Papa can protect me from Rudolph, surely Sister Mansa is mistaken. I write back and tell her to stay strong. Leave if she has to. Meanwhile I will write to Papa myself, explain things to him.

Rudolph writes too. He wants to visit me in Dakar. Papa must not have dealt with him yet. I reply and tell him not to come. Absolutely not. Even if I wanted him, this is not Ghana. Girls can't have boys in their rooms at night. I tell him no, and no and no: Don't come because I can't hide you in my room, what with a Senegalese roommate who will tell on me and get me thrown out of Cité Claudel and then where will I go? Don't come to Dakar because you don't have money for a hotel and I don't know where to put you. You can't bring Nigerian naira to Senegal because no one spends the naira, only the franc CFA. The banks will accept foreign currency only from America or England or France. If you bring naira, they'll give you a look that says you are an insect. Short and simple, stay in Nigeria.

CHAPTER THIRTY-ONE

HAVE WRITTEN TO Papa about Sister Mansa. Surely, he will act. Now I can enjoy myself. How I love it here. Dakar, Dakar, Dakar! Land of long-limbed women beautiful as roses. Land of wiry men tall as the trees. Land of restaurants in the sea like ships, of blood-red wine, brandy-drenched crepes, voluptuous food. The stringed kora seduces the air. Your breeze is a kiss and your sea a lover!

Sally and I love the beach so much we spend nights on the is-land, sometimes taking the canoe to the mainland for our classes, sometimes skipping them altogether. We eat couscous drenched with fish stew, and I drink more and more wine and laugh so hard I could burst with joy. I tell Sally about Rudolph but I say nothing about the abortions. I'm ashamed before this girl who is so free, who smokes, who has taken the train and traveled as far as Turkey where she ate shish kebab and slept on the train at night. I want to be like her except for the *wee* smoking.

True to his promise, His Excellency invites us to his residence and introduces us to the Ghanaian diplomats. There are Ghana-ians working for the United Nations, World Bank, USAID, every international organization in Dakar. These are the brains that drained here from Ghana to earn foreign money and build castles back home. We students get adopted by different families and I like my new guardians, a Mr. Ghartey with one short leg and a kind smile. His wife has a penny round face that glows pinkish from the bleaching creams she has used to peel off her black skin. Which is a shame because the new skin looks like someone recovering from a burn. They have no children except their dog Shabara, who might as well be their son. Every week, they invite me to their home and stuff me with so much food I can't breathe. I am happy in Dakar, but Rudolph writes again with Nigerian news that makes me sweat at night.

Nigerian politicians have robbed the country of so much money that electricity goes off for no reason and food prices are "too dear." The government blames foreigners, just like what happened long ago in Ghana. Now Nigerians have had enough. They say foreigners must leave, especially Ghanaians. Here we go again, foreigners responsible for money troubles. What Papa said has come true. Nigerians are retaliating for the time we drove them out of Ghana. I hope Rudolph will be safe. He can always return to Ghana, can't he? I won't worry.

One day, Sally and I return from the beach to find one of the Ghanaian students waiting for me in my room.

"You've got a cablegram," she says. "It's your man, Rudolph. He is arriving tonight." She shoves a paper the size of an airplane ticket at me.

"Tonight? Here, in Dakar?" I don't believe it.

"Yes," she says through pinched lips, her folded arms communicating her obvious disapproval of an engaged girl always disappearing to do God knows what on the beach with a half-caste girl.

"But I told him not to come!"

Sally grabs the cable from my trembling fingers and reads. "His plane will be here in four hours, Esi."

"But where is he going to stay? The bloody fool!"

Sally thinks for a moment. "Why don't we rent a room in a hotel?"

"But I can't afford to keep him in a hotel."

"Don't worry." She slips her arm around my shoulder. "You don't have to pay for it right away. He can pay when he gets here."

I am unconvinced but I can't very well leave him at the airport when he knows nobody in Senegal except me, can I? So, we head back into town where we find a hotel and make reservations. Then we take a taxi to the airport. At least, I warned him about money so I'm sure he has lots of dollars. Nothing to worry about.

He arrives bearing smiles that I strain to return. He presses his body into mine and lifts me up. "God, I've missed you, my wife!" I let my arms hang limp by my sides and turn my head so his kiss lands on my cheeks, not on my mouth. When he puts me down, I quickly introduce Sally to draw his attention away from me.

"Hello," Sally says. "Lovely to meet you." Then she digs her elbow into my side, whispering, "He's gorgeous, you lucky girl!"

If only she knew.

In the taxi from the airport, I explain things to Rudolph, since he obviously didn't understand my letter. "I can't have you in my room, you know, so I hope you brought enough money to pay for a hotel."

He gives me a don't-be-silly smile. "Come on, Esi, there is always a way to go around rules."

"But I told you, this is a Muslim country. You don't do things like that. I hope you brought some dollars because I had to book a hotel room for you."

"I didn't bring dollars, but I have four hundred naira." About three hundred pounds sterling.

"But I said you can't change naira here! The banks will only take dollars. Or francs or pounds sterling."

He tilts his head away, a smug look on his face. "What about the black market?"

"Didn't you read my letter? There is no black market! Even if one exists, I know nothing about it. I'm only a student, I don't want to get into trouble! Why don't you ever listen to me?"

He tightens his lips, folds his arms over his pink shirt, and stares ahead. I am trying not to cry as I turn to watch the waves breaking on the sand.

"So, how are things in Nigeria?" Sally asks helpfully.

"Fine," Rudolph says and clamps shut.

We ride in an itchy silence all the way to the hotel. When I hug Sally goodbye, she whispers, "Hang in there, dahling. See you tomorrow."

RUDOLPH AND I are lying on our backs on the bed in the hotel room, both staring at the white ceiling and the shadows of the overhead lamp. He reaches for my hand but I pull away. I don't know how to tell him I want to break our betrothal.

"I'm sorry," he says. "I really didn't believe you."

I turn to look at this stranger. "Why not?"

He sighs and looks at me. "I don't know. I'm sorry." His voice is a whisper and he is drawing closer. I shift out of reach.

"What's going on in Nigeria?" I ask by way of distraction.

He rolls onto his back again and puts his hand to his eyes, as if to close them against the inner memory. "They are herding up Ghanaians and flogging them until there is blood. People have been killed. Did you hear about what happened at the borders?"

"No, I don't have news."

"First, it was Benin. Hundreds of thousands of Ghanaians converged at the border, you know, between Benin and Nigeria. Benin refused to let Ghanaians pass, which means the Ghanaians were trapped on Nigerian soil, so what did the Nigerians do? Flog the Ghanaians, spit on them. I can't even describe it. People were dying. No food to eat. No water. No place to even relieve themselves. Finally, Benin had to let them pass through to Ghana." My stomach drops because pictures are flashing before me: Nigerians leaving Ghana, the shouting and hollering. Rudolph's head shakes with the weight of it. "Can you imagine? Already there is a drought in Ghana and a food shortage. And now the population has suddenly increased by two million."

For a country of ten million that's a lot. I can't imagine the strain of feeding everybody. I am also worried. "Will you be in danger when you return to Nigeria?"

He gives me a wry smile. "No. They think I'm from the mid-west because I have their surname. Also, people have seen me on TV."

"That's good then. And you still have your work."

He hesitates, then heaves onto his side, facing me. "Actually, I quit."

"Why?" And then it dawns on me. "You got a new position!"

"No, I didn't."

"Then why did you leave?"

He gives me a stubborn look. "I asked the director to increase my pay, but he refused. I told him I would leave if he didn't give me more money. Well, he didn't. So, I resigned. I deserve better." He bubbles with childlike eagerness. "See? I want to go to Hollywood. I want to be the next Eddie Murphy!"

"Who?" What is he talking about?

He props himself on an elbow. "You haven't heard of him? He is a black American making it in Hollywood."

"Good for him, but in the meantime, what will you live on?"

"I'll make it on my own." His eyes shift vaguely. "You see, I was born to be an actor. It's like a calling from God. I can't do anything else."

Fair enough. "What about rent? How will you pay for food?"

"I'll make it. I figure I can stay here in Dakar and see what opportunities lie here."

"What? Haven't you heard anything I've said? Where will you live? I can pay for this room only tonight. I can't use my scholarship money to pay for rent. It's barely enough as it is." I'm so angry I have to heave away from him before I start screaming. He says nothing. He is obviously hurt, but what am I supposed to do?

An uneasy slumber overcomes us both. In the middle of the night, I feel ants crawling around the edges of my nightgown. I brush them off but they keep coming. I snap awake up to discover the ants are Rudolph's fingers stealing under my nightgown. They creep between my legs, trying to pull my drawers to one side. His excited breath infuriates me. Pretending to be still asleep, I fling my arm out, whacking him hard. He holds still. From his fast breathing I know he is dying to come at me. When he thinks I'm sleeping, the fingers resume their creeping. I move and whack him again, then it's creep, whack, creep, whack until he understands it's not happening.

The next day, when we check out of the hotel, I avoid his eyes. I pay for the room and we catch a taxi to see my guardians, Mr. and Mrs. Ghartey with the bleached, penny round face. Mr. Ghartey drags his limp leg to the dining room where we congregate around the table with the flowery cloth. I paste a smile on my face and explain the situation with false confidence, praying they believe me.

"You're engaged?" Mr. Ghartey asks, looking from Rudolph to me.

"Yes," I say in an unconvincing voice. If I don't hold on to the engagement status, there is no way they will help me. Husband and wife exchange looks. Mrs. Ghartey's small eyes tell me nothing.

Mr. Ghartey looks long at me. "How come you never told us?"

"Erm, I didn't think it important to mention it." I'm giving them what I hope is a naïve look. The dog appears, wagging its tail, wetting my feet with several tongue flicks. Finally, Mrs. Ghartey says quietly without looking at Rudolph, "He can stay with us for a week." With that she gets up from the table to get a room ready. Mr. Ghartey smiles and asks Rudolph how things are going in Nigeria, which is a welcome change of topic.

We spend three restless nights with Mr. and Mrs. Ghartey. In the morning, I take the bus to school, then join the Gharteys and Rudolph for supper. At night I have no choice but to lie in bed with Rudolph, who does his finger-creeping thing and suffers more whacking from me. The fourth evening, the Gharteys are quiet and unsmiling at the dining table. I keep the compliments flowing. "Mrs. Ghartey, what a delicious thiéboudienne!"

"Hmmm," she says into her plate, not looking at me.

"How did you learn to cook Senegalese rice, this can't be the maid's cooking!"

"Hmmm."

"I mean, the rice is all separated, and the fish, the way you stuffed its side with spices."

"Hmmm."

I give in to the silence. The only sounds come from the forks and knives communicating with the plates. Finally, she dabs at her mouth with a cloth napkin, raises pointed eyes to mine. "I know you are wearing a ring on your finger, but how do we know you are truly engaged the Ghanaian way? We talked to our Ghanaian friends and they say something is not right."

Mr. Ghartey chimes in with an embarrassed smile. "There is

no way a responsible man engaged to a woman can arrive in a country without enough money to take care of her." He turns to Rudolph. "For all we know you are one of those people who have been driven out of Nigeria, and you've come here to stay. You don't have a job. We just can't have you live with us."

I want to crawl under the table and turn into a spider. I defend Rudolph feebly, but they won't listen. In fact, they wonder if I am not just being a bad girl pretending to be engaged so I can let a man eat me now that I am far from home. They don't want any trouble. What if I get pregnant? They won't condone my behavior. Rudolph has to leave tomorrow.

When we eventually face each other in bed, I tell Rudolph softly, "I'm sorry, you have to go to Ghana." He nods. A shimmer of tears covers his eyes. The way he looks shrunken, both hands pressed under his cheek, shoulders narrowed, makes me want to reach out from my propped elbow and stroke his hair. I don't.

"It's okay," he says. "I will visit Ghana and then I'll return to Nigeria. Try to find work again."

There is nothing to be said after that.

The next day we get him a flight on Ghana Airways. At the airport, I buy a bottle of whiskey and tell him to give it to Papa for me. I am so relieved to see him leave that I hug him tightly, rubbing my cheek against his neck. Then I wave and smile frantically until he disappears. When I see the plane climb into the sky, it's as if I'm breathing for the first time.

For weeks, I wait to hear from Papa about ending the betrothal, but time crawls by with no news. I write to ask how he liked the whiskey and if he spoke to Rudolph. He replies that he hasn't seen Rudolph, nor has he received any whiskey. *Is he in Ghana?* Confused, I write to Rudolph at the address in Nigeria. A week later, I receive his reply:

My dear Esi,
I am sorry I couldn't deliver the whiskey to your father. I ran
out of money, so I sold it to help me buy a bus ticket back to
Nigeria. I am very sorry. You can bring him another bottle of
whiskey when you finish your year-abroad program.
Love,
Rudolph

I am beyond incensed. What kind of man is so cheap as to sell
a bottle of whiskey destined for his father-in-law? And not have the
decency to let me know? I whip out pen and paper and urge Papa
to break the engagement, to go see Rudolph's parents, not wait
for him to show his face. Papa says okay, but first he must write to
Rudolph because that's the fair thing to do. Which he must have
done because after a month, I receive his reply as I am waiting for
Sally so we can go to the beach.

I am so happy I hug the airmail letter card to myself, rolling
on my bed. I know the letter's content without opening it. Papa
has broken the engagement, I'm free! Reading the letter deserves
a special ceremony. When we get to the beach, we'll find a quiet
spot. I'll order a bottle of wine. Only then will I pry off the flaps
of the airmail letter card to read Papa's precious words aloud. We
will clink our glasses and toast to my freedom, ha! I am singing
loudly when Sally opens the door. She's got the baseball cap and
jeans on. Her fingers are wrapped around the handle of her plastic
blue radio cassette player blaring reggae.

"Sally!" I jump off the bed and kiss her on the cheek.

"Hey, what's got you so happy?" She is laughing, setting down
the radio. I grab her by the waist and whirl her around in a mad
merengue.

"Stop making me dizzy and tell me!"

I let her go, grab my bag, and shuffle into my slippers. "I know exactly how I want to celebrate!"

"What's—"

"Ssh!" I put my finger to my lips and no amount of feet-stamping and shoulder-shaking from her moves me. Finally, she sweeps out of the room and I skip after her thinking how I'm going to devour brochettes of shrimp and lobster with the bottle of wine. Maybe I'll smoke *wee*, just to see what it is like, ha! Hmm, better not.

At the island, I plop down beside Sally, hugging myself until she grabs my shoulders and shouts, "Are you going to tell me or do I have to throttle you?"

"We need a bottle of wine."

"Come on, we can get a bottle of wine later. I'm dying here."

"Okay, okay!" I say, fishing the letter out of my bag. It's a bit creased, so I lay it on the towel to flatten it out. Using my fingernails, I carefully open the flaps and clear my throat. "Allow me to read it to you." It begins with the usual *My dear daughter*, and how happy he is to write to me, to give me words he knows I'll receive with reverence because I know I am precious to him, and then—

> . . . *Rudolph says you must have a boyfriend in Dakar*
> *because you never let him touch you. He says you're lying*
> *about the abortions. You just want an excuse to leave him. You*
> *made him feel unwelcome. I'll advise you to behave like a good*
> *wife and not make up stories.*

The letter falls through my fingers into the sand. My body crumbles. I can't speak. Sally's head shakes in confusion. She picks up the letter, brushes off the sand and reads:

> *I have always watched out for you and protected you, but you*
> *are a grown woman now. When I eventually leave this earth,*

*I want to know you are secure in a marriage and respected.
You see, a woman's glory is her husband, and I want you to
have that. Do not be a loose woman going from man to man,
despised by everyone. I really want you to do your best to make
this marriage work.*

  Your concerned father,
  Edward

Papa, Papa, Papa, don't you see? If I stay married to Rudolph,
I *will* become that loose woman going from man to man! Sally's
eyes oscillate up and down, then from the letter to me. "Esi.
Wha . . . what's this?" She kneels in front to search my eyes,
"What's going on?"

I've locked my arms around my knees. I am rocking on my
bottom, forward and backward. How could Papa believe Rudolph
over me? How could he believe the one who sold his whiskey and
took the money, the one who is not his son? They have met only
twice. Papa knows me. I am the child who yelled at him when he
read my letters, and when he slapped Auntie, but I am not the
child who lied when it counted.

Why are my insides whirling? Is this not the man who said it
was Sister Abena's fault that her husband nearly threw her out
the window? Wasn't it he who said the reason for Sister Mansa's
husband pummeling her was because she must have incited him?
How could I have ignored the signs? Being a woman means being
the one who is wrong. That simple. No matter how educated I
get, my womanhood will always be the veil he looks through to
see me.

"Talk to me, Esi." Sally's voice is soft. She rubs my knee repeatedly. I look at the love in her eyes, then I open my mouth and
everything pours out of me: Kayode, Auntie Biggie, the abortions with Rudolph. The words are vomit. I keep heaving them

out, tears running down my face. I heave everything out until I'm empty.

Sally sinks back onto her bottom, her mouth open, her eyes round. She is shaking her head gently. There is a long silence, then her eyes fill. "But, Esi, you're responsible for your own life. It's your body. It's your responsibility to protect it."

"I know." Tears of rage sting my eyes. "I have behaved worse than a baby who needs someone to point to the moon and tell her its name. The truth has always been there, right inside me. Rudolph did only what I allowed him to do. I could have insisted on him wearing something to stop him from getting me pregnant. Instead, I let him have his way." We lapse into silence again. I let my arms dangle between my knees, digging my big toe into the sand. "When a farmer plants a seed, the soil has no right to refuse. Soil has no life. A woman does. She is not soil, and no man may plant in her at will. No one may own another human being. I am the only one who should decide if I can take a pill or not. Anything done inside me is my choice alone. I am the queen of my body."

Sally nods softly. "Indeed, you are."

I heave a deep sigh. "Auntie Biggie too was the queen of her body. She chose to destroy it. I didn't snatch her life from her. I didn't have power over her."

"You bloody well didn't!"

We ease into a pensive silence. Overhead, birds caw. The sun is beginning to slide behind the coconut tree, still golden but turning a slight orange. It will drop into the sea and rise again to break dawn. All things die, and out of death, life begins afresh. Slowly, I pick up a fistful of sand. Somewhere in Nigeria, a denser, darker earth holds the denuded bones of Auntie Biggie. I've never wanted her to die. I trap the loose sand in my cupped hands, seeking a miniature outline of her, a shadow. Anything.

Nothing.

Too loose and free, the sand refuses my attempt to mold it. I spread out my fingers and watch it sift through them until my hands are empty. My eyes blur. *Goodbye, dearest Auntie Biggie. One day, I'll visit your grave. I'll press my cheek against your tombstone warmed by the sun. You're right, Auntie, it's love between us, one that doesn't end, right? I'll see you again, hopefully in the great beyond. Now it's time to let you go. It's time to stop the self-punishment.*

I blink away the gray haze of tears. I let go of her. I let go of Akwasi too. I let go of everything I can't control. The ropes I've wound around me are rolling off fast. I can breathe more freely. Taking a deep breath, I turn to Sally. "From now on, I'll take care of my own body."

"That's it, Esi!"

"And as for this evil engagement, it's over." I nod and nod and nod, wiping my cheeks with the back of my hand, smiling.

Sally's voice lowers. "Are you sure? I mean, if you've figured out your own culpability, do you think you could make it work with Rudolph? You say he's kind to you. He's damn good-looking too," she adds with a naughty smile.

Anchoring my hands behind me, I lean back to gaze at the fish-scale pattern of the water.

"Yes, he is kind and he isn't," I say. "I'm kind and I'm not. Neither of us can hoist a moral trophy over the other. What I do know is I can never press my body against his again. That part is dead. It's a symptom of something deeper. How long will it be before my heart, not just my body, throbs for someone else? I have to end it."

"Well, then, break it, Esi."

"I will. I'll go against tradition and dissolve it myself."

She shakes her head in wonder. "Gosh, Esi, what a girl."

I laugh softly. "And when I love a man again, I will deserve him, not give him up."

"That's it, my friend!"

I leap to my feet, a naughty grin on my face. "And the next time I lie with a man, I'll make sure I eat until I'm full as he is!"

"Yes, ha, ha!" She's bouncing on her feet like a little girl.

"Enough about this. We came here to enjoy ourselves. Let's do that!"

"Race you to the water?"

We run shrieking into the sea. Instead of removing my ring, I let the water well over it. I turn my head from side to side, waves of pleasure spreading through me as the bond slides off my finger and sinks. Down, down, down. Behind the orange clouds, my mother and Auntie Biggie are probably pumping their fists, *Yeei, go on, daughter.*

Every weight pressing me down has lifted. I am as unburdened as the day I slid out of my mother's womb, before the world loaded on me. I am. Not the great I AM of the Bible, but one of rightful existence. I am.

I slip off my bikini top and stretch out on my back, absorbing the sun's heat. I pull off my bikini bottom as well. The water runs over me, tickles into my vagina.

I am!

Dear Esi,

As you know, the Ghana government has closed down the universities because of student demonstrations. That means you are going to graduate a year later, so I've come to some decisions.

I want you to leave the university and come live with me as my wife. I'm tired of waiting and need you beside me. As a woman, your education is not as important as mine. Besides, you can join me in this acting business. We can go to Hollywood and make it. You could be a black Raquel Welch, I showed you her picture, do you remember? All the men will

want to chase you. I am not asking you; I am telling you to
come home.

    I love you.
    Rudolph

I hurt from laughing. Lord Rudolph, you want me to leave my
education, leave my future in your hands? You can take your deci-
sion and burn the sea. I rip the letter to pieces.

My dear daughter,
I am grieved that you want to break off your engagement to
Rudolph, such a fine man from such a fine family. What will
you do? A woman's glory is her husband. Without a husband,
you are nothing.

    Don't think too highly of yourself just because you have
gone to university. Look at Mr. and Mrs. Nortey. She was
a High Court judge, yet she condescended to marry a lowly
teacher, and they have lived happily ever after since. Now that
you have finished your year-abroad program, I want you to
go and live with Rudolph until the university reopens. Then
you can finish. I hope you will listen to what I say. I only want
the best for you, and that is respectability and security. Think
about it.

    Your loving father,
    Edward

What do I care about Mr. and Mrs. Nortey and their happily-
ever-after marriage, whoever they are? I know my father wants to
crown my head with glory, but this crown is one of thorns. Here's
how we're going to get there. He may not see it now, but because I
know he loves me, he will one day. Here are decisions of my own:

    I will remain in Dakar until the university reopens. I will work in an embassy. Someone is always looking for a translator. Do I not have spirit? I will save money and return the bride price Rudolph paid for me. That's the tradition. Bride price indeed. My father didn't sell me, but it adds up to the same thing: I have to buy back my freedom. I must also pay for the ring I lost. Whatever. I will buy back my freedom. If I don't, Papa will be liable. This is my fight.

I will return to Ghana and graduate from the university. Not with one, but two degrees: French and Spanish. It thrills me to laugh in the wind and let the sounds fall where they may, yes! For so long I've lived inward, far from the spirited little girl I used to be. Now I've rejoined her, except I'm twenty-one and stronger. I'll never again wish for a frog to turn me into a man. I'll light up my womanhood. I'll help my sisters. I'll help other women ignite their fires, blaze their paths through life, and leave behind embers to warm those who will come after them.

ONE YEAR LATER

■ ▮ ▮▮ ▮ ▮▮ ▮ ▮▮ ▮ ▮▮

I'S EVENING WHEN I arrive at my grandparents' house in Nigeria. Aunt Yetunde screams my name and rushes downstairs. She crushes me to her, gushing in her deep voice, "Welcome, Esi, welcome. We have missed you so much!" Her children crowd around me, jumping, pulling on my arm. Grandma waits on the balcony, a huge smile on her face as we come upstairs. She looks shorter and slightly bent, her hair whiter, thinner. She too says welcome, welcome. A shimmer of tears covers her eyes. I hug her tightly and next thing I know, she is dragging me to eat eba and okro soup in the parlor, Auntie Yetunde clucking at her children to go play and leave me alone. Grandma remains standing, barely blinking, as if I might disappear if she doesn't pay attention. As I sink into the couch, I let out a sigh of peacefulness. It's good to be back.

"Where is Kwabena?" I ask. I haven't seen him in more than a year and it's not like him to ignore my arrival.

"He is at Ikeja," Auntie Yetunde says, the couch dipping from her weight beside me.

I blink. "Ikeja? The area near the airport? What is he doing there?"

"He's spending the long holidays with Kayode," Grandma says.

Kayode. The name sets my heart pounding. "Kayode doesn't live here anymore?" My voice has gone an octave higher. A pit of disappointment opens in my belly.

Auntie Yetunde shrugs, looking away from me. "He has his own house now in Ikeja. Kwabena is always going there."

"I want to see him, er . . . Kwabena, I mean."

"That is not a problem," Auntie Yetunde says. "I have a taxi driver friend who can take you. He has been to that house a few times to deliver hair pomade for Kayode."

"I want to go first thing tomorrow morning," I say. "I'll probably stay for a few days before coming back."

She gives me a knowing smile but says nothing.

Grandma darts a look of anxiety at me. "You will come back, *abi* you will stay there?"

"I'll come back," I say. "I just want to greet my brother."

"And Kayode." She isn't smiling, but her eyes hold no anger.

"Yes, Grandma. But I won't stay more than a few days. I promise."

"*Oda,*" she says. "It's good." And she smiles, a warm buttery smile.

I get up and melt into her embrace, smelling her skin and the Lux soap she must have used to bathe. She is as comfortable as warm bread.

At nine o'clock in the morning, I am standing on Kayode's doorstep. It's a lovely bungalow on a quiet street, painted a pale cream. A home for a person who is neither rich nor poor. He must be at work already, but I'm sure Kwabena is in. Kayode's absence would be a relief, actually. I'll have time to talk to Kwabena, take my evening shower and calm myself before meeting him. Drawing in a deep breath, I knock on the green door. Kwabena appears. His mouth hangs open.

"Hello, little brother." I'm smiling but he is not.

"Esi?"

"Yes, it's me." I laugh. "Close your mouth before a fly flies in."

"I mean . . . " he gulps, "you are here. In Lagos."

"Yes, and yes. Where is Kayode?"

"He's at work. At the airport."

He looks thicker, older. His voice has deepened, and his chin displays a fuzz of hair.

"You look like a man," I say, punching his arm in my old, playful way.

His face breaks into a gruff smile. "And you, well, you look all right."

Taking my suitcase, he leads me into a spacious sitting room furnished with a brown leather couch and matching armchairs. It has the requisite television, stereo, and loudspeakers. After disappearing with my suitcase into one of three bedrooms, he draws me into a narrow but well-built kitchen, the kind you might find on a ship. I feel as though he is rushing me through a formality so he can move on to something else.

"What would you like to drink?" he asks.

I lean against the counter, watching him. "Do you have ginger ale?"

"Yes." He opens the white fridge and brings out a bottle. Then he reaches for a glass in a cupboard above the aluminum sink. He is silent, but I can tell words bubble inside his mouth as he hands me the fizzy drink. I thank him and sip, waiting for him to talk. He scratches his head and looks about before meeting my eyes. Finally, he says, "Esi, you can't stay here."

I put the glass down on the counter. "Why not?"

"Kayode is getting married."

"What?"

"I don't want him to change his mind. If he sees you, that's what will happen." My heart sprints, I have trouble breathing. First of all, I have never before known him to speak so forcefully. Also, I expected Kayode to have a girlfriend maybe, but getting married? I don't know what to say. Kwabena continues, locking eyes with me. "You have no idea what he's been through. You don't know how much you hurt him. He almost lost his job because of absences. I've never seen a man cry like he did. He nearly went crazy. Now he has come out of the gloom and found a woman. They are to be married next month. I don't want you ruining it for him."

"What? My own brother, talking to me like this?"

"Yes, you are my sister. My blood. But Kayode is my brother too. Did you know I had typhoid and spent three months in the hospital?"

I had no idea. "You didn't tell me. You never responded to my letters!" My voice is fierce. I want to hug and slap him.

"You know I've never been good at writing." That faraway look he gets in his eyes when he is sad overcomes him. "Kayode, he visited me every single day, even helped pay my hospital bills. And you know something else? When Grandpa was dying, he stayed up with us. He helped change bedsheets. He cried with us and gave us money. So please, leave him alone. Let him get married. Go back to Surulere . . . please. I'll come visit you there."

I don't know what to say. He is right. I have no business disrupting Kayode's life after he has managed to put it in order.

My eyes fill with tears. "I am sorry you were sick. So sorry. I wish you had told me. No one in Ghana knew."

He shrugs. "I am not like you, Esi. I don't know how to bring out everything inside me."

He tells me to spend the day with him and leave before Kayode returns from work. We reminisce about our childhood as he cooks and serves me rice and stew. I'm surprised at how delicious it is. I shouldn't be. Men have hands, tongues, and brains like women. The ability to cook isn't inscribed in our chromosomes.

At four o'clock, Kwabena is slipping his feet into his outdoor sandals, getting ready to see me off, when Kayode walks in. At first, he smiles politely, as if greeting a visitor he doesn't know, and then he stops.

"Esi?" He staggers back. "Is that you?"

I smile and nod. "It's me." My voice is calm, but my heart bangs.

He crosses the room to me and grabs my waist, pulling me to him. "Where did you come from? Senegal?"

"No." I give him a pleasant smile but I don't push against him. "I am back at University of Ghana to finish my degree." I step out of his embrace, easing myself into the armchair behind me. He sits at the corner of the couch, close to me, not taking his eyes off me. He shakes his head, surprise on his face. We lock eyes. This silence is comfortable, he is as familiar to me as my pillow. "Congratulations. I hear you are getting married."

He nods without smiling. Without blinking. "But I've never loved any woman as much as I love you."

Although his voice is soft, it slices through me. I don't know what to say. I look up and meet Kwabena's eyes. He is leaning against the kitchen door, arms folded across his chest, a warning look on his face, so I tease Kayode with my smile. "You can't still love me when you're getting married."

"I love you," he says calmly. There's a quiet confidence about him. "I even told my fiancée about you." He chuckles at the surprise on my face. "She wondered if I would leave her when I saw you again."

I reach out and touch his arm. It feels so warm I want to press my cheek against it. "You seem content. Look at this house. You're really doing well."

He smiles, taking my hand and swallowing it in his. "I'm fine now. I wasn't for a long time." He shakes his head, as if shaking off a bad dream. "When Kwabena told me you had left the Ghana-man,

I was delirious. I called your hostel many times. I wanted to propose to you, but they could never get ahold of you. I even left a number for you to call me but you never did. It broke me."

My mouth opens in shock and I blubber, "I never received a call, or any notice of one." Oh, wait, I remember . . . one time, coming from the beach with Sally, a Senegalese girl waving madly, saying I had a call from Nigeria. I didn't believe it, thought it was a joke. I never paid attention. I don't even remember whether she gave me a number to call. It must have been him, I'm sure now. I had no idea he would search for me. I thought he was too angry for that. I draw my hand back, cracking my knuckles. "I'm so, so sorry."

"It's okay."

He eases into silence. We are staring at each other. I'm remembering. My body heats at his nearness, but I can't forget what Kwabena said. I must choose my words carefully. "You are really getting married?"

He nods. "I need order in my life, Esi." His voice is quiet. "I want to settle down. You, on the other hand, want to go back to Ghana. To the university."

"Yes, I must get my degree, but . . . "

"Let me finish. I, too, want you to get your degree. I am proud of you. I just can't take the uncertainty. I will worry about you meeting someone else. I went through hell, Esi. I can't do that again."

"I know . . . Kwabena told me."

"Did he tell you how broken I was? People asked me, *Who is this Esi making you insane?* That kind of love that threatens my entire existence—I can't afford it anymore. I couldn't recover from its loss again. Not if you have to go away for another year. And I could never forgive myself if you left university because of me."

Silence. How weighty it can be. How conflicting. I too want

what is best for him. I guess that's what it means to love someone, to let him be. I can offer him no guarantees. I met him when I was a girl. After him came Rudolph. Then Papa surprised me. Maybe his view shifted from missing me, because when I handed him the money to dissolve the betrothal, he just said, "All right." No questions. End of betrothal. I didn't even have to be present. For the first time, I am free of entanglements. I am a woman who wants to finish university and figure out life for herself. It's not fair to ask Kayode to wait if he can't. Still, must he marry just like that?

"I want you to be happy, Kayode. Are you sure you want to marry a woman you don't love though? I'm sure you will meet someone else."

"No, Esi." His voice is firm. "I love this lady. It's different, hard to explain. She is like a lake, serene and still. With her, it's simply breathing. She's older than you, we are the same age. She is ready to settle down. I am also ready. You aren't, and it's okay."

I look at his steady face. The calm. The firm jaw. I have so much respect and love for this man. Enough to do the right thing. He needs a serene lake, not the cascading waterfall I am right now. I get up and move gently toward him. I sit on his lap, slide my arms around his neck. I look into his eyes, lean my forehead against his. Then I say softly, "You know what? Do exactly what will make you happy."

"Thank you," he whispers, burying his face in my neck.

It's all I can do not to press my lips against his, open my mouth and taste him. Instead, I take his hand, that hand that has stroked me, held me. I kiss its strength, then look at him. "No, thank *you*."

He cuddles me and I lay my head on his chest, hearing the *thump-thump* of his fast heartbeat, feeling his heat. Beneath me, I can sense him expanding, hardening. It would be so easy to slide my hand under his shirt, stroke his lentil of a nipple, slide down to his navel, touch the hair below. So easy to unbutton his trousers, push up my skirt and open my thighs over him, close my eyes and feel him deep inside me. But that will lead to confusion. I can't be selfish no matter how much I want him. I stand up, grab both of his hands, and pull him to his feet. "I have to leave. I am going back to Surulere."

"Stay the night," he whispers, hugging me. "I have a spare room. Stay, come on."

I look at Kwabena. His eyes are hard, his lips a straight line, but he needn't worry. I turn to Kayode. "I don't think so." Then I stand on my toes, using both of my palms to hold his face. I look into his black pupils ringed with brown. "I couldn't sleep under the same roof with you. It would be too . . . difficult." Then I press against him, rub my face in his shirt. "Thank you for loving me so much."

He nods, breathing warm air over me. We stay like this for a while. Finally, I disengage from him. Then I turn to Kwabena. "Let's go."

Kayode insists on taking my suitcase outside. He calls a taxi and I slide in. I should be sad, but I am strangely calm. Content, even. For an instant, there's a look of regret on his face, a sense of urgency. He leans into the open door. "Esi, when do we see again?" It's a spare expression of his that I love.

I give him a mischievous smile. "I'll send you kisses by air transmission."

"And I'll remember you in my dreams." He is grinning in the rascally manner he did when he laughed at my first love letter to him.

"Go away you," I say, scowling and pulling the door shut. And then we are all laughing, me feeling like a balloon lifting off as the taxi eases me away, into my future.

ACKNOWLEDGMENTS

Many, many thanks to my editor, Rakesh Saytal, who believed Esi's story needed to be told. His patience and consideration is without par. Thanks also to the team at HarperVia and HarperOne, especially Sam Tatum for his equanimity and guidance, my tireless publicist, Paul Olsewski, and to Jim Tierney for the stunning cover. So much passion went into the production. I am a lucky author.

My agent, Sharon Bowers, my champion and advocate, a thousand roses to you for believing in me. Thank you so very much for your agency.

Dave Eggers emboldened me to pen Esi's short story. There are not enough words to say thank you. He and Jordan Bass at McSweeney's were a delight to work with.

A toast to my crazy, Afrolit family, one to be savored in private. We have laughed, cried, raged, and danced in a certain room without color. You have cheered me on, introduced me to agents and editors, given me invaluable advice and nicknames. What should have been an awful lockdown was a thrill because of you. I love you all so much.

Baffour family in America, you are my siblings from other parents. Maame Fritzwa, Nyame *nhyira wo paa*. Mabel Bashorun, thanks for the inspiring conversations. Mimi Mignon, *mil remerciements* for the fake French job, chocolate, and laughter.

Thanks to my one-time TNBW family. Sharon Thatcher's sass and brilliance inspired me. You deserve a whole orchard of mangoes for pushing me. I owe Jeni Decker roses for reading and offering helpful comments. Robyn Webb edited earlier drafts and was a big help. There are not enough bottles of wine to thank you.

Many thanks to Akua Owusu for the many nights you listened. For the thousand and one aids you gave me. Your observations about Wesley Girls' provided needed balance. Jemimah Oware, my own Erot, gave me office space at desperate times, supplied meals. Afuah Laing, you know! I owe you all a debt of gratitude I can't pay.

My love and gratitude to Philip Mensah for his expert legal advice, kindness, and integrity.

All my love to my Adjepon-Yamoah family, especially big brother Kweku, my life-saver and comforter. Mamaa Fatimeh and Auntie Bintu, your memories endure in my heart.

Tolu, Tayo, and Ebo, here's to you!

NOTE FROM THE COVER DESIGNER

How can you faithfully encapsulate a novel like Bisi's—one that so fully embraces the broad human spectrum of sorrow, joy, pain, and pleasure—within a 6" x 9" rectangle? Esi's narrative is full of lush and striking images, but none nearly as captivating as the character herself. This book is a portrait, so it only felt right to give Esi her rightful place on the cover.

Bringing Esi's face to life was a careful and thoughtful process, with frequent help from Bisi in order to get her expression and features just right. I only hope I did her justice.

Here ends Bisi Adjapon's
The Teller of Secrets.

The first edition of the book was printed and
bound at LSC Communications in
Harrisonburg, Virginia, August 2021.

A NOTE ON THE TYPE

The text of this novel was set in Plantin, an old-style serif text font designed by Frank Hinman Pierpont and published by Monotype Corporation in 1913. Pierpont drew inspiration from the typesets of Robert Granjon. Plantin was named after Christophe Plantin, the French Renaissance printer and founder of the Plantin Press.

It is a Renaissance Roman typeface known for its dark, rich texture that works particularly well in editorial and book work.

HARPERVIA

An imprint dedicated to publishing international voices,
offering readers a chance to encounter other lives and other
points of view via the language of the imagination.

Enjoy this sneak peek of the Bisi Adjapon's next novel,

DAUGHTER iN EXILE.

Coming early 2023.

Sesa wo suban:
Change your character

This is the day that will determine my immigration status in America. After the trial, I'll no longer be a woman without a country. I'll either live legally in America or be deported back to Ghana within six months. I welcome either choice. I'm weary of peripheral living.

I've never voted in my life. When I was growing up in Ghana, the voting age was twenty-one. By the time they changed it to eighteen, I had already left. In America, I pay taxes but can't vote. I'm a skeleton of a resident without the flesh of belonging.

I've been up since three a.m.

The letter my mother wrote a week ago lies unfolded on my bedside table, like a staple pried open. It left spots of blood on my heart. I've read it so many times that even when I close my eyes, I can still see the looping cursive swimming before me:

My dear Akua,
It is a pity that you have not seen fit to write to me, your
mother, for such a long time. I hope you are doing well.
As for me, I am nearing the end of my life. Now my hair
has hoary streaks. I am afraid you may never see me again. I

*don't know if you hold the nuggets of wisdom I tried to impart
to you through those Adinkra symbols of old, but I cling to the
hope that you're living a good life.*

*I pray that the almighty God take care of you and keep you
safe when I am no longer here.*

Your loving mother

S. D.

Ten years. That's how long I've been away from home. Akua is
what my family called me because I was a girl born on Wednesday.
I used to hate it. What scant appreciation I had for our culture then.

I hated my western name too: Olivia. My mother's obsession
with the name felt like a nutmeg grater on my skin. I didn't care
that it belonged to her childhood best friend who died. My parents
had given the name to my big sister who had died at age three or
six, no one is sure. When I was born, they affixed the same name
to me, which left me feeling I was supposed to be a replacement
for my dead sister. I felt no connection to her, no sense I'd been
on earth before. The whole business kept me awake at night. I
imagined my sister's ghost hissing, "You're not me!" From the
moment I entered the university, I called myself Lola, a Nigerian
name I loved. The idea that their names are shaven from sentences
appealed to me. This fueled a letter from Mama about how I had
hurt her, how much Olivia meant to her. Now in America, I yearn
to hear her call me Akua, Olivia. Anything. Just to hear her voice.
This was my response to her letter:

My dear Mama,

*I'm so sorry for my silence. I know you think I've forgotten
you, but I haven't. How could I forget the woman I trusted not
to drown me when our car drifted off the road and ended up in
the sea?*

You've always insisted that at age three, I was too young to remember, that someone must have told me. Mama, to this day, the scene swirls in my mind. I was sprawled on the backseat when the sound of men shouting and water splashing yanked me out of sleep. I sat up. We were in water. Darkness covered us. Shadowy men surrounded the car, grunting, pushing, pushing. The water was so vast I couldn't tell where the sky ended and where the sea began. Somehow, I knew to be quiet as you hunched over, twisting and wrestling with the steering wheel. Right. Left. Like the windshield wipers. I didn't understand how you ended up in the driver's seat and why Dadda was slumped beside you, never to get up again.

The men pushed until, by degrees, the car turned around and we faced the sand, silhouettes of coconut trees rising to meet us. Then we were no longer rocking in water but on the steady sand. That's when you crumbled onto Dadda, shaking him, telling him to wake up, the scream ripping from inside me.

I don't know how, but you got us home.

You got us through the funeral. You got me through life. Because of you, I never felt the urge to dive under a blanket and remain there forever. You see, Mama, you are my safe place.

Yes, I think of the Adinkra symbols, now more than ever. Do you remember when I came home from university after skipping Christmas and Easter? You pointed to the San kɔ fa swan symbol hanging on the wall and said, "Why do you think she arches her neck all the way back to pick up the egg she laid and left behind? That's because she realizes it's the source of future life, the continuation of she. San kɔ fa! Never forget where you came from or you will be lost." I used to snort and roll my eyes, but how well I understand, now that an ocean separates me from home. Oh, to be the San kɔ fa swan, reach over my back and pick up what I left behind! I live for that day.

Your daughter always,

Akua.

Also known as Olivia

My hands tremble. I brush down my grey skirt suit. Breathe, I tell myself. I pick up my purse and sling it over my shoulder, car keys in hand. It's time to face the judge.

1995

▌▌ ▌ ▌▌ ▌ ▌▌ ▌ ▌ ▌▌

ƐSE NE TƐKRƐMA:
THE TEETH AND THE TONGUE

My coming to America began with a series of incidences that arranged themselves to catapult me across the Atlantic. You could say I entered America while living in Senegal, by way of my American friends, one evening, in a house near the sea, filled with the smell of salt, flowers, alcohol, perfume, tobacco breath and pheromones.

Americans had crossed my path, but never this many in one space.

Olga's house boomed with their loud conversations. They circulated around clutching wine glasses, bending over to reach for crackers and cheese laid out on the wicker table in the center of the room, fixed smiles on their faces. They didn't sit. They didn't break into dance, despite the Congolese soukous music thumping in the background. At twenty-one, I was a fresh university graduate. Everyone else was above thirty and married. I was the only African, one of three blacks. The other two were a couple whose masculine persona was laughing louder than anyone else. Olga had introduced him to me as Len George, or Lennard George, a man with a smile so broad his teeth seemed to begin from one ear and end at the other, strong and white. His wife, an oak-colored woman with green eyes and cotton-ball blonde afro, formed part of a clump of people complaining about Senegal.

"Can you believe it? The houseboy was playing with my son's toy car!" This was delivered with round-eyed indignation by a blonde who almost stamped her foot.

A collective "Nooooo!" arose from the group. They spurred one another on.

"They're so unbelievably lazy!"

"And the weather, talk about the heat!"

"I know, and then suddenly it gets cold and there's no way to keep warm!"

"No heat when it's cold. No AC when it's hot, Jesus Christ!"

"Get me out of here, that's what I say!"

"Back to DC!"

"Back to civilization!"

They groaned, avoiding my pointed stare. I had a good mind to throw in a sharp *Is life perfect where you come from?* But I was reluctant to ruin Olga's going-back-to-America party.

From behind me, a shrill voice announced, "*I love it here!*" That was Olga, striding towards the ladies. My heart warmed over. She stood tall above them, in a loose print dress and scarf tied over her head to form two cat ears. Her slanted, dark eyes flashed. "Gosh, I'm gonna miss it. Come on, you guys are so ungrateful. I mean, look at this house. And look at you all griping about servants. I'll give a hundred dollars to anyone who can point to houses like this and servants back in Kansas or wherever you came from."

No one spoke. A chill settled over them. I bit my mouth to stop from blurting *Hear! Hear!* Then Len George guffawed and the voices bubbled up again.

Olga's husband Barry appeared from nowhere and moved to the middle of the marble floor. He clinked his fork against his wineglass. "Yoo hoo!"

The voices subsided as we all drew closer. He grinned, revealing his wolfish teeth. "I'd like to thank you all for coming to our goodbye party. It's been a wild three years, but it's time to head back to America!"

Lennard nodded. "That's right! Raise your glasses, y'all. To Olga and Barry!"

"To Olga and Barry!"

At that moment, someone's glass shattered onto the floor. Wine splashed on my ankles. We gasped, sprang away from the watery shards. That was when Mr. George looked across at me with a benevolent grin and said, "Fatou, you go get rag and-" he made wiping motions "-mopez le floor."

I froze. Fatou was not my name. Evidently, Olga's introduction of me had washed over Len George. Before I could unglue my tongue, Olga said, "That's not the maid, she's my best friend, my best friend in Senegal!" Either Len didn't hear her or wanted to cover up his embarrassment, because he persisted, "Get rag, mopez le floor, haha!"

"*YOU* mopez le floor." I pivoted away from him.

Olga called the maid who mopped the floor while we spilled onto the veranda. Mindy, a blue-eyed lady, touched my arm, smiling apologetically.

"Let me fill your glass, Lola," her husband Ted said. "What are you drinking?"

"Sauvignon Blanc."

"Sauvignon Blanc it is."

I handed my glass to him, and away he went on sturdy legs, his shaggy black hair bouncing around his ears. I had the impression one could lean on him and not fall. Mindy nodded in Len George's direction. "What a fool."

"I don't want to talk about it."

"Yeah. Forget him. How are things going at the Thai embassy?"

I brightened up. "I love it. They're really nice. Did you know they eat plantains just like Ghanaians?"

"Huh, I didn't know that. Last year, I visited Vietnam and they ate plantains too. I imagine most tropical countries have them."

"You went to Vietnam? How come?"

She laughed as though it wasn't a big deal. "Yeah, for my USAID project." I wondered if Ted went too since he also worked for the same organization, but before I could ask her, he returned with my wine. I took a sip, savoring its chilled semi-sweetness.

He grinned through his glasses. "I take it you like it."

"I love it. Wine is the only alcohol I tolerate."

"So, you said you were writing a book. How is that going?"

"Not well. I wish I had more time to write."

Mindy mentioned a book she was reading titled the *Women's Room*. I was about to ask if she'd read Erica Jong's *Fear of Flying* when Olga grabbed me from behind, wrapping me in a hug. Only she would breathe cigarette over me, mixed with a primal scent from her armpit. She eschewed perfume, deodorant and under-arm shaving. When I turned around, she kissed my cheek.

"I'm going to miss you, Lola." She teared up for an instant, then flashed a naughty smile, her voice throaty. "You could come with us, you know. In whatever capacity you want. Mistress to Barry. Whatever."

"Olga!" I whipped around to see if Mindy and Ted had heard her, but they had drifted away and were now engaged in conversation with another couple.

Olga's slim shoulders went up in a careless shrug. "In some cultures, it's done, you know. I mean, Barry is always whooping about your breasts." She waved at her husband. "Hey, Barry! Tell Lola she must come with us."

He sidled over and pinched my butt. "You yummy thing," he said in a playful, raspy voice. I swatted his hand, whereupon he said ouch and slipped away, chuckling to himself. For all his constant pinching of my butt, he was a toothless wolf. Whenever he found himself alone with me, he'd stammer, hands glued to his sides and eyes on the floor. Olga loved to goad him.

"Can you blame him? You've got the most beautiful body."

"You're crazy, Olga. I can't believe you're thirty-eight and a mother of three."

She laughed, unrepentant. "Now, come on. Let's have it one last time."

I looked at her suspiciously. "Have what?" One never knew what percolated beneath her words.

"That song you taught us."

Ah, she was talking about a little ditty from *Treasure Island*. For reasons I didn't get, that song threw her into giggles each time I sang it. I didn't want those snobbish ears to hear me, but then I looked around and thought, why not give them one more thing to complain about? I lifted my chin and belted out the tune my mother made up:

Fifteen men on a dead man's chest,
Yo ho ho and a bottle of rum!

The room went silent. Olga threw her head back, a loud cackle erupting from her. A few guests giggled, then conversations resumed their buzzing. Her eyes misted. "God, Lola, what am I going to do without you? There's no one like you for fun! Listen, don't pay attention to Len George. What he said. He means no harm."

I rolled my eyes, shaking my head.

"Let's just dance," she said, striding towards the boom box and turning up the volume.

LEN'S CASUAL TREATMENT of me as a maid cut deeply. And yet, weeks later, when we bumped into each other without the presence of an audience, he greeted me as though he'd encountered a lost friend. "Lola! How *are* you? Good to *see* you! Why don't we grab a cup of coffee? Come on!" Reluctantly, I accepted, and was surprised to find him pulling a chair for me, smiling at me, pressing pastries at me.

Typical, I thought, as I bit into a chocolate croissant. "How come in the presence of whites, you mocked me, but now you're pushing chocolate and croissant at me?"

His smile disappeared. "Mocked you? What are you talking about?"

"*Mopez le floor*, remember? Fatou?"

"Come on, Lola, you know I was only kidding?"

"No, I don't know that. You called me Fatou. Olga had just introduced us, yet you called me Fatou. Fatou is what the colonialists called their maids when they couldn't be bothered to know their names." I was trying not to choke. "A name isn't . . . just a name. It's my family, my dignity. We have a whole ceremony, a whole day of feasting set aside just to give you your name after you're born. How could you dismiss me like that?"

He grew quiet, his coffee untouched. "Gee, I'm sorry. I didn't know you were that upset."

"You don't understand. At my university in Ghana, I used to trace the faces of American blacks in the Ebony magazines I found on the Formica tables in our cafeteria. I wanted you all to come home to Ghana. Then I come to Senegal and discover you black diplomats don't want to know us. We live in this layered cake society colonialism has created in Senegal, whites frosting over shades of brown. I don't blame you for distancing yourself, but don't expect me to love you for it."

He reached over and grabbed my hand. "Whoa, whoa, hold it there, girl. You do get off being an intellectual, don't you?"

I snatched back my hand and stood up, my chair scraping the concrete. "You know what, thanks for the croissant."

"Come on, Lola." He rushed around to block my way. "Look, I was only joking. That's what I do. When I'm embarrassed or something, I try to be goofy, you know, funny."

"I wanted to throw my wine in your face."

He laughed. "You should have. I'm truly sorry. Truth is, I totally forgot your name and just said Fatou. I thought . . . I don't know what I was thinking. Sit down. Please. Let me make it up to you." He walked back to the table to hold out my chair. He looked so wretched I found myself relenting, dragging myself to the table and slouching down. He returned to his seat, picked up his coffee mug, set it down. "You're so lucky, growing up in Africa. You've never walked into a room feeling you had to prove you belonged, have you?"

"Why would you need to prove you belonged?

He shook his head. "Wait till you go to America." He sipped his coffee. "By the way, do you know the head of the International Civil Aviation Organization? He's also from Ghana."

I sat back, surprised. "Mr. Koranteng? Yes, his son is my friend. A true brother."

"Ouch. A true brother, eh? Well, in a way, Mr. Koranteng's my boss. I work for the FAA, you know. In Africa, the FAA kinda falls under his jurisdiction. So, you see, I can't look down on you. You

Ghanaians are so smart." He shook his head in disbelief. "Man, that guy is fit. I mean, he's sixty, I'm forty, but he beats me at tennis every time."

Tennis? It was hard to associate the game with this man who irritated me so much. "I didn't know you played tennis. I always wanted to learn. At university, I tried to learn but the coach shooed me away because I hit all the balls into the bushes."

He smiled eagerly. "I could teach you. Listen, let's start over. No more goofiness from me. I promise." I said nothing, which prompted another "come on" from him until I yielded. "Aha! I see that smile. That's what I'm talking about. Now, are you ready for your lesson?"

"Right now? Isn't it dangerous to exercise after a meal?"

"You call a croissant and coffee a meal?" He pushed to his feet and held out his hand. "Come on, let's go. By the time you go home and get changed, what you ate would be long gone."

I allowed him to take me by the elbow. He ushered me into a white VW Beetle and zoomed away to my apartment building that was only minutes away.

"Wow," he said as he eased himself out of the car, swiveling around, taking in the grey, three-story building. "So, this is where you live? Not bad at all. Wow, Plateau. Are you rich or something?"

That threw me into giggles. "No, I'm not. This is the plebeian dwelling of the neighborhood." I pointed to a tall building not far from us. "Look at Immeuble Kebe with its uniformed doormen and garbage shoots. That's where Mr. Koranteng lives. His son Kwaku too, when he comes to Senegal. We don't even have an elevator. I have to climb to the third floor."

"Still. You're right across from the American Embassy. Wow."

"I'm within shouting distance, what of it?"

"This is great. I mean, I could stop by and say hello anytime

I'm in the neighborhood. Pick you up for tennis. Whatever. Wow, Plateau. The neighborhood of the rich. You live alone?"

"No, I live with my friend Joana, also from Ghana."

"Awesome. Wow, you Ghanaians are something else."

I was suddenly shy and hoped he wouldn't follow me up to the flat. As if guessing my thoughts, he leaned his elbows on the hood of the car. "I'll wait here while you get ready. You've got sneakers?"

"Yes."

I darted upstairs to get changed, feeling the budding of a friendship

We had fun. He showed me how to hold a racquet. He pulled two cans of balls out his bag and said, "These are yours. You're gonna hit them. Don't worry if they fly into the trees." He bounced the yellow balls in front of me and showed me how to pivot and swing the racquet to my shoulder. I kept hitting the ball out off the court, over the cage, but he never lost patience. "Keep trying. Just get the ball over the net. There you go! You're a natural. Come on, hit it."

I loved the way the ball and racquet connected with a resounding thwack. When I figured out how to hit the ball over net without it sailing into the sky, he trotted to the opposite side and fed me more balls. I chased them down, laughing and swinging away, thrilled at my power.

An hour later, I couldn't believe how quickly I had gone from hating to sitting beside him on a bench, our sweaty skins touching, expelling air into the Senegalese breeze.